After centuries...

Jack VanAll is a member of the... when he awakes... who resembles his late wife, he must prove his innocence or suffer the punishment: death. The problem? He doesn't remember a thing.

Sunshine Petersen's life as a vampire isn't getting off to a great start. She's got no control over her powers, can't find a job, and sexy Jack is being stand-offish. The only thing she'd like more than catching the creep who turned her is getting Jack into the closest bed. But, could Jack be the one who turned her?

When he and Sunny team up to find the culprit, Jack discovers feelings he hasn't had in years. But once Sunny finds out he's keeping a major secret, she disappears. Unfortunately, the man who turned her still has plans...

Other books by Stacy McKitrick

Bitten by Love Series:
My Sunny Vampire
Bite Me, I'm Yours
Blind Temptation
A Vampire Wedding

Ghostly Encounter Series:
Ghostly Liaison
Ghostly Interlude

Short Stories in the Following Anthologies:
Home for the Holidays
Love's a Beach

My Sunny Vampire
(Bitten by Love #1)

Stacy McKitrick

Mythical Press

Dayton, Ohio

Mythical Press

Mythicalpress.com

Copyright © 2013, Stacy McKitrick
Edited by Paige Christian
Formatted by Enterprise Book Services (EnterpriseBookServices.com)
Cover designed by Maria Zannini (BookcoverDiva.blogspot.com)

All Rights Are Reserved. No part of this book may be used or reproduced in any manner whatsoever without written permission, except in the case of brief quotations embodied in critical articles and reviews. The unauthorized reproduction or distribution of this copyrighted work is illegal. No part of this book may be scanned, uploaded or distributed via the Internet or any other means, electronic or print, without the author's permission.

This book is a work of fiction. The names, characters, places, and incidents are products of the writer's imagination or have been used fictitiously and are not to be construed as real. Any resemblance to persons, living or dead, actual events, locale or organizations is entirely coincidental.

Published in the United States of America
2nd electronic edition: October 9, 2017
2nd print edition: October 17, 2017
Print ISBN: 978-0-9967976-6-5

To Stephanie, my very first reader (and wonderful daughter). Your encouragement made this book possible.

Chapter 1

Jack VanAllen woke and immediately knew something was wrong. Contrary to many myths, vampires never slept, and since becoming one, he'd never passed out.

The cloying scent of wet cardboard and urine heightened his sense of wrongness and he bolted upright. Snow fell off his face and chest. What the hell? Close to six inches covered the ground. How did he end up in a narrow alley beside a dumpster? He searched his memories and came up with...nothing. Blank. Zip. Zilch.

"Shit."

Whatever that bum drank or snorted had sure done a trick on Jack. Damn Frank for wanting to go out in the first place. So what if it was New Year's Eve? It wasn't like he hadn't celebrated over two hundred of them.

Jack brushed the snow off his hair and gazed upward. Crap. The sky should be inky-black, not medium-blue tinged with pink. He scrambled upright, flinging snow in the process, and checked his watch.

Seven-thirty? The sun would rise in less than fifteen minutes. If he didn't get his ass in gear, he could very well fry, but where the hell was he?

He sloshed through the snow and stumbled over something solid, landing face first in the fluffy stuff. As he stood and spit out the ice crystals, the lump moaned.

"Frank?" He frantically brushed away the snow, uncovering the back of a hooded, blue coat and long, shapely legs. Well, she was definitely not Frank. And her shoes were missing. Damn, she had to be freezing. He pulled the hood down.

Red hair framed a flawless, creamy-white face.

"Clara?" His heart skipped a beat. No. Wait. Not Clara. This woman sure looked like his long-dead wife, though. Then it hit him. She'd been at the bar Frank had dragged him to. The reason he'd fed from that bum. So what was she doing out here?

"Miss?" He tapped her face. "Come on, sweetheart. Wake up. I can't stay out here much longer."

Her head lolled to one side. No, no, no. This couldn't be. Two bluish welts stood out on her slender neck, a couple of inches apart. Only venom injected into a human would leave those marks and they couldn't be hidden.

A vampire had turned her.

Damn it. Jack punched the side of the dumpster. The explosive sound echoed in the alley as the container slid several inches. Why? Was the vampire an idiot? There was no way someone had permission to turn her. As a Committee member, he'd have known about it. And why dump her in an alley as if she were trash? None of it made any sense.

The woman moaned, bringing him back to the present. Time was short. If he didn't get them to safety before sunrise, they were cooked.

After gently wrapping the coat around her and tying the empty sleeves to hold it in place, he easily lifted her. At least she hadn't been lying in filth. The snow helped in that regard. She moaned again, hitting him with whisky-rum-and-whatever-laced breath. Come to think of it, his breath smelled pretty rank, too. While he'd never drunk to excess before, could it be he'd just passed out? Would that explain his memory loss?

Whatever happened, maybe it was a good thing she was drunk. He remembered searing pain and begging for death during his turning. She was barely moaning and didn't seem far along in the process. Of course, the booze might have something to do with that and once it wore off… Oh hell. It was going to be a long day.

Happy fuckin' New Year.

My Sunny Vampire

Jack cautiously approached the street. He was closer to the safe house than Frank's, but still a good distance away. He'd be lucky if he made it there before the sun rose.

Each second that passed, the world became brighter. Any activity out of the ordinary might be noticed and carrying an unconscious woman through the city of Pittsburgh already surpassed ordinary. He trudged through the snow-covered sidewalk, but whenever traffic cleared, zipped down the plowed street. Thank God for the holiday and the light traffic.

Once he reached his street, he avoided the snow-covered sidewalks altogether and trotted in the plowed road. Zipping, or even running, would be faster, but not worth the risk of some busybody peeking out their window. He'd made it half a block when the sun broke the horizon.

Great, just great. Sunlight spread like greedy fingers over most of the street and the sidewalk he needed. He jumped the plowed snow pile to the shady side and used the houses, trees and bushes as a shield from the sun.

Up until this point, the woman had been relatively quiet. A couple of moans here and there, but no earth-shattering screams. Hopefully, those wouldn't come until he was safely inside.

He reached the old two-story house. Sunlight splashed across the front door.

"Shit." He kicked at a chunk of snow, sending it to the street. Wasn't anything going to turn out right? He took a deep breath to focus. Now was not the time to panic. He could do this.

Why the hell didn't the Committee buy a house that faced west? Because no vampire in their right mind would wait until the last minute to get to safety, that's why. Sure, he could use the back door, but he refused to toss her over the six-foot-high, gateless fence like a bag of trash.

He stared at the lighted front door. Exposure would be unavoidable, the quicker he worked the better. If anyone saw him, he'd take care of it later. He closed his eyes and pictured the route, taking calm, soothing breaths in the process. Once he was ready he opened his eyes. Keeping to the path with the most shadows, he hopped over the first snow mound, zipped across the street, hopped over the second snow mound and jumped up onto the porch, bypassing the four snow-covered steps. The sunlight hit him full on the back. A slow-burning, tingly sensation spread along his exposed skin.

With little effort, he adjusted the woman to free his arm and quickly punched in the security code on the keypad. A distinctive click registered the correct combination and Jack scooted inside. He kicked the door closed and leaned against it, welcoming the darkness that surrounded him. Relief rushed through him and he let out a long-held breath.

Sticking his elbow out, he flipped a switch. A dim light illuminated the small foyer and the stairway hugging the left wall. He carried her to the living room.

It had been years since his last visit and he'd forgotten how tiny the room was. And whose idea was it to cram it full of furniture? He walked around one of the two chairs flanking the couch and kicked the coffee table out of the way. The remotes to the high-definition television, DVD player, and game systems slid to the wood floor with a clatter.

After placing her on the couch, he straightened, hands on hips. She didn't appear all that comfortable wrapped up like a damn cocoon. The binding might actually cause her to panic. He bent over and lifted her, but she cried out. Either the booze was wearing off or her turning was gaining speed. Instead, he slipped his hands underneath and felt for the knot. Even this little bit of movement caused her to moan and each moan stabbed him in the heart.

With the sleeves free, he pulled the coat off and was greeted with the scent of roses. Her royal blue halter top, bunched up from the movement, barely covered her breasts and, damn, she wasn't wearing a bra. Quickly, he pulled the top down to her short black skirt, covering up her tan skin and taut belly. He went through the coat pockets and found fifty dollars in cash, a credit card and a Florida driver's license.

Sunshine Petersen. Twenty-seven years old. Not a bad age to be stuck in. He should know. He was stuck at twenty-eight.

He knelt beside her and gently brushed the hair away from her face. She didn't have freckles and her cheekbones were higher, still she bore a remarkable likeness to his late wife. His heart ached for the woman he'd lost over two hundred years ago.

Little Jack stirred to life. He stood and paced around the living room, hoping to slacken his arousal. Caring for Sunshine was going to be one hell of a test of his morality. Not to mention his libido. Why'd she have to go and look like Clara?

Listen to him. It wasn't her fault who she looked like. It wasn't her fault some deviant decided to turn her. Man, if he could only remember what the hell had happened.

So what drug would wipe his memory? He'd taken blood from inebriated donors before without any ill effects and always avoided donors who had taken an erectile dysfunction drug. But no vampire had ever lost their memory from feeding, so he never thought to ask what the donor had ingested.

Then there was Sunshine. The only thing he remembered about her, besides wanting to avoid her, was her klutzy friend who Frank had wanted to hook up with. Which reminded him, where was Frank anyway? He reached inside his jacket and came up empty. He checked every pocket--no cell.

"Great, just great." Hopefully, Frank was okay and had made it home. "He better have my phone."

After Jack found his friend and a phone, he'd have to contact the Committee Head. Of course, if the Committee had seen fit to supply the safe houses with phones and/or internet access, he wouldn't have to wait to call it in. Maybe now they would listen to him about upgrading to the twenty-first century.

Sunshine let out an agonizing cry as she began thrashing on the couch.

Jack went to her and held her head. She quieted to a moan and her movements stopped. He ran his thumbs across her cheeks and temples. "Easy, now. You'll be fine in a few hours. Try to relax."

His words were a joke. Relaxing was the last thing she'd be able to do, but his touch seemed to calm her, so he continued to caress her face.

Who was this woman and how did she end up like this? "I swear I'll get the bastard who did this to you. I just hope you remember more than I do."

Chapter 2

Pain. Unbearable, burning pain.

An agonizing scream sounded from a distance. Someone touched her face. The pain let up. That annoying scream stopped.

"Breathe slowly. Relax. You can do this."

Do what? Die? His gentle caress soothed her soul. His baritone voice calmed her heart. She concentrated on those and breathed like he suggested.

Her world became bearable until he moved his hand away. The pain returned, followed by that annoying scream.

She reached out and found a hand. Squeezed it. Another hand touched her face. Again, the pain let up, the screaming stopped. Oh. Maybe she was the one screaming.

"It's okay, Sunshine. I won't let you go."

She had no idea who Sunshine was, but she believed him and relaxed. With peace, sleep claimed her.

She awoke to humming. The burning pain had dissipated, but a dull headache took its place. When she opened her eyes, she could see…nothing. Panic gripped her chest. "Am I blind?"

The humming stopped. "No, sweetheart. The room is dark. Give your eyes time to adjust."

His soothing tone combined with the gentle caress down her cheek managed to alleviate the pressure in her chest. He made sense, but how would her eyes adjust? No light source existed in the room, not even from a window. Yet shapes started to take form.

She was in a small bedroom. Then again, lying in bed kind of gave that away. Curtains hung on the wall to the right and she turned her head to discover a dresser against the wall across from her. To the left, a door was opened to a hallway and a man was lying beside her.

What the--? She bolted from the bed and crashed into the wall. The burning sensation returned, although not with the same intensity. She hugged herself.

"Whoa. Easy, Sunshine."

Okay, so he was the guy who'd been talking. Still, what was he doing in bed with her? "Who are you? What's the matter with me? Was I in a fire?"

As soon as the questions left her lips, she knew that couldn't be the case. How was she able to move so quickly?

He scooted to the edge of the bed, swung his legs around, and sat. Darkness hid his face, but she could make out his wide shoulders. "You weren't in a fire. Your body is changing. If you just relax, I promise I'll tell you everything once your head is clear."

Her head seemed pretty clear right now, even with the pounding going on inside. She eyed the door. She could try and escape, but if she was a prisoner, wouldn't she have been tied up? Of course, if she'd been drugged… "What do you mean my body is changing? What did you give me?"

He stood, but made no move toward her. While he didn't tower over her, he wasn't some ninety-five pound weakling, either. One of his arms was as big as both of hers put together.

"I promise, Sunshine. I haven't given you anything. I'm only trying to help."

She could almost believe him, so maybe she wasn't all that together. Still, that was the second time he called her Sunshine. "Why do you keep calling me that?"

"Sunshine? Because it's your name."

"My name? No. That's not my name. My name is…think, stupid." What was her name? She rubbed her forehead. Empty. She couldn't remember anything. "Oh, God. Are you an alien? Have I been abducted? Did you wipe my memory?"

He lowered his head. "Shit."

What did he plan to do next? Probe her? She ran to the door, but he was quicker and grabbed her by the waist. Her face collided with his shoulder.

"Let me go." She pushed against his solid biceps to no avail. Pain ripped through her gut and she screamed.

He held her tight against his body. A body that could double for a wall. "Easy, I'm not an alien and you weren't abducted. I'm sure your memory will come back. Just relax. Please. I only want to help you."

How could she relax when she didn't know who she was and she hurt all over? "Why are you doing this to me?"

"I'm not doing anything to you. I found you like this."

"You found me, but you know what's happening to me?"

"Yes."

"So why won't you tell me?"

He rubbed her back, but made no move to release her. Apparently, he wasn't going to answer her, either. Not that she could blame him. He'd been a perfect gentleman--that she could remember anyway--so maybe he really was waiting for her to act more...with it.

Pain still gripped her belly, but she could live with it. She could function. She could behave. Besides, where could she go? For all she knew, she lived here, wherever here was.

"Who are you? Do I know you?"

"My name is Jack VanAllen. I am the wrong person who showed up at the wrong time. Or maybe the right time." He chuckled. "Whatever, I'm no one you know."

"So why are you caring for me?"

"Because you shouldn't be alone."

She looked up at him. No lamps magically illuminated the room, but now every detail of his beautiful face stood out--chiseled jaw, straight nose and shapely lips. But what nearly stopped her heart were his eyes. The color, a mix of blue and green, resembled the sea.

A sea she wouldn't mind swimming in.

* * * *

His Clara stared at him, but she wasn't his Clara. Sunshine was everything her name portrayed. Hair like the fiery sun. Crystal blue eyes like the sky on a cloudless, sunny day. She even smelled like the roses from his garden after the sun brought out their aroma.

My Sunny Vampire

Little Jack stirred. She was Clara, but she wasn't. How could that be?

She blinked. "I was alone?"

Her words snapped him out of his trance. Now was not the time to think of her as anything except a vampire in trouble. He needed to focus.

"When I found you, yes," Jack said. "I remember seeing you with another woman, but have no idea who she is."

She frowned, but relaxed in his arms. "You can let me go. I promise I won't run off. It's not like I know where to go."

He rather enjoyed holding her, but did as she requested. "How are you feeling?"

"Pretty good, considering I thought I was on fire not too long ago." She looked down at her long, lovely legs. "I wasn't, was I?"

He tore his gaze from her limbs and looked at her face, but that wasn't quieting Little Jack. Not at all. Focus, focus, focus. "No. No fire."

She grabbed her stomach and winced. "Should I be in the hospital?"

Oh great. Phase two was starting. Afterward, the hunger pangs would come. Teaching a new vampire the art of feeding wasn't his forte. Of course, first she needed to know what she'd become. Getting her to believe in something thought to be fictitious would be a chore. Then again, she thought he was an alien, and they didn't exist. At least as far as he knew they didn't. Maybe it would be easier than he anticipated.

He sat on the edge of the bed and pulled her down beside him. Her hand was small in his, and irresistibly soft, but he held it not just because he wanted to, but also because he could hear her thoughts this way. What he needed to say probably wouldn't sit well with her. "I'm afraid a hospital can't help you. You were bitten."

* * * *

Bitten? Like from something poisonous? Ice cold fear rushed through her veins. Was she dying? Then she should be in a hospital. If he wouldn't take her, she'd go on her own. She pried her hands away and bolted, promptly smashing into the wall. Pain sliced through her. Not in her shoulder, where she expected it, but in her stomach. Moving was definitely the wrong thing to do.

Jack was beside her in a flash, his hands on her shoulders. "You're not dying, okay? But you need to take it easy until you get used to your new body."

Her new what? She shrugged free and touched the indentation in the wall. What the heck did she just do? Was that dent there before? "What's going on?"

"Come back to the bed and I'll explain."

"No. Tell me--awww!" Pain ripped through her abdomen. She grabbed her stomach and doubled over. "Oh fudge."

Jack chuckled. "That's one way of putting it." He scooped her up into his arms.

"What are you doing? Where are you taking me?"

"Just to the bathroom. Your body is in the cleansing phase."

Cleansing phase? What the heck was a cleansing phase?

He reached inside the bathroom and flipped a switch. A light came on, brighter than she expected, and she brought her hand up to shield her eyes. Did he expect her to take a shower or bath? Another spasm struck and an urge followed. She rushed inside the bathroom and slammed the door hard enough to shake the walls.

She felt better after completing her business, as if she'd purged everything she'd ever eaten. Now, not only her memory was gone, everything else was, too. She cleaned herself and pulled down her skirt. Whatever happened to her shoes? And why weren't her feet cold? Something in the back of her mind told her they should be. A trickle of a memory, someone draping a blanket over her feet, then nothing.

Dang, she almost remembered something. Maybe he was right and she would get her memory back. But why was it taking so long? Had she hit her head or something?

She turned on the tap and washed her hands. Her mouth felt like one big, dry fuzzball. A tube of toothpaste sat on the counter and she squirted some over her finger, cleaning her teeth the best she could. The water looked inviting. After rinsing, she cupped her hands and drank. Beautiful, wonderful water. It left a cool trail down to her stomach. Her empty stomach. She couldn't stop gulping.

"What are you doing?" Jack asked through the door.

"Just cleaning up and getting a drink." Boy, was he nosy. What did he think she was doing?

The door sprang open. "Don't drink the water."

My Sunny Vampire

She looked up and the water spilled through her fingers. "Why? Is there something wrong with it?" What kind of place did he live in if the water wasn't safe?

"How much did you drink?" She nearly asked him why it mattered when her stomach cramped. Leaning over the sink, she vomited.

A wash cloth appeared in front of her. "Here. If you need to rinse your mouth, do it without swallowing."

"What's wrong with the water?"

"Nothing's wrong with the water. You've changed."

She threw the cloth on the counter. "Stop being so cryptic and tell me what's going on."

Jack rubbed his face. "I don't know how to tell you without sounding crazy, but I'm not crazy."

Well, he didn't look crazy. In fact, he looked scrumptious. Had she ever seen such a fine specimen of a man who didn't act like God's gift to women? She couldn't remember, but didn't think so. "Maybe you just need to say it then, and let me worry about what sounds crazy and what doesn't."

He nodded. "You were bitten by a vampire who injected you with venom. You're currently in the process of becoming a vampire."

A vampire? If he didn't look all serious, she would have thought he was pulling her leg. "Yeah, right. I hate to tell you this, but vampires don't exist."

"Just because you haven't seen one doesn't mean they don't exist. You've never seen an alien, have you? Yet you thought I was one."

He had a point there, sort of. She was out of it at the time. "So, how do you know this?"

"Because I'm one, too."

She stepped back. The man was mad. There was no other explanation.

"See? You think I'm crazy," he said.

Well, maybe just a little. He didn't seem dangerous, though. She turned toward the mirror and saw a face she didn't recognize. "Ha!" She pointed at her reflection. "If I'm a vampire, how come I can see myself in the mirror?"

He stood behind her and she saw him, too. "Because we're not invisible."

She ran her tongue over her teeth. "I don't have fangs."

He opened his mouth, showing perfect teeth. "And you won't until you're ready to feed."

Feed? "You mean...?" Her stomach started to churn. Didn't vampires drink blood? Oh, heck no. She wasn't doing that.

"I want to explain it all to you, Sunshine. Why don't we go downstairs to the living room?"

He started to steer her out of the bathroom, but she shrugged away. "That's another thing. You said I don't know you, so how do you know me?"

"I don't. I found this on you." Jack pulled a card out of his pants pocket and handed it to her.

A Florida driver's license. The picture resembled her reflection in the mirror and her address indicated she lived in Jacksonville, but it didn't trigger any memories. "So, you really don't know me?" Sadness tightened her chest. He wouldn't have the answers she sought.

"I'm sorry. I saw you briefly in the bar last night before I woke up next to you in the snow."

"Snow? Since when did Jacksonville have snow?"

"You're not in Jacksonville. You're in Pittsburgh."

"Pittsburgh? The city of the Steelers, the Pirates and the Penguins." The words just tumbled out of her mouth. How could she remember cities, but nothing about living in them?

His eyebrows popped upward. "You remember?"

Did she? If so, then who did she know in Pittsburgh? For that matter, who did she know in Jacksonville? Blank, all blank. Her driver's license wouldn't lie. Her name was Sunshine, yet the name didn't even sound familiar. She hit her forehead with the heel of her hand. "Dang it, dang it, dang it. How can I remember that, but not who I am?"

Jack pulled her arm down. "Stop it. Let's go to the living room and talk, okay?"

She looked at him. His eyes were even prettier in the light. He was crazy, wasn't he? He thought he was a vampire and he thought she was one, too, when clearly she had the flu or something similar. She needed to get out of here and find help. A doctor for her, a mental institute for him.

* * * *

My Sunny Vampire

Great, just great. Sunshine thought he was a nut case. Just like Clara had.

Every time he touched Sunshine's skin her thoughts were a direct link inside his head, a trait that vampires called screaming. Eventually she would learn control, but first she needed to accept the truth.

"I'm not crazy," Jack said. "If you don't believe me, go on outside. You'll find the sun very uncomfortable." He released her and motioned toward the staircase.

"You'll let me leave? Really?"

"You go outside and you'll see I'm telling the truth."

She skittered around him, leaving a rosy scent and a hint of mint in her wake. Grabbing the hand rail, she kept her gaze on Jack and side-stepped her way down the stairs. He followed at a distance, giving her space. When she reached the bottom, she opened the door. The sun's angle had changed since his arrival and she was safe if she remained inside.

Sunlight cut across the porch and a glare reflected off the freshly fallen snow. She raised her hand to block the light, but didn't venture outside.

What the hell was he doing? Hadn't she been through enough already? He couldn't bear to see her get hurt. "Don't. It's not worth it. Come back in. We'll talk."

She turned to look at him with a smirk on her face. "I don't think so."

"Fine. But don't say I didn't warn you."

She stepped out onto the porch and was bathed in light. A few seconds later she screamed. "Fudge! Fudge! Fudge!" She jumped up and down and smacked at her arms, as if putting out a fire.

He'd laugh if not for the fact she could be in serious pain. "Will you come back in now?"

She glared at him and then darted away.

"Shit." What was wrong with her? She was supposed to come back inside. He zoomed to the door and took a peek in her direction before pulling back to safety. Gone. What the hell? He glanced outside again. Footsteps in the snow made a path between the houses. He relaxed. She was in the shade. She was fine. For now. He marched over to the living room window. One way or another, he'd get her back to safety.

* * * *

13

Sunshine dashed between the buildings and nearly slammed into a tall wooden fence. Oh, great. A dead end. She leaned against the house and slid down into the snow. The top layer crunched, but the stuff underneath was soft. Fearsome tremors formed inside her gut and spread throughout her body, causing her to hyperventilate. Since when did the sun feel like an oven? It was winter for cripes sake.

The burning had stopped when she ducked into the shade. She examined her arms, looking for blisters she was sure had formed. Instead, her sunburn faded before her eyes. What the heck was wrong with her? If the sun scorched, why wasn't the snow freezing? She wasn't exactly dressed for the weather. In her haste to escape, she'd forgotten she wasn't wearing a coat or shoes. Wouldn't her butt be numb by now? Wouldn't her feet?

Oh, God. Could she actually be a vampire? No. Jack was crazy. And she was…what? Crazier?

The window above her screeched opened. Jack. She scrambled to the side of the neighboring house.

"I know you're confused. Are you ready to come back in and talk now?"

Why didn't he follow her outside? Did the sun burn him, too? "No. Tell me what's really going on."

"When you come inside. I'd rather not make this public."

"You sound like my father."

His eyebrows shot up. "You remember your father?"

Did she? Jack's words did sound familiar. Her response was automatic. Yes, she remembered standing in the front yard of a house similar to this one--her house!--and her father had stood on the porch with his hands on his hips. She had defied him. He'd been angry and didn't want the neighbors to hear. Holy moly, was she getting her memory back? She shot up. Big mistake. Knife-like pain cut a path across her belly. She grabbed her stomach and slid to the ground.

Something thumped in the snow and a hand landed on her shoulder. She jumped. Jack had crouched down beside her. "Let me help you."

She put her head back down. "Am I really a vampire?"

"Yes."

"Oh, God." She was sure tears would fall, but her eyes remained strangely dry.

My Sunny Vampire

"It'll be okay. Let's go inside."

Sunshine shook her head. "Can you make the pain go away?"

He smoothed the hair away from her face. "I probably can, but I'm not sure you're ready, yet. We need to go inside and talk."

"I'll do anything to make the pain go away. Make it stop. Please, just make it stop."

He lifted her chin and held her face, forcing her to look at him. "Your body needs nourishment."

So that was it? She was hungry? "Then get me some food."

He flattened his lips and leaned in close to her ear. His cheek brushed across hers. "Think about what a vampire eats."

Think? How could she think when his breath caressed her ear in a strange, enticing way and his mere touch flustered her? She nearly swooned. When the words finally sank in, when she realized what a vampire drank, she closed her eyes and started hyperventilating again. "Oh God. Oh God. Oh God."

He rubbed his thumbs across her cheeks and it felt oddly reassuring. "Sunshine, look at me."

"No. I can't. I can't drink..."

"I'm sorry this has happened to you. I'm trying to make it better. Can we go inside now?"

Inside would probably be better than announcing to the world what she'd become. She was about to stand when another cramp ripped through her body. She grabbed her stomach. This couldn't be happening. Maybe it was just a nightmare. She would wake up soon, right?

"Is everything okay?" A man in a red quilted coat appeared. She recalled seeing him shoveling his driveway and thought he hadn't noticed her. Apparently, he had.

"Everything's fine. I got it," Jack said.

The man looked at her feet and pointed. "Are you--?"

Jack stared at the man, cutting off his words, and within seconds, he pulled a one-eighty. Instead of heading for his house, he turned toward Jack's. Jack scooped her up into his arms. "Come on, let's get you inside."

"What did you do to him?" She didn't think he needed to carry her, but if she voiced her opinion, he'd probably ignore her anyway.

He walked over to the open window and slid her legs inside. Okay, so he wasn't going to answer her outside. She grabbed onto

15

the sill and eased her way in. When her feet hit the ground, her legs gave out and she landed in a heap on the floor. "Shoot." She tried to stand, but couldn't get her legs to hold her up.

Jack climbed in and shut the window. He picked her up and placed her on the couch. "Don't move," he said as he left the room.

Like that would be possible. Her legs weren't exactly working. But why'd he have to go sounding all bossy about it? Couldn't he just say he'd be right back?

Jack returned with the neighbor, who acted like he was sleepwalking. He removed his coat and sat beside her without acknowledging her or Jack.

She looked at Jack. "What's going on?"

He knelt beside her. "Nothing's going on. I brought you food."

"You want me to eat him?" Holy moly, that didn't come out right. "I mean…I didn't mean eat--"

Jack put a finger to her mouth and smiled. "You will take some of his blood."

The air seemed to have been sucked right out of the room and she struggled to take a breath.

He cupped her face, forcing her to look at him and not at the so-called meal beside her. "Hey, hey. Calm down. It's okay. You won't need much and he won't miss it."

She swallowed hard. "Why can't I eat regular food?"

"This is regular food. For us."

"What happens if I don't eat?"

He released her face and stood, hands on hips. "Turning takes a lot of energy. Going out in the sun didn't help. Try standing."

He didn't have to stand there looking all bossy. And sexy. Gee, where did that come from? Except he was sexy. His jeans fit perfectly, nice and snug. The not-so-small bulge in front held her gaze. Was it getting bigger? She looked away.

Dag-burnit. She needed to stop looking at his crotch and start paying attention. He was challenging her. Time to prove him wrong. She put her hands on her knees and pushed upward to a standing position. She was about to pump her fist in the air when her legs gave out.

Those big, strong arms were all that kept her from kissing the floor. His touch excited her to the point where she just wanted to rip his shirt off and tackle him to the ground. Dang. Where did that come from? Was she some kind of slut? What kind of person was she anyway? She pounded her hand on her forehead. Why couldn't she remember?

He grabbed her wrist. "Stop it. Hitting your head won't help."

"How do you know? You ever lose your memory?"

He lowered her to the couch. "As a matter of fact, I have. I can't remember what happened last night. I was hoping you would be able to shed some light. Maybe eating will help you get your memory back."

"Are you just saying that to get me to eat?" Because if he was, it was working.

He smiled. "Maybe a little. Truth is, turning is stressful to your body. Getting your strength back could be the trigger you need."

She had seen some glimpses of a past. A past which didn't make sense. But drinking blood? Could she do that? It just seemed gross.

Jack took the neighbor's arm and slid the sleeve up, exposing the skin. "If you bite right here"--he pointed to the inside of the wrist--"and suck for a minute, it should be enough."

"What, vampires don't bite on the neck?"

"They do when they know what they're doing, but the neck can be messy if you're not careful. You don't want to kill the guy, do you?"

No, she didn't want to kill anyone. She didn't want his blood, either. "Shouldn't I have fangs to bite?"

"They'll come when they're ready." He lifted the arm up to her.

She looked at the guy. Was he even aware of his surroundings? He appeared to be in some sort of waking coma. "Won't he feel it?"

Jack patted her cheek. "He won't feel a thing. I'll make sure of it." As if he knew the next question out of her mouth, he continued, "He won't remember any of this. Stop worrying. Now, put your nose next to his arm and smell."

Her mind screamed wrong, wrong, wrong, but Jack looked so sure of himself. Closing her eyes to keep from grossing herself out, she inhaled. Soap, sweat and something wonderfully sweet. That last one caused another stomach cramp and pain shot through her gums.

Her hand flew to her mouth. What the heck was that? Something pricked her lips.

"Sunshine, relax. It's only your fangs." He pulled her hand away. "I told you they would come. Now bite."

Fangs? She ran her fingers over two sharp points, just behind her eye teeth. A wonderful sweet flavor hit her tongue, it came from her finger.

He pulled her finger out of her mouth. "You need his blood, not your own."

Right. Blood. She could do this. She wasn't some wimpy baby. Or was she? God, she wished she could remember. She took the neighbor's arm. "How do I do this?"

Jack brought the wrist up to her mouth and positioned her fangs. "Place your lips against his skin like you're kissing and bite. You don't need a lot of pressure."

Her heart thumped nervously, but she followed his instructions. A light prick and a sweet, coppery flavor hit her tongue. Instinctively she started sucking. Wow. Who'd have thought blood would taste so wonderful. So exotic. She closed her eyes, savoring every second.

"Okay, now don't let go, but stop sucking."

Stop? She'd barely gotten started. Just a little more, that's all she wanted.

"Sunshine, look at me."

She opened her eyes.

"It's been over a minute. You have to stop."

Over a minute? No way! How would she ever be able to do this on her own? She stopped sucking, but the blood continued to trickle inside her mouth.

"Now lick the wound clean to stop the bleeding."

She licked and the wonderful sweet taste stopped. She pulled the man's arm away. "I'm sorry."

"Nothing to be sorry about. You did good. See, not a mark on him."

Jack was right. She'd actually healed the guy. "I didn't take too much?" The neighbor didn't appear to be unsteady enough to fall or anything like that, but what did she know?

As if to answer her question, he stood, put on his coat and left.

Chapter 3

"How'd you do that?" Sunshine asked.

Jack stood and ran his hand through his hair. She was full of questions, not that he could blame her. He'd been the same way many years ago.

"I told him to leave," he said.

"Like some kind of hypnotic suggestion?"

The corner of his mouth twitched. "Yeah, something like that. How are you feeling now?"

She rose from the couch and stretched. "Wow. I feel...strong."

"I bet you do. A vampire always feels strongest right after a feeding." It was a long-shot, but he had to know. "Do you remember anything?"

The elated look on her face morphed from hope to despair. His heart sank along with her expression. When she started pounding her head with her hand, he grabbed her wrists. "How many times do I have to tell you to stop it?"

She rested her head against his shoulder. "You said I would remember."

Her words sounded benign, but her thoughts of how good he smelled came through loud and clear, hitting his libido hard. Shit. He released her wrists and stepped back. "I said you might remember. Maybe you just need more time."

"How much more time? When I'm old and grey?"

Sunshine pouted and he started to hug her, but thought better of it and backed off. She wasn't Clara and until he got to the bottom of her turning, she was his responsibility. He needed to keep his emotions in check, regardless of how much she affected him. Bad enough Little Jack was straining to escape the confines of his jeans.

"Umm, you won't get old. Or grey."

She looked up, her eyebrows furrowed in confusion and licked lips just asking to be kissed.

Little Jack knocked on the zipper. Shit. He needed to focus. "Vampire? Immortal?"

"I won't get old?"

"I didn't."

She backed away and the tightness in his jeans let up a bit. Unfortunately, not near enough.

"How old are you?" she asked.

"I was born in 1750."

Her eyes widened. "Seventeen-fifty? That would make you..."

She started counting on her fingers and he chuckled. "Old. Yeah, I know."

She sank onto the couch. Her eyes flitted back and forth as if she were thinking of too many things at once. He sat next to her. It was probably a bad decision--hell, it was a bad decision--but Little Jack was currently doing most of the decision-making. If he gave in to all its demands, he'd strip her naked and devour her. In a good way, of course.

"I'll see all my friends and family die, provided I remember them at all." She chuffed. "Maybe it's a good thing I don't remember."

She covered her face with her hands and bent over.

"Don't say that, Sunshine. I know it's frustrating, but it'll come back. You just need to give it time." If he could make it better, he would.

She dropped her hands onto her lap and sat up. "I'm beginning to think I'm not a patient person. I'm sorry I'm being so difficult."

"Nothing to be sorry about. This wasn't your fault." He placed a hand on her back. Big mistake. The halter top did a lousy job of covering her and he caressed her skin. Soft and smooth, and he was sure the rest of her was, too. He wanted her. Oh God, but he wanted her.

* * * *

Jack's touch sent an electrical charge through her body that thrilled her. She turned and wrapped her arms around him. He smelled of sex and she wanted some.

Why did she keep thinking about sex? Was it her or a vampire trait? Or was it just Jack? Every thought centered on touching him, so she did. His arms, his shoulders. She wanted him naked. To feel…everything.

He lowered his hand. "Sunshine," he said on a groan. "You have to stop."

"Is there something wrong with me?"

"No, of course not."

"Then why?"

"Because this isn't right." His voice sounded strained and his heart beat raced. Seemed pretty right to her. She nuzzled his neck and inhaled his musky scent, which seemed to intensify with each passing second. She loved it. Her fangs extended and she rubbed them against his skin, so tempted to bite, not sure if she should. Instead, she kissed his neck and felt his rapid pulse against her lips.

He grabbed her wrists and attempted to dislodge her.

She held on tight. "Are you saying you don't want me?"

"That's not it."

"Then what?"

"I… I shouldn't."

He said he shouldn't, not that he didn't want to. Invitation accepted. She hiked up her skirt and straddled his muscular thighs. He hardened against her crotch. Control. She owned it, he was losing it. How much more could he take before he gave in? Keeping her mouth on his neck, she licked the salty skin and started sucking. Ran her fingers through his short locks. Ground into his growing erection. Dang, how big was he? Her panties were wet and his jeans were in the way. Maybe he wasn't the only one losing control.

"Shit," he mumbled. He grabbed her hips and held her against him.

Was he giving in? She lifted her head and stared into his eyes. Emotions flickered. Desire. Concern. Passion.

"Ah, hell." He grabbed the back of her head and pulled her close. His mouth covered hers with an urgency she returned.

She opened to welcome his tongue and he ran it over her fangs. When she explored his mouth, she discovered his fangs had also extended. Their blood mingled and it tasted good, but she wanted more. She reached for his belt.

His hand came over hers. "Not here. Upstairs. Hold on."

She wrapped her arms around his neck. When he stood, she wrapped her legs around his waist and he held her against his erection. With each step he took she rubbed up against him, sending her desire through the roof. Had she ever wanted anyone as much as she wanted him? She hoped not.

Jack kicked open a door. The bedroom. Yes.

Using his elbow, he flipped the switch on the wall, lighting a small bedside lamp. He laid her on the bed and climbed on top. With a devilish grin, he unhooked her halter and pulled it down. There were advantages to not wearing a bra.

"Beautiful," he said.

Hands that were rough and gentle at the same time caressed her breasts. He kissed her neck and rubbed up against her thigh. Finally. He wanted it, too. She unbuttoned his shirt and unhooked his belt. The dang zipper stuck half-way down and she tugged. He stood and finished the job, freeing the object of her attention.

Wow. She'd like to think she'd never seen anything so impressive and for some reason she wanted Jack to be the first. Hell, maybe he was.

"Do you have protection?"

His shirt joined his jeans. Smiling large, he climbed back onto the bed, and her. "You can't get any diseases."

"Nice to know, but I don't want to get pregnant."

He pushed her skirt up and pulled down her panties. "Can't get pregnant."

As he came back to her, she put her hands on his shoulders. "You can't have children?"

"No. Neither can you."

What? His words numbed her to the point she could no longer hold him up. When her arms fell away, he took that as an invitation to continue and suckled on a nipple. She wasn't feeling a thing. Instead her mind was racing.

She couldn't have children? Ever? She might not know who she was, but she was sure she'd want kids someday.

Jack slowly lifted his head. "Sunshine… I'm so sorry."

"Are there any more bombs you want to drop on me?" A slow-simmering anger started to take hold. It wasn't meant for Jack, he just happened to be convenient. She shoved him with more force than she intended and he bounced off the wall.

Guilt took hold of her heart and squeezed. She sprang from the bed and went to him. "I'm sorry. I didn't mean...are you hurt?"

He blinked several times. "I know you didn't mean it. Don't worry, I'm okay. I guess I'm not very good at this. It's just that newborns are supposed learn all this stuff before they're turned." He muttered, more to himself than at her, "Ah shit. They should have a checklist for this sort of thing."

She covered her face with her hands. Her heart ached with the loss of a child she would never have. "I hate him. Whoever did this to me, I hate him. He's taken everything away."

Jack embraced her. "Sweetheart, if I could turn you back, I would."

She sobbed with dry eyes. "Why me?"

"I don't know." He pulled up the halter straps and hooked them around her neck. "One of us is sure to remember eventually."

Remembering wouldn't fix anything. It was bound to make her more miserable knowing what she'd lost.

* * * *

Sunshine left the room and headed down the stairs. Jack breathed a sigh of relief. He had come darn close to making love to her. Luckily he had a big mouth or else Little Jack would be nestled deep inside her.

He needed to get it together. While a cold shower was useless when it came to lessening his libido, maybe the time away from her would cool his jets. He called down to her with his plans and suggested she watch TV.

Ten minutes later he emerged from the bathroom, clear-headed and less aroused. Now to keep his distance, both physically and mentally.

Talking would help. Might also give her memory the jolt it needed. Sunshine seemed to have some glimpses of her past. Maybe if he questioned her, it would eventually come back.

Going through the emergency stash in the dresser, he found a clean pair of jeans in his size and was zipping up when she yelled, "What kind of lousy call is that?"

He grabbed a shirt and put it on as he descended the stairs. The television was tuned to one of the bowl games. "You like football?"

From her position on the couch, she glanced his way. "I guess I do. You didn't tell me it was New Year's Day."

He sighed. Was he doing anything right? He felt like a total failure.

"I'm sorry," she said. "That came out ruder than I meant. I know you're doing your best." She lowered her head and played with the bottom of her top. "So I can't have children? Ever?"

"No female vampire has ever gotten pregnant. I'm sorry, Sunshine." He sat on the chair, wishing he could move it farther away. One whiff of her rosy scent brought Little Jack back to attention.

She shrugged, but kept her head down. "It's not your fault. I guess I have a lot to learn about being a vampire."

"Do you want to ask me questions or should I just tell you about us?"

She glanced at the TV for a second before gazing at him. "Do you mind if we don't talk at all for a while? I'd like to just sit here and watch the rest of this game, if it's okay with you."

It sounded great to him. It'd been a rough day for her and he wouldn't mind the distraction. He couldn't teach her anything until the sun set anyway. He turned the chair toward the TV. "So, who's playing?"

The sun had set by the time the game ended. It was nice sitting there with her, not worrying about anything but the outcome of the game. She picked up the remote and turned off the TV. "This is quite a set-up you have. You live here long?"

"I don't live here, I live in Atlanta. This is one of the safe houses."

Her eyes widened. "Safe house? Is someone after us?"

He smiled at her reaction. "It's not like that. Traveling vampires need a place to crash during the day. Most of the larger cities have one or more safe houses. Also, any vampire who owns a house is required to give refuge during the day. Technically, Pittsburgh has two. Here and Frank's."

"Frank? Who's he?"

"My friend. I'm up here visiting him. I thought we might go over to his house. He might know what happened last night."

"He was with you?"

"Yeah. After we saw you, we went outside to drink, from a drunk." Hearing the words out loud shamed him and he lowered his head. It certainly wasn't his finest moment. If it weren't for that stupid act, he wouldn't be in this situation and she might not have been turned.

"Vampires can get drunk?"

He nodded. "Most substances a human takes will affect us."

"So you can't drink alcohol, but you can get drunk from someone who has. Interesting. What happened after your…drink?"

"I don't know. That's the last thing I remember. I do know Frank liked your friend. If he hooked up with her, he might know where she lives."

Her eyes perked up. "Oh? What time is it? Is it dark out?"

"The sun set an hour ago."

"Well then, what are we waiting for? Let's go find him." She walked to the door, sashaying that fine ass of hers.

"Sunshine, you might want to go upstairs and look for some shoes. Anything you find up there, you're free to wear."

One look down at her feet and she laughed. "I guess people would notice, huh? I'll be right back."

As she headed upstairs, Jack found her coat on the floor and placed it on the couch. While coats weren't needed for warmth, they provided adequate camouflage during the winter months. No use drawing attention if it could be avoided.

A few minutes later Sunshine came down the stairs, wearing a Pittsburgh Steelers t-shirt, her skirt, socks and athletic shoes a size or two larger than her feet. "Are all the female vampires small? I felt like a giant trying to find something to wear."

"No, not all." It wouldn't do any good to tell her that he could probably count on one hand the number of female vampires taller than her. "Your feet don't seem big."

"That's because the only thing I could find were men's shoes, but my hips are too wide for any of the men's pants. Am I going to be some kind of a freak for a vampire?"

She wasn't a freak in his eyes. She was perfect. Her breasts filled his mouth just right and her hips were made for grabbing. Temptation returned and woke up Little Jack. Shit. Not again.

He forced the thoughts out of his head and smiled. "You're fine. Once we find your friend, you can get your clothes back. Those shoes look a little big. Let me go see if there's anything in the basement."

And while he was down there, he could get control of his raging libido.

****

Jack disappeared around the corner and she clomped into the living room. She itched to get a move on, but he was probably right about the shoes. Even the couple pairs of socks she wore didn't keep these suckers from slipping off her feet.

She grabbed what she assumed was her coat and slipped it on. The other jacket belonged to a man. She raised it to her face, the leather soft and supple against her skin, and inhaled, taking in the scent that was all Jack. She sighed. After he had dropped the baby bombshell on her, it pretty much killed the mood. She hoped she hadn't ruined any chance of them being together. He was sexy as all get out and she still wanted him. But she should wait until she talked to her friend. If she was happily married, it wouldn't be fair to her husband if she made love to someone else.

Of course, if she was happily married, what was she doing in a bar on New Year's Eve with a friend?

That thought brought a smile to her face.

The front door opened. A tall man in his early thirties with dark, unruly hair walked in as if he owned the place. "Jack? Are you here?"

"Frank," Jack said from the basement. "We were just getting ready to go find you."

"We?" Frank looked around the room. When he spotted her, his jaw dropped. "Sunny? What are you doing here?"

Sunny. *That* was her name. The revelation opened a portal inside her mind. She grabbed her head as the onslaught of memories bombarded her brain--her mother, her father, her home in Pittsburgh, her home in Jacksonville. It was all there. Memory after memory assaulted her senses causing sharp pains in her temples. Why did it have to hurt so much to remember? She fell to her knees and banged her forehead to the floor.

Someone gently grasped her shoulders. Her eyes stayed clamped shut as she tried to will the pain away. A memory of Jack loomed into view. The pain in her head eased as her gut simmered with anger. Son of a gun. He'd lied to her.

"What's the matter? Are you hurt?" Frank asked.

She opened her eyes and glared at him, shrugging off his hands as if he burned her. "Stay away."

"There's something different about you."

Jack barged into the room. "Frank, what'd you do?"

Frank stood and raised his hands. "I didn't do anything. What's she doing here, anyway?"

She attempted to stand. Jack was by her side in a flash and helped her up. "Sunshine, are you okay?"

He sounded sincere, but he couldn't be. He was a liar. He'd been lying to her all along. And to think she had wanted to make love to him. The pain of his betrayal slashed across her chest. She pushed him away and knocked him into the wall. "Leave me alone. Don't you think you've done enough already?"

He straightened his shoulders as if something were out of alignment. "What are you talking about? What did I do?"

Frank's eyes widened. "Oh my God. You turned her."

"I didn't turn her."

"Oh yes you did," she said.

"You remember?" Jack said.

"You bet your sweet patootie I do. You bit me. That's what I remember."

Chapter 4

If Jack's heart were mobile, it would have fallen to his stomach like a lead weight. Was he responsible? Could he have done what Sunshine accused him of?

Frank smacked him in the shoulder. "How could you do this?"

"I didn't. I couldn't. Weren't you with me, Frank?"

"What do you mean was I with you? I left with Carrie. Remember?"

Sunshine gasped. "Carrie? Did you turn her, too?"

Frank raised his hands. "Hey, I didn't turn anyone. Someone messed with your mind."

The situation was getting out of control and Jack needed to rein it in to get to the bottom of it all. First order of business, calm Sunshine. "Sweetheart, if you could just sit--"

"Don't you 'sweetheart' me. I know what I remember. You bit me." She stormed over to the door.

He couldn't let her leave, she was his responsibility. He rushed to her side and grabbed her arm. "Sunshine, wait. You can't leave. We need to discuss this."

Her icy stare sent shivers down his spine. "I'll do what I want. Discussion closed." She shrugged free and in a flash, she was gone. The slamming door rattled the walls.

Shit. His stomach churned from the accusation. Her memory had to be faulty, there was no other explanation. He started to go after her, but Frank's arm came across his chest.

"Frank, I have to get her."

"Oh no you don't. First you're going to tell me what the hell happened last night."

"I can't let her think I turned her."

"I really don't think she'll listen to you right now. Why don't you give her time to calm down, first?" Frank grabbed Jack's shoulders and turned him toward the living room. "I know where Carrie lives. We'll find her later. Now sit and tell me what happened."

Jack ran his hand through his hair and headed toward the couch. "That's just it. I don't know. I remember feeding and the next thing I know, I'm in a snow bank and she's turning."

"You sound like you have amnesia. Since when do vampires get amnesia?"

"I don't know, but that's what it is. I was hoping you could tell me what happened."

"Well, the last time I saw you and Sunny, you were drunk and she was mortal."

Jack collapsed on the couch. "This isn't funny, Frank."

Frank sat on the chair. "I'm sorry, but that's the truth. Could it be possible she remembers you fed from her?"

"Did I?"

"Yes, and more than once. I can't believe you didn't wipe her mind or distract her."

Jack hoped it was as simple as that. "Tell me what you saw."

"We went back inside the bar and introduced ourselves to Carrie and Sunny. I thought I might need to nudge Carrie, but I didn't have to. She liked me right off. Sunny took to you right away, too, not like that was a surprise. We sat together at a table."

Frank was grinning like a boy in love. Jack had missed that look. Ever since Frank's wife, Linda, had died a year back, he'd been a recluse. And he apparently drank. A lot. It was one of the reasons Jack came to Pittsburgh in the first place. He could kick himself for even going along with the drink, but at the time it had seemed innocent enough.

Frank continued, "You asked Sunny to dance and Carrie wanted to dance, too. The music was fast, Jack. You know how I hate bouncing around like that. In fact, I was surprised you asked Sunny, since you usually feel the same."

"Okay, so I asked her to dance. No harm there. Right?"

Frank leaned forward, placing his forearms on his thighs. "Well, not really. You went at her hot and heavy. I thought the two of you were going to fuck right there on the dance floor. That's when you fed from her the first time."

Out in public? Was he high? Oh wait, apparently he was. Jack bent over. It had been a long time since he felt sick and right now his stomach twisted in knots. "Why the hell didn't you stop me?"

"I tried. Sunny told me to go away. She was going at you just as crazy and since no one else noticed, I let you alone."

Jack's ego grew the tiniest bit. Sunshine must have felt something for him before her turning, unless he had manipulated her. Shit. Would he have been that crass? "Damn it, Frank. Didn't you think I was acting out of the ordinary?"

"Yeah, for a sober man. You weren't exactly sober. None of us were. Besides, I thought it was because she looked like Clara."

"I never treated Clara like that." In fact, he'd never treated any woman like that. Jack flopped back against the cushion and sighed.

"Well how the hell should I know? You never talk about her. The only reason I know she exists is because of that picture you carry around. Is it possible? I mean, could you have done it, thinking Sunny was Clara?"

That was the million dollar question. Could he have done it? He'd like to think the answer was no, even in his incapacitated state.

"Clara didn't want anything to do with me after I turned and I didn't force her. You're telling me Sunshine was interested in me, so why would I force her? It doesn't make sense."

"Maybe you didn't. Maybe she asked?"

Jack stared in disbelief at his friend. "Did she look like a woman who asked to be turned? She seemed pretty angry to me."

"Good point."

Jack leaned forward, resting his arms on his thighs. "So what happened next?"

"Beanie finally showed up."

"What?" Of all the people… Jack groaned. "What was he doing there?"

Harris Lobene, or Beanie to his friends, had been a pain in Jack's side ever since Jack had befriended Frank. But Frank's and Harris's friendship started long before that, and lasted up until two years ago when Harris's girlfriend, Ivy, killed herself. Harris blamed

My Sunny Vampire

Jack and Frank for her death and Frank hadn't heard from him since. Jack wasn't so lucky, since he was forced to see Harris once a year. Frank had taken it hard, though.

Frank grimaced. "He was that surprise I told you about. He called me two days ago. Said he was going to be in town and wanted to talk to both of us. He didn't think you'd show if you knew."

"He's not stupid, I'll give him that." Jack sat up. This bit of news lightened his spirits. "That's it. Harris turned her."

"What? No."

"Frank, think. If I didn't do it, and you didn't do it, he's the only other vampire around to do it."

Frank stood and shook his head. "You don't know for sure how many vampires are in the area and Beanie knows better. Besides, you wouldn't let anyone get close to Sunny. You practically growled at anyone who tried. Once he saw how wild you were, he left."

Wild? No one had ever used that word to describe him before. And what was with the growling? Shit. "He could have come back."

"I tried to get him to stay. He told me he'd call me later and set up another meet. I saw him drive off. About an hour after that, I left with Carrie."

Jack bolted off the couch. "You left me alone with her? Were you crazy?"

Frank grabbed Jack's shoulders. "Hey, calm down. It wasn't like that. You suggested we head to Carrie's, but Sunny didn't want to go. She wanted to dance some more and you jumped all over that. Said you'd meet up with us later. What was I supposed to think? You're my friend, but you're also a Committee Member. I've never questioned you in the past. I've never needed to."

Jack shrugged away and ran his hand through his hair. Now he didn't even have Frank's memory to lean on. It seemed to get worse and worse. "I'm sorry, you're right. It's just that I thought you'd be able to tell me more."

"When you didn't show at Carrie's, I tried calling you, but I went straight to your voice mail."

"Shit. I was hoping you had my phone."

"This doesn't make any sense," Frank said. "I can see where you might have passed out, but I've never not remembered where I was when that occurred. I've never not remembered what led to that situation. How can it be you don't remember anything?"

Jack stared at his friend. Maybe his drinking was getting out of hand. "How often do you pass out?"

Suddenly, something on the floor caught Frank's attention. "Not often," he muttered.

Not often, but apparently enough to look guilty. "Geez, Frank. Do you think that's wise? What if you passed out in the street?"

Frank pursed his lips and looked up. "How did this become about me? I'm not the one who's been accused of turning a mortal. Do you really think anyone will believe your amnesia story?"

No, he didn't. He could have the other Committee members probe his memories, but even that wouldn't solve anything. Many vampires knew how to hide their thoughts. "I'm sorry, Frank. I just worry about you."

"You don't need to, okay? So, you don't remember being with Sunny at all?"

Jack slowly shook his head. "When I woke up in the snow, she was beside me, in the process of turning. I got her back here just in time. I've been taking care of her ever since. We were just going to go out and find you after we--Oh shit. Frank, I have to get her."

"I don't think enough time has passed. Maybe we should look for your phone."

"No, you don't understand. She needs to feed."

* * * *

Sunny turned down Carrie's street breathing easily, as if she hadn't run the last ten minutes. Surprisingly, she hadn't broken a sweat and she'd run pretty fast, even with the clod hoppers she wore. Then again, did vampires sweat? Probably not.

Running hadn't helped her arrive any sooner, though. Maybe if she hadn't been so intent on putting space between her and Jack she wouldn't have gotten lost. Apparently, vampires weren't equipped with a built-in GPS. She'd stopped at a store to get directions, expecting the man behind the counter to give her a funny look due to her unusual attire. Instead he'd gone out of his way to be friendly. She must be giving off some kind of strange vibe because she didn't even have makeup on.

Sunny arrived at the small, three-story structure. She climbed the stairs to the second floor and opened the door to Carrie's apartment, grateful it was unlocked. "Hey, Carrie. I'm home."

Carrie came running around the corner, plowed into Sunny and wrapped her arms around Sunny's waist. At five-foot three, her head reached Sunny's chest. "Oh thank God. I thought for sure something bad happened to you."

Good ole' Carrie. Now this was more like it. Sunny might have only been gone a day, but it felt like a lifetime. And in a way, it was. She hugged her friend loosely, afraid of hurting her. "As you can see, I'm alive."

"Where were you? I expected you back last night." Carrie pulled away and did a quick examination. "Where'd you get those?" she asked, pointing at the over-sized shoes.

"I misplaced mine and had to borrow these."

Carrie cocked her head, causing her black hair to fall to the side. "Borrow? What did Jack do to you?"

Sunny crossed her arms. What did he do? He'd nearly made her fall for him. She wouldn't make that mistake again. "He turned me into a vampire, that's what."

* * * *

Frank's eyes widened. "What do you mean? Hasn't she fed at all?"

"No, no. She had some blood earlier, but not enough. Not near enough." Jack slipped on his jacket. "You gotta take me to Carrie's."

"Do you think that's wise? I mean, the girl accused you of turning her."

"What would you have me do? I can't leave her to survive on her own. It's not only illegal, it's cruel."

"That's not what I meant."

"Are you trying to tell me you turned her?"

Frank's jaw dropped as he stepped back. "Of course not. I would never do such a thing without permission."

"Well, neither would I." At least he hoped he hadn't. If he had, well, he would have to deal with that later. "We're just going to have to convince her otherwise. Right now we have to get her fed."

Frank nodded. "Yeah, you're right. As usual."

Jack was reaching for the front door when it burst open. Since when did Pittsburgh have so many visiting vampires at one time? When he got a glance at the intruder he nearly kicked a hole in the wall. Of all the lousy, rotten nights.

"Here you are." Harris stood in the doorway, looking downright pleasant and wearing clothes more suited for business than comfort. His eyes practically twinkled from the grin stretched across his face. "Hello, Jack. You sure look better. Did you manage to get that redhead home in one piece?"

Shit. Did everyone know about Sunshine? What exactly *had* he done? "Now's not a good time. We have someplace to be." Jack started to walk around Harris, but Harris blocked the way. All it would take is one push, one face-smashing push, and he'd be free to leave.

Harris shut the door. "Jack, wait. Please. This won't take long."

"I'm sorry we weren't in better shape last night." Frank one-armed Harris around the shoulders and ushered him to the couch. "But we're better now, aren't we, Jack?"

Great, just great. Jack wanted to hit something, Harris made a good target, but he reined it in. How the hell was he going to find Sunshine by himself? He had no idea where Carrie lived.

Harris chuckled. "It was a wild night, wasn't it? I don't remember partying so much on New Year's Eve when I was mortal. Sorry I didn't stick around. I felt like a fifth wheel."

"No need to apologize. I was at fault. I should have found you a girl, too," Frank said. When Harris looked away, Frank shrugged an apology Jack's way.

Oh, hell. Sunshine should be okay, provided she didn't overexert herself. Still, she'd left in such a rage, he wanted to see her, make sure she was okay. More than anything, he needed to know what she remembered. And until he discovered who turned her, the fewer who knew of the situation, the better.

"Okay, Harris, what did you want to talk to us about?" Jack leaned against the wall and folded his arms across his chest. Just because Harris wanted to talk didn't mean he had to be cordial.

Harris ran a hand through his dark mane. "I see you're back to calling me Harris. Guess I deserve that. I didn't exactly treat you guys like friends. I'm looking to change all that. New year, new life."

Harris, change? He couldn't be serious.

Ivy's death had been tragic. Jack's and Frank's actions might have contributed to the event, but if Harris hadn't gotten a bug up his ass about turning her without her knowledge, she'd probably still be alive today.

"So you're trying to tell us we're your New Year's resolution?" Jack asked.

"You mean, you're finally going to forgive me?" Frank asked with hope in his voice.

Harris hung his head. "I was way out of line back then. I just loved her so much, you know? It wasn't you guys' fault Ivy had a short wire in her brain. Maybe if I had listened to you in the first place..."

Frank scooted next to Harris and placed an arm around his shoulders. "You don't know how sorry I am it turned out the way it did. I didn't mean to cause--"

"I know you didn't," Harris interjected. "I'm just sorry I let it go on so long. I should have been there for you when Linda passed."

Jack stood by and watched it all play out. Something just didn't seem right to him, though. "Why now, Harris? It's been over two years. You never seemed interested in making amends when I saw you at the Committee meetings."

Harris stood and shoved his hands inside his pants pockets. "You're right. I wasn't. But this last Christmas was the worst one ever and I realized it was all my own doing. I alienated everyone I came in contact with." He turned and faced Frank. "Especially you, Frank. You're like a brother to me. We used to have such fun. I want that back."

Frank stood. "I want that back, too."

"Can we start clean?" Harris's dark blue eyes pleaded. "Start things out by grabbing a bite?"

No, no, no. That was the last thing Jack wanted. But Frank, desperate to be forgiven, spoke up first.

"Sounds like a great idea. Doesn't it, Jack?"

"Did you forget I have an errand to run?"

Harris looked between the two men and frowned. "We can do it another time."

"Jack's errand can wait an hour. Can't it, Jack?" Frank raised his eyebrows in question.

Was Frank hoping to get information from Harris or mend fences? Even though Jack would prefer to find Sunshine, he'd be stupid not to use the time to discover what Harris knew. He plastered a fake smile on his face and agreed to go.

* * * *

Carrie scrunched her face. "A vampire? Just how much did you drink last night?"

Sunny opened her mouth to explain, then closed it. Should she be telling Carrie this? Wasn't she supposed to keep being a vampire a secret? Well, Jack and Frank could go jump off a cliff. They were the ones who got her into this mess. She needed to confide in her friend and she was dang well going to do it.

"Something happened last night and you can't tell anyone."

"Bad?"

"Yeah, bad."

Sunny followed Carrie into the living room. Or should it be called sewing room? Carrie's sewing machine and current project covered the dining table, which she rarely used for eating. Two dress forms stood side by side and boxes, bags and bolts of fabric littered the floor. Her friend could use a good organizer.

"I see you got the sleeves done today," Sunny said.

Carrie ran her fingers over the partially completed dress. "Hey, if you can't use a holiday to sew, it's wasted time." She sat on the couch and Sunny sat beside her. "I wasn't sure I'd be able to do any work, though. I woke up with such a hangover."

Sunny wished that was the only thing she woke up with. "What do you remember about last night?"

"Besides drinking too much?" Carrie chuckled and pulled her hair back. "I left with Frank and Jack said he would take you home. Why? What happened?"

"Did Jack seem…okay?" Sunny might have remembered Jack biting, but the rest of the night was returning in bits and pieces and none too quickly.

"None of us were okay, Sunny. We were all drunk. Only thing is, I don't remember them drinking anything."

"Did Frank nuzzle your neck a lot?"

"Sure did, just like Jack did with you. God, it felt great. I thought I was going to come a couple of times. Don't you remember any of it?"

"Some." Sunny picked at the cushion. Could it be she remembered Jack feeding and not infecting her? She wanted to believe he wouldn't do such a thing. Maybe she needed to go a different route with Carrie. "Was Frank with you all night?"

Carrie shook her head. "Not really. He passed out shortly after we got back here. I curled up next to him. He sure is a hunk, isn't he?" Her eyes glazed over like they always did whenever she had it bad for someone. Sunny snapped her fingers. Carrie blinked her eyes several times and smiled. "Sorry. Anyway, when I woke up to use the bathroom, he was gone. Damn shame, too. I was hoping he'd stay."

"What time did you wake up?"

"Hell, I don't know. It was dark and everything was blurry." Carrie put her hand on Sunny's arm. "What happened that was so bad?"

"Jack and Frank are vampires and they most likely turned me into one, too."

Carrie placed her hand on Sunny's brow. "You don't feel hot. Are you sure you only drank last night?"

Sunny removed her friend's hand. "It's true and I can prove it."

She concentrated on Carrie's mind, but not knowing the intricacies of connecting, failed miserably. And of course, her fangs wouldn't cooperate, probably because she was afraid of hurting Carrie. There was only one thing she could do.

"Get off the couch," Sunny said.

"Sunny, it's okay. I believe you."

She knew when she was being placated and it wasn't acceptable. "Fine, if you won't get off, then hold on."

Sunny stood in front of the sofa, placed her hands underneath and lifted. This better work. Without thinking, she picked it up in the middle, not anticipating the uneven weight, and the couch dipped on Carrie's side. After her friend screamed and grabbed onto the armrest, Sunny adjusted her hold. Dang couch weighed practically nothing, almost like a piece of Styrofoam, even with her friend sitting on top. Wow. And she didn't even have muscles.

"Oh my God!" Carrie screamed. "How did you do that?"

"I told you, I'm a vampire. Now do you believe me?" Sunny asked as she lowered the couch.

"I believe you, I believe you. Tell me everything you know."

Sunny sat on the couch and told her friend everything that had happened. The more she told, the less nervous she became. Her friend absorbed every word with a rapt expression on her face, a huge relief to Sunny.

A cramp shot across her abdomen and she doubled over. Fudge. What the heck was that?

"Are you okay?" Carrie asked. "Did you hurt yourself?"

The pain subsided and Sunny straightened up. Why was she still cramping? What else had Jack forgotten to tell her? "I'm fine. Maybe I pulled a muscle."

"Sunny, if you can't go out in the sun, how are you going to make it to your interview tomorrow?"

Holy cannoli. Her interview. She'd completely forgotten.

Chapter 5

Sunny sat on the edge of her bed, willing the pain in her stomach to go away, as if it would do any good.

She had been talking to Carrie about her interview, trying to think of a way to actually attend, when pain ripped through her midsection. She should have known from the first cramp that she was hungry. Why couldn't her stomach just rumble like it used to? Why did everything have to be so much harder? When her fangs popped out, she'd thought she might bite her friend and had hightailed it to her bedroom to suffer.

She needed blood. The only problem was in getting it. The one time she'd fed wasn't all that difficult, but could she keep track of time on her own and stop before harming the individual? She couldn't even read Carrie's mind, how would she be able to mask the pain?

Maybe running from Jack wasn't such a bright move after all. So what if he had turned her? There wasn't much more he could do to her, was there? Then there was Frank. He might be able to help.

Should she go back and face them? Admit her mistake in leaving? It wouldn't be the first time she'd reacted without thinking. Wasn't that how she'd ended up in Pittsburgh in the first place?

All she'd ever wanted to do was live on her own terms, but her father had refused to listen to her, insisting she go back to college. Yuck. She'd hated high school and the few college courses she had taken were pure torture. Then she met Aaron, the photographer at one of her father's political events, and fell in love. With Aaron and photography.

While Aaron hadn't lasted, her love for photography had. But every time Sunny tried to get work in that field, her father managed to poke his fingers into her business. "It's a waste of time." "You'll never make any money at it." "You should concentrate on getting a real job." Sick and tired of being told no by the one person who should be proud of whatever she decided to do, she'd taken her portfolio, a week's worth of clothes and escaped to Carrie's without a word to her father.

Would life be any different as a vampire? Every time it appeared she was moving ahead, someone shoved her back. How the heck was she going to make an interview if she couldn't even eat?

Another painful hunger pang ripped through her stomach and she doubled over. "Oh God. Why can't I just die and get it over with?"

A knock on the door startled her out of her misery.

"Sunny? Are you okay?"

No, she wasn't okay. She wasn't sure she'd ever be okay again. "I'm fine. I just need some time alone."

The door opened a crack. "You don't sound fine." Carrie's eyes widened and she barged into the room. "You're so pale. Did you get sick?"

Oh, great. She had just gotten her fangs to retract. Sunny put her hand up. "Don't come any closer. I… I'm not sure I have any willpower."

Instead of obeying, her friend sat on the bed and tucked her hair behind her ears. Sunny got a whiff of Carrie's scent, but her fangs stayed imbedded and she wasn't drooling for any blood. Maybe Carrie was safe after all.

"You're not looking well," Carrie said, brushing her fingers through Sunny's hair. "What can I do to help?"

Offer a little blood? Oh fudge, what was she thinking? Carrie wasn't food. Sunny lay down and curled into the fetal position. "Nothing."

"Does it have something to do with being a vampire? Should I call Frank? I have his number." Carrie stood and pulled a cellphone out of her jeans pocket.

"You don't have his number. You said he left while you were asleep."

"He did. I got it when he was passed out. I added my number to his cell and then used his cell to call mine. Easy peasy."

Fear jolted Sunny upright and she grabbed for the phone right when another slashing hunger pang raced across her stomach. She hugged her belly and rolled over onto her side, moaning in pain.

Carrie knelt beside the bed. "Maybe I should call. I hate seeing you like this. No one should hurt this much."

Sunny panted through the pain. "Please don't call. Didn't you hear what I told you? It's because of him and Jack that I'm in this predicament."

"So, you *know* what's the matter?"

"Yes. Probably. Pretty sure."

"You gonna shed some light my way?"

The last thing Sunny wanted to do was confess, but pain and weakness took their toll. Plus, Carrie would probably bug her until she spilled. "If you must know, I'm hungry."

Carrie stood, slashing her hand through the air, dismissing Sunny's statement. "Is that all? I've got food here, you idiot. What did you want? A sandwich? Soup?"

Sunny covered her face and shook her head. Carrie wasn't that dense, was she?

Carrie plopped down on the bed. "Ohhh. You need blood."

"Bingo."

"Do you need a lot? I mean, you don't kill to feed, do you?"

"I didn't the last time, but I had help. I don't know what to do."

"So maybe I should call Frank."

"Nooo!" Dag-burnit. Didn't the girl understand anything?

"Fine." Carrie put the phone back in her pocket. "Can you take my blood? Would that help?"

"No way, no way." Sunny shook her head. "I can't ask you to do that. It doesn't seem right."

Carrie pulled her hair back and exposed her neck. "Is this how it's done?"

The vein in her friend's neck beckoned. The rise and fall of each pulse clearly defined, as if seen in slow motion. What was wrong with her? This was her friend. Besides, didn't Jack say it took practice to feed from the neck? She'd kill her friend for sure.

She tore her gaze away and did the only thing she could--she rolled over and let her back do the talking.

"If you can't take my blood, then you're leaving me no choice."

"You wouldn't." Sunny glared over her shoulder at her friend, or maybe it was former friend. "That's blackmail."

Carrie stood, hands on hips. "Call it what you want. Take my blood or I call Frank."

This was so unfair. Why couldn't Jack and Frank have left her alone? What did she ever do to them? God, she wanted to hit something.

"I'm not taking your blood and if you try to call Frank, I'll…I'll break your phone."

"You'll have to get it first."

Sunny glared at her friend. If only her telepathic skills worked, she'd show Carrie. But heck, she was a vampire and she did have other skills. Like speed. Sunny leapt from the bed, going for Carrie's pocket. Carrie squealed. Just as Sunny touched the phone, her stomach cramped as if someone grabbed hold of her innards and twisted. Clutching her belly, she screamed and collapsed to the floor.

"Oh my God, Sunny!" Carrie dropped to the floor and hugged Sunny close.

"Get out. Now." Sunny bared her fangs and shrugged away. She was an animal out of control.

Tears formed in her friend's eyes and she scrambled to leave. The door shut softly.

What did she just do? Guilt shamed Sunny. How could she go after Carrie that way and then bark at her as if she were the enemy? Sunny slowly stood, using the bed for support. Stupid stomach. Death needed to come and come quick. She was finished. She didn't want to be a stupid vampire. She just wanted to die. She deserved to die.

The bed called to her. She put on pajamas and crawled under the covers. If she was going to meet death, she might as well get comfortable.

* * * *

Leave it to Frank to suggest another bar. Was the man nuts? Or did he actually have a drinking problem? No way would Jack approach another drunk, at least, not anytime soon.

My Sunny Vampire

"Not hungry?" Harris asked after returning from his donor. Frank was still missing.

"Not for this." Jack leaned against the wall in the alley. Most of the foot traffic stayed on the street. Only those who needed to use the dumpsters would venture close. The scent of rotting food offended his nose, but at least he was alone. Or had been. It was a miracle he hadn't spent the day with Harris at the safe house. "So, where were you all day?"

Harris crouched down and started to pack some snow. "I was with Bailey."

Who the hell was Bailey? If Jack questioned Harris, he might grow suspicious.

Harris glanced up at Jack. "Oh, sorry. After I left you two at the bar, I hooked up with her."

"I guess you two really hit it off then."

Harris finished making a second snowball and placed it on top of the first. He started to pack a third. "Not really. After the fiasco with Ivy, I've given up looking for a relationship. I don't want to go through that again. Bailey won't remember me."

"You'll still remember her. How is that better?"

"There's not much to remember. I used her for sex and food. I didn't get into any conversation with her and she slept when I didn't need her."

As lonely as Jack's life had been, he'd never stooped so low. Wiping a donor's memory of the feeding act was one thing. For those times he found a woman who offered more, well, it just didn't seem right. Maybe it was his ego, but if he was going to remember the night, it only seemed fitting the woman did, too. Especially if she had a good time, which was always his goal.

"Harris, not everyone is like Ivy. You're not even giving them a chance."

"Since when do you care?" Harris shook his head. "Sorry, sorry. That's the old me coming out." He stared at the snowball in his hand. "I need baby steps, Jack. I want to fix our relationship first. I have a feeling that might take a while."

Jack would like nothing more than to distance himself from Harris, but the man deserved a chance at happiness. Everyone did.

Harris placed the third snowball on top, creating a miniature snowman. He stood and inspected his artwork. "You'll be at

Frank's tomorrow, right? I wouldn't want to intrude if you planned on being at the safe house."

"That's my plan."

Harris put his hands in his pockets and shifted his feet. "Listen, since you're being all soft-hearted and all, I want to ask you a question. Have you noticed Frank acting strangely?"

Funny Harris should mention that. The Committee had received an anonymous call about Frank's excessive drinking problem. The caller feared Frank might do something to warrant exposure, or worse, hurt himself.

The anonymous call made Jack suspicious, but the accusation held merit. Linda's death had devastated Frank and Jack should have been more attentive. If Frank really went off the deep end, Jack needed to help his friend and had been more than willing to take the assignment.

"Strange how?" Jack asked.

"I know I have no right to ask, and maybe he's been like this all along, but don't you think he's obsessed with drunks? He was rather wild last night. Don't you think?"

Frank? Wild? Jack wouldn't dream of telling Harris his memory of the night was currently in limbo-land, but it seemed strange how Frank had told Jack the same thing about him. Could Frank have lied? If so, why?

"It was New Year's Eve," Jack said. "I wasn't exactly sober, either."

"Yeah, but you weren't biting everything within dancing distance. I'm surprised you didn't belt him when he went after the redhead."

Frank bit Sunshine? Jack clenched his fists. Carrie wasn't enough? Frank had to go after his girl, too?

Whoa. Where did that come from? Sunshine wasn't his girl. She couldn't be either. How would that look to the Committee? He smiled at Harris, pretending it was nothing. "You don't say. I must have missed that."

Harris nudged him, shoulder to shoulder. "So, how was the redhead anyway? Sunny, right?"

Everyone seemed to call her Sunny, but Jack couldn't. To him, she was Sunshine and always would be. "I enjoyed her company."

"You sly dog. Listen to you, 'enjoyed her company.' You and Frank kept her so busy on the dance floor, I never got a chance to actually see her."

Jack relaxed. Thank God. If Harris had gotten a good look at Sunshine, he'd probably notice the resemblance. Clara's picture wasn't exactly a well-kept secret.

"What are you two doing standing out here? I thought we came to eat." Frank approached them without swaying, not a hint of a slur. If he was drunk, Jack couldn't tell.

Harris pulled out a pack of gum and put a stick in his mouth. He offered a piece to Frank, who waved it off. "Maybe if you picked a place with fewer inebriated patrons, Jack would have joined us. I think maybe he had too much alcohol last night." He offered a stick to Jack.

"No thanks," Jack said.

Harris put the pack back inside his pocket. "Why don't we go somewhere where there are fewer drunks? A hospital, maybe?"

Oh God, no. That was the last thing Jack wanted. Would this night never end? He wanted to find Sunshine. Make sure she was okay. Hell, he just wanted to see her. "I'm fine, really. I hate to cut this short," he glanced at his watch to make it look convincing, "but I need to be someplace right now. You know, Committee business." He hoped it was enough to keep the questions at bay.

"Oh, yeah, sure," Harris said. "How long are you in town for? Maybe we could hook up later."

"Jack told me he's here until the seventh. Except for today, he's been staying with me."

Harris's face lit up with his smile. "Great. Maybe I'll come visit in a couple of days, then? Catch up on old times?"

When a grinning Frank slapped Harris on the back, Jack nearly groaned. He and Harris had never gotten along, even before all the tragedy came their way. The last thing Jack wanted to do was reminisce.

"What a great idea," Frank said. "I'd like that."

Since Jack arrived in Pittsburgh, he'd rarely seen Frank so animated. First with Carrie, now with Harris. How could he ruin something clearly beneficial for his friend?

Jack took a deep breath. Harris mentioned baby steps. Maybe that's what he needed, too. Oh hell, it wasn't like he'd have to live with the guy. He'd keep it brief.

If Sunshine had her memory back, he'd find out who bit her. Then, once he determined Frank didn't have a death wish, he would haul her down to Atlanta and hand her over to the Committee with a clear conscience and get back to life as usual.

"We'll see you in a few, then." Jack did his best to convey a warm smile. Thoughts of Frank being happy made it easier. And it worked. Harris's grin stretched, making the sides of his eyes crinkle.

Harris jogged off and Frank turned to Jack. "Thanks. I know you don't care for the man."

"I didn't care for the man he was. Maybe he's changed." He still had his doubts, but it was better than telling Frank what he really thought.

"So, did you find out anything about last night? Did I give you enough time to question him?"

"Is that why you were gone so long? Geez, Frank. I wish you had told me. I don't want Harris knowing about Sunshine and I certainly don't want him to know I don't remember."

"You don't still suspect him, do you?"

Harris was at the top of his short list. So was Frank. He hated doubting his friend, but what choice did he have? "I don't know what to think. Not until I've accessed Sunshine's memories. Can we go find her now?"

Noise blared from inside Frank's pocket and he pulled out his cellphone.

"What the hell is that?" Jack asked. "It sounds like a cat screeching."

"I'm not sure. I just wanted a ring tone to get my attention. The clerk found the song for me. I have no idea how to change it." Frank looked at his phone. His mouth opened and his eyes widened.

"What is it?" Jack asked.

"It's Carrie."

"Carrie? Damn, Frank. You gave her your number?"

Frank shook his head. "I swear, I didn't. She must have gotten it some other way. That's not the worst."

What could be worse than a mortal having a vampire's cellphone number? Losing his patience, Jack snatched the phone out of Frank's hand and read the message.

SUNNY NEEDS BLOOD. CAN YOU HELP HER?

My Sunny Vampire

What was worse than a mortal having a vampire's cellphone number? The mortal *knowing* she had a vampire's cellphone number, that's what.

Chapter 6

Jack and Frank approached Carrie's apartment building. Surprisingly, it wasn't far from the bar where they'd met the girls.

"How do I look?" Frank tugged the hem of his flannel shirt.

"We're not here for a social call. Damn, I still can't believe she told her." Of course, it wasn't like Jack told Sunshine every rule. And she had apparently forgotten how to eat. Or maybe she hadn't, but just didn't know how to hide it. That was most likely the case. He should never have let her leave.

"What's the big deal? So we wipe Carrie's memory. Just don't wipe out last night. I think she likes me and I don't want to have to start over."

The lightness in Frank's voice caused Jack to observe Frank in a whole new manner. The way he kept pulling his shirt down like it would do any good to hide the wrinkles. Or the way he combed his fingers through his hair. He acted like a nervous suitor. "She that important to you?"

Frank shrugged. "I don't know. Maybe. I only know I liked being with her, Jack. I haven't felt like that in a long time."

Well, whaddya know. Frank was smitten. Jack shook his head. "You look fine. Quit fidgeting."

Jack followed Frank to Carrie's apartment and Frank knocked on the door. It swung open to a pixie of a girl. Jack had no memory of Carrie standing so the height difference came as quite a shock.

At six-foot three, Frank stood like a giant in front of her. He grinned like a love-sick boy.

My Sunny Vampire

Her eyes widened and she flung herself at him screaming, "Frankie!" He caught her and she put her legs around his waist, all while planting one seemingly messy kiss on his lips.

Jack was pretty sure Frank had nothing to worry about in making an impression on the young woman. She seemed to like him just fine.

Jack cleared his throat. When Carrie looked at him, he waved. A nice shade of pink crept onto her cheeks.

"Oh. Sorry." She climbed off Frank, who frowned at her departure. "Guess I got carried away. Sunny's in the bedroom. You can help her, can't you?"

Jack followed Frank and Carrie inside and shut the door. "What exactly did Sunshine tell you?"

"That she's a vampire and that you turned her." She led them into a small living room. Every available wall space had a bolt or two of fabric leaning against it and patterns covered the table. "Excuse the mess. I wasn't expecting company."

"I can't believe you betrayed me," Sunshine yelled from down the hall. "After I die, I'm coming back to haunt all of you." The rant preceded several seconds of moaning.

Carrie gasped and brought a hand up to her heart. "She's dying?"

A snort nearly escaped, but he stopped it in time. Carrie might not see the humor in Sunshine's words. "No, she's not dying. She's probably just hungry." And scared.

"That's what I thought, but when I offered my blood, she refused to take it. Even though she said you don't kill humans. In fact, she said you probably both sampled my blood last night. So is that true? Are you vampires?"

The woman was downright giddy. If the Committee thought all mortals would react this way to the realization of vampires, they would have come out long ago. Unfortunately, most humans would not react as favorably. Instead, they would see vampires as a threat to their existence, if not their lifestyle.

"That's sweet," Frank said. "You offered your blood?"

"She's my friend. I'd do anything for her."

"Let me go see her," Jack said.

"She's in the room on the right."

Jack walked down the short hallway and turned the knob. He thought he might find it locked, but Sunshine hadn't bothered.

49

The small bed and dresser took up most of the space in the room. Facing away, she was curled up under the covers as if she were cold. "I think I'll haunt you first. Since you're the one who did this to me."

After shutting the door, he walked around the bed, and sat beside her. "You're not going to die from lack of blood and I'm pretty sure I didn't do this to you."

"I remember. You bit me." She grabbed her stomach and hissed through clenched teeth.

"According to Frank, I did some nibbling. That's probably what you remember. If you'll let me have access to your memories, I can show you." He reached for her arm, but she pulled away.

"Don't touch me."

"Sunshine..."

"And don't call me that. My name is Sunny. But you can call me Ms. Petersen."

Damn pigheaded woman. Clara had never acted that way. She'd known better than to argue, had done what was expected. Shit. He mentally slapped himself. Of course she had. Life had been different in the eighteenth century. Who's to say she wouldn't have turned out like Sunshine if she were raised in the twenty-first century?

And Sunshine was definitely a twenty-first century woman. Fine, he could play her game. "Ms. Petersen, then. I need to link into your memories. If I see I truly did inject you, then I'll turn myself in, but I believe I only fed from you."

She stared at him. "What do you mean turn yourself in?"

"It's against our laws to turn a mortal without permission. One who does will be punished by death."

"Death?"

She lifted her head and her expression intrigued him--furrowed brow, worried eyes. She liked to talk big, but apparently cared something for him. Otherwise she'd be cheering, wouldn't she?

* * * *

"I don't want anyone to die." Except maybe herself. It would surely be less painful.

"Then may I?" Jack placed his hand on the bed, palm up.

Sunny stared at it. Less than twelve hours ago he'd had that hand on her body and she remembered every touch. She couldn't touch him now. If she did, she might not stop with his hand. Oh

My Sunny Vampire

why couldn't he have stayed on the other side of the door? It was taking everything within her not to run into his arms, not that she was in any shape to bolt out of bed.

Was he telling the truth, could her accusation get him killed? She thought she hated him, but she didn't. Not really. She certainly didn't want him dead. Maybe it would be better if she died. It would make everyone else's life easier.

She sat up and pulled her knees in close, waiting for tears to flow. Her chest ached for release, but her eyes remained dry. Dang it, she couldn't even cry anymore. A profound sadness overcame her. How much more would she discover she'd lost? She lowered her head to her knees and sobbed.

"Sun--I mean, Ms. Petersen--"

She wailed louder. Why was he so mean to her? Now he sounded impersonal. She wanted personal.

He hugged her and she buried her head against his chest.

"Don't call me that anymore." Another pain sliced through her abdomen and she clutched at his back.

The chuckle reverberated in his chest and almost caused her anger to flare up. Was he laughing at her? Then he caressed the back of her head. Didn't seem like he made fun. Well, maybe she was acting silly. Getting control of her wild emotions wasn't an easy accomplishment, especially when they changed without notice.

"Why don't I get you fed first, then we can determine what I should call you. Afterward, we'll figure out what happened. How does that sound?" he asked.

"I don't know. Will it always be this bad when I'm hungry? If it is, just kill me."

He let out an exasperated breath and pulled her back. "Will you stop? You're not dying and I'm not going to kill you. I'm sorry I've mucked this up. The first few weeks are the hardest on a new vampire and require more blood than normal. I should have taken you out as soon as the sun set. I'll make it better for you. I promise."

The words didn't sound like they came from someone who would have turned her and dumped her in the alley. Then again, she'd ended up beside him, or so he said. She didn't know what to believe. Maybe once she ate, she would think more clearly.

He stood and offered his hand to her. At this moment she might make a deal with the Devil himself if it meant she didn't have to hurt any more. But could she touch his skin? No. She was weak in more ways than one.

She grabbed his covered arm and stood. When the sheet fell, his eyes widened and he gasped. Fudge. She'd forgotten about her pajamas. Not that a tank top and bikini panties would be considered pajamas to other people. Having her nipples stick out like they did wasn't helping any, either. All of a sudden she felt exposed.

"Maybe I better change first, huh?"

He scrubbed his face. "Yes, maybe you better."

Was it wrong for her to enjoy his frustration? It gave her a sense of power. Unfortunately, that power vanished the second she released him to hunt for her clothes. One step and her legs decided they'd rather see the floor up close and personal. Jack reacted quickly enough and kept her upright by grabbing her waist. The soft leather of his jacket did nothing to hide the muscular arms underneath. She looked up. His lips were inches from hers and she closed her eyes to keep from leaning in for a kiss. As she adjusted her stance, her thigh rubbed up against his erection. Dang. What she wouldn't give to be feeling one hundred percent right about now.

He lowered her to the bed. "Sit and tell me where your clothes are." His voice cracked just a bit. Maybe he wished the same thing.

She indicated where to find her jeans and sweater. After slipping the clothes on over her pajamas, she bent over to tie her shoes and another cramp skittered across her stomach. She moaned. He took over the task as she straightened to catch her breath.

"I can carry you if you want."

She shook her head. Not only to indicate her answer, but to clear the blurry memory that surfaced. He had danced with her, grinding his body against hers and she had liked it. A lot. Had their chemistry started before her unfortunate event? Maybe she got it wrong. Maybe what she felt now had nothing to do with her being a vampire. She would have to ask him later, though. Once her stomach stopped hurting. "I think I'll be okay as long as I can hold onto you."

"Then hold away."

Their trip to the living room didn't burn up any carpet. Each step was torture. She couldn't concentrate on walking when her mind was focused on the arm around her waist, but she wasn't some baby who needed to be carried. She would walk if it killed her and at her rate, death would probably come soon.

* * * *

Jack timed Sunshine as she sucked on the second donor's wrist. They were currently between two houses, out of sight from the general public. Finding two donors was a streak of luck he wasn't taking for granted. She hadn't been in any shape to go farther than a block or two, but apparently some people enjoyed their nightly walks regardless of the season.

Although mind manipulation should have been second nature to her by now, there were a few cases where the new vampire needed to be taught. In order to teach her, he needed her strong and clear-headed, thus the second donor. After her indoctrination in Atlanta, she would be on her own and would need that skill to survive. He couldn't be with her forever, not that forever was a bad idea.

When she had crawled out of bed and uncovered that luscious body of hers, Little Jack had nearly exploded. Maybe once he solved this case, she wouldn't mind him visiting every now and then. He certainly wouldn't mind seeing more of her. First, he needed to clear his name. What good was making plans if it turned out he was the culprit?

The second hand crossed the one minute mark. "Time," he said.

She licked her puncture marks and pulled back. Good, no mess this time. In her frenzy to feed, she had squirted blood all over the first guy's arm, which had to be cleaned before Jack would release him.

The second donor walked off and continued on his journey, oblivious to anything out of the ordinary.

"When are you going to teach me that?"

"I was thinking we could practice on your friend before we wipe her memory. You might be more comfortable--"

She grabbed his arm, cutting him off in mid-sentence. "What? Why do you need to wipe Carrie's memory?"

"Humans aren't supposed to know about us. It has to be done."

"She's not going to tell anyone. If you wipe her memory, I'll just tell her again."

If he were built of springs he would have sprung them all. Damn woman, she was impossible. He scrubbed his face, trying to calm down. Yelling might also help, but he didn't need to draw a crowd or get her more defensive than she already was.

"Please don't." She sounded like a defeated child, as if he'd given her a fight, when he hadn't said a word. She plopped down into the snow. "She's the only person I can talk to."

He crouched beside her. "I know it's tough. I can take you to a female vampire if it would make it easier for you."

"I don't want a female vampire. She's not going to help me. Carrie can."

Oh, this had to be good. "Explain."

Her face lit up, as if she thought he might give her a chance. "A female vampire couldn't help me get to my job interview tomorrow."

* * * *

Sunny stared at Jack. He must reconsider. Now that she was fed and stronger, she could make her interview, but only with Carrie's help. How else could she get there during the day?

He furrowed his forehead. "Job interview? You can't go to any job interview."

"Why not? Don't I still have to make a living?"

"Sure, once you have a new identity and all."

Dag-burnit. He was doing it again. Feeding her information in bits and pieces and frankly, she was sick and tired of it. She stood and brushed the snow off her butt. "What new identity?"

He rose with her and took a step back as if he thought she would strike out at him. Heck, she just might. "All new vampires have to start over. Before DNA testing, any old body could be used to report a death, as long as it was unrecognizable. We can't do that anymore, so you'll be reported as missing. You might be able to keep your name, but you won't be the same person, at least not where the government is concerned."

His words swam in her brain. Was he telling her the life she knew was dead and gone? "But why? I don't understand."

"In case you didn't notice, you're different now."

"I'm not that different. Carrie didn't say anything."

He glanced behind her and pulled her toward the back of the house. "That's because you told Carrie you're a vampire," he whispered. "But you can't tell anyone. Not your family and not

My Sunny Vampire

your friends. You won't be able to live with them. They'll notice you don't go out during the day. Or that you don't eat. Imagine what questions they'll have if they see you get hurt, but recover within hours. You can't even go to a doctor. These are things you have to learn to camouflage."

He continued to hold her arm and his presence fogged her mind. Dang her stupid hormones. It had to be that, why else was she all hot for him when she should be mad? Between his touch and his words, she needed to keep her distance. She welcomed the anger, no matter how tiny the seed. After tugging herself free, she paced up and down the narrow passageway between the two homes. He made her life sound like hell. To know her friends were out there, but she couldn't contact them? To know they grieved and she couldn't comfort them? She wasn't dead, dang it.

"You're telling me everything is gone. All because someone"-- she stopped and shoved him in the chest--"maybe you, wanted to turn me into a vampire. Well, I won't stand for it. It's not my fault this happened. Do you hear me? It's not my fault. So quit punishing me."

"I'm not punishing you, but there are rules."

"Oh yeah? And who made you the ruler?"

* * * *

This discussion couldn't have happened in a worse place. One neighbor already peeked out the window. Jack needed to keep Sunshine quiet. "We need to talk about this at Carrie's."

"You don't want to talk. You just want to tell me everything I can't do anymore."

Sunshine sounded bitter, but he couldn't blame her. It did seem like he was always bursting one bubble or another. He approached her, ready to retreat in case a fist flew. "Yes, there are some things you can't do anymore, but there are also things you can do. Please, let's discuss those in private."

She folded her arms across her chest and backed up as if he were the threat. "Why should I trust you? Sure, you've taken care of me, some. Shown me how to feed. For all I know you did all that because you turned me. I mean, wouldn't you be here if that were the case? Maybe you just want to get me alone to brainwash me or something."

"Will you listen to yourself? We're alone now. Am I brainwashing you?"

She stopped and frowned. "How the heck should I know? Do people being brainwashed know they're being brainwashed?"

He shook his head. There wasn't anything he could say to her accusations. Damn, if he could only remember. "I know you don't have any reason, but I hope you'll trust me. Let's just go back to Carrie's."

He reached for her elbow to encourage her to return to the apartment, but she whipped her arm away. In the process, she smacked an older gentleman in the chest and he went flying to the pavement.

"Oh my God," she wailed. "I've killed him!"

Jack went to the man. "Will you hush? He's not dead." At least, not yet.

Out cold, the man had landed hard on the cement and blood oozed from one ear. Nothing wrong with his heart rate, though.

"Oh." She covered her mouth.

"Stand back. You'll be okay."

"So you say. Your teeth didn't just pop out."

"Breathe through your mouth and avert your eyes."

The unconscious man was the same person who had peeked out of the window earlier. Jack concentrated on the building and heard one heartbeat. Great, just great.

"Is he going to be okay?" Her words were said with a lisp. Most likely her fangs hadn't retracted.

Before he could answer or come up with any plan, the door to the house opened. A petite white-haired lady poked her head out. "Albert? Is everything okay?"

"Fudge," Sunshine muttered.

"Get back," he whispered to her. "Don't let her see you." He stood and approached the old woman. Her eyes widened and she backed into the doorway. "Ma'am. I think your Albert fell on the sidewalk."

With the snow on the ground and the sidewalk icy in places, it wasn't hard for the woman to believe Jack. Her eyes widened and her hand went up to her neck. "Oh my. What happened?"

"I think he slipped on some ice. You might want to call 9-1-1."

She nodded and went back inside the house. Jack took the opportunity and cupped his hands on the gentleman's face for some mind manipulation. It might be harder to send a suggestion to an unconscious recipient, but not impossible, especially when

My Sunny Vampire

they touched. "*Albert, when you came outside, you found the neighborhood deserted and you slipped on the ice.*"

Jack repeated the message several times until the man's wife came back, wearing her coat and carrying a blanket and pillow. She covered Albert the best she could without moving him too much. The woman laid the pillow down on the ground beside Albert and sat upon it. After a few moments, she started shivering.

"Why don't you go on inside?" Jack said. "I'll stay with him."

"That won't be necessary." She took hold of Albert's hand. "But you could be a dear and fetch me another blanket."

That he could do, and brought out several. She thanked him for his kindness, yet Jack felt anything but kind. If it weren't for him and Sunshine, the man wouldn't even be in this predicament.

While Jack waited with her, she introduced herself. Her name was Mabel, and she and Albert had been married fifty years. She told Jack how she and Albert met, never once letting go of her husband's hand. It seemed to give her great comfort.

After the paramedics were on the scene, Albert started coming around. Jack tensed, waiting to see if his suggestion took. When Mabel asked what happened, Albert responded as instructed. Jack let out a long breath. Thank God. But that wasn't the biggest miracle. No, that honor belonged to Sunshine. She'd actually listened to him for once and stayed hidden during the whole ordeal.

The paramedics took Albert to the hospital and Mabel followed in her own car. Once she was out of sight, Sunshine emerged from between the buildings. "You were awfully kind to her."

"Why wouldn't I be kind?"

"Most people would have probably walked away once someone took responsibility. You were nice to her and kept her calm. You didn't have to do it."

She stepped out of the snow-covered grass and stomped her feet on the sidewalk, knocking the snow off her shoes. Her demeanor had changed. She was more relaxed, less angry. This wasn't the woman who nearly punched his lights out earlier.

"I'm ready to go to Carrie's and talk."

Well, hallelujah. Would wonders never cease? Maybe punching the old guy did her some good. Maybe she could see she needed to control her emotions better and maybe he'd impressed her just a bit. He smiled, hoping he had, as he offered his elbow to her. She

57

took it and the corners of her mouth curled slightly. Not a full-blown smile, but more than he expected.

Chapter 7

Sunny sat on the couch with Carrie while Jack and Frank explained all the wonders of being a vampire. Wonders, indeed. Leave it to Jack to lay out the facts in a business-like manner, listing the events she could no longer do along with the tasks she was now required to do. The only thing missing was the whiteboard and markers so he could put a check mark next to each item. As if sensing Sunny's spiraling depression, Frank counteracted by speaking animatedly, assuring her of the incredible abilities vampires possessed.

"Wow, how cool is it to be a vampire?" Carrie said. "Super speed. Super strength. Super everything. You don't even have to sleep. I can't even imagine what it's like to never be tired."

It might have sounded cool to Carrie, but Sunny was anything but upbeat. She only heard about the things she'd lost. Food. Children. Sunlight. A career. Her freedom. What good was it to live forever if you couldn't have any fun? And then Jack wanted to wipe Carrie's memory, which meant Sunny would lose her best friend, too. The pity party she was having weighed heavily upon her heart. She lowered her head and stared at her lap.

Jack crouched in front of her. "Hey, it's not the end of the world."

Sunny wanted to be mad at him, but he made it darn hard sounding all sincere-like. "That's easy for you to say. You at least have friends."

"Hey, what am I?" Carrie said. "Chopped liver?"

Sunny turned to her friend. Here was something she could get mad about. "Why don't you ask these two what they plan on doing to you. Then ask me that."

Frank sat on the armrest beside Carrie and played with her hair. "We might not need to."

Jack looked up at Frank. "Aren't you the one who reminded me?"

"Yeah, but that was before I knew how well she took to us."

"What the hell are you talking about?" Carrie interjected. "Is something going to happen to me?"

Sunny stared at Jack. Was Frank on her side? Was it possible she wouldn't lose her best friend after all? Hope started to form and she held on to every bit she could.

Jack stood and spoke to Carrie, "It's customary to wipe the memory of any mortal who finds out about us."

"Wipe my...? Frankie? Is this true?" Carrie looked at him as she worried her bottom lip.

Frank stroked her hair. "Now, baby, it's not as bad as it sounds. You wouldn't forget us. Only that we're vampires." He turned toward Jack. "Is it really necessary? She's not threatened by us and I kind of like not having to lie. I'm sure she won't tell anyone if we ask her."

Carrie nodded. "I won't. I promise."

Jack rubbed his head and face. "Frank, are you saying you'll take responsibility for this mortal?"

This mortal? Sunny hated the impersonal tone he projected. Carrie wasn't just some mortal. She was a person with feelings. "Why does anyone--"

Jack raised his hand in a stop motion, cutting Sunny off in mid-sentence as if she were some child to be hushed. How dare he.

"It's okay, Sunny," Frank said. "That's just the Committee Member in him coming out. If that's what it takes, Jack, then yes, I'll take the responsibility."

Was that why Jack seemed so official, so cold, while he laid out her duties as a vampire? If having to report to Atlanta once a year wasn't a duty, she didn't know what was. "You're part of this Committee I have to report to yearly?"

"Jack?" Frank looked at his friend. "Didn't you tell her that already?"

"I never got around to it."

My Sunny Vampire

"You're a cop?" She bolted off the couch. If she kept staring at Jack's sexy blue-green eyes, she could very well throw him to the ground and jump his bones and she wanted to be mad at him more than anything. Anger seemed to dampen her sex drive. A little, anyway.

"Not quite."

What kind of answer was that? And why did she desperately want to kiss him? Dang it. Was he putting some kind of mojo on her to let her guard down? Could he control her emotions? Because she was certainly doing a lousy job of controlling them herself.

She took a deep breath and focused. "If you're not a cop, then what?"

"More like a judge."

A judge. It all made sense now and was exactly what she needed to feed her anger, but if she hit him could he arrest her? She was almost tempted to find out, but kept her fists to her side. "So let me get this straight. You're a judge, you're supposed to enforce the rules and it's possible you broke a huge one turning me."

* * * *

God, she was beautiful. The fire in her eyes, the scent of her desire. And she desired him, all right. If not for the room full of people and his will to remain professional, he'd have taken her right there on the couch.

"I told you earlier I might be able to prove I didn't bite you, but to do that, I need to access your memories." Jack put his hand out, palm up. "Will you let me now?"

Sunshine stared at it for a moment then looked him in the eyes. "You can read my thoughts and memories from a touch?"

He nodded. "You can, too. It just takes--"

"You've been able to read my mind all along?" She poked him in the chest, her eyes wide with panic.

"Not intentionally, but you've been known to scream a few times."

"Scream? What's that supposed to mean?"

She was on the verge of a meltdown and he was her target. She clenched and unclenched her hands, probably deciding whether to hit him or not. How could he blame her? He should have told her long before now.

He grasped her shoulders, hoping it would calm her. "It means your thoughts are close to the surface."

She jerked out of his hold and folded her arms across her chest. "What if I don't want you to read my mind? What then?"

He clenched his teeth. "Damn it. I'm being nice here. Technically, I don't have to ask."

"Easy, Jack," Frank said. "She doesn't understand."

She got up in his face. "Technically, I shouldn't be a vampire. Why in the world should I trust you?"

Jack wanted nothing more than for her to trust him, but was failing miserably. Would he ever be able to get on her good side again? Because if he couldn't, he might as well just turn himself in.

Carrie went to her friend. "Sunny, why are you so angry? If Jack says he can prove he didn't do it, why won't you let him?"

"How do I know he won't be manipulating my memories? If he could wipe your mind, he could easily change mine."

"That's not true," Frank said. "When you were mortal, yes, we could change your memories. You're not mortal anymore. Vampires can only access memories from other vampires. No manipulation."

It all started to make sense. "Is that what you're afraid of?" Jack asked.

Sunshine lowered her head. "You never actually explained it like that."

At this rate, it would only take a couple more shovels before he dug a hole deep enough to bury himself. He kept forgetting she wasn't prepped to become a vampire. What she must think of him. "Forgive me. I didn't mean to cause you any more stress. I only want to get to the truth."

She plopped down on the couch. "Fine," she said in a tone that was anything but. "What do I need to do?"

He sat beside her and took her hand. An electrical charge passed between them and she tensed. He'd felt it before, when they almost made love, but he contributed it to her hormones and his lack of willpower. She should be way past any hormonal changes by now, so what was happening? Maybe someone else should be reading her thoughts.

Then he remembered something Frank had said about his first encounter with Linda. How he had known she was the one for him. One touch and he knew. Could that be what Jack was feeling?

My Sunny Vampire

Because he'd touched every vampire since becoming a member and never felt this stimulated. Could Sunshine be his one? Great, just great. If she was, the Committee would only see her turning as a desperate act to keep a mate. This didn't bode well for him at all.

Images of being kissed by him, and her mental ranting of "*Oh God, Oh God, Oh God,*" were enough for him to release her hand. His mind cleared when the connection broke, but Little Jack was well on his way to knocking on the zipper of his jeans.

"What is it?" Frank asked. "You weren't at it very long."

Sunshine was clearly distraught. Head down, eyes closed. She practically panted. He had to make this right. Not just for himself, but for her, too. He placed his hand on her lower neck, using the sweater as a shield, and found her as hard as a rock. Slowly, he massaged the area. "I think maybe we need to bring in a female."

"But Jack, the more people who know…"

"Doesn't matter. Do me a favor. Give us a few minutes alone. Take Carrie back to the bar and see if you can hunt down my phone."

Carrie sat on the other side of Sunshine and pulled her hair back. "Is that okay with you? I can stay if you want."

Sunshine took a deep breath and looked at her friend. "I'll be okay."

Carrie kissed Sunshine on the cheek and then glared at him. She opened her mouth as if to speak when Frank took her elbow.

"Why don't I take you roof-hopping? It's the closest thing a vampire can do to simulate flying."

It didn't take much to change Carrie's demeanor. Her eyes widened and she squealed. "That sounds like fun. Let me go get my coat."

Sunshine remained mute, watching Carrie and Frank, offering an occasional lift of a smile whenever Carrie looked her way. The sprite knew how to take her time, or she purposely slowed down, enjoying Frank's attention. After what seemed like an eternity, she finally finished and the two of them departed.

The apartment became quiet. Jack stood and moved to the opposite side of the room, giving Sunshine her space. Apparently, he affected her just like she affected him. He didn't know whether to be happy or scared that she might feel something for him. Right now he only wanted her at ease and comfortable, and if distance, or another vampire, could bring that to her, then he was all for it.

"What's wrong with me?" she asked.

"What makes you think something is wrong?"

"It's just...whenever you're close. Are all female vampires sluts?"

He bit back the laugh that nearly escaped. She really did have a way with words. "Let me ask you this. Do you feel the same when you're near Frank?"

She paused as if in thought and then smiled. "No."

"I'm also guessing you were attracted to me before your turning. Is that true?"

She lowered her head and stared at her lap. "Maybe."

Maybe, his ass. He risked it and sat beside her. "I remember being attracted to you when I saw you in the bar. According to Frank, I behaved horribly, and for that, I'm sorry. I'm pretty sure I felt something for you during that blackout period. Because I'm certainly feeling something now."

"So it's not just me?"

"Hardly. What are you afraid I'll see?"

She looked up at him. "It's not what you'll see. It's what I might do."

"So maybe it would be better to have a female vampire read your thoughts."

Her eyes widened. "But Frank said...no. No. I can do this. Take my hand."

Before he could react, she grabbed him and, like the rapids of a river, the current flowed through them. God, he wanted her, but he needed to get to the answer.

He closed his eyes, slowed his breathing and connected to her memory.

His face came into view. He pulled her close while they danced. When he nuzzled her neck, she tilted to give him better access. He bit. She let out a whimper.

Dammit, he didn't even mask the act from her. "Show me every episode similar to this."

The memory flickered to another song, another dance, another bite. He had fed from her at least three times. But what about Frank?

"Did Frank dance with you?"

My Sunny Vampire

"Once." The scene played out, showing them dancing, but no neck nuzzling. Either Frank blocked her memories--what any sane vampire would do--or Harris lied.

"Do you remember any bite producing searing pain?" A vampire wouldn't be able to block the injection of venom.

"No."

"Did anyone besides us dance with you or approach you?"

"Not that I remember."

"Show me the last thing you remember before waking in pain."

Jack held Sunshine's hand as they left the bar together. She reveled in the snow and twirled around in the falling fluff. Losing her equilibrium, she started to tilt. He laughed and grabbed her around the waist. Leaned in and kissed her. Then the vision went black.

"Shit." She didn't remember the injection. Anyone viewing this would see one drunk vampire obsessed with a mortal. If he hadn't turned her, then the person responsible had done a thorough job of hiding his or her presence, setting Jack up big time.

* * * *

Sunny couldn't stand it any longer. Was he responsible for turning her life inside out?

Jack didn't seem concerned about the biting incidents. Even she was beginning to think he'd only fed from her. It wasn't until everything went dark and he cussed, that she began to worry.

She squeezed his hand and prayed. "*Don't let it be him. Please don't let it be him.*"

"Sunshine."

She'd told him she didn't like being called that, but she'd lied. She liked only him calling her that. Made her seem special to him.

"You are special to me," he said.

Fudge. He'd heard her. Their hands. They were still clasped. "Am I screaming?"

The room was eerily quiet and then she heard, "*...hear me?*"

She stared at him. Did he just talk in her head?

"*You heard me, didn't you?*"

Wow. It was the first time one of her vampire skills actually brought a smile to her face. "How'd I do that? How'd I hear you?"

He caressed her cheek and smiled. "All you have to do is open your mind. In the first case, I practically punched a hole in it, but once I got through you seemed to hear me fine."

"So, is that how I manipulate minds to feed? Just talk to them mentally?"

"Pretty much. You can probably practice with Carrie. I don't think she'll mind."

Joy surged through her. For once something was working right. But wait. What about Jack? What did he find out? The exuberance was short-lived and quickly snuffed out. "So, what did you find out? Did you turn me?"

A frown marred his beautiful face. "I still don't believe I did, but while your memory doesn't show me doing it, it certainly looks like I had the opportunity."

"Fudge. Why can't I remember?" She stood and paced the small room, pounding her forehead with the heel of her hand. "How can I remember everything else but not that?"

When she turned to pace in the other direction, she collided into him and he grasped her hands together.

"Stop it. This isn't your fault." His lips gently touched her forehead and something inside her ached for more. Before she knew it, her arms were around his neck and her mouth over his. Energy flowed between them, sexually charging her body. She grabbed the neck of his shirt, ready to rip it off, when his hands covered hers. "Sunshine, stop."

No. No stopping. She nuzzled his neck and took in his scent. The bulge in his pants encouraged her and her fangs popped out. Just as she began to pierce his skin, he pulled her head back.

Pain flashed in his eyes. "I can't do this."

Talking was difficult with the extra teeth in her mouth, so she communicated mentally. "*Why not? You want me. I can tell.*"

"Doesn't matter what I want. *The Committee wouldn't understand.*"

He probably didn't mean for her to hear the last part, but it came in loud and clear in her mind. "*What does the Committee have to do with us?*"

He released her and stood back, breaking their connection and her ability to speak without lisping. She was still charged up and it frustrated her to no end. Ripping his shirt sounded good about now, and it wasn't because she wanted it off. She just wanted to tear.

"Now's not a good time. Maybe after we find the person responsible."

My Sunny Vampire

"Maybe?" So much for being special. His rejection hurt her to the core. They had something going, she could feel it, he admitted it and he wanted to throw that away? Apparently, his precious Committee meant more to him than she did. Anger slowly took over, erasing the pain and retracting her fangs. She welcomed it. Fed on it. "You can go jump off a cliff, Jack VanAllen. Now get out."

* * * *

If her glare could throw daggers, they would certainly strike deep within his heart. Sunshine was furious with him--her eyes bright, her nostrils flared. Jack hadn't meant for her to hear his thoughts. He didn't mean to cause her any pain.

Whatever possessed him to say maybe? He couldn't have uttered a worse word or a more untrue one. He'd never wanted anyone more than he wanted her and it had taken every bit of willpower to push her away. Oh, the curve of her hips. The sweetness of her lips against his. It was a miracle he could resist her at all. But what choice did he have?

If he gave in to her, if they became an item and the Committee found out, he might as well hand them the stake. Oh hell, even if she decided not to accuse him, it probably wouldn't matter. The Committee prosecuted based on the facts. And when the facts were unavailable, their assumptions. One look at Sunshine and her memories, they would assume a lot.

Why did she have to look like Clara? If Sunshine ever found out, that would be the end of it. He needed her on his side, not against him. Once he cleared his name, then he could tell her, but not before.

Of course, he was doing a pretty lousy job of getting her on his side.

She went to the door and held it open. She couldn't stay mad forever, could she? Maybe some distance would calm her and make her see reason. Or at least forgive him.

He walked over to the opening. "I'm sorry I hurt you. That wasn't my intention. Once you've thought about everything, you'll see I'm right. I'll leave you for now, but I'll be back tomorrow. We have work to do."

"Whatever."

The door slammed in his face. Oh yeah, he'd mucked this up all right. Maybe he could get Carrie to help calm Sunshine. She seemed to have a level head.

He sat on the floor and leaned against the wall. Where the hell were Frank and Carrie? And how long did it take to find a phone? It was either there or it wasn't. The bar wasn't that far away and if Frank was roof-hopping, it shouldn't have taken more than fifteen minutes.

Thirty minutes later, giggling echoed through the stairwell. Not long after, the door flew open and Frank stumbled into the hallway with Carrie on his back. He released her when they arrived at the apartment.

"Hey, Jack." Carrie waved wildly as she tilted to one side. "What're you doing out here?"

Jack stood and the scent of beer assaulted his nose. "You're drunk."

"Maybe a little."

Frank wasn't looking too well, either. His eyes were bloodshot and he swayed on his feet as if the Earth were unsteady. He held onto Carrie, but Jack wasn't too sure she'd keep him upright.

"What the hell were you two doing?"

Frank leaned back against the wall. "Hey, is that any way to treat the friend who found your phone?"

"You found it?" Glory to God. At least one good thing had happened.

Frank grinned and dug inside his pocket. "Sure did."

"Yeah, the bartender wasn't going to give it to us until Frank asked if he could get it to ring, could we have it then? I don't know why he just didn't use his mind control thing."

"Sometimes it's more fun if I don't." Frank tossed the phone. It went wide, but Jack caught it before it hit the wall.

"Damn it, Frank. Couldn't you just hand it to me?"

"Geez, lighten up. You caught it, didn't you?"

Ah, his cell. He flipped it open and went to his log. He felt his face drain of blood. Barnet's number filled the screen. Jack scrolled down and counted thirteen until he got to a phone call he made at two a.m. A phone call he made to Barnet. Shit. His stomach churned. What the hell did he tell the Committee Head to generate thirteen calls and two messages?

"Is your phone okay? It's not broken, is it?"

My Sunny Vampire

Hmmm. If he broke it, could he claim ignorance? Unfortunately, Barnet still wanted to talk and would most likely find another way to get in touch. Jack snapped it closed. "It's okay. So, what took you two so long?"

Carrie wavered on her feet. "Frankie thought you'd need more time alone with Sunny, so he bought me a couple of drinks."

Needed more time or wanted more to drink? He pocketed the phone. "Beer?"

She shrugged, but in her inebriated state, lost her balance. Frank reached out and settled her. "There was beer involved," she said. "Frankie called it a boilermaker. Man, what a kick it had, too. I hope I don't wake up with a headache in the morning." She turned in Frank's arms and pulled his head down, giving him a long and thorough kiss on the mouth. "I better go check on Sunny. Will I see you tomorrow night?"

Frank hugged her back. "Just try and keep me away."

She bid them goodnight before entering the apartment.

Maybe this wasn't the time, but Jack needed to know. "You fed from her, didn't you?"

"I might have had a sip or two. Couldn't let her drink alone, now could I?"

A sip or two? Or maybe he'd sipped from more than one person. "Don't you think you drink a bit much?"

Frank narrowed his eyes. "Don't you think you should mind your own business?"

"Hey, I'm worried about you. Even Harris thought you were overdoing it."

"I haven't seen you in months and Beanie in nearly two years, now all of a sudden you think I have a drinking problem? Geez Louise, give me a break."

If Frank didn't have a drinking problem, why get all defensive? Jack would have to keep a better eye on his friend. "You're right. I'm sorry."

"So what happened with Sunny?"

Too much. Not enough. "I'll tell you on the way home."

Once there, he'd have to find out what kind of mess he'd gotten himself into where Barnet was concerned.

* * * *

Sunny sat on her bed reading. Not that she could concentrate on the words. She'd heard of sexual frustration before, but never experienced it until now. Being a vampire had nothing to do with it. Jack did.

When he had touched her, her memory of the night became clearer. Thank God he only wanted to see when she was bitten. She couldn't believe how aggressive she was toward him. He didn't reject her then, so why now? Was it because he only wanted mortals? Could that be it?

She refused to believe that. He'd nearly made love to her earlier and she was a vampire then. Of course, that was before she accused him of turning her. She put the book down and fell back on the pillow. That's it. She'd hurt his pride and he hid it behind the Committee.

She punched the bed. Well, he should know better. How the heck was she supposed to know the difference between feeding and turning?

Jack was letting something stupid get in the way of some awesome sex.

The front door opened then closed. She sat up. Was it Jack? Was he coming back to apologize?

A knock on her door was followed by its opening. Carrie poked her head inside. "You okay in here?"

Her heart sank at the sight of her friend. What did she expect? She'd practically told the man never to return.

Sunny sat up. "I will be."

Carrie smiled and leaned against the door jamb. "I couldn't help but notice Jack sitting in the hallway when we returned. Did he do it? Did he turn you? Was that why he was out there?"

"The memories I have don't show anyone turning me."

Carrie frowned. "Oh, sorry. So why was Jack in the hallway?"

Because the guy was a stupid idiot. "I don't want to talk about Jack. Did you have fun with Frank?"

Carrie jumped and clasped her hands together. "Oh yes. I never knew how exciting it was to jump roofs. It felt like we were flying." She raised her arms out like a plane, did some jittery jumping moves and bumped into the dresser. "He was more graceful than that, though. Hardly jerked me around. Man, I really like him."

Sunny went to her friend--who reeked of beer--and helped her stand. "You're drunk."

"Maybe a little." Carrie tottered as she pinched her forefinger and thumb together. "After we got Jack's phone, we had some drinks. Frank thought the two of you would need more time alone."

Sunny steered Carrie over to the bed then sat beside her. "Frank drank?"

"Yeah, from me, silly. I didn't mind. It kind of feels nice when he does it, especially now that I know what he's doing. Makes me wonder what it would be like during sex."

"You two haven't had sex yet?"

Carrie shook her head. "He's been a perfect gentleman."

Yeah, a perfect gentleman who liked to get his date drunk so he could drink her alcohol-infused blood. "Listen, what are you doing tomorrow morning?"

Carrie fell back on the bed. "I gotta work, but the store doesn't open until ten."

The store she mentioned sold fabric and patterns and was located near the mall, the opposite direction from Sunny's interview, which meant Carrie would have to drop her off around nine-thirty for an eleven o'clock appointment. She could make it work. She just had to. "Can you take me to my interview tomorrow?"

Carrie's eyes widened. "I thought Jack told you not to go."

"Jack doesn't own me. Can you do it?"

"But, Sunny, how? I mean, the sun will be out."

"You own an umbrella, don't you? That should work." At least, she hoped it would. When she sat in the shade earlier the sun hadn't bothered her, not that she noticed anyway. "Besides, I won't be out in it long."

"I don't know. It doesn't sound safe for you."

"If you can't do it, I'll take the bus, then. I'm going to this interview and no one's going to stop me."

"Okay, okay, I'll do it. I just hope you know what you're doing."

She did, too. But how hard could it be?

Chapter 8

Jack tossed his jacket on the back of a chair in the spacious living room. An oriental rug Linda had picked out long ago lay over a hardwood floor he had helped Frank install.

Frank's home, built by him during his mortal years, was a modest two-story situated in an older neighborhood, similar to the safe house Jack stayed in with Sunshine the day before. Unmarried, and no family to call his own, Frank was able to keep the building after his turning.

Jack headed for the stairs. He'd nearly told Frank about the messages, but thought better. Maybe the messages weren't important. No reason to worry until he got to the bottom of the matter. He'd tell Frank only if he needed his help.

Frank plopped down on the couch. The television blared to life. "Where are you going? I thought you might want to watch a movie."

"Maybe later. I need to make a phone call."

Frank clicked the TV off. "Why'd you come here? I've asked you plenty of times to visit. What made you choose now?"

Tell him the truth or lie? That was the question. Jack had hurt his friend enough. If Frank knew Jack was only in town to check up on his drinking habits, it might cause a deeper depression. Maybe if he'd visited more often, no one would have needed to call the Committee regarding Frank's behavior.

"Because I realized you're the only family I have. Does it matter? You want me to leave?"

My Sunny Vampire

"No, I don't want that. So, you just came because you wanted to? There's no ulterior motive?"

Lying wasn't his forte. Manipulating the facts? Now that he could do. He sat on the couch next to his friend. "I was wrong not to come earlier. Please don't make this any more than it is."

Frank displayed his famous lopsided grin. "Forgive this old guy. Guess maybe I did have too much to drink. It's made me a bit melancholy. I like being with her so much."

"You don't need to drink to impress her, Frank. She seems to like you just fine."

His eyes lit up. "You think so? You're not just saying that?"

"Are you telling me you haven't read her thoughts?"

Frank shook his head. "She's not a screamer and I didn't want to pry. I like her, Jack. I want to do this right."

"I'm sure you will." Jack stood and patted his friend on the shoulder. He left Frank flipping through the channels. The television noise would help camouflage Jack's conversation.

He took the stairs two at a time and entered his room. Located at the back of the house, the room contained one painted-over window that looked out over the side yard. A double bed took up most of the space, not that he'd ever used it for anything but sitting. He sat on the edge of the bed and played the first message.

"Jack, this is Barnet. I think we got cut off. Please call me as soon as you can." Barnet's voice sounded fine. No concern. The second message, received three hours and ten calls later, said pretty much the same thing, but his tone was uneasy. And why wouldn't it be? It was unlike Jack to not return the Head's call.

What exactly had he told Barnet? Only way to find out was to call. He punched in the number and waited.

Barnet answered on the first ring. "Jack. Are you all right? I was about to send someone out there to locate you."

Shit. That was the last thing he needed. "I'm fine. I misplaced my phone and just got it back."

A strained chuckle resonated in Jack's ear. "Good, good. You want to tell me what your phone call was all about?"

There was no dodging that question. He sighed in surrender. "I wish I could tell you. I don't remember the call."

"You don't remember calling me and telling me you're in love and asking permission to get married?"

Married? The pit of his stomach heaved. "What else did I say?"

"Jack. What the hell is going on?"

He couldn't tell Barnet the whole truth. Not until he proved he wasn't involved in Sunshine's turning. "I lost about nine hours of my life. I'm still trying to put the pieces together."

"Lost? You mean you passed out?"

"No. I called you, didn't I?"

"But Jack, vampires don't get amnesia."

"This one did. So far I haven't discovered doing anything illegal." Which was the truth. Then a brilliant idea came to mind. "I do intend to go back to the bar and see if I can find the donor I fed from. See what kind of drug he was on. He had to have taken some strange combination for me to lose my memory like I did."

"What the hell were you doing at a…oh. Frank. How is he doing anyway?"

Good. A change of subject. The television blared downstairs, but Jack kept his voice low, just in case it carried. "I think Frank might have a drinking problem, but maybe things will turn around for him. He's met someone."

"Mortal?"

"Yes, but she knows."

Barnet groaned his apparent displeasure.

"Don't worry about her. She's okay with it. If she becomes a threat, I'll wipe her memory. I don't think I'll have to resort to that, though." Wiping Carrie's memory would probably kill Frank, not to mention himself once Sunshine got a hold of him.

"I'll leave that at your discretion, then. So, I guess you're not looking for permission?"

Permission? Jack's heart stopped for a moment. Had he actually asked to turn Sunshine? Then he remembered. Not permission to turn. Permission to marry. Although why he'd need permission… Jack shook his head. Who knew what he was thinking that night? His heart beat returned to normal and he laughed, relieved he hadn't made such a blunder. "I think I was in love with the high. If I'm engaged to be married, no one told me. I can honestly say that marriage is the last thing on my mind."

"That's too bad. I'd never heard you so happy before. Guess it was the drug talking."

Had Sunshine made him happy or the drug? Would he ever find out? "That's scary. I'll look into it some more. I don't like not

My Sunny Vampire

knowing what can knock a vampire for a loop like this. It's certainly a frustrating feeling, not remembering."

"I can't even imagine. How long do you think you'll be up there?"

How much time would he need to find the vampire to clear his name? A few days weren't nearly long enough, but if he said weeks, Barnet might get suspicious. "Frank expects me to stay until the seventh. If I need more time, I'll just play it by ear, if that's okay with you."

Barnet was on board with that plan and Jack breathed a sigh of relief after disconnecting the call. So far, so good. But what was he doing? He had practically lied to the Head of the Committee. Or was it considered a lie if he just withheld information? Jack should have come clean. He should have told them about Sunshine. They would find out eventually. If anyone else on the Committee had done what he had, he wouldn't hesitate to request their seat be vacated.

Of course, it was quite possible the Committee could help and not accuse. They were the closest he had to a family. But he couldn't take the chance. As long as Frank was on his side, he should be able to find out who turned Sunshine. Maybe tomorrow he could try reading her memory again. She had to remember something substantial. And he needed to recognize it.

Unfortunately, getting to her memory might be harder than finding the criminal.

* * * *

Sunny turned off the television and set the remote down. She'd been a vampire for a day and already she was bored with the life. It wasn't like she could sleep to pass the time. She'd finished the only book she possessed and basic cable was all Carrie could afford. Her choices were limited and unappealing.

She needed to get out. Sitting around doing nothing drove her crazy. She grabbed some money, her keys and camera and headed out. There must to be a store open that sold books or magazines or something to keep her busy. If not, she could try and take pictures. Her outdoor options were now reduced to night shots.

When she left the building she looked up at the rooftops. Roof-hopping sounded fun, but how did Frank get up there? The apartment building didn't have a fire escape to the top. She would have to ask Frank since Jack would probably tell her it was dangerous and not necessary.

She remembered passing a gas station on her run to Carrie's earlier and headed that way, taking pictures of the few businesses that advertised with neon lights. Using different speeds, she purposely moved to swirl the colors. After viewing the photos, she smiled. They turned out kind of cool. She could have fun with that.

An old building on the corner caught her attention. The street lacked any illumination, but she could make out the detail. Would her camera? If she couldn't hold the camera still, she could always go back and get her tripod. What else was there to do?

She held her breath, aimed her camera and focused. After leaving the lens open for several seconds to gather enough light, she closed the shutter and viewed her picture.

Holy moly. The photo turned out perfect. She was sure she would have caused it to blur. Holding a camera for any length of time without blurring the image was impossible without a tripod. Until now. Could she do it again? She repeated the process and obtained the same results.

In fact, both times she never even felt the burn to breathe. As an experiment, she held her breath and using her watch, counted the seconds until they became minutes. After three minutes and still no burn or light-headedness, she stopped counting. Dang. Jack never told her about that. What else had the guy forgotten to share?

Her spirits rose. Taking night shots could be fun. She could probably get some great pictures, not to mention from unusual places once she learned roof-hopping, and never need a tripod.

The gas station was open, but didn't have any books. She pulled five different celebrity and entertainment magazines from the rack. As she stood at the counter to pay, she glanced at the candy bars and sighed. No more chocolate. That just didn't seem fair. How could she survive without ever having chocolate again? Then again, no one said she couldn't eat. Like the water, she would probably upchuck it later. Chocolate would be worth that.

She grabbed a chocolate bar and paid for her purchases. Once she was outside, she ripped open the wrapper and tentatively took a bite. Oh, the sweet, wonderful chocolate. It hadn't lost its luster. Not one bit. Her tiny bites turned into bigger ones. In a matter of seconds, the chocolate disappeared.

My Sunny Vampire

She tossed the wrapper in the trash and headed back to Carrie's. Maybe she could still eat chocolate and not gain weight. Wouldn't that be great? If this was going to be her life, she was certainly going to find the perks.

By the time she reached the end of the block, her stomach started churning. She rubbed her belly. Another half block and she rushed to the curb. Pain erupted in her stomach. Her throat clenched. She fell to her knees and vomited on the street.

Chocolate was so not worth it.

After kicking some dirty snow to hide the mess, she ripped out an ad from one of her magazines and used it to wipe her mouth. A napkin or tissue would have been kinder to her face, but it would do.

Looking for a dumpster or trash can, she headed between two buildings and stopped. A bum emerged, smelling of stale beer and sweat. His oily hair, grimy jacket and torn pants did nothing to dissuade her assessment, either. Her heart pounded frantically. Maybe coming out alone wasn't such a good idea.

But wait. What did she have to be afraid of? She was a vampire now. If she couldn't take care of one measly bum, what good was she?

Before Carrie had gone to bed, Sunny had practiced the mind manipulation on her friend. Successful only a third of the time, she couldn't tell if she was bad because Carrie was drunk or she was just bad. Even worse, the few times she had control, Carrie looked like a zombie. It had freaked her out and she had stopped, afraid she was hurting her friend.

Now, she couldn't care less if this guy turned into a zombie. She just wanted him gone.

Concentrating as if she were shooting a laser beam out of her head, she sent out a mental signal. *"Go back where you came from."*

She nearly laughed. She sounded like an alien asking to be taken to the leader.

The man smiled at her, displaying massive gaps between his teeth. "Whatcha got there sweetie?"

"No, no, no. You need to go away," she muttered. She concentrated harder and tried to sound more natural. *"Go back where you came from."*

The zombie look came over his face. He turned around in a jerky manner and walked back the way he came.

"Whoo hoo!" She pumped her fist above her head. She was starting to get the hang of being a vampire. That interview in the morning should be a breeze. Dang Jack and his can't-do-this and can't-do-that attitude. He was as bad as her father. She could do anything she wanted.

* * * *

Jack stomped the snow off his shoes before entering the house. After his call to Barnet, he and Frank had headed back to the bar in hopes of finding the donor.

Frank kicked his shoes off. "I wish I thought about asking when I was there earlier with Carrie."

Before or after he drank Carrie's boilermaker-laced blood? Okay, that was unfair. Frank apparently had an illness. One Jack never thought could happen to a vampire, but all the symptoms were there. The man was an alcoholic.

"He's probably still recovering from the night before. Maybe we'll find him tomorrow." Jack plopped down on the couch, feeling useless. Soon it would be daylight and he'd be trapped inside.

"You never told me. Were you able to access Sunny's memory?" Frank tossed his jacket on the chair as he settled on the other end of the couch.

"Yes, but don't get your hopes up. She doesn't remember who turned her. I do have a question for you. Did you feed from her?"

Frank's eyes widened. "Why? What does she remember?"

Hmmm, touchy. "It's not what she remembers. It's what Harris told me."

Frank rubbed his chin and grimaced. "Maybe I hoped you wouldn't find out. It's your fault. You kept going on about how sweet her blood was. You insisted I take a taste."

"And?"

"And, she was good. But so was Carrie." Frank shrugged. "Then again, you always did prefer the negatives."

Negatives? Could the answer be that simple? With his memory gone, there wasn't any way he would have known since her blood had changed once the venom entered her system. "She had negative blood?"

"O negative, to be exact."

Jack stood and paced the room. O negative. His favorite, too. He wished more than ever he could remember feeding from her.

My Sunny Vampire

What she must have tasted like. He'd never know now, not unless his memory returned. Still, it solved a minor puzzle. "That's it. That's how I'll find the rogue. The donor I fed from was B negative. He must have known I'd go for a negative donor." His heart lifted in glee until Frank continued to shake his head. The high slowly crashed. "Why not?"

"Jack. Everyone knows you prefer negatives. You haven't narrowed your search one bit."

Damn it, he'd forgotten. He hated it when Frank was right. Two years ago during the June meeting, some asinine vampire had asked Jack in front of the whole crowd why he disliked prostitutes. The question had confused him. What the hell did prostitutes have to do with anything? Then a small group roared in laughter. Apparently, the man overheard a conversation and mistook Jack's dislike of positives for a dislike of prostitutes. It had been the highlight of that Committee meeting.

Jack collapsed onto the couch. "So we're back to square one."

Frank patted him on the shoulder. "Maybe not. We still have a chance in finding that donor. If you work with Sunny, it's possible she'll remember more. I mean, she does like you."

Yeah, but that was before he rejected her and she threw him out of the apartment. Of course, if she didn't care, she wouldn't have gotten so angry. So, maybe there was hope after all.

Chapter 9

Having finished reading the magazines hours ago, Sunny flipped through the channels and stopped on the weather. Cold and sunny. That figured. She didn't care about the cold, but why couldn't it be cloudy? It would have been a lot easier on her eyes.

Carrie's alarm went off. It was quickly silenced and no sounds of movement followed. Sunny shook her head. Carrie and mornings didn't go together.

Sunny entered Carrie's bedroom carrying a mug of coffee. After shaking her friend's leg, she knelt beside the bed and waved the steam toward Carrie's face. "Get up sleepyhead or we're gonna be late."

Carrie moaned as she rolled over on her back. She rubbed at her eyes. "What time is it?"

"It's eight. We need to get going if you're going to get me downtown before you head to work."

"Eight? Na-ah. My alarm will go off at eight."

"It already did. Come on. I have coffee for you."

"Coffee?" Carrie sat up and grabbed her head. "Damn. I told Frank that drink would get me this morning. Remind me never to drink boilermakers again."

Boilermakers? Fudge. Was Carrie even fit to drive? "I thought you just drank beer last night."

"I wish. God, I feel like shit." Carrie's eyes widened and she covered her mouth. "Oops. Sorry."

My Sunny Vampire

"Just because I don't cuss, doesn't mean you can't. It's a free world." Sunny handed her friend the mug. "Here, maybe this will help."

Carrie took a long sip and then laughed. "You cuss. You just use made-up words."

"Yep, and I'm not embarrassed when a five-year-old hears them, either. Now get up and get dressed. I don't want to be late."

"Yes, mother." Carrie climbed out of bed and padded to the bathroom.

Forty minutes later she emerged looking clean, but not better.

"Are you okay?" Sunny asked. "Your eyes are all bloodshot."

"I've had better mornings. I need more coffee." Carrie held out her empty mug.

Sunny refilled it, wishing she could join her friend. She loved the taste of coffee. Now if she drank any, she would only throw it back up. Just like chocolate, she didn't love it that much.

"Is that a new outfit?" Carrie pulled a Pop-Tart out of the box and sat on a chair.

"Yes, I bought it for the interview." Sunny brushed some lint off the black pantsuit. She wanted to look professional. First impressions were everything, especially for a dream job like this. "I look okay, don't I?"

"You look spiffy." Carrie picked up the portfolio. "This is new, too, huh?"

"You don't think it's too much, do you?"

"No, not at all. You sure you still want to do this? It's an awfully bright day today."

Sunny couldn't argue that point. She had peeked out the window earlier and was nearly blinded. Even wearing sunglasses didn't seem to help with the glare. However, she wouldn't be outside long. "I've got my sunglasses and an umbrella. I'll be fine."

"I don't know. If that's all it took, wouldn't more vampires be outside during the day?" Carrie alternated between eating her Pop-Tart and sipping her coffee while she fidgeted with her hair.

"How do you know they aren't? Just because Jack says so, doesn't make it so. For all I know he's been lying to me since the beginning." Information didn't flow from his lips like she expected.

"I guess we better get going if I have to go downtown. I don't want to be late for work today. I've got a class to teach at ten-thirty." Carrie popped the rest of the pastry in her mouth and washed it down with the remainder of her coffee.

"How's that going anyway?" Sunny slipped on her coat and then picked up the portfolio, which contained her ID and some money.

"Better than I thought. It's fun when they want to learn and they already know how to sew. I'm mainly there to help with their projects instead." Carrie pulled her hair out from under her coat and zipped up. "I can pull the car up to the apartment building if you want."

"No. If this isn't going to work, better to find out now."

Carrie locked up and Sunny followed her down the stairs to the first floor and the door to the parking lot. The sun shone across the entrance and Carrie walked in it as if it was nothing. And it was nothing for her. Sunny stopped short of the exit. Her heart raced and threatened to climb up her throat.

This time going out into the sun should be a whole lot different. Shouldn't it? She was completely covered for one thing, not wearing a skimpy halter top and short skirt. The umbrella would shade the parts she had unprotected--her head and her hands. If it didn't work, she would find out soon enough. She slipped on her glasses and readied her umbrella.

"Here goes nothing." Sunny opened the umbrella as she stepped outside, fully expecting a full-on burn and smiling when it didn't occur.

Taking advantage of her vampire speed and the deserted parking lot, she zipped to the vehicle and slid onto the passenger seat. She pushed the knob to collapse the umbrella. Something prevented it from closing, almost as if some evil elves were at work against her. Sunlight hit her hand and soon the prickly burning sensation spread across her skin. After two more tries and an urge to toss the stupid thing in the parking lot, the umbrella obeyed. She slammed the door shut.

Fudge. What was she thinking, sitting in the front seat? The sun hit her full in the face.

Carrie started the ignition. "Buckle up."

"Wait, I'm going in the back." Sunny threw the umbrella and portfolio in the backseat and climbed after them. Her jacket caught on the headrest, keys and cell clattered to the floorboard and a button popped off. Certainly not her brightest moment--the car

My Sunny Vampire

was way too small for her large frame--but it beat going outside, even for a moment.

"Here." Carrie handed her the button, along with a small sewing kit.

Sunny offered a smile of gratitude. "I think you're the only person I know who carries one of these around. Thanks."

While Carrie drove, Sunny slid from side to side, avoiding the side the sun decided to visit. Re-attaching the button during all this movement took longer than normal, but by the time they reached her destination, she had accomplished her task and the button looked none the worse for wear. Too bad she couldn't say the same for her.

"Good thing my appointment isn't until eleven. It'll give me time to freshen up."

Carrie pulled over into the shade and turned around in her seat. "Your building should be down there." She pointed to the street on the right. "I won't be able to pick you up until two. That's when I get off for lunch."

"That's fine. I brought a book to read." One she would read for the third time unless she found a place to buy more.

"Please be careful." Carrie's forehead was furrowed and her bottom lip jutted out. If she twisted her hair any tighter, she'd end up with a bald spot.

Sunny placed a hand on her friend's shoulder. "I will. Thanks again for doing this. I really appreciate it. Now quit worrying. I'll see you a little after two."

The shade was a blessing and made it easier for Sunny to maneuver to the building without having to resort to the umbrella. She waved goodbye as Carrie drove off. A quick trip to the restroom and she emerged looking fresh and new. Even the burn on her hand disappeared. Talk about healing fast.

With an hour to kill before her appointment, she strolled along the foyer and gazed out the windows, keeping a safe distance. Jackpot. A bookstore was across the street. Her heart leapt with excitement. No more long and boring nights.

Only one problem: getting to the store. Sunlight drenched that part of the street and the sidewalk. She could zip, but someone might notice her speed. What about the umbrella? It worked getting to the car, why not to the bookstore?

After adjusting her sunglasses, she stepped outside and opened her umbrella, which seemed more tolerant than it did when closing it earlier. She ventured into the sun, pushed the walk button and then backed into the shade to wait for the light to turn. Her eyes scratched and burned. Stupid sunglasses. She would just have to buy some darker ones if this became routine.

Once the signal indicated she could walk, she hurried across trying to appear normal, but then who walked around in the winter with an umbrella on a bright, sunny day? There was no getting around looking weird.

Again, the umbrella put up a fight as she attempted to close it before entering the building. Not that she was superstitious or anything, but the door was too narrow to accommodate an open umbrella. Pin pricks of pain spread across her hands.

"Dag-burnit," she muttered. "Close already."

As if it heard her command, the umbrella cooperated and she dashed inside the bookstore. The pain eased once she was protected.

"Is it raining out there?"

Sunny turned and found a Hugh Jackman clone, sans the Aussie accent, grinning at her. God, he was cute. And tall. In fact, he was someone she would have flirted with before her unfortunate accident. Or would that be before she'd met Jack? She liked Jack, even with the way he irritated her. Although, she suspected he was a sweet teddy bear under that cold, official exterior and hoped they could get to know one another better.

She didn't have to be rude to Hugh, so she smiled. "No rain, nor snow. My body doesn't like sun, though. I burn easily."

"I guess you're doing something right. Your skin looks flawless." His eyes flashed with desire and he took a good long look at her body.

Well, fudge. No one ever looked at her like that before she turned. Except for Jack. But when Jack did it, her panties got wet. This man did nothing for her sexually. She would have to ask Jack how to turn off the vampire vibes she emitted.

She thanked him and excused herself. An hour wasn't that long, and the store was larger than anticipated. Upon investigation, she discovered they would hold her order until close of business. She found a basket and started selecting books that piqued her interest.

My Sunny Vampire

Sure beat walking around a foyer and she could wait for Carrie here after her interview, too.

Her stomach cramped and she paused in her book search. Nothing painful. Just a minor twinge. The burns on her hand probably took extra blood to heal. She would make sure not to burn them again.

Her time up, she handed her selection to the clerk and headed back for her interview. She approached the entrance and stopped. Fudge. Pushing the walk button to the store had been easy since she could wait in the shade. This side of the street wasn't as blessed. The instant she stepped outside, she opened the umbrella and used it as a shield, keeping her hands and face away from the direct sun. She huddled under it and waited for the light, bouncing up and down as if that would get it to change quicker. Each second that passed, the spasms in her stomach increased in strength. And with each spasm, her energy waned.

Was there a hole in the umbrella? No, but the material was some thin, gauzy, waterproof substance and light filtered through. Still, her hands and face weren't burning, so it must be working. Wasn't it? Then again, she was cramping and feeling drained. So maybe it wasn't working.

The light finally changed and she stepped onto the street. She planned to run across, but could barely move one foot in front of the other as if she were in some kind of slow-motion land. That or the air had turned to honey. Each step was slower than the last and her shady destination seemed farther and farther out of reach.

A car honked as she inched along, as if that would make her move faster. She glanced at the agitated man behind the wheel. He raised his arms in the air as if that would help. What if she were an invalid or elderly woman? Would he honk at her then? She'd like to give him the finger and tell him who's number one, but she didn't do that sort of thing. Besides, she'd probably drop the umbrella, not that it was doing such a splendid job. The driver whizzed around her.

Hugh had crossed the street ahead of her and turned around. He grabbed her elbow and helped her to the curb. "Are you okay? You're awfully pale."

No, she wasn't okay. Something was playing a game of tug-of-war in her stomach. Once she reached the safety of the shade, she dropped her umbrella and doubled over. Stupid sun. How the heck was she going to make it to her interview? She could barely walk. She could barely talk.

Blood. That's what she needed. Could she get him into a corner and feed without him knowing? Without anyone else knowing, either? She could at least take advantage of his Boy Scout mentality. If he wanted to help, he could. She straightened up. Big mistake. Her midsection felt like it held some kind of campfire party, but dang if she was going to fold again.

"I'll be fine if you could help me inside the building."

He picked up her umbrella and closed it easily. Dang it. Was everything against her going to this interview?

"Do I need to call 9-1-1? You look like you're ready to collapse."

"No. No 9-1-1." A hospital wouldn't do at all. Wouldn't Jack just kill her then? She grabbed onto her helper's arm to steady herself. She hadn't grabbed him too hard, had she? Would he notice her unusual strength? Or had the sun eaten that all up? Her whole body felt like rubber and the shade wasn't giving her any relief.

He opened the door to the building and guided her to a bench off to the side. They were still in the open, but her options were slowly disappearing. About the only thing possible would be to hide behind one of the pillars. Pretend they were having a little make-out session and hope no one would bother them.

She concentrated and prayed her mental command worked. *"Take me behind the pillar."*

His eyebrows furrowed in confusion. "Why are you scrunching your face like that? Are you in pain? Is there someone I can call for you?"

Dag-burnit. He was being too helpful, but not in the way she needed. What the heck was the matter anyway? Couldn't he hear her? She concentrated harder and sent the same command.

This time his eyes glazed over, getting that zombie look like Carrie and the hobo, and he guided her to the pillar. Relief bathed over her. Finally, something went right. She pressed him against the support. *"Relax. This won't hurt. It will feel good."*

She ran her fingers over his neck, his vein throbbing an invitation. His cologne was musky, but nothing compared to the sweet scent of his blood. Food. That's all he was at the moment. Her fangs emerged. She leaned in and was positioned just right to pierce his skin when a bright flash blinded her. Some object in the street reflected the sun back toward the building just as someone opened the door. Her midsection exploded in pain and the Earth started trembling.

As she headed for the floor and Hugh reached out for her, she realized the Earth wasn't moving. She was having a seizure.

Chapter 10

Hugh placed his cellphone back inside the holder looped on his belt. Sunny had tried to tell him not to call 9-1-1, but no words came out. She tried to stand, but that required control and she'd lost it all when it came to moving. Her stomach burned. This was so much different than those cramps. What the hell was wrong with her? She thought clearly, saw everything, heard everything. But move? Communicate? Not so much. She'd never been so frustrated.

He knelt beside her, placed something soft under her head and tenderly brushed the hair from her face. He truly looked concerned. "I don't know if you can hear me, but help will be here soon. Just hold on."

Holding on wasn't her problem. Going to the hospital would be.

The timing couldn't have been worse. She was within seconds of replenishing her blood supply when the seizure struck. Stupid sun. Stupid, stupid sun.

Sirens echoed inside the building. A gurney clattered across the threshold of the entrance, squeaking its arrival as it rolled across the floor. Somehow she must stop them before they took her away.

Unfortunately, none of her mind powers were working. She had tried numerous times to get Hugh to disconnect his call, all to no avail.

A male paramedic with a nametag stating his name was Garcia, wrapped a blood pressure cuff around her arm and started

My Sunny Vampire

pumping. Good thing her heart still beat, but what kind of pressure did a vampire have anyway?

"Can you tell me your name?"

She opened her mouth and moaned. No surprise there. The pain in her gut decided to invite her lungs along for the ride. Still, she sounded like some stupid imbecile.

"Her ID lists her as Sunshine Petersen." Hugh presented her driver's license to Garcia.

He went through her things? How dare he? He had no right. If she could voice her opinion, she'd let him have it.

"You visiting someone in Pittsburgh, Ms. Petersen?" Garcia asked.

Yeah, right. If she couldn't answer her name, what made him think she could answer that?

He wrote something on a clipboard before removing the cuff. His face didn't indicate anything good or bad. If her blood pressure was abnormal, he wasn't letting on. He flashed a light in each eye and wrote some more. Did she look dead or just paralyzed?

"Let's get her on the gurney."

No, no, no. This wasn't happening. If her blood pressure was normal before, it certainly wasn't now. Her heart wanted to take off into outer space. Why couldn't she speak?

Garcia nodded to the other paramedic and they lifted her to the gurney. The action jolted her and pain slashed across her abdomen. Two straps came around her. One bound her chest, the other her legs. Most likely to keep her from falling, they made her feel like a prisoner. With all her effort, she tried screaming at them to stop, but only another moan escaped.

"Easy, ma'am. We're going to take care of you." Garcia's eyes narrowed and he opened her mouth. "Hello. What are these?"

Shoot. Her fangs. They hadn't retracted during her seizure. He must have seen them when she tried to scream. He ran his thumb over the points and nicked his skin. Sweet heaven, he was bleeding right inside her mouth. One tiny drop flooded her tongue with ecstasy and before she knew it, her teeth were imbedded in his finger.

"Fuck!" He removed his hand, but not before her tongue lapped up the miniscule amount of blood he seeped. "She bit me."

Fudge. What was wrong with her? Did she want to get herself a padded cell? But the taste triggered something primal inside her.

Probably survival instincts. What did she know? If she possessed survival instincts, why the heck didn't her body wait until she fed before betraying her? It's not like Jack had told her anything about this. She needed to get herself under control. But how? She couldn't even get her fangs to retract.

"That'll teach you not to wear your gloves," the other paramedic said. "You think she's got rabies? Or maybe she's a vampire?"

Sun of a gun. Could he say it any louder?

"A vampire? No, Danny. I don't think…" Garcia stopped when he saw his partner snicker. After wiping his finger on his pants, he checked the wound.

Danny peered over his partner's shoulder. "I thought you said she bit you. I don't see any teeth marks."

Thank God for small favors. In her desire to ingest every drop she could, she'd healed him. Garcia looked a bit relieved, too. When Danny handed him some gloves, he snatched them and put them on.

"Come on, let's get her out of here." Garcia placed her portfolio on her stomach and started rolling her toward the door. And sunlight.

Hugh. Where was Hugh? He must stop them. Didn't he remember what she told him about the sun? In her mind, she fought to get free. In her mind, she yelled at them to stop. In actuality, her movements were sluggish, her speech slurred.

Despair rolled over her. Would she burst into flames? Would she turn to dust in front of their eyes? Would she feel any pain? To think she had wanted to die yesterday. Now all she wanted to do was live.

* * * *

After two movies, three hours of mind-numbing video games and reading the same page over and over, Jack couldn't stand it any longer. He needed to know how Sunshine was doing. Hearing her voice would be nice, too. The day must be boring for her. Hell, he was bored and he had Frank.

Jack tossed the book on the end table. "Do you happen to have Sunshine's number?"

Frank was lounging on the couch, reading. His head was perched on one arm and his legs hung over the other. He peered over the book, shaking his head. "Sorry. How about Carrie's?"

My Sunny Vampire

"Do you think she'd give it to me, or would she be more apt to give it to you?"

Frank marked his page and closed the book. "Don't know, but I like having an excuse to call her." He put the book down and pulled out his cell. A few beeps later, a grin spread across the man's face. "Hey babe. Whatcha doing?"

Listening to Frank talk to Carrie, Jack almost felt like a voyeur. But where was he going to go and *not* hear? Still, it was nice hearing the joy in his friend's voice and seeing the sparkle in his eye return. Linda had done that to him and more. Frank had planned to spend eternity with her and then some stupid accident had taken that all away.

"Yeah, I can't wait to see you either. Before you go, can you give me Sunny's number?"

Jack pulled out his cell, ready to punch in the numbers, but apparently Carrie was having second thoughts.

"Nothing important. We just want to see how she's doing. Is she still mad at us?" Frank shrugged and continued to listen.

Patience had flown out the door hours ago and Carrie was driving him batty. He wiggled his fingers for the phone. "Let me talk to her."

When Frank hesitated to hand it over, Jack grunted and grabbed the cell. "Hi, Carrie. It's Jack. I just want to apologize to Sunshine."

"Oh, that's so sweet," she said all gooey-like. He nearly rolled his eyes. "Like I was telling Frank, I don't think she has her phone on."

"Fine. Then I'll leave her a message."

"Well, see, that won't work. Sunny will most likely delete it, since she won't recognize the number. You see where I'm going with this? Let me have her call you."

Something wasn't right. Carrie sounded nervous.

"Is she okay?"

"Why wouldn't she be okay? Is there something you're not telling me? Should I have stayed with her today?" Panic set in her voice and Jack backed off. The last thing he wanted to do was worry her.

"No, no, no. Nothing like that. I'm sure she's fine. Have her call me as soon as possible. Okay?"

"Sure, Jack. I gotta go back to work. Tell Frank bye for me."

He handed the phone back to Frank. Disappointment tugged at his heart. He'd been looking forward to speaking with her. Something was up. Why would Sunshine turn off her phone? It didn't make any sense. If he didn't hear from her soon, he was liable to venture out into the sun and make a visit.

* * * *

Garcia pushed the gurney much quicker than Sunny wanted, the exit looming closer and closer. If she could flail herself off the contraption, she'd get their attention, but being strapped in made that move impossible. The tiny bit of blood she'd gotten had done zilch for her. Her voice remained mute.

Danny opened the door and Garcia shoved through, jostling her over the threshold. Even the shade couldn't protect her as the sun glinted off the office windows and blinded her. She closed her eyes. At least they worked.

People gathered to watch and she could hear them talking among themselves. Nothing like being the top news story on a slow day.

Fudge. Besides the non-stop cramping going on in her stomach, a different kind of sickness seeped in. She prayed someone had robbed a bank and the cops were chasing him down the road. Or the President said something stupid. Anything more news-worthy than her. If she thought Jack would be mad with her going to the hospital, she could only imagine how furious he'd be with her escapade spread all over the news.

Thunk.

Her feet dropped down as the gurney landed in the street. A warming sensation traveled up her body. When it reached her hands it felt like millions of tiny pins attacking her skin. The gurney shook, sending sharp pains through her abdomen. She cried out, emitting a lousy moan.

Thunk.

Blazing heat reached her face and the sun seared her eyes, even though they remained closed. If this didn't kill her, she was sure she'd be scarred for life. She might even become blind. Did the lobster feel this much pain when he was tossed in the boiling water? The burn intensified and she couldn't even scream in agony. She couldn't grab onto anything for relief. The sun continued its attack on her and there wasn't a darn thing she could do.

My Sunny Vampire

The gurney's shaking took on a violent turn. With any luck, she would fall off.

"She's seizing," Danny said. "Look at her face. Maybe she is a vampire."

Oh, so that's why she was moving. She was the cause.

"Shut up, Danny," Garcia said.

The people on the sidewalk spoke in muted tones, but one word came out loud and clear. Vampire. The crowd had apparently heard Danny. Could it get any worse?

Suddenly, the gurney thrust forward. The light disappeared. The burning stopped. All was still. The pain in her face and hands subsided. She could almost relax and risked opening her eyes. Yes. Inside the ambulance. Safe.

Garcia climbed in after her and Danny shut the doors. Soon the engine started and the sirens blared to life. They were on their way.

"I guess you don't like the sun, which seems kind of funny since your name is Sunshine," Garcia said.

Yeah, it was a riot. Couldn't he see her laughing?

Even with this brief intermission, she still hurt. Her arms and legs ached with the need to move. Her hands and face were stinging, as if badly burned. Her stomach tightened with each stabbing pain. All she wanted to do was curl up into a ball, but she didn't even have that in her.

The sound of drawers opening and closing drew her attention back to the paramedic. He pulled her sleeve up and swabbed her arm. Next, a pin pricked her skin. What was he doing? He taped a needle to her arm and attached a bag filled with a clear liquid. Flashing that darn light again, he examined her eyes. What, she wasn't blinded enough by the sun?

"Danny thinks you're a vampire." He stared down at her and seemed to examine her face. His fingers lightly touched her cheeks and forehead. "I wouldn't listen to him. He must have forgotten that vampires are dead during the day. You're in shock, but you're not dead." He patted her shoulder with a chuckle. "We'll get you to the hospital soon."

Danny was the least of her worries. She had heard the people on the street and could see the headline now: "Pittsburgh Invaded by Vampires."

Oh fudge. Jack was so going to kill her.

Liquid trickled down her arm. It must have trickled on Garcia, too, as he looked down at the source. "Shit. How did this pop out?"

The needle had come free and the contents of the bag dribbled from the tip. He pinched the line closed and cleaned up the mess. Once he found a new needle, he re-swabbed the area and re-attached the bag. She didn't know what kind of liquid he was flowing through her veins, probably some sort of saline solution, but at least she wasn't getting sick. Of course, she wasn't getting better, either.

The vehicle jerked to a stop and the sirens died. When the doors opened, Garcia climbed out and pulled on the gurney. Oh, no. Not again. Preparing for another round of the blaring sun, she closed her eyes, but was greeted with nothing. The ambulance bay protected her. She breathed a little easier.

"What do we have here?" a female doctor asked.

"Twenty-seven-year-old female. Two known seizures. Unresponsive to stimuli, but seems aware of her surroundings."

The doctor came around the gurney. "Luis, is this any way to attach an IV?"

Even with all the turmoil in her belly and the panic of things to come once the doctors got a good look at her, she smiled. Whether or not her face displayed her amusement was another matter.

So, her body wouldn't accept needles. Interesting. Maybe she *was* in a self-preservation mode.

* * * *

Jack plopped down onto the chair and turned on the television. Did someone actually want to buy a car from a shark? *Click.* Now some whiny woman complained a man didn't love her. *Click.*

Crap. *Click.* Crap. *Click.* More crap. TV during the day sucked.

"I'm sorry about Sunny," Frank said.

"What do you have to be sorry about? You're not the one she's mad at." The moment Jack heard Carrie's explanation, he knew she was lying. For whatever reason, she didn't want to give him Sunshine's number. He could respect her for that. It made her a good friend.

But damn. Thirty agonizing minutes and no call. The truth hit him hard and it hurt. Sunshine was still mad. How long could the woman hold a grudge, anyway?

Click. Click. Click.

My Sunny Vampire

Frank snatched the remote out of Jack's hand. "Damn, you're irritating. What is it you do all day anyway?"

Jack shrugged. "Search the web. Read the news. Take a swim. Work on my car."

"Never got a computer, don't have a garage and there's no place to put a pool, but there is one thing I can do." He punched in some numbers. "Here. Watch the news."

News? He sighed. News wouldn't fix him. Only Sunshine would. Why'd he have to get her mad anyway? If he'd only explained things better, he could have spent the day with her. But no, he had to reject her advances. All because he thought impressions would matter to the Committee. What a joke. One look inside his mind and they would know what Sunshine meant to him. One look at her memories and they would see a vampire smitten with a mortal.

"I was thinking of taking Carrie out dancing tonight," Frank said. "I mean, after we check out the bar for that donor. You think she'll like that?"

Dancing or drinking? Jack nearly asked, but having one person mad at him at a time was all he could stand. "I think she'll like doing anything with you."

"You could come along. If you want."

He should go along. Besides being bored out of his mind, how else was he going to observe Frank's drinking problem? "I'll think about it."

Weather--his favorite part of the news--ended. The rest of the news didn't interest him. He would risk the sun and head over to Carrie's. The worst Sunshine could do is not let him in, but at least he'd know she was okay. He was reaching around Frank for the remote when the anchor said, "Is it possible we have a vampire in Pittsburgh? Story after these messages."

Frank straightened up. "Did that guy say what I think he said?"

"It's probably some kook looking for attention." Jack had seen his share of vampire stories since every accusation had to be taken seriously. It wasn't unusual for a vampire to become disgusted with his life and announce their existence to the world. In those instances, the Committee would have to step in and clean up the mess. To have a story like that on a local news station was odd. Most of them ended up in the tabloids. Jack chuckled. "Must be a slow news day."

He'd stick around and see what the story was about. It was his job, after all.

After the commercials, the anchor returned. "A young woman had a seizure downtown, causing witnesses to question the woman's origin. Many believe her to be a vampire, as witnesses reported seeing fangs and her skin appeared to burn in the sun."

The screen switched over to a grainy recording showing several people hovering around an ambulance. When the paramedics loaded the seizing woman onto the vehicle, long, red hair came into view.

Jack's heart landed in his stomach.

"Get Carrie on the phone. Now!"

Chapter 11

Sunny lay on the bed, staring at the covered window, trying to breathe through the waves of pain as her stomach continued to cramp. How did her life get screwed up so fast? All she wanted to do was go to a simple interview. All she wanted was to make a name for herself and not ride on her father's coattails. Why did her turning have to change everything?

Another spasm slashed its way across her abdomen and she winced. Hunger had taken control of her actions and twice she came close to biting someone. A doctor had examined her face, which she assumed was burned due to its tightness, and his thumb had traveled too close to her mouth. Even though he wore gloves, the scent of latex did nothing to overpower the scent of his blood. Once her nose got a whiff, she snapped her teeth, but missed her mark--his reaction quicker than her sluggish one. Another doctor, curious about her fangs, had decided to take a look. If she possessed any kind of control, she would have waited for the right moment. Unfortunately, she had bitten down too soon. Or maybe she was just too slow. Now, no one came near her mouth.

The nurses had strapped her wrists to the bed, not because she was grabbing for anyone, but because they thought she was pulling out her IV. Minutes after being re-inserted, it would slip free. And it was free once again, the sheet around her arm was wet.

She had been poked and prodded, but most of the nurses had been gentle. When the uncovered window caused her to squint, they shut the curtains and turned out the lights. The technicians had taken her blood, though. Would they find anything unusual with it? Thank God tests took time. So long as she wasn't seizing and her vitals appeared normal, the doctors didn't seem too interested in her. So what if she couldn't move or talk? Those attributes probably made her a model patient.

The door swished opened. She kept her head turned away because moving it took too much energy. The last time she moved, the doctor thought she was seizing, which drew a crowd. The less people who saw her, the better. Maybe if whoever came in thought she was asleep, he or she would leave her alone.

"Damn. How do you keep doing this?"

Out of all the nurses who could have visited, why did it have to be Nurse Billy? The last time he changed her IV, he told the crudest jokes. Probably thought he held a captive audience.

His gloved fingers touched her chin and pulled her head toward him. A flash of light blinded her and she closed her eyes. Did he just take a picture?

He tugged on her chin. "Come on, open up. Let me see those fangs of yours."

Fudge. What kind of scum worked here, anyway? Jerking her body, she moved her head to the side.

"Hey, now. Don't make me hurt you."

"*Yeah, well, if you continue, I might hurt you. Now, go away.*" No matter how hard she tried, she still couldn't get her telepathic powers to work. She had nothing. Nothing, nothing, nothing.

He turned her head back and yanked down on her jaw. She tried to clamp her mouth shut, but with no control, she lost that battle. He brought a cellphone up and another flash went off. Fudge. The man was going to blind her.

"Shit, that didn't work," he mumbled as he examined the device.

He flipped a switch and the fluorescents above her head flickered to life. At least she had control over her eyes and closed them to the irritation.

He climbed onto the mattress and straddled her body. The man had some nerve. Frustration turned to anger and she tried to buck him off, but all she managed to do was jerk her body around.

"Hold still, will you?" Billy placed one hand on her chin and held her mouth open. With his other, he pointed the phone at her. Suddenly, he stopped and sat up. The phone landed on the bed.

My Sunny Vampire

"Am I interrupting something?"

Jack. Thank God. Relief rushed through her. So intent on the nurse, she hadn't heard the door open. How the heck did he find her? Oh, who cared? He'd found her. That's all that mattered. She'd hug and kiss him if she could.

Billy climbed down and sat on the floor. Jack worked at removing the straps. "How're you doing, sweetheart?"

Emotions welled up inside and her heart constricted. She wasn't the type to burst into tears, but if she could, she might have done just that. Oh God, he looked good.

"Cat got your tongue?" With the smile accompanying the question, she was sure he meant it as a joke, but when she didn't answer, he furrowed his brow in concern. "Can't you talk?"

If he'd just touch her skin, he'd find out. Then again, her silence should be a big give-away.

He removed the last strap, setting her free. Too bad she couldn't move. He pushed a button and the head portion of the bed lifted. She started to lean to one side and he adjusted her, releasing her once she remained in place.

He sat beside her and then quickly stood. "What the--" Discovering the IV, he removed the tape and draped the tube on the pole. He found a towel of some sort and placed it on the wet spot before sitting on the bed. "That's better," he said as he gently took her hand.

"Oh, Jack. It's been awful. How did you find me? How'd you get here? How're you getting me out?"

"Easy, now." His smile nearly melted her heart. "Why don't we get you fed first, then worry about the rest? Do you have any objections to using this guy here?"

"No. The guy's slime."

Jack rose and the nurse took his place. He took Billy's wrist and positioned it over her mouth. "This won't be near enough for you, but it should get you mobile. Just relax and let your body take over. I'll remove him when it's time."

Relax? Was he kidding? What if someone walked in? Then the sweet scent of blood filled her nose and all other thoughts left her head. She let her teeth do the work. Within seconds, the coppery flavor hit her tongue, sending her mouth to heaven. She must have gotten messy, as Jack wiped her chin with a tissue, but she continued to suck the life back into her.

Moments later she was able to bring her hand up and hold onto Billy's arm without Jack's help. Energy flowed from her midsection to her extremities and the pain ebbed. The tightness in her face receded. What a rush.

Jack placed his hand on her jaw. "I know you need more, but I also know you don't want to kill the guy, so let go."

Reluctantly, she did as he said, licking the site to remove her fang marks.

"What's this?" Jack held Billy's phone in his hand.

"That's his cell. He was taking pictures of me." She felt her eyes get big. Oh sweet heaven. She talked. She actually talked.

"Here." He tossed her the phone. "See if you can delete them and I'll go find your clothes."

Control. She finally had control over her body. She cherished every little thing she could do. She found and deleted the photos while Jack gathered her clothes and placed them on the bed. He took the phone and returned it to Billy's pocket.

"Do you need help getting dressed?"

"I don't think so."

He faced the wall and waited. While she didn't mind the view of his butt, he didn't seem to want to watch her. Was he that mad? Was she that disfigured? She touched her face.

"I don't hear you moving. You sure you're okay?"

"Am I scarred?"

He turned around. "What? No. You healed nicely."

"So why the back?"

"I was just trying to give you some privacy." He turned back around.

Her hero was chivalrous. She smiled. Her movements weren't the quickest, but at the moment she wasn't complaining. She had no problems getting dressed until she had to stand, then she asked for Jack's help. He even got her shoes. Through it all he remained quiet and smiled politely. It unnerved her, like waiting for a bomb to explode.

"Why are you being so nice?" she asked. "I thought for sure you'd be furious with me."

He finished placing the shoes on her feet, his hands gentle and strong at the same time. Then he looked up with those beautiful blue-green eyes and smiled. "I am furious with you. You ready to go?"

My Sunny Vampire

"Oh." Her heart fluttered. Dang, if that was furious, how might she react to happy? She swallowed. "I need my coat and portfolio."

* * * *

Jack couldn't stop staring at Sunshine.

Her blue eyes sparkled with life, her red hair aflame. Quite a contrast from the woman he found a short while ago.

He had expected to find her helpless, since no one contacted him or Carrie, but she shouldn't have lost her abilities to begin with. Could it be because she's a newbie? He hoped that's all it was.

He found her items in the closet and handed them to her. "Once we're in the clear, we'll get you some more food. Right now we have to go."

She nodded and slipped on her suit jacket and then her coat. When she slid off the bed, she teetered over and dropped her portfolio.

He caught her. "Are you going to be able to walk?"

"Yes. I just lost my balance. I'll be okay."

If it weren't for the fact he wanted to get out without making a scene, he'd just pick her up and carry her. And he might have done just that, except there were at least five people in the area and he could only manipulate two, maybe three minds at once. So he'd hold on to her and hope for the best. He picked up the portfolio and slid his arm around her waist. Damn, she felt good. All soft and curvy. The aroma of roses invaded his senses. He'd missed her.

Jack opened the door. "Put your head on my shoulder so you look like a grieving visitor."

"What about Billy?"

Who? Oh, the nurse. "He'll be asleep for a while."

He pulled Sunshine into the hallway. The nurse's station was several doors down and no one was looking their way. Coast clear, he led her to the stairwell.

The simple act of descending the stairs took its toll on Sunshine. Her breathing became labored and she grabbed her stomach several times. Jack breathed easier once they reached the garage level. If he could find a convenient donor on the way home, he'd make sure she fed.

He opened the door, sending squeaking noises echoing in the garage. Carrie squealed and dashed into Sunshine, nearly knocking them both over.

"Hey, Carrie." Sunshine hugged her friend and winced. "Why are you here?"

Jack gently pried the sprite loose and answered. "Frank doesn't know how to operate a computer. I take it everything is okay?"

"Yeah," Carrie said. "It was so cool. I felt like a spy. No one even bothered us."

"That's because I suggested they ignore us," Frank said. "All records and tests regarding Sunny have been deleted, as well as other patients. Carrie thought it would look better if they thought they had some kind of computer glitch."

Jack smiled. "Good thinking." He handed Carrie the portfolio. "Take this back to Frank's and we'll meet you there."

"I'm not driving you?"

"It's okay, babe," Frank said. "Our way is safer. Besides, we might beat you there anyway."

Jack wasn't sure about that. Sunshine needed blood, soon.

Carrie hugged the case to her chest and furrowed her eyebrows. "You okay, Sunny? You look kind of pale."

Sunshine smiled broadly at her friend. "I'm fine. Go on and we'll see you later." She watched Frank accompany Carrie back to her car. When they were out of sight, her smile faded and she leaned against Jack. "If vampires slept, I'd sleep for a week."

And he'd want to sleep right beside her, but before anyone did any resting, they needed to get as far away from the hospital as they could. "Let's go. We don't need to wait for Frank."

"So how are we traveling during the day? You're not having me walk through sewers or anything like that, are you?"

He took her hand and led her through the parking garage, staying between the cars and the wall. "Yes and no, sort of. There are more than sewer tunnels underground. Some were actually built for pedestrians."

"Did vampires build these tunnels?"

Jack laughed. "Not that I know of."

Frank caught up to them before they reached the exit. However, when they approached a line of sunlight, Sunshine froze.

Her eyes were wild and she trembled.

Well, he'd wanted her to be afraid of the sun. "It's okay. We're not going into the light. There's a door, right there to the left." He pointed and she blinked several times before following his direction.

My Sunny Vampire

She gripped his hand and stayed close beside him as he headed for the door. When he opened it, he silently cursed. The sun had moved and a beam filtered into the stairwell. In order to get to their destination, they must cross the sliver of light.

Frank zipped through as though the sun didn't exist. A little exposure was normally fine. However, Sunshine had experienced more than her fair share.

She planted her feet and shook her head. "No, no, no."

"What's the matter?" Frank asked.

Jack glanced at his friend and then turned to her. Panic flashed in her eyes and her breathing became erratic. He couldn't make her do it. He wasn't sure she should try.

He caressed her cheek. "We'll wait until it's safe."

She nodded and breathed slower. Trust replaced the panic in her eyes. He would make sure he wouldn't lose her trust, either.

"It's not safe for her here," Frank said.

Jack turned to his friend. "You go on ahead. We'll hide. It shouldn't take more than an hour. If you don't hear from me in two hours, come looking."

"Are you sure? I could stay."

"Carrie will freak if you don't show up. You need to go."

Frank relented and descended the stairs. Alone with Sunshine, Jack set upon finding an appropriate hiding spot. A car approached. In order to hide her, he positioned himself to simulate a couple talking intimately.

Her rosy scent swirled around his head and Little Jack stirred. Shit. Not now. He took a step back.

"I'm sorry," she said, lowering her head. "I really screwed things up, didn't I?"

He focused on the job at hand. Not her scent and certainly not Little Jack. "We'll talk about that later. Right now we need to get you out of sight. I don't know how long it will be before someone checks on you, or notices Billy has been gone too long."

The garage quieted once again. He took her hand, ignoring the electric flow that always seemed to affect his groin, and led her to a row of parked cars. He needed something large, like a van, and one that looked like it might be parked all day.

He tried the doors to several vans, all locked. Frustration tried to weasel its way into his head and he came close to punching the last vehicle. If he carried any kind of wire, he might have been able

103

to pick a lock, but he hadn't planned on breaking and entering. Then he found an old, beat-up Chevy panel van. When he turned the handle, it moved.

Ushering her inside, he followed and closed the door behind him. He could see why it was unlocked. Who'd want to steal this junk? Buckets were stacked or strewn about, paint rollers and sticks looked as if they'd been tossed inside and several McDonald's bags littered the area between the front seats. Sunshine cleared a spot to sit against the wall. As tempted as he was to be beside her, he sat across instead. Little Jack was still giving him fits and distance seemed the best course.

"What happens when the owner comes back?" Sunshine lightly touched her stomach and winced.

"I guess you'll feed, then. How bad is it?"

"It's been worse." She leaned her head back. "So, you gonna yell at me now?"

"What makes you think--?"

"Because that's what you do, Jack. You tell me not to do something. I disobey. You yell. Well, maybe not out loud, but I can tell you do it in your head."

His bit his lip to keep from laughing. "So if you know I'm going to do this so-called internal yelling, why do you disobey?"

She chuckled. "Why do you have to be so bossy?"

"How am I bossy?"

She played with the button on her blazer. "Because all you ever tell me is what I can't do. I really didn't think going to a little interview would cause so much trouble."

"Because you didn't think."

"Hey!"

"I told you the rules. I told you how things are different for you now. Do you know how close you came to becoming a caged animal? To exposing all vampires? When are you going to realize that we need mortals more than they need us? If that means we live in secrecy, then we do."

* * * *

Sunny had asked for his wrath, got it and then some. Her defensive shield went up. "I didn't ask for this life."

Jack scrubbed his face. "I know, but that's not the issue is it? It's your life now and you have to face those facts. Just like when you lived as a mortal, there are rules you must follow."

My Sunny Vampire

"What happens if I break them?"

"There are consequences. Right now the Committee will be lenient. You're new and were turned illegally." He lowered his head and shook it. "I should have taken you to them at the first opportunity. Someone else would have done a better job than me."

What? No! Her heart broke at those words. He was the only good thing about being a vampire and now he didn't want her? Why the heck did she have to accuse him of turning her? Pretty much killed any desire he felt for her before. Now all he did was push her away. "Maybe you should. Then I wouldn't bother you anymore."

He leaned forward, his expression softened. "You're not a bother to me."

"Could have fooled me. Before I turned, you wanted me. You kissed me and held me close and I liked it. Even when you fed, I liked it. Now you act like I have the plague or something. Did I change that much?"

He picked up a stick and played with the trash. "You keep forgetting I don't remember you then. But you couldn't be further from the truth."

"So why?"

He flicked a cigarette butt into the air. "It's complicated."

She crawled on her hands and knees, brushing the debris away. "If I say I don't care who turned me, or better yet, say I wanted you to turn me. Would that make it better for you?"

"While I appreciate the offer, your memories don't lie. It doesn't matter what you say. It only matters what you remember and what you remember can--"

"Get you killed. I get it." She stared at his lips. Lips she desperately wanted to kiss. "I don't want you to die."

He smiled. "That's good to know. I just wish it mattered."

"I'm beginning to dislike this Committee. They seem strict. Have you thought about hiding me?" Not that she would like that, but if it kept him alive...

He chuffed out a laugh. "I can't even keep you from an interview. What kind of luck do you think I'd have hiding you?" His hand cupped her cheek and he gazed into her eyes, causing her heart to flutter. "Besides, you'd hate that. I'd rather die than see you unhappy."

He would? His lips beckoned and she leaned closer. She ached to kiss him. She yearned for his hug. Would he push her away again? Just then, her stomach cramped and she folded in on herself. Fudge.

Trash skittered against the walls of the van, most likely pushed away by Jack. He grabbed her shoulders and gently lowered her to the floor.

He kissed her forehead. Not exactly what she was aiming for, but it felt nice all the same. "I'm going out to find a donor."

"Be careful."

"It's not me they're looking for, sweetheart. Hang tight. I won't be long."

This stomach cramping business really got on her nerves. So far this whole vampire thing chafed big time. Would she ever have fun again?

The driver's door opened. Why was Jack back already? And why up front?

"What's the matt--?" The words died on her lips. He wasn't Jack.

The bald man turned around. "Well, hello there. What are you doing in my van?"

* * * *

Jack loitered near the elevator. He'd prefer a lone person disembark. Picking someone out of a group only caused more complications. Couldn't something go easy for once?

Of course, once he got Sunshine fed, would she continue her quest for a kiss? He had nearly given in before she collapsed. He had to face it, he had no willpower against her.

While he waited, he called Frank and let him know they were okay and that he would call him back in an hour.

The doors opened to a semi-full load. Shit. Too many.

A burly security guard approached him. "Sir, did you see a young woman, a patient, with red hair walking around down here?"

Hmmm. Maybe his luck was turning. Bad news the staff noticed Sunshine missing, good news they sent a guy alone. "Was she tall, around five-ten?"

The man's eyes lit up. "I don't know. Where did you see her?"

"I'll show you." The passengers dissipated and were finally out of ear-shot. "*Don't say a word and follow me.*"

My Sunny Vampire

The guard's tag identified him as Sgt. Robbins. Fat rolled over his belt and he seemed to have trouble keeping his pants up. As they approached the van, Jack heard Sunshine sobbing. She wasn't that bad off when he left. Panicked, he rushed and flung open the door. A man with blood on his neck lay lifeless on the floor. She was leaning over him, wailing.

"Oh God, Jack. I think I killed him."

Chapter 12

"*You saw the redhead you were looking for drive off in a white sedan.*" Jack confirmed the message with a vision. Once released, Sgt. Robbins trotted toward the elevators. At least that should buy them some time.

Jack climbed inside the van and shut the door. "What the hell happened?"

Sunshine's face and collar were splattered with blood. Worry lines marked her brow and she hyperventilated as she spat out the words. "He just...showed up...and I thought...I could do it...on my own. But then...he fought me."

The man's chest rose, slow but steady. Jack went to her and placed a hand on her shoulder. "Look at him. He's breathing, so that makes him alive."

She stared at the body for a moment and then closing her eyes, rocked back on her legs. "Thank God. Thank God."

He looked around for a rag and found a roll of paper towels. He tore one off and handed it to her. "Here. Clean yourself up."

With shaky hands, she took the towel and moved up front to use the mirror. "I'm so sorry. I just didn't know what to do." She licked the paper and wiped at her chin. "Do you think he'll be okay?"

"You're not the first vampire to take too much. He'll probably be weak, but he'll live. How are you feeling?"

"Better than I should." She lowered her head. "How am I ever going to do this without you stopping me?"

My Sunny Vampire

"You just need some more practice." He moved up behind her and placed his hands on her shoulders, only to offer comfort, but she turned around and hugged him, catching him off guard.

"I'm never going to get the hang of this. I'm probably the worst vampire around. I don't know what I'd do without you."

Jack's heart warmed to her. How did she get wrapped up in his life so quickly? No one ever needed him before. Not even Clara. Especially after he turned.

"You'll be fine, I promise." His arms slipped around her and she nestled her head on his shoulder. He could get used to this. Feeling connected. Feeling needed. But what she felt couldn't be real. She'd been through a trauma and was probably clinging to the one person who helped her--him. Some sort of hero worship. He'd heard of it before.

If he gave in to his feelings, he'd only be taking advantage of hers. Once she became accustomed to being a vampire, her need would fade. Of course, none of that would matter if he was guilty of turning her. He'd be dead.

She deserved his tact. Rejection wouldn't fare well with her right now, no matter what his intentions were. He loosened her hold on him, tearing a hole in his heart. "Better take care of him before he wakes."

* * * *

Sunny didn't want to let go of Jack. He was like the home she always dreamed about. But he was right. An unconscious man needed looking after.

"So, what do we have to do?" she asked.

He crawled over the body. "Not we, you."

"Me?"

"You made the mess, you clean it up. You want to learn, don't you?"

Oh, fudge. She hated it when he was right. Heck, she hated being wrong. She frowned.

A chuckle escaped Jack's lips as he sat back against the wall. "It's not that bad and with all that extra blood in your system, you shouldn't have a problem."

Extra blood was right. What a rush. What a mess. Unprepared for the onslaught, she had gotten more than her mouth could hold and panicked, most likely severing her link to the man. He fought back. She had done the only thing she could think of, fed until he passed out.

Sunny assessed the situation. The man no longer bled, but she'd left a mess. She should have fed from his wrist, but when he'd come after her like some wild beast, he had landed on top. There was his neck, just begging to be bitten and she got greedy. At least she had the sense to pull his shirt away. The excess blood had dripped on her.

Without water available, she resorted to licking him clean. Even that small amount gave her mouth a zing and her fangs extended. How annoying.

"Will I ever have control over these things?"

"Concentrate on something else. I'm sure you can pick out another scent that will make them retract."

Another scent. Another scent. She closed her eyes and mentally scanned the interior. Hmmm. Musky. Manly. Intoxicating.

Fudge.

Jack's scent not only kept her fangs extended, but caused other parts of her body to perk up. She spotted a McDonald's bag, opened it and took a whiff. Yes. Mustard.

Her teeth retracted. Maybe she needed to carry something like that around with her. Her version of smelling salts.

She replaced the bag. "He's all clean. Is that it?"

Jack folded his arms. "What do you think?"

"You sound like my therapist."

His eyes widened. "You have a therapist? Why am I not surprised."

She planted her hands on her hips. "What is that supposed to mean?"

"Sorry." He put his palms up in surrender. "It was uncalled for. Please forgive me."

Sunny hadn't thought of her therapist in years, so why did she even bring it up? That part of her life was in the past, where it belonged.

She stared at Baldy. What else could she do for him? He was unconscious. When he woke up he'd be clean. And totally confused. Of course. She needed to put him behind the steering wheel.

Being able to lift such a heavy man without any effort still surprised her, but the small confines of the van made maneuvering awkward. How in the world could she get him over the seat without hurting him?

Walking on her knees, she pushed him into a sitting position and tried shoving him between the seats, but his legs hit the dashboard before his hips were in position. Bending his knees didn't help as they kept falling over. The man was as limp as a wet noodle. She punched the seatback. "Dag-burnit."

Jack snorted. "How the hell did you get him over the seats to begin with?"

She looked at him sitting there as if he had all the time in the world. Frustration burned its way out her mouth. "I didn't. I just thought 'come here' and he came."

He rubbed his face and smiled. "That would do it."

She would show him. It couldn't be that hard to get Baldy on the seat. He did crawl over on his own. Realizing her mistake, she angled the man's legs over to the passenger side and eventually lifted him onto the driver's seat. After she positioned his feet over the pedals, his head slumped over and landed on her chest, his mouth on her boob.

Jack snickered.

"Hey! Don't make me come over there and hit you."

Would it kill him to lend a hand? Finally, she propped the man up, making it appear as if he took a nap while waiting on someone. She brushed her hands on her thighs, feeling pretty smug about herself. Then it hit her. He would remember her. Nerves fluttered in her stomach.

"Jack, I don't know...I mean, I've never done..."

"Sunshine, take it easy. You got into his head once."

"Yeah, but Jack, he was conscious then. How would I know?"

"You can do this."

Uncertainty clouded her mind. How could he be so sure? She wasn't sure. If she missed something or screwed up, the man would remember her. What then? She buried her head in her hands. "Please don't make me do this."

Hands touched her shoulders and she jumped. Jack moved to her without making a sound. Would she ever be that good?

"What would you do if I weren't here?" he asked. "You'd try, wouldn't you?"

"I tried to feed without you and look where it got me."

"Look at the positives. You got into his head. You fed from him. And he's not dead. Those are big positives."

"Yeah, but--"

"No buts. You're smart. I have faith in you."

She stared into his eyes. He had faith in her? Oh, fudge.

"If you give him a command to perform when he wakes, you'll know if you got through to him."

The butterflies in her stomach eased. "If he doesn't, then I repeat it when he's conscious?"

He smiled. "Exactly."

"So we're staying until he wakes up?"

Jack sat back against the wall of the van. "Why not? Where else are we going to go? The sun doesn't set for another three hours."

Hmmm. Three hours in a van with Jack? She could live with that, especially since she felt two-thousand percent better.

So, what kind of believable memory could she leave behind? What would cause *her* to fall asleep behind the wheel? Then an idea struck.

"You might want to hold his head," Jack said. "Sometimes the contact helps when they're unconscious."

Grabbing Baldy's head, she concentrated--because she really had no idea how it all worked--and transmitted, *"Upon waking, you will yell 'Mother.' The last thing you remember was entering the van with a raging headache. You leaned back hoping the pain would go away."*

She smiled. If it got through, it would be believable. She didn't stop there. *"When you feel better, you'll clean up the inside of your van."*

"Okay, I'm done."

"Now we wait."

She sat beside him. "Thank you."

"For what? I didn't do anything. You cleaned this up all by yourself."

"Not about this. For rescuing me. I'm sorry for causing you so much trouble."

His hands were in his lap and she yearned to hold one. To touch him anywhere. He'd probably pull away if she tried.

He looked at her. "I'm sorry for not realizing how important your old life was to you. In my need to clear my name, I guess I forgot you're a victim in all this. I don't mean to hide you, I really don't, it's just--"

My Sunny Vampire

"I know. You want to find the person who turned me before the Committee finds out about me. I get it. So how can I help?"

Baldy groaned and yelled, "Mother."

Holy moly. It worked? She stared at Jack and smiled. He leaned into her ear. "I take it that was your code?"

She nodded. "He's up sooner than I thought. It's too soon to leave, isn't it?"

Jack shrugged. "I could always get him to drive us home."

Baldy grabbed his head and groaned.

"I don't think he's in any shape to drive," she said. "Can I suggest he go to the ER? Then we can stay here a little longer. Besides, with his blood loss, he should probably see a doctor, don't you think?"

Jack raised his arm in an invitation.

She concentrated on the man's head. "*You're sick and dizzy. Go to the ER.*"

Baldy opened the glove box and scoured through the contents.

She knew it had seemed too easy. At least he hadn't seen or heard them yet. After three more attempts, she balled her hands into fists, ready to punch something.

Instead, she pounded her forehead with the heel of her hand. "What am I doing wrong?" she muttered.

Jack held her wrist. "Quiet. How many times do I have to tell you not to do that?"

"I'm broken."

"You're not broken. You're just making this harder than it is." He massaged her shoulders, and dang, if that didn't feel good. Maybe too good. "Relax. You don't need to scrunch up your face like you're sending out a laser beam."

"I don't know how else to do it."

"Close your eyes." His hand came up and covered her eyes, causing her heart to skip a few beats. "Breathe deep and send the message."

He made it sound so easy. How would closing her eyes work? But she did what he suggested.

A door opened and then slammed shut. She opened her eyes. Baldy was gone.

She hugged Jack and kissed his face, over and over. He grasped her shoulders and pushed her back. He said, "That's enough." But his thoughts of wanting her filtered through her head.

Why was he still pushing her away? Maybe he just needed her to make the first move. It was now or never. She held his face in her hands and planted her lips over his.

* * * *

Sunshine assaulted his senses. Willpower and common sense flew out the window. Her lips were soft and yielding and her tongue sought his mouth. He opened and welcomed her. She tasted as sweet as he remembered.

Jack fisted his hand in her hair, wanting to get closer. All thoughts of pushing her away were stripped from his mind. He wanted her and he wanted her now.

He found her breast and squeezed. She moaned into his mouth. While Little Jack strained for freedom, he lowered her to the floor and unbuttoned her blazer.

The passenger door opened.

Like a slap in the face, it was all Jack needed to gather his wits. This was no place to make love to her, but he was sure as hell headed that way. He pulled back.

"No, no, no," she pleaded. "Send him away."

"Where's my God-damned wallet?" the man muttered.

Papers scattered and Jack held still. The van's owner could see them if he bothered, but he was too preoccupied with his search. If Jack didn't let the man finish, he'd only come back later.

"There you are." The door closed.

Jack sat back on his heels and sagged in relief. He looked down at Sunshine. She reached out and touched his face and he took her hand.

"I'm sorry," he said. "I shouldn't have done that."

"If I recall, I kind of started it." She straightened up and leaned in for a kiss, but he held her back.

It killed him to reject her again, especially after she offered to help.

"Oh." Pain flashed in her eyes.

He moved to the side of the van. "We should be able to leave in another hour. The sun will be low enough then."

Sunshine leaned against the opposite wall and closed her eyes. "Whatever."

My Sunny Vampire

He had come too damn close to ripping her clothes off. She deserved better than the back of a van. She also deserved time to come to terms with her new life. Until he knew her feelings for him were real, he couldn't take advantage. He only hoped he hadn't screwed it all up. Damn, he had to face it, he was falling for her.

Chapter 13

The music blared just as loudly as it had two nights ago, but fewer people visited the joint. Jack and Sunshine were sitting at a high-top table in clear view of the entrance while Frank and Carrie were out on the dance floor.

Despite the cold shoulder in the van, Sunshine seemed in better spirits. Maybe she'd finally realized her feelings for him were false. If so, it didn't mean he couldn't try courting her later, when this whole mess was solved. Provided he was innocent.

"I think he's using her," Sunshine said, snapping him out of his ruminations.

"Who's using who?" Jack tore his gaze from the entrance and stared at her. The blue dress she wore complemented her eyes and made her hair look like fire. The low-cut neckline showed off ample cleavage. If he were courting her now, nothing would stop him from ravishing her. Instead, he had a case to solve, although she made it damn hard to keep his mind on the task at hand.

"Frank. He plies Carrie with liquor and then feeds from her. Is that normal?"

He looked back at the door. A couple entered. Not his man.

"The feeding can be, but he's not asking her to drink."

Frank promised he wouldn't do anything Carrie didn't offer. That wasn't to say…

"Oh come on. You mean to tell me he's not using his mind mojo on her?" she said, wiggling her fingers over her head.

My Sunny Vampire

He stifled a laugh. "Mind mojo? No, I don't believe Frank would do that to her. She's the first woman he's shown an interest in since his wife died." It did seem strange how Carrie's glass was never empty. Could he really trust an alcoholic not to drink? Because he was pretty certain Frank was one.

She raised her eyebrows. "You can marry?"

"Sure, why not? Don't you think we're entitled?"

"It's not that. I guess I just never gave it much thought. So, how long was Frank married?"

Jack remembered Frank and Linda's wedding day as if it were only yesterday. "Almost seventy years."

She propped her elbow on the table and rested her head in her hand. "Wow. I can't imagine being married that long. What about you?"

"I'm not married."

He kept his peripheral vision on the door. Three men entered the bar. Still no sign of the donor. Of course, what were the odds he'd be here on a weeknight?

She tilted her head to the side. "Well, duh. I kind of figured that, even though it's nice to actually hear the words. Were you ever?"

He couldn't help but smile at her. She was a nut, but an adorable one. "When I was mortal, yes."

"For how long?"

"We'd been married one year when I went to fight in the war." She raised her eyebrows and he leaned in close. "Revolutionary."

"Oh. Wow. Any children?"

His heart ached for the son he had lost. "No. I was turned before we had a chance to start a family."

She placed her hand on his arm. He intentionally wore a long-sleeved shirt, so no inadvertent thoughts would slip to her mind. They had gotten him into enough trouble already.

"Oh," she said. "Were you changed against your will, too?"

The way her mind veered from one subject to another boggled him, but at the moment the change was welcomed. The last thing he wanted to discuss with her was his life with Clara. "Sunshine, most of us were changed against our will. Our rule of getting permission was enacted in 1930. Since then, there's only been one, well, I guess now two instances." Death was apparently a good motivator to behave. So whoever turned Sunshine was one crazy vampire.

He continued to monitor the door. Five women departed and only two women entered. No men. Where were the men? Where was *his* man?

"How did Frank's wife die? Did she do something illegal?"

"No, nothing like that. Linda was a model citizen. She died in an accident. A little over a year ago, she was driving back from a friend's house when a tanker truck plowed into her. It ignited on impact. She might have been able to escape, but didn't have enough time to free herself before the flames overtook her."

She brought her hand up to her neck. "That's awful. Frank must have been devastated."

"He was."

Jack nearly groaned as seven more people departed and no one entered. At that rate, he wouldn't need to stay much longer.

"What happens when a vampire dies publicly like that? That would be a lot of minds to wipe."

"You're right. It would be impossible. In that case, the Committee has to create a life. We add information instead of deleting. We make it look like she was a normal person living a normal life."

She looked out over the dance floor. Frank was nuzzling Carrie's neck. Did Sunshine see? Did she know what he was doing?

"Do you think Linda's death triggered Frank's drinking?"

Dammit. She saw. He leaned back in his chair. "I don't think that's what he's doing now." The lie tasted bitter in his mouth, but Sunshine didn't need to think of Frank that way. Bad enough he did. "He took Linda's death hard. Just going out on New Year's Eve was a big step for him. I think Carrie's helping him turn his life around."

Movement at the entrance caught Jack's attention. Still no sign of his guy.

"Well, you know him better than I do." She continued to stare at the dancing couples. "Do you want to dance?"

He'd love nothing more than to have an excuse to hold her in his arms, but what would stop him from going further? Sitting beside her was torturous enough. Of course, now that he really looked at the dancers, not one couple touched. "That's not dancing. That's people jumping around."

"No, I don't suppose they are dancing to you. I guess you're used to waltzes or something like that?"

"I don't see any reason to dance if you're not touching your partner. Regardless, I need to keep an eye out for the donor. I don't want to miss him if he happens to show." Not that that was looking like a possibility.

She frowned and slouched, clearly disappointed in his answer. He had told her the night might be boring, so what did she expect?

A man wearing a shiny red shirt with the top few buttons missing, baring more skin than was called for, approached their table. "Care to dance?"

Sunshine sat up straight and looked at Jack, raising her eyebrows in question. Was she looking for his consent? He wasn't the one who brought the man over. Frankly, Jack was surprised at her pick. He could have sworn the guy eyed him several times.

"You wanted to dance," he mumbled.

Turning to the man, she smiled broadly. "Yes, I would."

She took his hand and stood. Had it been only a few hours ago she complained she couldn't control a mortal? What kind of game was she playing?

* * * *

Sunny sighed as the man led her to the dance floor. This wasn't what she envisioned after that wonderful kiss in the van. No matter how much Jack's rejection stung, she knew they had something special and she planned to prove it to him, but when they'd returned to Frank's, Carrie had stuck around and Sunny never got a chance to get Jack alone. She thought for sure something would happen here, but Jack was all business.

"I'm Derek, what's your name?"

"Sunny."

She glanced back at Jack. Why the frown? He had invited the guy over, she hadn't. Maybe he was regretting his decision. Well, she could really make him regret it, even if she didn't like the view. Derek's silk shirt exposed a shiny, hairless chest and his skin-tight leather pants revealed more than she cared to see. Even his hair seemed too shaggy, since she preferred Jack's short locks.

It was just a dance, not a date, so she would dance. Music set her soul alight and she got caught up in the beat. So what if her partner's gaze seemed to ravish her body? She would just ignore him and enjoy herself.

Derek grabbed her hips, causing her to jump. She promptly removed his hands and released him. "I don't know you well enough for you to touch me."

He closed the gap with a few dancing steps and brought his head close to hers. "So what do I need to do for you to get to know me better?" His breath tickled her ear and reeked of beer.

"'Cause I'll do it."

"I just bet you would," she muttered and opened up the expanse once again. "I only agreed to the dance. Let's not make it more than that, okay?"

She swayed her hips and concentrated on the music, closing her eyes to Derek and everything else. Everything else, except Jack. Back on New Year's Eve, Jack had loved the way she danced and he couldn't keep his hands off her. Touching, kissing and a whole lot of biting. She missed that Jack.

The music lived inside her. She could almost feel Jack's gaze caressing her body and was dancing solely for him when arms came around her from behind. Derek's stench assaulted her senses. Ugh. Just when she was starting to have fun he went and spoiled things.

Derek pulled her close, grinding his erection, or whatever he stuffed in his pants, against her backside. "You're sexy, you know that?"

Dang, stupid idiot. He had definitely moved into the creep category. "*Let me go.*" He didn't respond. Oh, fudge. Was she ever going to get the hang of the mind mojo thing? She unhooked his arms and spun to face him. "What did I say about touching?"

He cupped her face and planted a wet, smoochy kiss on her lips. She clamped her mouth shut to keep him from shoving his tongue down her throat. "*Gross, let go!*"

Yet, Derek continued to assault her with his mouth. That did it. She placed her hands on his chest and was about to give him the shove of his life when an arm came across her waist and pulled her back. Derek stood motionless in front of her.

"Easy, sweetheart," Jack whispered into her ear. "You don't want to do anything rash, now do you?"

* * * *

Jack held Sunshine close and felt her heart race. Listening to their conversation wasn't his proudest moment, but he was thankful he had. The frustration in her voice alerted him. Sure enough, she nearly went ballistic. One news story about vampires

My Sunny Vampire

in the city was already one too many. "Why didn't you just control him?"

Sunshine turned and glared at him as if she wanted him to burn.

"I tried," she said through clenched teeth, then stormed off to their table, leaving him with Derek.

So much for thinking he was gay. The man deserved to be decked, but not in a crowded club, and certainly not by a vampire.

"*You're bored with the women here and you will go back home.*" Jack released the man's mind and returned to his table.

Sunshine rested her head on her arms as if asleep, but he knew better. He couldn't blame her for being frustrated. How could she invite the guy over to dance, but not get rid of him? It didn't make sense.

"I'm sorry," he said as he returned to his stool. "I thought you were getting the hang of it."

"I did, too," she muttered. "Thank you. If you hadn't intervened, I might have flown him across the room. That wouldn't look too good, would it?"

It was nice to know she didn't hate him, but it pained him seeing her so down. "If you still want to dance--"

"You've done enough," she interrupted. "God, I can't seem to do anything right."

He wanted to hold her close and comfort her. Tell her he'd help her through it. But that was a promise he couldn't make. "That's not true, you just need--"

"More time. More practice," she said with a sarcastic tone. She turned her head and glared at him. "Did you? Did you need so much time when you turned?"

No, he hadn't. Mind control kicked in first thing for him. In fact, he'd sent suggestions to several people before he even knew what he was doing. "Everyone is different."

"Yeah, and I'm at the bottom of the learning curve, apparently. Nothing new there, though. So, have you located your man yet?"

Shit. He'd been occupied watching her dance, the guy could have come and gone. "No. I'm beginning to think this is a waste of time."

"Maybe I can help. What does this guy look like anyway?"

Now, why didn't he think of that? All this time he'd been looking and he could have had an extra set of eyes. He unbuttoned his cuff and rolled up his sleeve. "Touch me and see."

He meant for her to place her hand on his arm. Instead, she took his hand and intertwined their fingers. Just that simple touch woke up his libido and then some. Little Jack stirred.

"I don't see anything." She pulled away. "I knew it. I'm broken."

He cleared his throat to keep from laughing out loud. Even whiny, she was adorable. "Sorry, my fault." He brought his memory of the man to the surface. "How about now?"

This time she touched the back of his hand and he struggled to keep the man's face at the front of his mind. She furrowed her brow in concentration, something he might want to tell her wasn't necessary, but then again, maybe not. She was just so damn cute. Watching her wasn't helping his concentration any and he set his sights back to the entrance.

"He's the guy you fed from?"

"The one and only."

Carrie and Frank returned to the table. Carrie grabbed her drink and chugged it down.

"Whatcha doing?" she asked, her voice slightly slurred.

Sunshine turned toward her friend. "Remember that guy who hit on us on New Year's Eve? The one who was high?"

High? All of a sudden, the inside of Jack's mouth turned dry. His worst fears confirmed.

"That wasn't any guy. That was Bobby Foxx. I thought you knew that. Why you wanna know?" Carrie asked.

Sunshine's eyes widened. "Bobby Foxx? Nooo, really? What the heck happened to him?"

"You know the guy?" Jack asked.

"Yeah, we went to high school with him," Carrie said. "Big football star. Then he got injured and lost his scholarship. I think it's been his downfall ever since."

"Do you know where he lives?"

"No, but I'm sure it's easy to find. I think he still lives with his mother."

Sunshine sat quietly and stared at her hands as a frown marred her face. Jack touched her shoulder. "Are you okay?"

She looked up and smiled. "Yeah, sure."

Something was up. Maybe there was more to this Bobby guy than she was letting on.

My Sunny Vampire

Carrie stared at her empty glass. "Frankie, sweetie, can you get me another?"

Sunshine grabbed Carrie's arm. "I think you've had enough. Since when do you drink so much?"

"But I'm thirsty."

"Then get a Coke."

Carrie slumped down in her chair. "Okay, if you insist." Frank left to purchase her drink. Jack was still reeling over the news. The donor had a name and could be found. If nothing else, he could find out exactly what the man ingested to cause his amnesia. The bonus would be to find out if another vampire was involved.

"So what were you doing dancing with Derek?" Carrie asked.

Sunshine leaned up against the table. "Jack thought he was doing me a favor and had him come over to ask me to dance."

"I didn't bring him over. I thought you did." Jack wanted to hit the guy even more. He had given the creep the benefit of the doubt, assuming Sunshine lured him.

"Oh. Maybe it was my vibes. You're going to have to show me how to turn that off."

"Vibes? What vibes are you talking about?"

"You know. I smile and men fall over me."

He looked around. "Where are these men?"

She smacked him in the shoulder. "You know what I mean. I must be giving out something. Most of the time I'm not even wearing makeup and they practically drool over me."

Jack chuckled, picturing a bevy of men drooling over her.

"It's not funny," she said.

"I'm sorry. But you're right. You are different now. You project an aura where unknowing mortals see you in a favorable light. They won't notice your grubby clothes or if you're in need of a shower. It helps us blend in easier."

"Only problem is," Carrie said, "I don't think she's Derek's type. Would that make a difference?"

"Oh? How would you know what type he likes?" Sunshine asked.

"I've bartended here on occasion. The owner calls me when he's short-handed. I know a lot of the regulars. Every time I saw Derek, he was with a guy."

"No way." Sunshine shook her head. "He came on to me."

123

Carrie shrugged. "Maybe I'm mistaken. I could have sworn the guy was gay."

Jack was pretty certain, too, which meant only one thing. He slammed his hand on the table and stood, knocking the chair over. "Shit."

Sunshine jerked in her seat. "What? Do you see him?"

"No," he said. "He was here. Don't you get it? The rogue was here."

Chapter 14

Jack rushed outside with Sunshine on his tail. How stupid could he be? How blind? He had sent away the one person who might tie him back to the vampire. This wasn't happening.

The sidewalk was empty, as were his hopes of finding the fiend. "Damn it. I was so close."

She grabbed his arm. "How can you be sure he was here?"

"I'll give that he might have wanted to dance and chose you. But it took some programming to get him to come on to you. He didn't do that on his own."

"Thanks so much. You sure know how to flatter a girl."

Her frown confused him. Hadn't she hated the kiss? So why the disappointment? Would he ever understand her? Did he want to?

"Besides, why would the rogue do this?" she asked. "Huh? Maybe it was just my vibes. Or maybe I did call him over without realizing it. Carrie could be wrong about the guy."

Sunshine had a point. Why would the rogue go to all this trouble? There was enough evidence right now to convict Jack, why not contact the Committee and get it over with? Because then the fun would be over? Someone was playing with him, but unless he was willing to confess that she resembled his late wife--and he wasn't, not yet--he couldn't explain it to her. Still, he wouldn't mind messing around with her a little.

"Okay, so let's say he was interested." He moved in closer, making her retreat until her back hit the wall. Her eyes widened and he nearly grinned, giving it away. "Then how 'bout I tell you that I hated seeing you dance with him. That I might have ripped the man's head off when I saw him kiss you and the only reason I didn't was because I thought you were playing some kind of game that got out of control?"

"I wasn't trying..." She swallowed. "You did?"

Her rosy scent took hold of his good judgment and he placed his hands on the wall, trapping her. Oh, who was he kidding? He wasn't messing with her. He was fooling himself. He'd hated seeing her dance with that guy, the jealousy nearly ate him alive. No more rejections. She belonged to him and no one else.

He heard her heart pumping away and she licked her lips, drawing his attention. God, she was beautiful. Little Jack stirred. He leaned in and brushed his lips against hers. Exquisite. Simply--

"Did you find him?" Carrie asked.

He jumped back. Damn it all to hell. Carrie sure knew how to spoil the mood. She hugged herself and bounced, most likely trying to keep warm.

"No, he already left," Sunshine said. "What now, Jack?"

He'd like to forget the whole thing, take her home and ravish her, but that wouldn't be fair to her. She deserved to know who turned her. While losing Derek was bad luck, he still had his donor. "Time to find Bobby Foxx."

* * * *

Dressed for the weather in dark-colored clothes so as not to draw attention to themselves, Sunny and Jack headed for Bobby's house. Bobby was still living with his mother and Sunny knew the address. A girl didn't forget where her first crush lived.

Jack had surprised her with the invitation to join him. He even suggested driving--Sunny hadn't known he owned a car--but she wanted to be closer than a car would allow so she suggested walking. The best part was when he took her hand and continued to hold it. Whatever happened to make him change his demeanor, she wouldn't complain.

"What if he's not there?" she asked.

"Then we'll wait or come back."

Just walking down Bobby's street brought back an old ache in her heart. "I grew up a few blocks from here."

"I thought you were from Florida."

"No. Dad grew up in Jacksonville. Mom grew up in Pittsburgh, and that's where we lived until her death. After she died, he wasted

My Sunny Vampire

no time moving back." She had barely gotten a chance to say goodbye to Carrie and she certainly hadn't had enough time to mourn. There hadn't been anything in Florida to remind her of her mother and she'd had no friends to confide in.

"I'm sorry about your mother. How old were you?"

"Sixteen. It's been eleven years and I still miss her."

He squeezed her hand. "Losing your mother is hard at any age. I'm sorry you lost yours so young. Is that why you had a therapist?"

"Yes and no. I guess I was a handful for my father. He didn't want to deal with me, so he sent me to Dr. Landry." She still hated her father for not being there when she needed him the most, and while she had initially fought seeing the doctor, she'd been grateful someone listened to her. She would never admit that to her father, though.

"I can't imagine you being a handful," he said sarcastically.

She laughed and batted her eyes. "Right, because I'm such an angel."

"I think we're here."

Bobby's house was dark, but that didn't mean unoccupied. It was three in the morning and he most likely slept.

"Can you tell if he's home, standing way out here?" she asked.

"Sort of. I can tell if someone's alive inside. You can, too. Just listen for a heartbeat."

She stared at the house and concentrated, but didn't hear anything.

Jack chuckled. "You're cute, you know that? But you don't have to scrunch your face."

She sighed and lowered her head. Would she be able to do anything right? Just once, she'd like to get some praise for her abilities. Not more criticism.

"Hey." He lifted her chin up, but she kept her eyes down. Looking at the pity on his face would only make things worse. "I didn't mean to hurt your feelings. I just think you're trying too hard to do what should be easy."

"Nothing's easy for me. Don't you get it?"

"It's probably me. I haven't been the best teacher. When this is over, someone else might be able to help you better."

His words caused her heart to lodge in her throat. Someone else? She didn't want someone else. "Sometimes it's not the teacher, it's the student." She took the shoveled walkway up to the covered porch and sat on the steps. "It wouldn't be the first time I screwed up."

He sat beside her and rubbed her back. "It probably won't be the last time, either."

"Thanks so much for your vote of confidence."

"You know it's true. You're a wild person, Sunshine. And I wouldn't want you any other way."

She looked into his beautiful eyes. Had she heard him correctly? He ran his fingers behind her neck and gently pulled her toward him. All she saw were his lips. Closing in on hers.

His mouth touched hers ever so softly and her heart sped like a freight train. She closed her eyes, refusing to make any move. She'd done it enough and got rejected. But she wanted his body next to hers. She wanted to feel more.

She got her wish.

Jack scooted closer and his tongue sought access. Opening up, she let him explore. Once she was satisfied he wasn't stopping, she slid her arms around his neck and held him tight.

He deepened the kiss and ran his fingers through her hair, igniting her nerve endings. She trembled with pleasure. Oh, if only they weren't sitting on the porch. Oh fudge. The porch.

Reluctantly, she broke away. "As much as I'm enjoying this, shouldn't we check on Bobby?"

He was breathing heavily and his eyes were darker, if that were even possible. "He's not home," he said and then proceeded to kiss her some more.

With nimble fingers, he flicked at the buttons of her coat and like magic, it was open. He tugged it off her shoulders and nuzzled her neck.

Her mind was a jumbled mess. How many times had she dreamed of making love to him, and now she was stopping him? Would someone examine her head please? She pushed him back. "I can't do this on the porch. Is there someplace we can be more private?"

He cupped her face, running his thumbs over her cheeks. "Any place?"

"Any place private."

* * * *

Jack caressed Sunshine's face. Guess he couldn't blame her. Even at the late hour, it was possible someone could spot them.

My Sunny Vampire

How many times had he nearly taken her in an inappropriate place? First the van, then the bar, now out on the porch? There was an empty house behind them. Probably had a bed. If it didn't, he'd improvise.

He settled the coat back on her shoulders and took her hand. When they stood, she headed for the sidewalk, he toward the front door.

"Oh no, this way." He pulled her along and grabbed the knob, not expecting it would turn, but pleasantly surprised when it did.

"We're breaking in?"

"I didn't break anything. The door's unlocked."

She tugged on his arm. "You know what I mean. How is this private? What if he comes back?"

"Sweetheart, we'll hear him long before he opens the door."

He stepped inside and paused. Death.

She covered her nose. "Pew. What stinks?"

There wasn't anything wrong with her sense of smell. The stench of decay didn't take long to form, the weak odor inside the house indicated the death happened recently. Mortals probably wouldn't have noticed. "Don't touch anything and stay here."

"No. I'm staying with you."

Of course she was. When did she ever listen to him anyway? Letting his nose lead the way, he walked up the stairs to the short hallway and one open door.

Sunshine gasped. "Bobby."

Damn it all to hell. His one shot at getting answers was lying on the bed with a needle up his arm.

"We need to get out of here." He took her hand, but she held still.

"Shouldn't we help him?"

"Sunshine, he's beyond help. We have to go. Now."

He urged her down the stairs and out the door. Using his shirt, he wiped the knob. Not that it was likely anyone would dust it for fingerprints, but Jack believed in being cautious.

She sat on the porch steps. "Can't we at least call it in? Who knows when he'll be found?"

He knelt in front of her. "And tell them what? Nothing plausible, that's for sure. This is our life. We help when we can, but for the most part, we stay out of it. We have to." He stood and offered his hand. "We need to get out of here."

129

She started to take it, then hesitated before looking back at the house.

"He's gone, Sunshine. What's in there is an empty shell, nothing more."

Worry lines feathered her forehead for a moment before smoothing. She took his hand. They had walked a block before she spoke. "He was the first one to talk to me after my mother's death. The first one who understood, anyway. I feel I should do something for him. We don't need to go back yet, do we?"

"We have all night. What were you thinking?"

Her lip curled a bit at the corner and she raised one eyebrow. "Ever been to Heinz Field?"

Chapter 15

Jack ran a hand through his hair and gazed up at the fence. This was sheer madness. How did he let her talk him into such a crazy idea?

Sunshine looked up as if surveying her strategy. Granted, if she was going to do what he suspected, she had picked the correct side. She put her hands on her hips. "I know vampires can climb and vampires can jump. Can they break bones?"

"Yes."

She swiveled to face him. "Yes? I can break a bone?"

"If you land incorrectly, but you will heal. Eventually."

"Too bad they cleared the snow. Might have cushioned my fall." She shrugged. "Oh well. I guess I better not fall, then." She rubbed her hands together before lacing her fingers through the fence. When she hoisted herself up, he grabbed her arm and pulled her down.

"Hold on, Spiderman. What exactly is your plan anyway?"

She raised one shapely eyebrow and huffed. "To get to the field." The word *dummy* was implied.

"I gathered that. What for?"

Her face softened. "Bobby's dream was to play for the Steelers. I want to stand on the field in his honor. Besides, I've always wanted to go inside." She returned to the fence, but stopped. Her brow furrowed. "I can do this, right? I mean, I have the ability?"

He hated seeing the uncertainty on her face and he wanted her to have more confidence. He just wasn't sure this was the place to do it. "You have the ability, but I'm not sure it's wise."

"Of course it's not wise. Wise isn't fun." She laughed and climbed up the fence.

Shit. If he didn't stay with her, who knew what kind of mess she could get into? He hooked his fingers through the fence and followed. By the time he reached the top, she was already running down the aisle toward the field.

She leapt off the wall and disappeared. "Whoo hoo!" echoed inside the stadium. He rushed to the bottom of the aisle.

"Oh. My. God. This is so awwwesooome!" Her arms were extended, as if she were flying, her coat and hair billowing in the air.

Even in the few days he'd known her, she'd never looked so happy or so free. This woman who resembled Clara was nothing like his late wife. Clara had never been spontaneous, carefree. She'd known her role, performed it without question and he'd loved her for it.

But times were different back then, certain things expected. He still lived by the code he grew up with: Get a job, do it well. Nothing else mattered. Fun wasn't part of the equation. Hell, it wasn't even in his vocabulary.

Sunshine twirled around in the center of the field and then fell backwards, laughing with unadulterated joy. She was having fun. Why couldn't he?

He jumped down to the field and rushed to join her.

* * * *

The city lights made it hard to see the stars, but the bright ones shone through. If someone had told Sunny she'd lie in the middle of Heinz Field one day, she would have asked them what they were smoking.

She closed her eyes and silently prayed for Bobby. Having a crush on a football player was one thing, having him console you when your mother died, another. Who knew what her life would have turned out like if she hadn't moved to Florida? Or his, for that matter?

Now his life had ended before he'd even had a chance to live it. She wouldn't let him go without some kind of memorial. Even if it only consisted of lying on the football field he would have loved to play on.

Bobby was the boy in her past, but Jack was the man in her present and hopefully future. Sure, they still had this issue regarding her turning, but she honestly didn't believe he had done it. The Committee would see that too, wouldn't they? If not, she'd make them.

Suddenly, Jack appeared, kneeling beside her with a big grin on his face. She smiled back and her heart expanded, sending warm fuzzies outward. When had she ever seen him look happy? And at her?

"Is it what you expected? Coming here?" he asked.

"No," she said seriously. He frowned at her answer and she laughed. "It's so much better."

He leaned over, placing a hand on either side of her body and her heart nearly stopped. Would he finish what he started on the porch?

"So, what did you want to do next?" he asked.

Kiss him. Love him. "You in a hurry to leave?"

He shook his head and moved in closer. His breath tickled her face.

"Me, neither," she whispered. A moment ago she couldn't tell if it were hot or cold out. Now heat flowed between them. If he didn't kiss her soon, she'd have to take matters into her own hands. "Jack--"

Her words were cut off when he claimed her with his mouth. This was no soft kiss, but a possessive one. There wasn't anything she wanted more than for him to possess her, heart and soul. He plunged his tongue inside and she sucked on it, tasting him. Parts of her body clenched in need. Why the heck was she wearing clothes?

He pulled away, but only long enough to move to her neck. "Is this place private enough?"

Before she could answer, he flicked the one button holding her coat together and ran his hand over her breast. She arched into his touch.

"I'll have you know, you'll be the first," she said.

He leaned back and stared at her. "You're a virgin?"

She smiled. He was just too easy. "To doing it outside, yes."

Shaking his head, he said, "You're incorrigible."

She sat up, shed her coat then reached for his jacket zipper. "Is that a good thing or bad thing?"

"I'll let you know when I know." His jacket went flying, along with her sweater. "Damn, you're beautiful."

He kissed her, hot and heavy, making it hard for her to concentrate. The man certainly knew how to rev her engines. She fumbled at his shirt buttons, but it seemed like there were millions of them and she nearly ripped the shirt apart when the last one came undone. The shirt joined the jacket and sweater and she rubbed her hands over his arms, shoulders, chest. So muscular, so beautiful.

The bra came next and he lowered her back down onto her coat. After caressing her breasts, he captured one with his mouth, laving her nipple. Pleasurable sparks surged through her body and she moaned. He moved down her stomach, doing evil things to her with his tongue while managing to pull her shoes and socks off. God, she wanted him.

He unbuttoned her jeans and slipped them off, taking her panties in the process. It seemed strange to lie on the ground outside, stark naked. Even stranger not to feel the cold. She didn't want to be the only naked one, though, and didn't have to wait long. He kicked off his shoes and removed his socks and jeans in record time. Standing there in all his glory, he was a wonderful specimen of the male sex. But he was too far away.

As if he read her mind, he knelt at her feet. He rubbed his hands over her legs, inside her thighs, up and over to her stomach, missing the best part. He kissed her stomach, grabbed her butt, and ran his tongue over her skin. Going down, down, down, until he reached her clit. Her breath hitched in her throat as he sucked on her.

He caressed the inside of her thighs before slipping a finger inside her. Each lick of his tongue and suck of his mouth built up an intense pressure, she thought she would burst.

"Come for me, sweetheart," he said. "Don't hold back."

She wouldn't. She couldn't. Her world exploded and wave after wave swept her away. He kissed her mouth as he positioned himself to enter her.

* * * *

She was wet and ready for him, his Sunshine. And she was his. He wasn't giving her up. Not for anyone. He slipped inside and felt

My Sunny Vampire

like he'd come home. So tight. So wonderful. With each thrust, she arched to meet him.

She ran her fingers down his back and grabbed his ass, leaving a sensitized trail. Heaven help him, he wouldn't be able to last much longer. He nuzzled her neck, taking in her scent. His fangs extended and without thinking, he bit down. The sweet flavor flooded his senses. He'd never tasted anything quite so exquisite.

"Oh God, Jack." She came for him, convulsing and squeezing his cock. He lifted his head and saw the bloody mark he left behind. Before he could lick her clean, she leaned forward and ran her tongue over his nipple, her own fangs grazing his skin. That was all it took to release. Arching his head back, he spilled inside her, crying out her name.

He knew at that moment, he would never be complete without her.

Chapter 16

Using her hair like a paint brush, Jack swirled the red strands around her tanned shoulder. Eventually the tan would fade and she would become pale, but there wasn't any sense in telling her that. She'd had enough bad news and he didn't wish to ruin the moment.

"I'm surprised that doesn't tickle," Sunshine said. "Instead, it feels nice."

What felt nice was having her in his arms, one arm and one leg splayed across his body, lying beneath the stars. But if he lay here much longer, he'd want to make love to her all over again, and they didn't have the time.

"It'll be light soon and we need to feed before we head back."

She stretched and rubbed her hand over his pecs, flicking his nipple. He inhaled through his nose. Now, why'd she have to go and do that? He was having enough difficulties keeping Little Jack at bay. Her actions brought him back to life.

She looked down at his growing member. "You call your penis Little Jack?"

Oh shit. He'd been so relaxed, he'd forgotten to put his guard back up.

"Not out loud, I don't."

"Oh, Jack. I hate to tell you this, but there's nothing little about him." She smiled before planting a brief kiss on his lips. "So, why the name?"

My Sunny Vampire

That kiss wasn't nearly enough and he was tempted to roll her over to do it right, but if he didn't get his ass in gear, they'd never get out of there in time. He stood and located his jeans. "It's silly. Now don't just lie there. Get dressed."

She stood and found her bra. "Some girl named it, huh?"

Could she drop it? No, of course not, that wasn't her. What did he expect? It was his fault she had found out at all. He zipped up his jeans and searched for his shirt. "Not just some girl. My wife."

* * * *

Sunny started pulling up her panties and stopped at the word wife. He'd said he'd been married when he was mortal. When was that again? Sometime in the eighteenth century? She shook her head and continued dressing. "I didn't know women went around nicknaming a guy's junk back then."

"Junk?" he asked, his eyebrows scrunched together.

Didn't he know every term associated with a penis, or did he only like Little Jack? Although, she had to confess, she kind of liked his version.

His face softened as if he got the joke. "Oh, you mean... No, it wasn't like that."

She slipped her sweater on over her head. "So tell me, how did your wife, a woman back in the seventeen hundreds, come to name your penis?"

Jack found his shirt and slipped it on. While he buttoned up, he said, "She had problems with using the proper word. When I hurt myself down there, she wanted to see the damage. When I refused to let her inspect it, she insisted on seeing 'Little Jack,' afraid I had ruined any chance of siring children. It ended up being our joke."

His voice drifted off, as if the memory was too painful to remember. She picked up her shoes and socks. He did the same. They sat on the ground and finished dressing.

"I'm sorry, I didn't mean to pry," she said while tying her shoe.

"If I didn't want you to know, I wouldn't have told you. No one else knows, though."

She smiled, glad he felt he could confide in her. "Your secret's safe with me."

He stood, laughter bringing a twinkle to his eyes, and offered his hand to her. "Good, because I'd hate to be the laughingstock of the vampire community."

They headed back to the end of the stadium where they had entered. Jack grabbed her hips and hoisted her to the seating section. His hands were strong and felt oh, so good. She hated to leave. Would they spend the rest of the day exploring each other? She certainly hoped so.

Turning around, she offered her hand. He hesitated for a moment. Didn't he think she could help? Then he grabbed hold. With no effort at all, she pulled him up. Wow. Her strength would never cease to amaze her.

Jack indicated she go up the fence first--being a gentleman or hoping to catch a look? She climbed over the top and started to descend when her coat snagged in the metal. She tugged to free the material.

"Just rip it," he said.

"No. I don't want to leave anything behind. Besides, I don't want to ruin my coat."

"Hold still, let me look at it." He climbed over the top and swung his leg around. Straddling her, he studied the tangle of fabric and fence.

Now here was a position she could get used to. She moved her hips a smidgen, feeling the bulge in his pants become larger. Too bad they were on the fence. Heck, they were vampires, maybe they could do it on a fence. What would he do if she said, *"Oh yeah, baby. Take me here."*

He chuckled, his breath tickling her ear. "And you wanted privacy."

"You heard?"

He rubbed his cheek against hers. "You all but screamed it in my head."

"You keep saying I'm not broken, so how is it you can always hear me, but I rarely hear you?"

"You're not broken, so stop it. And we'll talk about this later." The material started ripping and he stopped. "I see where it's stuck. Hold here and here," he said, indicating the coat and fence. "When I lift you up, that should free it."

Sunny put one hand next to the snag, and the other on the fence, hoping her strength was enough, because she would be the only thing holding them up. "Wouldn't it be smarter if I climbed back over?"

Jack grabbed her hips. "And deny me this pleasure?"

My Sunny Vampire

His hands did feel good. The little massage on her rump wasn't too bad, either.

"Don't worry," he said. "As long as you don't let go, we'll be fine."

"What are you two doing up there?"

The voice came out of nowhere and she jumped, releasing the fence just as Jack freed the coat. Panic froze her for a moment too long. She reached out for support, but her fingers simply grazed the metal. Gravity took hold and pulled them to the ground. They landed with a sickening crunch.

* * * *

Pain ripped across Jack's lower back and exploded in his head. Little Jack wasn't feeling too chipper, either, since Sunshine's rump was situated right over his crotch. What the hell just happened?

The man who spoke was a police officer. "Whoa! Are you two okay?"

She scrambled to a standing position and turned toward the man. At least she wasn't hurt, she moved as if nothing happened. Jack wished he could say the same. His back screamed in agony, his head throbbed and his nuts were on fire.

"Hey, aren't you the missing woman?" the officer asked.

She lifted her hand in a stop motion, scrunched her face and the policeman halted, his eyes glazed over like a zombie's. Did she just control him? *"Way to go, sweetheart."*

She turned her attention back toward him. "Oh God, Jack. I'm so sorry. Are you all right?"

She knelt beside him. Her hands hovered over his body, as if she were afraid to touch him. A panicky look flashed in her eyes. He grabbed her hands and her thoughts slammed into his head. Fear and guilt being the main topics.

"Calm down. I'll be all right." And he would be, but he had most likely broken his back and that would take hours to heal. They didn't have that kind of time before the sun rose.

"Broken back?" She buried her head on his chest. "Oh, God. It's all my fault."

Shit, he needed to keep his thoughts blocked. "Sunshine, listen. I don't even know if I broke it, but I'll be all right. Do you understand? It will heal."

"That's right. You'll heal," she said more to herself than him. She lifted her head and chuffed in relief. "Can you move now? What can I do?"

"You have control of that man. I need you to feed from him. You're going to need your strength if you have to help me home. While you're at it, find out how he recognized you." A new pain formed in his stomach. Shit. He needed blood.

Worry lines formed on her forehead. "No. You should feed first. You're injured."

She raised a valid point, but the man was definitely a positive donor. Jack could wait. He hoped. "I will, but you go first. You can do this." He then said the words that would work best. "I need you to do this for me, Sunshine."

Distraught, she nodded and went to the officer. She glanced at his wrist before reaching for his neck. For some reason her closeness to another man irked Jack. He wanted her mouth only on his neck, not another man's.

"Sunshine, stick with the wrist. It'll be less messy. Stop when you count to one hundred." Technically, he didn't lie, but it sure felt like it.

She brought the man's wrist to her mouth, closed her eyes and fed.

Slowly, Jack moved to one side. Pain sliced through him and he hissed through clenched teeth. Yep, he had broken something. He would require her assistance to set him straight.

The officer blinked several times.

Oh shit.

Just as the officer turned to look at Sunshine, Jack intervened and took over control.

She opened her eyes and pulled away. "Wow! I did it. I really did it." She turned toward Jack and grinned. "Why didn't you tell me about the counting before?" She lifted the officer's arm. Blood dripped from holes and she cleaned it up, healing the wounds.

"To tell you the truth, I just thought of it." Jack only wished it had worked, but he couldn't bring himself to tell her.

She held the officer's hand. A frown marred her lovely face and turned into a scowl. When she stomped her foot, Jack remembered he'd told her to read the man's thoughts.

"I'm sorry, I have him," he said.

"Is that why I'm getting static?"

"Yes. Only one vampire can control at a time."

"Then how were you able to control Derek if the rogue was?"

"I wouldn't have, but since I could, Derek was either programmed to react the way he did or the rogue relinquished control before being detected." Which only proved to Jack the rogue was on the stupid side for picking a gay man in the first place.

"So then how did you control the officer if I had him?"

Jack wanted to hold her as he told her the bad news, but that would require standing and he wasn't able to do that quite yet.

"You lost him while you counted."

"Oh." She frowned then perked up. "But I did have him, right? I guess I need to practice doing two things at once, huh?"

He laughed at the change in her attitude. Pain slashed through his lungs, turning his laugh into a groan.

"You're not okay," she said. "You're hurting."

"Nothing for you to worry about." Of course, she wasn't buying that for a minute. Probably because he winced with every word he spoke.

She stood over his body. "What can I do?"

"I need to straighten my back to help speed up the bone alignment."

She grimaced. "Yuck. Is it hard to do?"

"No. Granted, it would be better with two people, but we can improvise. Take off my shoes and move me over to the fence so I can hook my toes underneath, then pull my shoulders. That should work."

"What about the officer?"

"Shit." Jack had forgotten all about him. When Sunshine pulled, he would most likely disconnect with the man, not a good thing.

"Undo him," she said, waving her fingers in the officer's direction. "I'll read his memory and send him on his way."

Why not? If she succeeded, it would certainly bolster her confidence. If she failed, he could quickly take charge. He lifted a hand in an invitation. "He's all yours."

The policeman became alert. "What's going on? Weren't you just--?"

His eyes glazed over in a zombie stare. Jack really needed to show her how to avoid that look. It was downright creepy. At least

141

she controlled the man, and her attitude flip-flopped. Such a major step for her and he beamed with pride.

She held the man's hand once again and concentrated. How many times did he have to tell her she didn't need to scrunch her face as if she were calculating a difficult math problem in her head? Still, he smiled. Maybe he didn't want her to stop.

Her eyes widened. "Oh fudge."

The man was still staring out into space, so no loss of control. Something else had upset her.

Her eyes pleaded for forgiveness. "I'm so sorry."

* * * *

Sunny briefly shut her eyes. Jack was going to kill her, she just knew it.

"You're sorry about what?" Jack asked.

"Later. Can I send him away?" The man's zombie look was starting to creep her out. Mortals always appeared normal when Jack controlled them. What was she doing wrong?

"If you're finished with him, go ahead."

Sunny concentrated and sent the message. After the second try, the policeman walked away, out of sight.

"What did you tell him?" he asked.

She chuckled. "That he saw two squirrels on the fence."

"That's a good one." His laughter turned into a cry of pain, slicing her heart.

"Oh, Jack." If it hurt that much to laugh, what would he feel when she straightened him out? Oh, why did she let go of the fence?

He tried to convince her he felt fine, but she didn't believe him for one minute. Still, he needed her help. She gritted her teeth as if she were the one in pain and dragged him to the fence. His face contorted, but not a sound left his lips.

She walked around to his head and grasped him by the arm pits. "I don't know if I can do this. It's going to hurt."

He patted her cheek. "I won't lie, it will hurt, but I'll feel better once it's over. It's a good thing this stadium is big." He smiled. "Maybe no one will hear me screaming."

She would notice and it tore her heart apart. He wouldn't be in this mess if it weren't for her.

"Just count to three and--"

My Sunny Vampire

She pulled, cutting him off. He screamed. Bones cracked. She wanted to cry.

"You can stop, now." He took a deep breath and closed his eyes. "Much better. I'll just lie here for a while."

After replacing his shoes, she sat against the fence. She never wanted to go through that again. "So, what's next?"

He glanced at his watch then pulled his cell out of his front pocket and examined it. "Wow. Still works." After punching in some numbers, he placed it up to his ear. "Hey, Frank. Where are you?"

Jack had said he felt better, but he seemed stiff, as if he were in a lot of pain. And why wouldn't he be? He broke his gosh-darn back. Could he walk back in his state? Could he stand? They had run to the stadium from Bobby's and it still took some time. Walking back would be way slower. Did they have enough time before the sun rose?

"Can you get her keys and drive over to Heinz Field?" he asked. "Thanks, buddy. We'll see you soon." He snapped his phone shut and stared at her. "While we're waiting for Frank, why don't you tell me what you found out from that nice officer."

Oh, fudge. Her heart started racing. He would be so mad, she just knew it. Then he might yell and hurt himself. She deserved it all, that wasn't the point, but he didn't need to exert himself. He needed to get better, first. "We need to find someone for you."

"Someone? Oh, you mean a donor. You can call them that, Sunshine. I'll let Frank help there. I don't feel like walking right now anyway. So tell me what you found out."

Of course he didn't want to walk. How stupid could she be? She swallowed hard. How to start. Maybe at the beginning? She clasped her hands and lowered her head because she couldn't bear to look him in the eye. "Promise me you'll wait until you're better before you yell at me, okay?"

"What makes you think...?" Jack paused, only causing her more concern. "I promise. Now will you tell me what you found out?"

"First, maybe I should tell you who my father is."

"Governor Ward of Florida? Yes, I know."

Her head snapped up. "How?"

"Carrie told me at the hospital. She thought it might cause a problem if they found out." Then some flicker of knowledge flashed across his face as if he realized where she was going with her confession. "Damn it. They found out, didn't they?"

She nodded. "I'm sorry. I know it's all my fault. If I hadn't gone to that job interview, none of this would be happening."

"The vampire who turned you is at fault here, not you." He looked up at the sky. Maybe he couldn't bear to look at her. She wouldn't blame him.

"I really didn't think my father cared. He's probably being forced to act."

He turned his head back toward her, his expression softened. "He's your father. Of course he cares."

She shook her head. "He only cares about himself. I'm nothing but a problem."

"Was he abusing you? Is that why you left?"

"No, nothing as simple as that."

"So why did you change your name?"

Good ole' Carrie. She mentions her father is the Governor of Florida, but not how her name came to be different.

"I didn't just change my name. I got married."

His jaw dropped for a microsecond before snapping back. "What? You're married?"

"Not anymore. I was young and foolish. Thought I was in love. Didn't hurt that my father hated the man, either. A week in I knew it was a mistake, but I tried to make it work. I couldn't have my father say 'I told you so.' After a month, I couldn't stand it anymore, and I filed for divorce."

"Why didn't you just get it annulled?"

"Are you kidding? I figured it was my ticket away from Dad. Using my ex's last name was a gift I wasn't giving back." She pulled her knees up and propped her arms on top. "He knows where I am now, though. That can be a problem. Not just because of my new circumstance, either."

"Your father is not the problem. We've made people disappear before. You won't be any different."

"Disappear as in a new life? As in giving up my old life?" She regretted the words the instant they left her mouth.

He closed his eyes and exhaled loudly. Was he in pain? Or just exasperated with her? "Sunshine, your old life is gone. You have to come to grips with that."

My Sunny Vampire

"I know. I'm trying." And she would, eventually. Especially if Jack was in her life. He would certainly make the change bearable. Oh what was she thinking? He'd make it exciting. "So if my father's not the problem, who is?"

"The Committee, that's who."

* * * *

Jack concentrated on breathing. It was better than concentrating on the pain. That fall had caused some major damage to his back and healing would go slowly until he fed.

Headlights appeared, coming in their direction. Ever since he'd mentioned the Committee, Sunshine hadn't said a word. They weren't exactly her favorite people. Whether or not she saw the problem like he did--publicity of any kind made it harder to work under the Committee's radar--there wasn't anything he could do at the moment. Right now, all he wanted was to get back home, relax and maybe snuggle with her. Snuggling shouldn't hurt and even if it did, it'd be worth it.

Frank pulled up and stuck his head out the window, wearing a goofy grin on his face. "Did someone call a cab?" His speech slurred.

Oh, shit. Jack hadn't noticed any abnormalities over the phone. "What are you doing on the ground?"

Sunshine grabbed his hand *"He's drunk. Which means..."*

"Which means nothing. He could have gone out while she slept." A real possibility, but one he highly doubted.

She glared at Jack. *"He shouldn't be driving."*

Even drunk, a vampire's reflexes were superior to a mortal's, but now wasn't the time to discuss this with Sunshine. Jack needed Frank's help to find a suitable donor and didn't need to piss him off. If that meant acting more hurt than he actually was, then that's what he'd do.

"I was showing off and fell off the fence. Can you help me up and sit in the back seat with me? I think I broke some bones and I'll need help finding a donor."

Sunshine's mouth opened slightly, but she remained quiet.

Frank climbed out of the vehicle and went to Jack. "That'll teach you." He looked at Sunshine. "Are you okay?"

She nodded.

Together, Sunshine and Frank helped Jack stand. Jostling only made the pain worse and it appeared he didn't have to act hurt after all. He couldn't wait to feed and speed up his healing.

Sunshine got behind the wheel. "Where am I going?"

"Find the nearest hospital," Jack said. "I should be able to find a suitable donor there."

She put the car in gear and started driving. "So, what are the plans after we get you fed?"

Frank spoke up. "If you don't mind, you can stay at my place. Carrie doesn't have to be at work until noon and I'd like to stay with her."

Her back stiffened. Jack was sure she wasn't happy with those plans, but at least she didn't say anything.

"Okay, I can drop Jack off and then take you to Carrie's."

"You're not dropping me off," Jack said. "Frank can drive back."

"I have stuff I need at Carrie's." She gave him a warning look through the rearview mirror. "But if you'd rather we all stayed there instead…"

"No," both he and Frank said at the same time. At least Frank had the same idea.

Jack wasn't going to win this one. Not in his shape. "Okay, but you're not going to have much time to get back."

"I don't plan on staying long."

When they arrived at the hospital, Jack suggested she park out of sight. He didn't need anyone recognizing her. Just in case, he remained with her in the car. Frank left to get the donor.

"You're worried about Carrie, aren't you?" Jack asked.

"She's the only real friend I have. My only tie to the past. I swear, you better never wipe her memory."

"Hell, if Frank is as attached as I think, she may end up being one of us."

Her head snapped around. He was sure she was going to blow up at him, but she laughed instead. "She would probably love that, too, but wouldn't she lose her usefulness then?"

"Sunshine, you don't know he's using her."

She faced forward, her spine like a rod. "And you don't know he isn't."

Frank saved him from continuing an argument that would only get him in trouble. The mortal, a young man in scrubs, climbed in

My Sunny Vampire

the back seat next to Jack. The interior of the small vehicle filled with the stench of cigarette smoke.

Sunshine held her nose. "Oh yuck." As Frank settled on the passenger seat, she set her sights on him. "Couldn't you find a non-smoker?"

Smoker or non-smoker, Jack needed blood. Sinking his teeth into the man's neck was easy once he held his breath. The rush of energy flowed through him and he felt the healing process speed up.

"Hey, he was the only negative outside," Frank said. "I wasn't about to go searching inside." He grinned at Jack. "You can thank me later."

Jack didn't want to thank him at all. It was bad enough most vampires thought he was a little nutty, he didn't want Sunshine to think it, too. With his mouth currently busy, he couldn't tell his friend to shut up.

"Negative? Negative what?" she asked.

"What, didn't Jack tell you? He only likes negative-type blood."

"There's a difference?"

"Besides their scent, I don't notice one. You probably don't either. But Jack here, says there is. It's probably the same for Coke and Pepsi lovers. If you have a favorite, you notice the difference. If you don't care, they probably taste the same. Jack is the only picky vampire I know, though."

Sunshine turned around and placed her arms on the backrest. Her face was full of mirth. She reached out and touched his hand. "Feeling better?"

Jack stopped sucking and healed the wounds. "Yes. Almost good as new."

She furrowed her eyes at that statement, seeing right through his lie. While his back pain no longer stabbed him, it'd be awhile before he could move around without wincing.

The man left the vehicle and walked back to the hospital, courtesy of Jack's suggestion. Sunshine put the car in gear and drove off. Jack was ready for some peace and quiet and leaned his head back. However, Frank apparently wanted to chat.

"Beanie is expecting us around nine tonight. You're coming, right?"

Shit. Not Harris again.

"Who's Beanie?" Sunshine asked.

Jack said, "His name is Harris Lobene and he's an old friend. We'll see how I'm feeling. I won't promise anything."

"You'll be fine by then. Bring Sunny. We'll have fun."

"Are you nuts? He doesn't know about her."

"Jack, I hate to tell you this, but he probably already knows. She was all over the news."

"Shit." He ran a hand through his hair. Taking her out to the bar with mortals was one thing. Harris was quite another. Just because he said he wanted to turn over a new leaf didn't mean he wouldn't jump at the first opportunity to report Jack to the Committee.

"It's okay," Sunshine said. "I can stay with Carrie."

"Carrie's coming," Frank said. "Come on, Jack. Let him prove himself to you."

"I don't have to go if you don't want me to," she said as she pulled up to the house.

That she would be okay hiding to save his ass said a lot. "I'll think about it."

Jack slowly climbed out of the car. His back protested. So far, nothing seemed to be going his way. Would he ever get a break?

"Need help inside?" she asked.

Worry lines marred her beautiful face. Well, maybe one thing had gone his way. He'd made love to one pretty terrific woman tonight. He smiled at her. "No, I can manage. Don't be long."

* * * *

Sunny's heart ached as Jack struggled to climb the steps. Guilt. It ate at her insides. He wouldn't be hurting at all if she'd only held on to the stupid fence. Would she ever be able to make it up to him?

"You better get moving if you want to make it back in time," Frank said.

That would be her luck, getting stuck with Frank and Carrie. Sunny put the car in drive and took off. Jack would probably be furious with her, but she needed to know what Frank's intentions were. "Do you care for Carrie?"

"Yes, I do. Very much."

"Then why are you using her?"

She expected him to avert his gaze. Instead his steely grey eyes widened in shock. "What makes you think I'm using her?"

"How else do you explain her drinking?"

My Sunny Vampire

Now he averted his eyes. She knew it. He was guilty.

"I thought she always drank like that. You saying this is a new behavior?"

"Yeah, that's exactly what I'm saying."

"Are you sure? She told me your last visit was more than two years ago."

That part was true, but she knew her friend. No way was Carrie an alcoholic. She'd never shown the signs before and nothing in her life would have triggered it. Frank was lying. He was the problem. "I think she's drinking for you."

He shook his head. "No. I swear, I've never asked her to. She's been the insistent one. I've tried to talk her out of it, but she wouldn't listen."

That didn't sound like the Carrie she knew. "Why didn't you just suggest it to her, then? Wouldn't that get her to stop?"

"A suggestion to an alcoholic would only stop her temporarily. If she has the disease, nothing I could say would change that. She has to stop on her own."

Sunny pulled into the parking lot and found an open spot. After turning off the ignition, she handed the keys to Frank. "So why do you feed from her?"

He shrugged. "She asks me to, says she doesn't want to drink alone. I think she just likes me biting her. She means a lot to me, Sunny. I would never do anything to hurt her. But if she's an alcoholic, she has to help herself. I can't. No suggestion will change that."

Maybe Frank couldn't suggest it, but nothing would stop her from trying. Carrie was not an alcoholic, and she would prove it.

When they entered the apartment, Frank plopped down on the couch and turned on the television, keeping the sound low. Sunny went into her room and shoved some clothes and her purse inside a backpack. Leaving the pack on the bed, she tiptoed over to Carrie's room. Heck, who was she fooling? Frank could probably hear everything if he wanted.

Carrie lay on her bed, the covers twisted around her legs. Sunny could never share a bed with her friend, she took up too much space for such a small person. Of course, now Sunny didn't have to share a bed with anyone, since she would never sleep again.

"*You will no longer desire alcohol. The taste will repulse you.*" She sent the message three times, just in case. While her abilities seemed to be improving, however minutely, they were still inconsistent. How she controlled the policeman, she'd never know. Her thoughts at the time only centered on Jack's welfare. Maybe he was right. Maybe she was trying too hard.

Deciding to let Carrie rest, and afraid she might not make it back before sunrise if she did wake her, Sunny returned to her room and slipped on the backpack. She poked her head inside the living room, ready to announce her departure when she saw Carrie's project sat untouched. It wasn't like her friend not to work on it at all. Sadness weighed her down. Could Carrie really be an alcoholic? Or was Frank just keeping her busy? Things should change with her suggestion. She hoped so, anyway.

"Tell Carrie to call me when she wakes, okay?"

"Sure," he said as he stood. "You don't need to worry about her. I'll handle things differently now that I know."

Differently, how? In hiding it or actually helping? Trust didn't come easy for Sunny. A person had to earn it and Frank hadn't done that yet.

She bade him goodbye and ran back to Jack. The more she thought about him, the quicker her steps became. The lightening sky didn't hurt any, either.

Chapter 17

Sunny arrived at Frank's house without incident and before the sky got too light. When she opened the door, she found Jack standing in the living room, wearing a big grin.

"You made it."

"I certainly didn't want to spend the day with Frank." She slipped the pack off her back and it landed on the floor with a soft thud.

"That's good to know."

If she didn't know any better, she would never have guessed he'd been hurt, but then he wasn't moving, either.

"Why aren't you lying down?" Her coat joined the backpack. "Won't that aid in the healing?"

"Probably, but I was waiting for you."

"Waiting for me to do what? Jack, you've been hurt. You need to rest."

He moved over to the couch and sat slowly, like an old man might. "I'm fine." He patted the cushion beside him. "Come here. Sit with me."

The guy was seriously out of his mind. "No. I'm not sitting with you. Just lay down on the couch."

He rolled his eyes and gave an exasperated sigh. "I don't want to lie on the couch. There's no room to snuggle."

Snuggle? She closed her eyes momentarily and shook her head. He whined worse than a five-year-old. But if lounging beside him got him in a horizontal position, who was she to argue? "Can you make it to the bed?"

"Of course I can. I'm not an invalid." He might have been more convincing if his face didn't twitch several times in the process of standing.

He hurt and it was all her fault. Why wasn't he yelling at her?

Jack stood in front of her and caressed her cheek. "Hey, I'm all right. Honest. Stop feeling guilty. It was just an accident."

"An accident I caused. You don't know how sorry--"

He reached behind her head and pulled her in for a kiss, cutting off her words. It started off slow and tender and progressed into something more passionate. Afraid of hurting him, she stood still and kept her arms to her sides even though she craved holding him. He ran his tongue across her lips, seeking entrance and she opened up, inviting him in. As he thoroughly explored her, the lower half of her body clenched in need.

He broke away, winded. She might have thought it was due to his injuries if her breathing wasn't also coming in spurts.

"I've been wanting to do that ever since we made love." His lips curled a bit on the ends and his eyes twinkled. "That, and make love to you again."

Sounded good to her, too, if only... "You're not exactly in any shape for physical activity. Are you resting down here or upstairs?"

* * * *

Little Jack strained to escape, causing pain in more ways than one. Maybe the kiss wasn't the smartest thing he could do, but it was oh so worth it.

Jack looked at the stairs. They would be his greatest challenge. If he wished to convince Sunshine of his well-being, he needed to stop wincing every time he moved. Then again, he kind of liked the bossy way she acted. No one had ever wanted to take care of him before.

He took her hand, but about half-way up, he nearly squeezed the life out of it when his back objected to the exertion of climbing the stairway. The pain increased with each step, from a dull throb to knife-slashing. "*Breathe through it. Breathe through it.*" It worked for mothers in labor, why not him?

"Breathe through what?"

My Sunny Vampire

Damn it. By concentrating on getting through the pain, he'd apparently stopped blocking his thoughts. He ignored her question. Only four more steps and he'd be at the top.

"Dang it, Jack. You're making it worse, aren't you? I knew you should have stayed on the couch."

"And I told you I didn't want to."

Every time he whined at her, she rolled her eyes and mumbled. Something along the lines of the male sex being such babies. Aggravating her was fun. Made him want to whine harder.

He reached the top, finally, and by that time, the bed practically called his name. After kicking off his shoes, he scooted toward the middle of the mattress and leaned back. That was more like it. He patted beside him. "Next."

Sunshine remained in the doorway with her hands on her hips. "I don't think that's such a good idea. You need to remain still and rest. How do you expect to heal if you keep moving around?"

"I didn't come up here to be by myself. If you don't lie beside me, I'll just go back downstairs and watch TV." He truly didn't think he could make it back down without falling, but she didn't know that.

While slipping her shoes off, she mumbled some more about him being a baby. He smiled. He'd better enjoy getting his way now because once he healed, he was pretty sure she'd tell him to screw it. Not those exact words, since she apparently had something against using actual swear words, but it would mean the same, however she said it.

"No funny business," she said.

"How funny can I be if we're fully dressed? Now, if you want to sprawl naked beside me, I won't promise anything. I won't object, either."

"And you thought I was incorrigible." Any other time she would have smacked him and he missed it. He'd have to try harder.

"Just snuggle up next to me. You can put your head on my shoulder."

"Do you need anything first? A blanket? Extra pillow?"

"Quit stalling and come here."

She slowly placed one knee on the bed, followed by the other. In the time it took her to position herself against him, he could have fed off three donors.

She settled in and moved close. Her hair was a wild being and he smoothed it out of the way. "That's better. Now, close your eyes and relax. Let your body unwind."

"Shouldn't I be telling you that?"

"Hush. If you relax, I'll relax."

She closed her eyes, but she was still tense. He lightly rubbed her back and then kneaded her neck and shoulder.

"That feels good," she said. "Please don't over-exert yourself."

"I'm barely moving. Quit worrying."

"I can't help it." She snuggled closer. "But keep talking. Why don't you tell me how you became a vampire?"

If talking got her to relax, why not? He stroked her hair. "During the Battle of Monmouth I was mortally wounded and left to die."

"They just left you there?"

"War was different back then, sweetheart. No time to help the un-helpable. Besides, they might have come back, but by then I was gone. That night, a vampire couple was scrounging through the wounded and found me. They were looking to start a group and pretty much turned anyone worth turning. Basically, they saved me, so they earned my allegiance. A lot of vampires were created from that war."

"Did you have to leave your wife then?"

"No. But I was told if I wanted to stay with her, I had to turn her, too. I probably went about it all wrong in telling her what I'd become. She ran away and returned with the doctor, thinking I had injured my head and gone crazy."

She looked up at him with widened eyes. "Oh, Jack. I'm so sorry."

"What are you sorry about? You couldn't stop it."

"No. I mean about thinking you were crazy, too."

He smiled and pressed her head back against his chest. "You came around. That's the important part."

"I take it she didn't."

"Yes and no. I mentally convinced the doctor I was fine. After that, she noticed the differences in me and didn't want anything to do with me. Thought I'd lost my soul and she didn't want to lose hers. Nothing I said could convince her otherwise because for all I knew I had lost my soul. I wasn't about to force her to be like me. I wanted her to want it." And he desperately needed to change the

My Sunny Vampire

subject before he blabbed about how he had returned to Clara for a second chance only to discover she and his son had died in childbirth. If he had only known she was pregnant, he'd have never left her.

"I can understand that. I just can't see why the Committee cared if she was turned or not."

"Oh hell, they weren't the Committee. My group was a rag-tag bunch that only cared about numbers. They drove me nuts. If I had known the Committee existed at all, I would have turned them in. As it was, the Committee found us about two months later."

"Is that when you became a Committee member?"

"No. I wasn't eligible until 1878. Didn't stop me from attending every meeting and helping out whenever possible, though. Lucky for me a position opened up in my year of eligibility. By then, everyone already knew me. I won by a landslide."

"So I guess it's not like our politics. You don't have terms?"

"Nope. We're there until we no longer wish to serve, get voted out or die."

"Die? You mean get killed, don't you?"

"Same difference." He continued massaging, feeling the curve of her neck, the line of her jaw. Her skin velvety soft, so perfect. A sigh of contentment left her lips.

He could get used to this. Lying next to her, touching her. Always touching her.

"Give me a kiss."

She lifted her head and smiled. Slowly, she moved to her knees, leaned in close and brushed her lips lightly across his. What the hell? She called that a kiss? He held her head and deepened it. Feeling mischievous, he slipped one hand under her sweater and found her breast. Her nipple hardened through the material of her bra.

She tried to pull away, but his hand was on her neck and he held her still. She yanked his other hand off her breast.

"If you can't behave, I'll have to tie you up."

"Oooh, sweetheart. I like this side of you. Where's the rope?"

"I'm serious."

"So am I."

Her mouth dropped open. In one swift movement, he pulled the sweater over the back of her head and hooked her with it, holding her close. Her knee brushed against Little Jack and he grew harder.

"Guess I don't need rope."

She struggled in his embrace. "I'm going to hurt you."

"Not if you hold still." He knew one way to get her still, he only hoped he wouldn't pay for it later. He rolled over.

She gasped.

So did he.

His back disapproved, but he certainly liked this position better. "I got you now." He smoothed the hair from her face and kissed her. Her scent excited him, drove him crazy with need. He reached behind her and unhooked her bra, freeing her breasts. Heaven, that's where he was. Her nipple hardened at his touch. If he weren't hurting, he'd bend down for a taste. She stopped squirming and moaned. He loved the way she reacted to him. In fact, he loved everything about her. Her life had changed dramatically when she turned, but so had his. He couldn't see his life without her in it.

* * * *

Jack was driving her wild with desire. His fiery touch consumed her whole. Sunny wasn't sure she could hold out much longer. She wanted nothing more than to wrap her arms and legs around his body, but his wince during that move cautioned her.

He stopped kissing her mouth and moved to her neck. She turned her head to give him better access. His fangs scraped across her skin, sending a thrill down her spine.

"Bite me." Maybe her blood would help him heal. Oh, who was she kidding? His bite turned her on big time.

"My pleasure." His teeth pierced her skin and he rubbed Little Jack up against her. Even with her pants on, she reached a pinnacle she never thought possible. When he played with her nipple, she cried out his name.

"Open your eyes," he said softly.

She did as he requested and gazed upon his adoring face, riding wave after wave of her orgasm.

"I love you, Sunshine."

"What?" she choked out. She couldn't have heard him right.

Jack brushed his thumbs over her cheeks. "I know I should wait until my name is clear, but my heart won't let me keep quiet. It wants what it wants. And it wants you. I think it's always wanted you. You just weren't born yet."

My Sunny Vampire

Ever since high school, she had wondered if someone would love her. Not like a relative. Not like her mother loved her, or her father, if he loved her at all. Not because she was related to someone famous, but because they wanted to, because they loved her. For that someone to be Jack was better than she could have ever hoped. "You're not just saying that?"

He brushed his lips against hers. "No. I love you. Do you hear me? I. Love. You," he said, punctuating each word with a kiss.

She had never felt such joy fill her heart, it nearly burst. "Oh, Jack." She wrapped her arms around his neck. "I love you, too. I don't ever want to lose you."

"Then we'll just have to make sure we do everything we can so that doesn't happen." He rolled on his back and grunted, taking her with him.

"You stupid man. Was that all worth it?"

He grinned. "Oh yeah. It was definitely worth it. I'll be good now, I promise." He paused for a moment then said, "Say it again."

She nestled her head on his shoulder and smiled. "I love you, Jack VanAllen, and there's not a darn thing you can do about it. Is that what you wanted to hear?"

"I'll make it right for you, Sunshine. I promise."

God help her, she believed him. But there must be something she could do. "Can this Beanie help? Is he one of the Committee?"

"No and no. We've had a falling out and he says he wants to make amends."

"So, you can use that? Right? If that's what he wants, why not let him prove it?"

"I don't feel comfortable having him meet you."

"If I'm in the news, wouldn't it be worse if you hid me?"

"I don't know. Maybe."

"Jack, the media can be ruthless. If they smell a story, they won't stop."

He scrubbed at his face. "Shit. You're right. It would be worse." He kissed her forehead. "You win. I'll call Frank later and tell him we'll meet them. But right now, I just want to lie here, hold you, and heal."

She could live with that. For now.

Chapter 18

"What time is it?" Sunny's head was still on Jack's chest. She would have thought her neck would eventually get a crick, but she felt fine. Or that she'd be bored, but she wasn't. She loved being close to him.

"Ten-fifteen." He stretched one arm over his head and sighed.

"Finally. No pain."

She lifted her head. "You're okay now?"

"Sweetheart, I'm always okay when I'm with you. But I am pain-free now." He sat up and twisted his back. She held her breath, waiting for him to yell out or wince. He did neither. "I think I'm going to take a shower. Care to join me?" he asked, flashing his eyebrows.

"That sounds like fun, but I need to check my phone first. I asked Frank to have Carrie call me, and I think it went off a while ago." At least she thought she'd heard something.

"It did at nine-thirty."

"Oh, great. Then you go ahead and start without me. I'll come in later." She found her sweater and, when she tugged it over her head, he pushed her back and sucked on her breast. She smacked him on the head. "Jack, cut that out."

"Ah, but it was just out there asking to be sucked on. I don't think I can wait." He flicked his tongue on her nipple, getting it hard.

Her willpower was waning fast. "Please, Jack? She'll be leaving for work soon."

My Sunny Vampire

His sigh tickled her skin, but he released her. "I get it. You just want some privacy to talk with your friend." He kissed her on the mouth. "She better not talk your ear off. I want to show you all the wonderful things you can do in a shower."

Wonderful things? A lump formed in her throat and she tried to swallow it down. Oh God. She wanted that, too. He pulled her up into a sitting position as he climbed off the bed. Grabbing the bottom of his t-shirt, he slipped it off over his head, his muscles rippling in action. His movement was effortless, as if he'd never been hurt.

"I thought you had a phone call to make."

"Oh, yes." She stood and put on her sweater. He yanked off his jeans just as she scrambled out of the room.

The rat was laughing as she hurried down the stairs.

She pulled her purse out of the backpack and found her phone. Sheesh, the thing was on vibrate and they both heard it? Guess her hearing worked okay. Did vampires ever have any privacy?

Sitting on the edge of the couch, she called Carrie and sank into the cushions when her friend answered the phone sounding clearheaded. Thank goodness. Carrie would have had problems speaking if she'd been drinking all night like Sunny feared.

"Are you and Jack coming tonight?" Carrie asked. "Frank hopes maybe you can talk Jack into going."

"Tell him not to worry. Jack plans on calling him later." The next bit of news was hard to say, but necessary. "Carrie, Bobby's dead. Looks like he OD'd."

"Aww, gee. I suppose he's in a better place now. I'm sorry, Sunny. I know how much Jack wanted to talk to him."

"How are you doing, Carrie? Is Frank treating you okay? If he's not and he's in the apartment, don't say anything. I'll take that as a no."

"Listen to yourself, would you? Why are you so suspicious? He's been nothing but a gentleman to me. Probably too much of a gentleman." There was a pause and then Carrie softened her voice. "God, you don't suppose he's gay, do you?"

"Where is that coming from? You've been with the guy, don't you know?"

"I've been with him, but I haven't been with him, if you know what I mean. He hasn't even tried to kiss me. I've initiated it every time."

"Well, I'm pretty sure he's not gay. The guy used to be married for like, seventy years."

"Wow. He never said anything. I guess he's not afraid of commitment, huh?" Carrie chuckled. "Maybe he's just afraid to start. I can deal with that."

Sunny told her friend she'd see her later that night, said her goodbyes and hung up. The shower was still running and she got up, intending to join Jack, when she remembered something else she wanted to do in private. She felt bad about missing her interview and wanted to apologize. Perhaps set up another one for the evening. The job wouldn't require working on site, and even if she couldn't accept the job, she still wanted to know if she was qualified.

Scanning through the address book on her cell, she located the phone number and pushed send. The number rang once. "I'm sorry, the number you have dialed is no longer in service."

"How can that be?" She stared at her phone. Mr. Rivers had called from that number. Did Frank have a phone book? She searched the living room with no success, but found one in the kitchen. Flipping through the pages, she located the business. Different number, but the book was two years old. Oh well, what did she have to lose? If it didn't work, at least she'd tried.

She punched the number on her phone and hit send. She got another recording, but for the business. Having no idea how to find the extension she needed, she pushed zero for the operator.

"How may I direct your call?"

"I'd like to speak to Mr. Rivers, please."

"I'm sorry. No one by that name works here."

"It's possible I got his name wrong. My name is Sunshine Petersen. I had an interview set up yesterday at eleven-thirty with him in the art department. I wanted to apologize for missing it and see if I could reschedule."

"Hold, please."

Instrumental music played while she waited. The shower continued to run upstairs. She hoped this wouldn't take long. Number one, she wanted to join Jack. Number two, she didn't want him to know what she was up to.

"Ms. Petersen, I'm sorry to keep you waiting," the operator said. "No one in the art department had any interviews scheduled for you yesterday or any other day for that matter. In fact, there are

My Sunny Vampire

no job openings in that department. If someone called saying they were from this company, then I'd say it was a prank. I'm sorry."

A prank? An achy pain radiated in her chest. "Thank you. I'm sorry to have bothered you."

Stunned, she stared at her phone. Who would do such a thing to her? And why?

* * * *

After thirty minutes, Jack turned off the water. Apparently, Carrie was talking Sunshine's ear off. Too bad. He was now stuck with an erection that wouldn't go away. Oh, but maybe he could get her off the phone and then do something about it.

He grabbed a towel off the rack and dried himself. After tossing the towel on the floor, he walked into the hallway. No use getting dressed, not when he wanted her out of her clothes.

The house was eerily quiet. His hearing would have picked up Sunshine's conversation regardless of who spoke. He got nothing. He checked the bedrooms and paused at Linda's office. Frank hadn't changed a thing since her death. Jack shook his head and went downstairs.

When he reached the bottom of the steps, he found Sunshine sitting on the couch, staring straight ahead as if she were in a trance.

He rushed to her. "Sunshine? What's the matter? Did something happen to Carrie?"

She looked up at him as if she just noticed he was in the house. "Oh. Hi, Jack. No, Carrie's fine."

Now he felt ridiculous standing there naked and wished he'd kept the towel. He sat beside her and smoothed her hair away from her face. "What's the matter then?"

She closed her eyes and her bottom lip trembled. "Nothing."

"It's not nothing. You're upset."

She played with the bottom of her sweater. "If I tell you, you'll just be mad."

Which was code for: I did something you told me not to do. "If I promise not to get mad, will you tell me?"

It took several moments before she finally spoke. "I called that place I had an interview with."

He closed his eyes and pinched the bridge of his nose, concentrating on remaining calm and not lashing out. "Why would you do that?"

"I wanted to apologize."

"And set up another interview?"

"Maybe." She turned and buried her head against his chest. "Doesn't matter. They never heard of me, there was no interview, there is no job. I knew it was too good to be true."

He hated seeing her so down. Hugging her didn't seem to be enough, but what more could he do? "I don't understand. Didn't you apply for the job?"

"No. They called me. Said they saw my work and wanted to interview me for a position. Lucky for me I had my portfolio or else I would have had to go back home to get it. Like it mattered anyway. I just can't figure out who would do this to me."

Who, indeed. "Sunshine, when did you get this call?"

"Day after Christmas. I was thinking of going back home for New Year's, but then I got the call, so I stayed."

That was the same day the Committee got word regarding Frank. Someone wanted both Jack and Sunshine to be in town. There were two known vampires in town who could do it, too, Frank and Harris. Wouldn't the responsible party want to remain in town to see how everything played out? Maybe the upcoming evening activities would give Jack the information he sorely needed. He'd make sure to get one of them to slip up.

"I tell you, if I ever find out who did it, they're gonna wish they were nicer to me because I'm so going to let them have it. Even if I only give them some mind mojo."

The snort escaped before he could stop it.

She looked up and smiled. Then she ran her hand over his chest and glanced at the rest of him. "How come you're naked?"

"Well, see, I was in the shower waiting for you and when you didn't show, I thought I'd..." Oh hell, it sounded better in his head.

"Dang. I missed the shower." She straddled him and Little Jack sprang to life. "Sure you're not still dirty?" She tugged on his ear and peered behind. "I think you might have missed a spot."

"It's highly possible. You think I need another shower?"

She cupped his face and smiled sweetly. "Oh, most definitely."

He almost wished he was dirtier. 'Cause getting clean with her was looking like a whole lot of fun.

Chapter 19

The traffic whizzed by and the air stank of exhaust, but none of that mattered because Sunny was walking to the club with Jack beside her. After their bout of lovemaking, she'd been excited about going. They were actually a couple now, a couple on a date. Now if she could only get him to hold hands, the night would be perfect. Instead, he was more fascinated with her hair.

"What is your problem?" Sunny pulled her braid out of his hands. "Ever since you saw me with my hair up, you've been acting funny."

"I don't like it like this. Why can't you wear your hair down?"

"Gee, you got some cheese to go with that whine?" She chuckled. His bewildered look only made her laugh harder. "I can't help it if it got frizzy after our shower. I would have thought a vampire's hair would be perfect. Apparently, I still need my hair care products. Am I that repulsive?"

He frowned. "No, of course not. I just like your hair down."

He might be on the whiny side, but she still loved him. She gave him a quick kiss on the lips. "Tough. Deal with it."

As Jack reached for the door, Frank and Carrie came around the corner. One look at Sunny and Frank's eyes widened in surprise. Vampires. They must think all women should wear their hair down.

While waiting for Harris's arrival, they found a table and ordered the requisite soft drink, except for Carrie. She upgraded her normal margarita to a Long Island iced tea.

"Gee whiz, Carrie. Doesn't that have, like, five different boozes in it?" Sunny asked. What happened to her suggestion of not desiring any alcoholic drinks?

"Don't you go starting on me again. We're here to have fun, aren't we? It's not like I'm driving anywhere. So, lighten up. Ever since you turned, you've been a stick-in-the-mud."

Sunny wouldn't be such a stick-in-the-mud if Carrie stopped drinking. Was it a coincidence that Carrie's drinking and Sunny's turning occurred almost simultaneously? She didn't think so, but what did she know?

Sunny hated thinking Jack had anything to do with her turning and she highly doubted Frank would bother, seeing how he fixated on Carrie. Maybe seeing Harris, or Beanie, or whatever his name was would trigger a memory.

"Why are we at this place again?" Jack continued to fiddle with her braid and she yanked it from his fingers.

"Stop it," she whispered.

"Because I get a discount on the drinks," Carrie said.

Shoot. Was Frank right or was he controlling her? Or did Sunny's suggestion fail, like so many others had? And why didn't Frank do anything? Carrie would listen to him.

Jack kissed her temple. "Come on, let's dance."

"Dance? I thought you didn't like to dance."

"I never said that."

"You implied it."

He stood and offered his hand. "Are you going to get up or argue about it?"

No arguments. She took the extended hand and followed him to the floor.

He pulled her into his arms like Fred Astaire had held Ginger Rogers in one of those old dancing movies. Wow. She'd never danced like this before. It was more intimate than she expected, especially from him. Following him was really easy, too. They were like one person.

The music changed to something more lively, but Jack continued to hold her close. At this point, she didn't really care about Carrie or Frank or whoever turned her. The building could burn and she wouldn't want him to let go. Being in his arms lightened her mood and excited her. He'd made love to her three times during the day and her body still craved his.

My Sunny Vampire

"I'm sorry Carrie's upset you."

"She hasn't upset me. I was just hoping it worked."

"Hoping what worked?"

She told him about her conversation with Frank and the suggestion she left with Carrie.

"Why do you think your suggestion failed? And don't say it's because you're broken. Think about it."

She still thought she was broken, despite what Jack said. "I know that alcoholism is a disease, and if Carrie was an alcoholic, then I can understand my suggestion not working. But I'm telling you, she's not an alcoholic."

He kissed her temple and kept his lips close. "Did you want me to try? Is that it?" Before she could answer, he continued, "If it doesn't work, will you consider the possibility that you might be wrong?"

It hurt too much to believe Carrie was ill, but she needed to know. "Yes."

They danced quietly. She assumed Jack was doing his thing and she didn't want to interfere. A couple bumped into them, but he twirled them away before any real damage was done.

"Okay, I sent it. I hope you're right, but if you aren't, you have to admit she has a problem. As much as it will kill you, just be her friend. Stop antagonizing her. It won't do either one of you any good."

No way she could stand back and watch Carrie ruin her life. Even if Frank eventually turned her, what guarantee would there be that she'd stop craving alcohol? Apparently Frank hadn't. Which got her thinking... "How do you turn someone? Why can't I remember it happening to me?"

"You're not thinking of turning her are you?"

"No. Why? Can't I?"

"You could if you have her permission and the permission of the Committee. She would have to wait, unless you got someone else to do it. Your venom won't come in until you've been a vampire for a year. We don't know why it takes that long, it just does. As for remembering, I can only assume you were not conscious at the time since you don't remember being injected by venom."

"You mean I would have felt something?"

"Yes. Venom burns immediately. The new vampire is in agony for at least half a day. There's no way for us to block the pain."

Half a day? She remembered the pain, but not for that long. "So it was a good thing I was drunk?"

Jack shrugged. "I can't say. I've never heard of alcohol working before, but then I've not witnessed any turnings until you. I only know what I felt and what others have said."

"Never?"

"No reason for me to. I never turned anyone."

"So if I could remember who knocked me out, then that's probably who turned me?"

"Yeah, but you don't remember that either, do you?"

She sighed. "No." Resting her head against his shoulder, she listened to his heartbeat. She didn't even need her ear next to his heart. What a wonderful sound. One she would never tire of hearing. "I want you to know, if this didn't happen to me and we continued to see each other after New Year's Eve, I could see you maybe turning me."

* * * *

Jack was sure his heart swelled ten times due to her statement. How close had he come to never knowing her? A shudder ran through him with the thought. He released her waist and stepped back enough to hold her face in his hands. "I don't think you'll ever know how much you mean to me. I love you."

He kissed her there, out on the dance floor, and the world seemed to stop. Her arms came around his neck and she leaned into him and damn if he didn't feel a charge race through his body. He was addicted to her.

A hand landed on his shoulder, but Jack continued to kiss Sunshine. Only one person would bother and he could bug off.

"I'd tell you to get a room, but Beanie's here." Frank chuckled.

Jack stiffened at the news and broke the kiss. "Shit. I was hoping he forgot."

"Not likely." Frank departed and headed back to Carrie, who seemed to be dancing just fine alone.

Jack gave Sunshine a kiss, wishing he could escape with her instead. "I guess we should go back to the table."

"Just remember, he might be able to help." She brought her hand up to his cheek, but he took it and kissed the palm.

My Sunny Vampire

Harris could only help if he confessed to the crime. Jack wasn't holding out for that to occur.

"I'll do my best. For you." He offered his elbow and she took it. The dance floor had become more crowded since their arrival and he weaved them around the dancing couples. When they reached a clearing, someone yanked Sunshine away. She yelped.

"Hey! Aren't you the vampire girl?" A dark-haired man in his early twenties held her arm.

She scrunched her face again, probably trying to control the young man and failing miserably. It troubled Jack's heart that she was still having difficulty.

Maybe he could get out of this without mind control and she wouldn't feel so frustrated. "Please unhand her. Didn't your mother teach you any manners?"

"Oh, I'm sorry." The man released her, appearing remorseful. "It's just that you look just like her."

She offered him a smile he clearly didn't deserve. "I get that all the time."

Her smile affected the young man. He looked at her with love-sick eyes. "You sure could be her twin. You're real pretty."

Great, just great. She couldn't control the man, but her--what did she call it?--vibes were working just fine.

Sunshine frowned. "Umm, thanks?"

Jack placed a hand on the small of her back and guided her to their table. "You okay?"

"My pride's a little bruised. I tried to get him to leave."

"You scrunched your face."

She sighed. "Trying too hard. Yeah, I get it."

"Give it time. Soon it will be second nature to you." He kissed her temple. It should have been second nature by now, but everyone was different. He hoped he hadn't lied to her. "Of course, you could have just told him to go away. It works for mortals all the time."

She stopped and faced him. "My vibes seem to be working in full swing, though. They think I'm coming on to them when I'm clearly not interested. You know that, right?"

He laughed. He knew, but loved to hear her say it.

As they approached the table, sure enough, Harris was looking their way. His eyes widened when he saw Sunshine. Why'd she have to wear that braid? With her hair pulled back, she could almost be Clara's twin. Not that Harris wouldn't notice her likeness otherwise. Dammit, dammit, dammit.

She grabbed his hand. *"I don't have something on my face, do I? Everyone keeps looking at me funny."*

"You look fine. Harris probably wasn't expecting to see you."

Jack pulled out her chair and she sat. He took the seat beside her and waited for the grenade to go off.

Harris leaned over the table. "I thought that was her on the news. Sunny, right? I'm Beanie."

She relaxed and smiled, probably assuming her TV appearance was the reason for Harris's reaction. "Hi. I'm sorry. I don't remember you."

"I didn't dance and feed from you, if you wondered. Still, I don't suppose you would remember me. I didn't stay all that long."

Harris sent an accusing look Jack's way.

"I found her in the process of turning," Jack said. "She doesn't remember who did it."

"Seems mighty convenient for the perpetrator, now doesn't it? So why is she here and not in Atlanta? Wouldn't that be the proper protocol?"

Jack could almost see the gleam in Harris's eyes. He was probably ecstatic thinking Jack had done something illicit.

Sunshine took his hand and squeezed. *"It's okay."*

Jack wasn't sure anything would be okay. Not until he found the culprit. But he loved how she worried about him and returned the squeeze before refocusing on Harris. "The proper protocol would be to investigate the case as soon as possible, and that's what I'm doing. The responsible party is most likely still in the area and she might remember something later on. I'll take her to Atlanta once I solve the case. Until then, there's nothing they can do."

A server approached and placed another Long Island iced tea on the table, then took the two empty glasses away. Sunshine pulled free as she watched the whole process. How long had they been out on the dance floor? Jack could almost hear her fretting.

Carrie returned with Frank on her heels and plopped down on her chair. "Oh goodie!"

She grabbed the drink and downed it as if Jack's command had never been received. He glanced at Sunshine. She was staring at her friend and worry wrinkles marred her beautiful face.

My Sunny Vampire

"Carrie, this is Beanie," Frank said. "Carrie is Sunny's friend and knows about us."

Harris raised his eyebrows. "Isn't that disallowed?"

Jack cut him off. "Frank's taking responsibility for her."

"Boy, you two have been busy, haven't you?"

"Carrie?" Sunshine asked. "Are you okay? You don't look so well."

And she didn't. Apparently that last drink tipped the boat. Carrie stood and tottered on her feet as her hand came up to her mouth. Oh great. She was about to spew.

Sunshine came to her aid and whisked her away. Frank stood to follow.

Jack pulled him back to his chair. "Why do you keep buying them for her?"

"I'm not. She's ordering them."

"And how much have you had?" When his friend averted his eyes, Jack inhaled deeply. No wonder Carrie was such a mess--high alcohol, low blood. That would do it.

"I didn't realize how much Sunny resembles a certain picture," Harris said.

Jack's heart skipped several beats and Frank's eyes widened.

Jack knew that braid was a mistake. He should have ripped it out when he had the chance.

"And now she's one of us. If I didn't know any better, I'd say you turned her."

"We don't believe Jack turned her," Frank said.

"What's that supposed to mean?"

"It means I don't remember," Jack confessed. "I woke up next to her in an alley on New Year's morning."

Harris raised an eyebrow. "That seems mighty convenient, now doesn't it?"

"Only convenient if someone wanted to set me up. Like you, for instance."

"Me?"

"Jack, this isn't the place." Frank grabbed Jack's arm.

"You in on this, too, Frank? I told you I was with Bailey that night."

"Whose memory you said you scrubbed," Jack said. "Not much of an alibi."

169

"You want to read my memories? Is that it? Go ahead." Harris pushed up his sleeve.

"Like that would prove anything. Anyone with the skill can manipulate their own memories. You know that."

"Jack, Beanie, please. We can discuss this at my place."

Harris shot out of his chair, knocking it over. "What's to discuss? You're both trying to set me up for something I didn't do. And to think I wanted your forgiveness. Apparently what's good for you isn't good for me, and I think the Committee should hear about this."

He stormed off. Frank followed, calling his name.

Great, just great. Jack knew better than to upset Harris, yet he just couldn't stop himself. If he didn't get some answers soon, Harris would only make him look more guilty.

Frank returned alone. "What the hell, Jack. You couldn't wait to discuss this in a civil manner? He's not listening to anything I have to say now."

Why would he? Harris and Jack weren't the best of buds even before Ivy's death. Jack felt his world starting to cave in. Losing his position on the Committee would be tough, but if Sunshine remained in his life, he could bear it. Of course, if the Committee sentenced him to death… Oh hell, he didn't want to think that far ahead.

* * * *

"How you doing in there?" Sunny stared at the stall door. Carrie had been throwing up on and off for the last five minutes, but had become eerily quiet. She was breathing and her heart beat rapidly, but that didn't mean she hadn't passed out.

"I feel like shit and my head is about to explode." Carrie moaned some more, followed by the dry heaves. "Oh God. This place really stinks, you know that?"

Sunny agreed. With her heightened sense of smell, she could tell more than one person had thrown up, the sanitary box needed emptying and at least one patron had missed the toilet. She looked under the stall where Carrie was kneeling and hoped it wasn't that one.

Sunny bit her lip. She had nearly cried when Carrie had downed that last drink. Apparently, Jack's suggestion didn't take any more than hers had. Was Carrie an alcoholic?

My Sunny Vampire

The door to the bathroom opened and Harris, or Beanie, came through. "Is it just the two of you in here?"

"Yes, but--"

He cut her off. "Listen, I don't have a lot of time here. I think there's something you should know about Jack."

The way Jack went on about Harris, she had expected him to be some boorish oaf, but in fact the man was rather good looking. Standing eye level to Sunny with an air of confidence, he stared at her with the darkest blue eyes she'd ever seen, they were almost black, like his hair. She had hoped seeing Harris would trigger something, but got nothing. He did seem familiar, though, and his admission of being at the club on New Year's Eve might have been the reason. Still, her radar went up at the mention of Jack's name.

No sound came behind the stall door. "Carrie?"

"She's okay," Harris said. "I have her. She doesn't need to hear this unless you want her to."

"So what did you want to tell me?"

"Is it true you don't remember who turned you?"

She sighed. "I remember being with Jack and leaving the bar with him. Then nothing until I woke up feeling like I'd been set on fire."

"But you do remember. You were with him. He had to have turned you."

She put her hand on her hip. "What makes you think that?"

"Do you know he was married before?"

"Yes, he told me. What does that have to do with anything?"

"Do you know you look like his late wife? Could be her twin, actually?"

A small pain radiated from her chest. She willed it away and tried not to over-react. Listening to Jack and Frank talk earlier, she knew Jack and Harris were not friends. So maybe Harris was only trying to break them up out of some sort of strange feud. "How would you know? Did you know him then?"

"No, but Jack carries a picture of her."

"A picture? From the seventeen-hundreds? Come on. I know better than that."

"It's a photo of a painting. A small likeness he keeps in his wallet. I tell you, he's manipulating you. You need to report him to the Committee."

"Jack and Frank said one vampire can't manipulate the mind of another. You saying they lied?"

He waved his arms in the air. "No, no, no. Not that kind of manipulation." He paced the room, clearly frustrated. "He's playing you. Probably getting you to trust him so they'll be lenient. Has he done anything to find out who would have turned you?"

"Yes. We went to find the donor who he believes caused his memory loss."

"And? Did you?"

"We found him dead before we could talk to him."

"Kind of convenient, isn't it? As is his memory loss. I'm sure if you look, you'll see he's doing a lot of things that aren't in your best interest. It's best you get out while you can." He reached inside his back pocket, pulled out a wallet and thumbed through it. "Here's my card. My number is listed. When you realize I'm right, call me. I can take you to Atlanta. They'll take care of you there."

Vampires kept cards? Heck, what did she know regarding the vampire race? Barely anything. She took the card. It listed him as a manager for Vantage Accounting and Management Personnel Services, the fake company the Committee hid behind.

"Don't wait too long." He rushed out the door.

The toilet flushed and Carrie emerged, her hair flying every which way, oblivious to what just went on. "I think I want to go home." She went to the sink and turned on the faucet. "I'm sorry I spoiled your night."

"You didn't spoil my night." That honor would go to Harris.

Carrie stared at Sunny through the mirror. "Then why do you look like someone just killed your pet?"

Or nicked her heart. Sunny straightened up and slid the card in her pocket. "Sorry. Guess I was having a pity party in my head. Being a vampire isn't all it's cracked up to be."

Carrie ran her fingers through her hair like a comb and once she seemed satisfied, splashed water on her face and grabbed a paper towel. "They all seem so normal though, don't they? Could you tell they were different?"

Did she need to remind her friend that she was now one of them? "No, they seem pretty normal to me."

"I think I can pass for the land of the living now," Carrie said. "I'm going to have Frank take me home. You staying with Jack again? You two seem pretty tight now. Things going good?"

My Sunny Vampire

They were up until a moment ago. "Let me take you home. Frank doesn't need to be with you all the time. Let's just go home and veg out in front of the TV."

"If I can stay awake, that sounds good."

They headed back to their table. Like the gentlemen they were, Jack and Frank rose and held their seats. Sunny couldn't sit beside Jack, not so soon. Not until she sorted things out in her head. Harris had to be wrong, but what if he was right? She should give his accusations her full attention and Jack's presence would only be a distraction.

"Where's your friend?" she asked.

"He decided to leave. I guess he didn't want to make amends after all," Jack said.

"That's too bad. He might have been able to help." Unless Jack didn't want Harris's help. Oh fudge. Was she going to question every comment he made? She grabbed her coat. "I'm going to take Carrie back home. I'll be staying with her tonight."

Hurt flittered across his face. "Did I do something wrong?"

She flashed him a giant smile, but felt no joy behind it. "No, silly. I think Carrie needs some girl time. I'll see you at Frank's after she's asleep."

Frank helped Carrie with her coat and she gave him a kiss goodbye. When Jack tried to help Sunny, she avoided the gesture, turned to face him and gave him a peck on the cheek. Big mistake. He grabbed her arm and pulled her close.

"Something is wrong." He stared at her intently, as if he could read her mind and she did her best to look neutral.

"I'm just worried…" She couldn't finish the statement or even think it.

His face softened. "I'm sorry, Sunshine. I'm sure she'll be all right." He kissed her on the lips, so sweet and tender, it took everything in her not to hold onto him tight. "I'll miss you."

Pain slashed at her heart. She loved him so much, but did it make her blind to the truth? She would do everything she could to come up with a flaw in Harris's accusations.

Chapter 20

At three in the morning, while the snow softly fell, the streets were deserted. Surprise, surprise. Even without the noisy traffic, a nice, peaceful feeling filled the air, as if the snow muffled every other sound around. Sunny had never actually walked in falling snow without freezing her butt off. And if she could stop thinking about what Harris had said, she might enjoy the walk.

She meandered through the neighborhoods, kicking at the snow, hoping the quiet solitude would ease her mind. She'd already put off this trip since ten. Carrie had crashed by then, but Sunny wasn't ready to face Jack. So she attempted to read and took a shower, but nothing purged Harris's words. When she realized what she'd been doing, believing someone she just met over someone who had done nothing but care for her, she fixed her hair the way Jack liked it, left Carrie's and headed for Frank's. Jack loved her. She'd seen it in his eyes, in the way he treated her. But did he love her or a reflection of his late wife?

Fudge. All night she had asked herself questions of that nature. She was driving herself nuts. Jack would be able to explain. She trusted him.

As she approached Frank's street, a thud, followed by grunt, came from behind.

She'd been so caught up in her thoughts, it never occurred to her that she might be followed. At such an early hour, who else would be out here? She twirled around, hoping to catch whoever in the act, but found the sidewalk empty. Empty of a person, but not

My Sunny Vampire

from a clue. Whoever was following apparently forgot it was snowing.

A five-foot holly hedge lined the sidewalk. Snow clung to its dark green leaves except for a spot that someone had knocked clean. Hand prints and skid marks obliterated her footprints and tracks disappeared around the bush. No one knew about her, so why the need to hide? She cautiously approached the hedge, the fresh snow compacting with each footstep.

Branches rustled.

Sunny stopped. A cat cried down the street, but two heartbeats thumped from the other side of the hedge and the scent of perspiration and beer hit her nose. If her vampire skills couldn't outwit two drunken mortals, she might as well hang it up.

* * * *

"That's it." Frank grabbed the remote out of Jack's hands. "Call her or go outside, but stay away from the television."

"I can't call her. She'll think I don't trust her. Besides, it's your fault I'm not with her now." Jack shouldn't have said that last part, but he couldn't stop himself. He'd never felt a bond with a woman like he did with Sunshine and being apart nearly killed him. Maybe if she hadn't left in such a strange mood, he'd feel better, but she had acted funny back at the bar. Almost like she was trying to avoid him.

Why would she want to avoid him? Harris got him so paranoid, he was seeing things. Sunshine was concerned about Carrie and she had good reason to be. Frank might not be controlling the woman, but he certainly took advantage. Sunshine had the right idea by splitting up Frank and Carrie.

"How many times do I have to apologize for that?" Frank asked. "You know I'm worried about Carrie, too."

"If you're so worried, you'd stop feeding from her. But you can't, can you?"

Frank stood and threw his book down. "This has nothing to do with me feeding from her. She wants me to. I'm not asking her. Do you know how that makes me feel? I feel like I matter. I don't care what her blood is laced with. If she asks, I'll do it."

Jack rose and went to his friend. "You matter, Frank."

"Sure. That's why so many people have visited since Linda's death."

Ouch. "How many times do you need me to apologize?"

"It's not just you, Jack. Beanie was like a brother to me. Sure, Ivy's death devastated him, but to not show up for Linda's memorial service...that hurt. I realized then I only mattered to one person and she was taken from me."

Jack placed a hand on Frank's shoulder. "You matter to me. Your friendship means a lot. And you matter to Carrie, I can tell. But Frank, this isn't the way to start a relationship. She needs help."

"I know. I tried to get her to stop. When Sunny told me Carrie's behavior was new, I thought maybe someone had manipulated her. Maybe the same person who turned Sunny. So I did some manipulation myself, but nothing I told her did any good."

That made three of them trying and still Carrie continued to drink. Sunshine would just have to face the fact, her friend was an alcoholic.

"Have you tried talking to Carrie about her drinking?"

"Yes, but she only gets angry. I don't want her angry at me, Jack."

Frank never could handle confrontation. Why would Jack think he would be different now?

He patted Frank's shoulder. "I'll go outside and wait for Sunny. You can go back to reading."

When he opened the door, he smiled. Fat snowflakes filled the air. He'd forgotten the forecast called for several inches. Maybe once Sunshine arrived, he could take her out and play. He'd enjoyed making snow angels as a child and she always seemed in the mood for fun.

He looked at his watch. Ten after three. She said she would return after Carrie went to bed. How late did her friend stay up, anyway?

* * * *

"I know you're there," Sunny said. "You might as well come out."

Two men emerged. The shorter of the two, a blond, held his hands behind his back. The taller, dark-haired one had accosted her in the bar. Fear tingled down her spine and her heart raced. He had called her vampire girl. That couldn't be good.

"See? I told you it was her," tall, dark and stupid said.

"You followed me home?" Didn't these guys have anything better to do on a weeknight?

My Sunny Vampire

"It's not every day you see a vampire."

The short one approached. "Do you have fangs?"

"Hold up there, buddy." She put her hand out. The would-be vampire hunters stopped and flinched, raising their arms to their faces, as if her hands were some kind of ray guns. She wished she had that kind of power. Wouldn't that be cool?

They reeked of beer, but she suspected alcohol was the least of her worries. If Jack could get rid of them without controlling them, maybe she could do the same. "Why don't you two go on home before you get yourself in trouble?"

"We don't want to hurt you," Shorty said.

He sounded like a bully just before shoving his victim in a locker. Well, she was no one's victim and wouldn't stick around to see what they had planned.

"Goodnight, boys." She turned and headed for Frank's. Meandering didn't seem so tranquil any longer, or safe. She picked up her pace.

The tall one ran in front of her, blocking her path. Fear turned to anger and she clenched her fists. "Get out of my way."

He put his hands on his hips. "Make me."

Fine, if he wouldn't move, she'd just walk around him. She took a step to her right and he moved in the same direction. Stepping left did no good, either. He mirrored her movements.

"*Do not move.*" His eyes glazed over and seemed to look right through her.

Whoa! It worked? It must, he looked like a zombie. Not wasting any time in case it didn't last long, she walked around him, glad to finally pass. Zipping would have been better, but how many times had Jack warned her to look normal? So normal she would look. Besides, she didn't need to give Stupid's friend any ammunition on the whole vampire business.

"Hey! What did you do to Tom?" Shorty caught up to her and pulled her arm back.

Dag-burnit. Can't they get the message? She whipped free and her coat popped open. "Let me go."

Her link with Tom disconnected. Next thing she knew she was sandwiched between fiddle-dee-dee and fiddle-dee-dum. In a fit of panic, she shoved Tom and he went flying into the bushes.

Fudge. She hadn't meant to do that. Sunny rushed to his side. Was he dead? He blinked several times. No, but she smelled blood.

She leaned over him and sniffed. The scent came from his head. Scratches. That's all. She sighed in relief.

Shorty yelled.

She turned just as he charged her with a raised hand. What the heck was he doing? He tackled her to the ground. Snow puffed outward. Shooting pain radiated from her chest. She screamed in agony.

"Tom. She's bleeding. She didn't turn to dust. You said she would."

Tom scrambled out of the bushes. "They always did on Buffy. Come on, let's get out of here."

"We can't leave her lying in the middle of the sidewalk. Shouldn't we move her?"

Son of a gun. The stupid idiot had stabbed her. Probably thought he was some sort of vampire slayer. And if her coat hadn't opened up, he might not have succeeded in piercing her skin. Her thin, light blue t-shirt was currently turning dark with her blood around the piece of wood that stuck out of her chest. Sunny tried sitting up, but it felt like someone was sitting on her chest. She couldn't even move her hands to pull out the stake. She was paralyzed. Oh no. Not again.

Maybe the last time she deserved what she got, but this time she hadn't done anything wrong. Was she a jinxed vampire?

"We'll put her in the bushes," Tom said.

No, no. Not the bushes. She might not be spotted until morning, if she survived the sunrise. *"Don't touch me."* When Tom grabbed her shoulders, she knew she hadn't gotten through. What good was having powers if she couldn't use them consistently? Pain ripped through her chest and she cried out again. Shorty lifted her by the ankles and they shoved her into the bush. Each push aggravated the wound, making her wish she could pass out from the pain. Branches poked her side and scratched her face. She might be paralyzed, but she could certainly feel.

"You can't leave me here." She was grateful her voice, although weak, at least worked.

"You shouldn't have tried to bite my friend," Shorty said.

The sounds of their footsteps faded while sirens wailed in the distance.

My Sunny Vampire

Her back to the street, she relied on sounds. Besides the sirens, the area was quiet. No heartbeats. Not even her own. Those two idiots just left her here to die? Or was she dead already?

* * * *

A woman's scream echoed down the street. Jack sat up straight. Was that outside? He descended the steps and started walking toward the sound. Another cry of torture. He stopped. The woman was outside and needed help.

As he rushed toward the scream, the sound of sirens came closer. Someone must have already called for help. Should he investigate or go back and wait for Sunshine?

"Jack...Jack...Jack...Jack."

Her voice was faint, but recognizable. "Sunshine?"

The chanting continued.

It was her. "Sunshine!"

"Jack? Thank God. Help me."

A lump formed in his throat as he rushed toward her voice, in the direction of the screams. When he reached the intersection without any sign of her, he called, "Sunshine, where are you?"

"Over here, in the bushes."

To the right. Down the street. He ran. Footprints in the snow caught his attention and he skidded to a stop.

"I'm here," she said.

He looked down at the limp body, lightly dusted with snow, squished into the shrubbery. "Oh, sweetheart. What happened?" he asked as he knelt beside her.

"I don't know. The guy stabbed me and now I can't move. I'm so glad you heard me." Her raspy voice sounded strained as if she held back a cry of pain.

"Stabbed?" He grabbed her arm and pulled. Stuck in the branches, she cried out and it nearly ripped his heart in two. "I'm sorry. I can't get you out without hurting you."

The door to the house owning the hedge opened. An old man stuck his head out through the opening. "I'm sorry I can't help you, but I called the police."

The sirens. Jack only had a minute or two to work.

He stared at the old man. "*Go back inside. Call the police and tell them it was a mistake. You only heard cats fighting.*" He waited until the man retreated back inside the house before turning his attention to Sunshine. "He's gone."

"Oh God, Jack. The sirens. You gotta get me out of here. I'll be quiet."

The sirens died. Jack doubted the old man was that fast. Most likely the police were responding to another call or they had entered the neighborhood.

"It's okay, we have time." Not much, but he didn't want to cause her any panic. He shoved his hands under her body and with one jerk, freed her, branches snapping their disapproval in the process.

She gritted her teeth, but didn't yell.

A narrow cylindrical piece of wood protruded out of her chest. It must have pierced her heart if she couldn't move. "I'm going to remove this and it might not be pleasant."

"I don't know. I'm kind of growing attached to it."

He kissed her forehead. Even in pain she could be sarcastic. "I'll cover your mouth, so if you need to cry out, at least it'll be muffled. We don't need to disturb any more neighbors." Or have any more calls to the police.

"No. Neighbor waking wouldn't be good." She blew him a kiss. "I'm ready whenever you are."

She closed her eyes as he covered her mouth. When he grasped the stick she moaned, but when he pulled it out, she screamed in agony. He nearly screamed with her. Blood oozed from the wound. He caressed her face, trying to soothe her. "It's out, sweetheart. You'll be okay, I promise."

"I'm going to hold you to that," she said between heavy breaths.

The wooden stick looked like some kind of arrow without the metal tip. After cleaning it off, he stuck it in his back pocket, making sure the sharp end stuck up. He didn't need to poke himself in the ass.

Lights flashed and reflected off the falling snow. The police car arrived with barely a sound. Whether or not the officer respected the late hour or was hoping to catch a perpetrator unaware, Jack didn't care to know.

"Dang it, I don't want to go back to the hospital."

"You won't. Don't worry." He would never allow that to happen. Smoothing the hair away from her face, he noticed she wore her hair down. "You got rid of the braid."

A small smile formed on her face. "You didn't like it."

My Sunny Vampire

And he thought she'd been avoiding him? If so, why would she care what he liked or didn't like? His heart swelled with love for this woman and he kissed her lightly on the lips. "I'll get rid of him and then we'll go."

Before he could send a message, the radio announced the false alarm. The officer acknowledged, but said he would check the area anyway. When he climbed out of the car, Jack sent him a message. *"The only thing you found were some cats fighting. Get back in your car and drive away."*

* * * *

Sunny moved to sit up. Her chest ached and a painful cramp skittered across her abdomen.

Jack placed a hand on her shoulder and held her down. "Wait until he leaves. I don't need him noticing us here," he whispered.

Fine with her; she wasn't in much shape to sit up anyway. At least she could move and her heart was beating. It had started out slow, like a truck driving up a steep incline, but steady, and brought a smile to her lips. She grabbed his hand. *"Can I feed from him?"*

He shook his head. *"Someone could be watching."*

The cop returned to his car and drove off. The street became dark once again.

"It's not fair," she whispered. "You do it so easily and the guy doesn't even look like a zombie when you do it. I don't think I like being a vampire. I never got into so much trouble when I was mortal."

"You do seem to get into some interesting predicaments." Jack lifted her to a sitting position. "How do you feel?"

"Like I've been staked." She peeled the shirt from her skin. Her wound puckered and the bleeding stopped. "This was different than before. I could still talk. Why?"

"A stake to the heart will render a vampire paralyzed, but not speechless. Before, the sun drained your energy. In essence, you were starving. If you lost more blood this time, you might have lost the ability to speak. Plus, you're new. The older you are, the more resilient you become." He stood, offering his hand. "Do you think you can walk?"

She grabbed onto him and rose, but her legs wouldn't support her. He scooped her into his arms before her butt hit the ground. "So, what happened?" he asked as he headed toward Frank's.

She wrapped her arms around his neck and told him about Tom and Shorty and how her mind mojo didn't work. She even admitted she was probably trying too hard.

"Then Shorty thought I was biting Tom and he decided to be Buffy and stake me. I think he was disappointed I didn't turn to dust."

"Buffy?"

She stared at him. "Buffy the Vampire Slayer?" He shook his head. "You don't watch much TV, do you? We'll have to remedy that."

Jack stopped at the steps to Frank's house and turned around.

"What is it?" The street was deserted and she'd been too busy talking to hear anything unusual.

Jack climbed the steps. "Nothing. Can you reach the knob?"

Another cramp rippled across her midsection just as she reached back, causing her to wince. Dag-burnit. She was going downhill fast.

He stepped through the doorway and kissed her temple. "We'll take care of you soon."

She would have preferred a kiss on the lips, but it was better than nothing.

"What happened?" Frank stood as he put his book down. The only light in the room came from a small lamp he used for reading.

"Someone staked her," Jack said. "Pull that thing out of my back pocket, then go out and find someone for her. She needs blood."

Frank pulled the stake out and examined it. "Staked her? Like Buffy?"

"Exactly," she said. "See, he watches TV."

Frank put the stake on the table. "You picky like our friend, Jack, here?"

"Not that I know of," she answered, then thought better. "Well, maybe I am. No smoker, okay?"

He smiled. "Got it."

Jack carried her upstairs and placed her on the bed. She sat on the edge so as not to get any blood on the covers. He helped remove her coat and examined it before placing it on the floor. When he reached for her t-shirt, she stopped him. "I'm not wearing a bra and I don't have a spare shirt."

"So? I've seen them before."

My Sunny Vampire

"Yeah, but Frank hasn't." Not to mention the donor he was getting. Sure, the man or woman wouldn't remember anything, but it would feel like getting undressed in front of a dog. Just because dogs didn't speak, didn't mean anything. They always looked with interest and it creeped her out.

"Good point." He placed a finger along his cheek and seemed to be thinking. When his face lit up, he said, "Don't move."

Was he kidding? Any kind of movement made the cramps more severe. "Can I ask you a question?"

He stopped and turned back. "What'd I do now?"

She laughed, he was such a man, but it caused her stomach to cramp and she leaned over. "Will it always hurt like this when I'm hungry?"

He knelt in front of her and caressed her face. "No, sweetheart, it won't. But I'm afraid that won't be for several months. Your body is still getting used to the change. I promise, it'll get better." He gave her a brief kiss on the lips. "I'll be right back."

He returned with a towel and wet washcloth. He placed the towel across her lap. "You can use this to cover up after I get your shirt off."

She lifted her arms. Her wound screamed in pain. Okay, his plan failed. "Never mind. I'll just keep it on."

"No, no, no." He wagged his finger in the air then zipped out of the room again. When he returned, he held scissors. "I'll cut it off."

"Is this really necessary? I can wear the bloody shirt."

Seemed it was. Snip, snip, snip. He began cutting at the bottom without any problem until he reached the wet blood stain, then the material proved to be difficult.

Those scissors were aimed straight for her. Maybe it would be better if he started at the top. "Jack, why don't you--"

"I got it." He shoved the blades upward. The fabric parting caught him off guard apparently, and he clipped her chin.

"Oww!" A new pain bloomed on her face and blood dribbled onto her chest.

"Oh, shit. Sunshine, I'm sorry."

"I haven't lost enough blood yet?" She brought her hand up, but he took the washcloth and pressed it against the new wound.

"It will heal." He grinned and raised an eyebrow. "Of course, I could heal it sooner."

She smiled and lifted her chin. "Be my guest."

He removed the washcloth and licked the wound, his tongue soft against her skin. Moving his hand behind her head, he held her in place. Her body clenched in need for him and her nipples hardened.

She grabbed onto his shoulders. "I'd say you did it on purpose just to get a taste. But since I'm covered in the stuff, that kind of blows my theory."

He chuckled as he left a fiery trail of kisses from her chin to her mouth, where he sought entrance. She obliged, wanting more, and shucked the shirt off her shoulders. Holy moly, he knew how to get her motor running. Too bad most of her body protested in pain.

Jack broke the kiss. "I guess I should've waited until you're healthier, but I've been wanting to kiss you since you said goodbye at the bar."

"Jack, you always want to kiss me." And she always wanted to kiss him, so she supposed that made them even.

"That I do, sweetheart. That I do."

"You can't, by any chance, heal this wound, can you?"

"Sorry, sweetheart. Even if it hadn't closed up, it's a little too deep for my tongue. Don't worry. I'll get you taken care of." He began cleaning up the blood on her chest.

She smiled. How could she ever doubt his love? Because she didn't doubt his love, she doubted who he loved.

Oh fudge. Not again.

He stopped cleaning. "Why are you frowning? Am I hurting you?"

Was she frowning? Shoot. She needed to stop thinking about Harris's accusations. "Just a little. Let me do that."

Not that she wanted to finish what he started. She loved the attention he gave her, but didn't know what else to say. He sat back on his legs and watched with interest as she wiped the blood away. Dang. Even his look got her all hot and bothered. "How long will it take for me to get healthier?"

Jack wrapped the towel around her breasts. "It's different for everyone and you're new, so I'd guess about three hours after you feed."

She'd have to wait three hours? She supposed it could be worse. As a mortal, she'd have been sore for weeks, if not flat out dead.

Her stomach seized and she doubled over, causing the towel to open up.

"The towel's not working, is it?" Jack pulled his t-shirt over his head. He slipped the neck opening over her head and laid her back. He sat beside her and helped her with the sleeves.

"I'll go see what's taking Frank so long." A brief kiss on the lips and he disappeared.

Sunny rolled onto her side, trying to find a comfortable position and spotted Jack's wallet on the bed. It must have fallen out when he sat. Was there a picture of his late wife inside? Should she check? If she didn't she'd only wonder later on.

The wallet was thin. He certainly didn't keep much in it. A Georgia driver's license with a birth date indicating his age at thirty-one. She knew the age was wrong, but what about the day? Would he make that up, too?

A credit card and cash completed the contents of his wallet. No pictures. A warm feeling embraced her heart. Harris had lied. She couldn't be more pleased.

He just moved up to the top of her suspect list. Now if she could only find proof.

Chapter 21

The tub came from another era, an older-style model with claw legs, not built into the wall like its modern cousins. Jack reclined inside with Sunshine between his legs, her back against his chest. Normally, he hated bathing--and sitting in dirty water--but this bath he could enjoy.

Frank had resorted to bringing in a neighbor for Sunshine, a practice he tried to avoid. Jack didn't see why it mattered where the donor lived, but Frank said he didn't live there for the convenient food source. More likely, Frank liked his neighbors and didn't want to use them, just as Sunshine didn't want to use Carrie to feed. Jack never got attached enough to any mortal to give a shit.

After Sunshine fed, it took nearly thirty minutes for her to get some strength back, but he knew she would need to feed again before daybreak. He took her out and found suitable donors for both of them. Just the boost she needed. His suggestion to make snow angels in the park around the corner had brought a smile to her face. He felt like a kid, playing in the snow. All because of her.

It pained him seeing her difficulty with mind control. Would she always be flawed that way or would it just take more time? She was only four days old. Still, he'd never seen any other newbie have such problems. They all took to mind manipulation right away and for good reason. A vampire who couldn't control a mortal was in a serious world of hurt when it came to feeding.

He took the soapy wash cloth and gently rubbed it over the fading scar on her chest. By tomorrow no one would be able to tell

My Sunny Vampire

she'd been staked, not that he'd want anyone but him viewing her chest. Her breasts gleamed in the light and he abandoned the cloth to massage them with his hands. Such perfect beauties.

"*I think you woke up Little Jack,*" she transmitted, wriggling her ass against his growing erection.

"No. *You woke up Little Jack. I'm cleaning your breasts.*" He tweaked her nipples and she gasped.

"As much as I'm enjoying this, we need to talk about Frank and Carrie."

"We can talk about them later." Her nipples hardened like pebbles and he continued to play with them.

"That's what you said earlier. Now it's later. We need to do something about those two."

Frank and Carrie were the last thing on his mind. Her body was so much nicer and Little Jack wanted to play. He kissed her neck and she arched into it. "We have all day to talk, I want you now."

"I think I created a monster."

"There are some who would consider us monsters, sweetheart." He turned her head and claimed her mouth. When she sucked on his tongue, desire surged through him. He grew harder. And she called him a monster.

She spun around and straddled him, her lips never leaving his. She found Little Jack and stroked him. Even in the water, her touch charged him. He choked on his breath and nearly took her, but her actions gave him pause. Maybe for once he should let her take charge. Just what did she have in mind?

Light, feathery kisses trailed from his lips to his chest as she slowly lowered herself. She sucked on his nipple and flicked it with her tongue, making the nub highly sensitive. Damn, she knew all the right buttons to push. She grazed her teeth against his skin, but managed to keep her fangs at bay. How she withheld their emergence was beyond him, his had already extended. He wanted to bite her. Hell, he wanted her to bite him. Of course, if she bit him, he'd probably come right there in the water, but would that really be so bad?

Instead, she continued the tease as she ran her tongue down his chest and over his abs. Dipping her head in the water, she brought her mouth over Little Jack. He nearly exploded. Oh, sweet Jesus. Each swirl of her tongue put him closer to coming and then she sucked and sucked and sucked. He held his breath and gripped the sides of the tub, fighting to remain in control, a war he was currently losing.

No woman had ever sucked him off before, and he never thought to ask. Women gave him sustenance, he gave them pleasure. Even-Steven. Asking for more would have been greedy.

Just as he reached the point of no return, she rose up and rode him, taking him full inside. Grabbing her hips, he wanted to pleasure her, he wanted her to come first, but after her mouth, he couldn't control anything. "*So tight.*"

"Tight?" she asked. "You want tight?"

Before he could answer her, an amazing thing happened. She squeezed Little Jack.

"Come for me, baby," she said.

Damn. One more stroke and he was a goner. He cried out her name as the explosive orgasm rocked his world.

* * * *

"You got your hair wet."

Sunny rested her head on Jack's chest and looked at the wet mess plastered there. His heart rate was slowing, but still raced. She'd never made anyone lose control like that and she liked it. Made her feel powerful. "So it is. It'll dry."

"It'll dry?" He shook his head and chuffed. "Last night you cursed me for getting it wet."

"Last night we went out." She lifted up and kissed him on the mouth. "I promise I won't braid it, okay?"

He smiled. "I'll hold you to that. Guess you discovered you don't need to breathe so often. Very impressive."

She'd almost forgotten, too. When her face hit the water, she hadn't planned to be down there for long until she remembered she could hold her breath. Oh, the things she pictured vampires doing underwater made her tingle with excitement. "How long can you hold your breath?"

"I don't know. Maybe five minutes. It's not something I need to do often. Comes in handy, though."

"We still need to breathe?"

"Yes. If you hold your breath too long, you're liable to pass out, just like a mortal. I've heard of one vampire holding his breath for twenty minutes before that happened."

Twenty minutes? She was happy to hold it for three.

My Sunny Vampire

"You did well with the fangs. How did you manage to keep them under control?"

She'd been afraid they would pop out without notice. "I didn't think you'd want me to bite you down there, so before I went under water, I concentrated on smelling the soap. I figured it worked with the mustard."

"Smart girl. However, I am sorry I lost control," he said. "That wasn't my intention."

"Don't be sorry."

"But I didn't satisfy you."

"Sure you did." She held his face in her hands. "Jack, I don't have to have an orgasm to have a good time. Watching you was all the satisfaction I needed."

He took one of her hands and kissed the palm. "You're a remarkable woman, Sunshine. I don't deserve you."

"You might rethink that when I tell you it's time we talk about Frank and Carrie."

"Sweetheart, the way I'm feeling, you can talk about anything you want."

The door burst open and Sunny practically jumped out of her skin. Water sloshed over the sides as she turned back to hide her nakedness. Jack pulled her close.

"Dammit, Frank. Can't you knock?" He reached over her and the shower curtain scraped across the rod before it abruptly stopped, well short of covering them. She felt exposed.

"It's my house. I can enter if I want. Especially when I keep hearing my name mentioned like I'm a naughty child."

Shoot. When would she remember how easily a vampire could hear? Frank's hearing must be better than hers, because she never heard him come up the stairs. No, that couldn't be, because Jack seemed just as surprised as she did. Maybe one vampire couldn't hear another vampire being sneaky.

While she wanted to discuss the situation, she certainly didn't want to do it naked. "I'm sorry. I only wanted to find out when the best time would be to get us all together. I didn't plan on talking behind your back."

"Oh. Well why didn't you say so?"

Jack slid out from under Sunny, gave her shoulders a reassuring squeeze, and climbed out of the tub. She sat in the water and hugged her knees, keeping her back to the gentlemen. At least her rump wasn't exposed now.

"She didn't need to, Frank. Why the hell were you eavesdropping in the first place? I thought we had an agreement."

"I...I didn't mean to." Frank was acting flustered. Could it be from the accusation or the fact Jack stood in all his nude glory?

"Sunshine, you can get up now."

She turned and discovered a large towel held out, blocking Frank's view. Carefully, she rose and took the offered covering, wrapping it tightly around her body. Relief flowed through her once she no longer flashed Frank.

"You owe her an apology." Jack's demand might have been more effective if he wore a towel, or robe or something.

"It's okay, Jack. It did seem like I was talking behind his back." She hugged the towel close, making sure it wouldn't fall. "Frank, I'd like to discuss your relationship with Carrie. Can we talk downstairs after we get dressed?"

Frank hung his head and turned to leave. "I'll see you downstairs."

"Go on and get dressed. I'll clean up in here," Jack scrubbed his head and flattened his lips.

"Everything okay?"

"It's fine. Just get dressed."

After dressing in silence, he took her arm and led her down the stairs. Frank stared at the television, slouched on the couch. He glanced up when they approached.

She settled on the chair as she struggled with a way to broach the subject of Frank's obsession with Carrie, but Jack saved her the trouble.

He sat on the armrest and played with her hair. "What did you do when Sunshine and I went out earlier?"

Frank straightened up. "Am I being interrogated for something I should know about?"

"Just answer the damn question, Frank. You went out, didn't you?"

"Of course I went out. I was hungry."

Jack rubbed his chin. "You were hungry? Didn't you get enough from Carrie at the bar?"

Frank stood, shoved his hands in his pockets, and walked to the unused fireplace. "What are you trying to get at?"

Jack stood. "You're drunk, aren't you? After feeding from Carrie all night, you went out and found another drunken soul and fed. Didn't you?"

"No, I uh…"

Frank turned and stared at Sunny. A chill ran down her spine. "You bastard. You went to Carrie's."

The man possessed no morals whatsoever. She flew out of her chair and into his face faster than Jack could stop her. She pulled her fist back. Her momentum came to a sudden halt as Jack grabbed her wrist and wrapped his arm around her waist. Frank could have stopped her if he wanted, but he just stood and stared at her, as if he was begging for her punishment.

She struggled in Jack's strong arms, but couldn't get loose. She wanted to hit something. She wanted to hit Frank.

"Sweetheart, you need to calm down."

She twisted, still to no avail. "I don't want to calm down. She's my friend. Who knows what he did to her?"

Pain flashed in Frank's eyes. "I didn't hurt her. I would never hurt her."

Her cellphone went off, playing the theme from *Friends*. Only two people were assigned that ring tone and one of them was currently holding her. "Let me go. Carrie's calling."

Jack released her and she sprinted up the steps to her bag, where she stored her phone. She answered it before the call transferred to voice mail. "Carrie, are you all right?"

"I could use an aspirin, but besides that, I'm fine. Why do you sound worried?"

"Frank visited you last night." Sunny hated the way it sounded so blunt and rude, but Carrie deserved to know the truth.

"Oh, so he told you. Sunny, you need to quit worrying about me."

Her words sunk in and lit a fuse. Frank not only used Carrie for food or alcohol or whatever, he manipulated her mind, too. Jack appeared in the doorway as Sunny paced the small room. "Dang it, girl! How can you say that? You don't know what he's capable of."

"I know he cares about me. That's all that matters, so drop it. I called to warn you, anyway."

"I can't drop it, Carrie. I--What? What do you mean warn me? About what?"

Jack raised his eyebrows in surprise and appeared beside her in a flash. She held the phone out so he could hear, too.

"Your face has been plastered all over the news. Didn't you think your father would eventually find out?"

"So what if he does. It's not like he cares."

"He cares enough to send someone. The guy wouldn't leave until I told him where you were. I didn't think you wanted him to have your phone number, since you apparently haven't given it to your father."

If she had done that, she might be forced to talk to him. Or be yelled at. "Thanks, Carrie. We'll take care of him."

"And stay away from Frank. He hasn't done anything wrong. I asked him over last night after you left. If you want to remain my friend, I expect you to keep your nose out of our business."

Carrie's words stung and Sunny's chest tightened. She couldn't lose her best friend, but how could she look the other way? Jack gently squeezed her shoulder as if he understood her dilemma. "I don't want you to get hurt," she said.

"Right now the only person who's hurting me is you. I'm a big girl and Frank hasn't done anything to me that I haven't asked. So be my friend and butt out, okay?"

"Fine." Although she was anything but. Dang it. She hated giving in. If Frank gave her any cause, though…

"I mean it, Sunny. I love you like a sister, but this isn't your problem."

"All right. I get it. I'll leave him alone." Just saying the words left a bitter taste in her mouth.

"Thank you. I'm going to head on out to work. Let me know how it goes with your father's aide and I'll see you tonight, okay?"

"Yeah, I'll call you later." She disconnected the call and lowered her head.

Jack came behind her and massaged her shoulders. "I know how it looks, but Frank isn't a bad guy. Why don't you give him a chance to explain?"

"I can't do it right now. I'm sorry, but I just don't trust the man. And I don't see how you can, either. Are you sure he didn't turn me?"

"Frank may have issues, but I don't believe he'd stoop that low. If you must know, he's tried to get her to stop drinking. You have to face the fact, she's an alcoholic."

My Sunny Vampire

She couldn't believe that. Someone was lying and she'd get to the bottom of it. She turned around and wrapped her arms around Jack, the only person she trusted, the only one who mattered. "I can't stay here another day. I know he's your friend, but... Can we stay at the safe house tomorrow? Please?"

* * * *

Jack held Sunshine close, as if he could protect her from all the miseries she encountered. The pleading in her voice tugged at his heart. He couldn't blame her for disliking Frank. The man hadn't been at his best. But the safe house? "Yeah, about that. Harris is probably there."

"Harris? I thought he lived in the city."

"He used to. He moved away a couple of years ago."

She pulled back, her crystal blue eyes beseeching. "Then how about your place? You have a car, right? Can we get there in one night?"

He ran the back of his fingers along her cheek. "Sunshine, as much as I would like that, it wouldn't help in finding the person who turned you. He's probably still here."

"I don't care who turned me. I only want to be with you."

And he wanted to be with her, but at what price? If he didn't find the vampire responsible, he could possibly be charged with the crime.

Her eyes widened. "Oh, fudge. I didn't mean... I mean, I don't want..." She laid her forehead on his chest. "We can't leave until we find him, huh?"

"That would be the best thing, yeah." A chuckle escaped. "Although, I'm doing a pretty crappy job in locating the monster." Falling in love could be quite a distraction, but it was no excuse for his behavior. Maybe he should visit Harris and see what the bastard was up to. If only he could figure out a way to do that without Sunshine knowing.

"How well do you know Harris?" she asked.

Shit. Was she reading his mind? "Well enough. Why?" A chill ran down his spine. "Did he talk to you last night?"

"Yes, he told me--"

"Hey, Jack. Are you expecting company?" Frank asked from downstairs.

Sunshine groaned and met Jack's gaze. "Oh, man. I really don't want to deal with him. What should I do?"

Jack would rather hear what Harris told Sunshine, but first things first. "Why don't we see what he wants and then decide."

Chapter 22

The last time Jack had to associate with a young lady's father, he was courting Clara. Not that the businessman who stood on the porch was Sunshine's father, but for all intents and purposes, he played that role.

Sunshine opened the door a few inches. While the grey clouds offered no protection from the sun's harmful rays, the sun's angle and the porch roof kept her protected, so apparently she wasn't willing to offer the man entrance.

"May I help you?" she asked sweetly.

So, she was going to play it coy, huh?

The man shoved his hands inside his coat pockets and shivered as he kicked the snow off his shoes. "Sunny, you know who I am. Are you going to let me in?"

"Why should I?"

"So the whole world doesn't know our business?" He arched a thumb over his shoulder.

Sunshine poked her head out the door with Jack right behind her. Cameras aimed their way clicked frantically. He quickly pulled her back.

"Shit. What did you do? Advertise?" Jack rushed the young man inside and closed the door behind him.

"Hell, no. I was hoping to be discreet. They were already here when I arrived." He held out his hand. "By the way, I'm Gary Porter. I didn't catch your name."

"That's because I didn't throw it."

Gary frowned at his statement. Sunshine's attitude was starting to rub off. If Jack hoped to impress, he needed to behave. He took the offered hand and felt the warmth for a split moment until his body temperature matched Gary's, who most likely wouldn't notice the change. "I'm sorry, bad day. It's Jack. So what can we do for you?"

"I came to take Sunny home." Gary rubbed his hands together and turned toward her. "Although, I have to say, you look in better shape than I imagined. I thought you were burned."

She put a hand up to her face, flawless and beautiful as ever. No hint she'd ever had any kind of burn. "It was a…rash," she said. "So you see, there's nothing wrong with me. If Dad really cared, he would have come up here himself."

"Sunny, be reasonable. The media has been hounding your father for the last couple of days, ever since your picture showed up on the web. Don't you think you owe it to him--?"

Anger flashed in her eyes and she raised her hand, palm out, cutting him off. "I don't owe my father anything. I think we both know he just hates bad publicity. So go back and tell him I'm fine, or tell him you didn't find me. I don't care. I'm not going back to Jacksonville."

Gary shook his head. "I guess you haven't changed a bit. You never did consider how your actions would affect those close to you."

She narrowed her eyes, pursed her lips and clenched her hands. Jack held onto her shoulders, just in case she attacked. The woman certainly had a short fuse. "I didn't do anything wrong. I've never done anything wrong. Why don't you just go back to wherever you came from?"

"I don't think so. I didn't come all this way to be thrown out." He strolled into the living room as if he were invited and removed his coat. "It's freezing in here. Forget to pay the heating bill?"

The only reason the house had a heater at all was to keep the pipes from freezing and it was currently set at sixty. Without an appropriate warning of the visit, Jack hadn't had time to turn up the heat.

"We like to keep the cost down. Besides, isn't that what sweaters and quilts are for?" Of course, his excuse would hold more weight if he wore a sweater, but he and Sunshine both wore t-shirts.

"I guess." Gary slipped the coat back on. "So, what are your plans with the media? Are you going to make a statement?"

Jack wanted to manipulate Gary's mind, but it wouldn't get rid of the problem at hand. Too many people took pictures of him coming inside. And someone sent him. If Gary didn't leave on his own accord, he could be replaced and Jack wouldn't play that game. Eventually, Sunshine's supposed death would solve everything, but until then, Jack would have to deal with things manually. No way would he have Sunshine make a statement, but Gary didn't need to know that. "What kind of statement are you talking about?"

Gary looked at Sunshine as if she had asked the question. "For one, some seem to think you're a vampire. So maybe if you just went outside and told them there was a misunderstanding, that you walked out of the hospital of your own free will. You did walk out on your own, didn't you?" He glanced briefly at Jack. "No one coerced you?"

Breathing heavily through her nose, Sunshine's eyes widened and she grabbed onto Jack's arm. Her grip would probably leave marks, but he felt no pain. "No one coerced me and I will not go out there. I didn't do anything wrong."

"So you keep saying. For some reason I don't believe you. Is this man holding you against your will? Do I need to call the police?"

"How dare you. You think you can just come in here and threaten me?"

This was getting out of hand. One more accusation and Sunshine might do something rash. Jack needed to get rid of the guy. "Gary, you're not helping by upsetting her. Why don't you let her think about what you said? Do you have a number where we can reach you?"

Gary narrowed his eyes at Jack.

"I swear, I'm not holding her against her will."

Gary pulled a wallet out of his back pocket and fished out a business card. "My cell is listed. If I don't hear from you tonight, I will be back. With the police."

Even though Gary offered the card to Sunshine, Jack snatched it. "She'll call." She opened her mouth, ready to speak when he stared her down. "You'll call."

"We need to nip this in the bud before it gets any wilder. I mean, vampire? Really? What would even make them think such a thing?" Gary walked over to the door. "Do the right thing, Sunny. You owe it to your father."

When he opened the door, cameras clicked briefly before falling silent. Guess the photographers had enough pictures of Gary.

After the door shut, she turned toward Jack. "Why did you tell him I would call?"

"What the hell is going on out there?" Frank bellowed as he emerged from the basement stairwell. "The neighbors are going to have a field day."

Jack's legs felt limp, as if someone let the air out. He collapsed on the edge of the couch and cradled his head. One down and how many more to go? Acting spontaneously was not his forte. He much preferred to have a plan of action. "Someone tipped off the reporters."

"Do you think those two guys who attacked me this morning are responsible?"

He looked up at her. He hated worrying her any more than necessary. When he had carried her, after her stabbing, she had asked what was wrong. He'd heard a noise, but took it for a cat or neighbor. Could they have been followed? "I doubt it."

She sat beside him and took his hand. "What about Harris?"

"Beanie wouldn't do it," Frank said. "He's…well, he just wouldn't."

She glanced between him and Jack. "What if he thought one of you turned me?"

"Is that what Harris told you last night?" Jack asked. "He thought it was one of us?" Damn Harris. What kind of game was that man playing? No wonder she'd avoided his kiss. Harris had filled her with doubt.

"He might have mentioned it."

"What else did he mention?" Jack shuddered to think that Harris might have told her about Clara.

She averted her eyes. "Nothing. I told him he was nuts."

Jack wanted to relax, but her eyes told him she held back. She couldn't even look at him. But if Harris had told her about her resemblance to a certain woman, she'd say something. Wouldn't she?

My Sunny Vampire

"If Beanie thinks one of us turned you, then he'd tell the Committee, not the media," Frank said.

"Which is exactly what he threatened to do. Shit, like it matters now. If she's all over the news, they're bound to hear it." Jack leaned back onto the cushions. "Damn. I'm screwed."

"Don't say that." Sunshine cupped his face. "We just have to find out who called those reporters. If it wasn't Harris, then it has to be the vampire who turned me. Right? What other vampires are in the area?"

Her crystal blue eyes shone with hope and her hands were soft against his face. He took one hand and kissed the palm.

"She's got a point," Frank said. "If the vamp responsible didn't want to bring attention to himself, he could have called the media knowing the Committee would find out."

Meaning Harris could still be involved, covering his ass.

The hope on her face morphed into one of dread as she pouted. "Fudge."

Jack chuckled and hooked a stray hair behind her ear. "What brought that horrible curse word to your lips?"

"I just realized I'll have to talk to the media after all."

He sat up straight. "No you don't. I never intended for you to talk to them."

"You implied it with Gary."

"I was getting him off your case, but I never said you'd talk to the reporters."

"But if I can help--"

"No. That's not helping. We need to keep you out of the news."

An incessant ringing came from upstairs and Sunshine looked in its direction. "That's not my phone."

"Mine's here." Frank held one in his hand.

Jack patted his front pocket. Empty. Shit. Only one person could be calling him. But was he calling about Frank or Sunshine?

* * * *

Jack rushed upstairs and soon after his phone stopped ringing the door clicked closed. Why would he need privacy? Unless... Sunny looked at Frank. "Barnet?"

"That would be my guess."

Not good, but good, too. That meant Jack would be busy for a while. Now was her chance. She rose and put on her coat.

"What do you think you're doing?" Frank asked.

She pulled her hair out from underneath the coat and buttoned it up. "I'm going to talk to the press. They have to know who tipped them off."

"Didn't Jack just tell you he didn't want you in the news?"

"I'm not going to tell them anything. I just want to get information."

She walked to the door and stopped within two feet. Scratches and dents marred the surface, giving testament to its age. However old, this door stood as a barrier to the outside world, to the sun. Fear glued her feet to the floor. Why did she think she could do this? Hadn't she been out in the sun enough already? She was crazy.

No, no, no. The porch was safe. She must do this for him. For them.

The brass doorknob gleamed at her, daring her to turn it.

"I wouldn't do it if I were you," Frank said.

That was all the encouragement she needed. "Well, I'm not you."

Holding her head high, she opened the door and stepped onto the porch. She closed the door behind her, held her breath and leaned against the house. No burning, tingling sensation. Thank goodness. She let out the breath and loosened muscles she didn't realize she'd tightened. The dreary clouds blotted out the sun, but made the shadows barely discernible. Where could she stand and not get burned? Afraid to be a guinea pig, she stayed close to the house.

Cameras clicked away, but the mob stayed to the sidewalk. Guess they didn't want to be caught trespassing or they just didn't want to get their feet wet.

Sunny's mob turned out to be three reporters. Two women and one man were converged and huddled in the cold. They were dressed for the long haul, wearing caps, scarves and gloves. Cameras hung around their necks.

"Ms. Petersen, I'm with *Truth or Fiction?*. Can you answer a few questions?" a female reporter, wearing a light blue puffy jacket, asked.

"I'm with *Real Stories*," the man said. "Is your vampirism the reason your father sent you away?"

My Sunny Vampire

"The readers of *Bitten* would like to know how long you've been a vampire."

Tabloid reporters. Fudge. Maybe Jack was right. Maybe she shouldn't have come out here.

* * * *

Jack pulled the phone out of his other jeans, still damp from the snow angels he and Sunshine had made earlier. "Hey, Barnet," he said as he closed the door to the bedroom. Not that the door would prevent the other occupants of the house from hearing, but it would make them more honest.

"Hello, Jack. I'm surprised you haven't called back."

"I'm sorry about that. I haven't had much private time."

"I take it the news isn't good?"

Jack looked at the door. Frank eavesdropped earlier and the door to the bathroom had been shut. What would stop him from doing it again? "Yes and no. I can't get into it now. I'll try and send an e-mail tonight. I might be able to locate a computer."

"You're not at the safe house?"

"No. I'm staying with Frank. The safe house doesn't have a working computer, either. If I recall, you didn't think it was worth replacing."

"That's because most everyone else has those smarter phones."

"You mean smart phones, don't you?" Jack was lucky his cell took pictures, let alone searched the internet and Barnet had been known to disintegrate his whenever he lost his temper.

Barnet chuckled. "Whatever they're called. Can't blame you for not having one. I can't stand them myself. Guess I'll just have to wait for your e-mail. But Frank's not the only reason I called, though."

Jack's heart skipped a couple of beats. Uh-oh. Did Harris go through with his threat? If so, wouldn't Barnet have led with that bit of information?

"I'm not sure how much news you've been watching, and since you don't have the internet, maybe you don't know. We've seen stories about a woman in the Pittsburgh area labeled 'Vampire Girl.'"

Jack sighed in relief and his heart slowed to normal. So far so good. He wouldn't have to lie. "I've seen the stories, too. I'm checking into it."

"Did you notice anything unusual about the woman?"

"The only reports I saw were of her being transported on a gurney to the hospital." And that was also the truth. He hadn't seen any other stories since, although he was sure there were plenty out there, especially with the reporters camped outside. Once Barnet saw their pictures, Jack would no doubt be in trouble.

"When you see her, you might want to prepare yourself."

Okay, here it comes. "Prepare myself?"

The door to the bedroom burst open and Frank stood in the doorway. "Your girlfriend just went outside."

All the air left Jack's body, as if he'd been hit with a sucker-punch. What the hell did she think she was doing?

"Jack," Barnet said. "Did he say girlfriend?"

Shit. Jack plopped down on the bed. There was no escape. What other word could be mistaken for girlfriend? "I need to call you back."

"What's going on? Is everything okay?"

"I'll explain later. I gotta go." He disconnected the call and stared at the phone. Sunshine was out talking to reporters and he'd just hung up on the Head of the Committee. Imaginary walls crumbled down upon him. How would he ever get out of this mess unscathed?

Chapter 23

Jack rushed down the stairs. Of all the stupid, idiotic things she could do, talking to the media made the top of the list. With clenched teeth, he swung open the door. The sky was a dreary grey, but it did nothing to keep the snow from glaring and stinging his eyes. He squinted and raised his arm against the annoying light while his eyes adjusted. "Get in here, now."

Sunshine's hair flew like a red banner as the wind whipped across the porch. She turned at the sound of his voice.

"Ms. Petersen. Who are you talking to? Is he another vampire?" A female reporter wearing a black parka held up a recorder, as did the others, waiting for an answer.

"Dammit, Sunshine. What did you tell them?" He should go out on that porch and drag her ass inside. Unfortunately, that would instigate more pictures.

She smiled at the reporters and stepped back toward him, keeping her gaze forward. "Take it easy, I haven't said anything to them. They're only speculating," she said from the corner of her mouth.

Jack took the opportunity of her closeness and reached out for her arm. No need to cause any suspicion with the media. Just a couple more inches.

Click, swoosh.

The arrow struck him in the left shoulder. Sharp, shooting pain ran down his arm. Blood bloomed on his shirt. Shit. Who the hell shot him? As if on cue, the reporters turned toward the street, probably wondering the same thing.

"Damn it, I told you to hit the girl," a man whispered from across the street.

"I tried, stupid," another man answered.

"What the heck was that? Who's trying to hit me?" Sunshine looked over her shoulder at Jack. Her eyes widened. "Oh my God! Are you okay?"

Click, swoosh.

"Get down!" Jack tugged at her arm, but it was too late. The arrow found its target.

She arched her back and cried out. "Fudge! What's going on? Who's shooting at us?"

That's what Jack wanted to know. The reporters scrambled and ran toward their vehicles. One way to get rid of them. Of course, one of them could end up calling the police. Just another complication he didn't need.

Silence settled upon them once the cameras disappeared. Jack scanned the area. Somewhere their shooter was hiding, but where? If it was night out, he'd be over there finding the fiend, but right now he felt like a target on a shooting range. He went to help Sunshine.

Click. Swoosh.

The arrow struck him, piercing his lung. Goddammit. He inhaled to yell, but sharp pains shot through his chest, as if his lung was filled with shards of glass. Coughing up blood, he lost his balance and fell to his knees. Sunshine composed herself and grabbed him under his arms, lifting and dragging him toward the door.

Click. Swoosh.

She screamed, loosening her grip. He landed on his back and she fell to the side. Two arrows protruded out of her back.

Frank stood behind the door. "Where are they coming from?"

"A...cross...the...street." Jack had never had such trouble speaking before. Each word gurgled in pure agony.

Frank crawled on his stomach toward Jack and extended an arm. Jack grabbed hold with his right hand. As he was pulled to safety, Sunshine followed on her hands and knees.

Click. Swoosh. Thump.

An arrow hit the side of the house. An inch closer and it would have pierced her head.

"It has to be Tom and Shorty. It just has to. If I ever get my hands on those bozos, they won't see tomorrow," she muttered as she inched her way inside.

Frank closed the door, but they were far from safe. A siren wailed in the distance.

"Fudge. What are we going to do?" Her hand went up her back, but she couldn't reach the wood.

Jack went into survival mode. Mind control worked best in minor situations, but this was escalating into something major. With witnesses possibly recording the event, Jack must make the scene appear innocent. If he couldn't get this under control now, the mess would only get bigger and then the Committee would definitely become involved.

"Remove...arrows. Frank...help her?" Blood sprayed from his mouth and talking was almost impossible. He sat up and examined the wood--plain, no ornamentation. In fact, the arrows looked similar to the stake those bastards had used on Sunshine. He pulled the one out of his shoulder. It came free easily enough, but hurt more coming out than it did going in. He inhaled on instinct, causing a painful, bloody coughing fit. The stake clattered on the floor as he grabbed at his chest. Damn, it felt like he was coughing up his lung.

Frank saw the simplicity of the arrows and went to Sunshine. "Hold still while I pull these out."

In all the years since Jack's turning, he'd never been staked. He'd been stabbed with a saber during the Revolutionary War, but he'd been mortal and the memory of that pain long gone. Now he could appreciate what Sunshine had gone through when he pulled the wood out of her heart. The memory of this pain would likely stay with him forever. What he wouldn't give to never have this experience.

Once the coughing subsided, he grabbed the arrow in his chest and pulled. He screamed profanities as sharp pains spread across his chest. Blood seeped through the two holes of his t-shirt and met, making one large spot. Painful cramps flitted across his stomach. He flopped back to the floor, too exhausted to sit up any longer.

The siren was getting louder.

* * * *

Sunny put her brow to the floor and lay still while Frank removed the arrows. Ouch, ouch and double-ouch. What was with all the staking, or did she just get lucky that way? While her coat offered her some protection and prevented the stakes from penetrating too deeply, it didn't stop them from causing major pain. She could just strangle those two idiots, shooting at her like some target at a carnival. She'd like to give them a prize they'd never forget.

Jack cussed words that burned her ears as he ripped the arrow from his chest. So much blood. From his mouth. From his chest. The front of his shirt became one big red mess. Guilt crushed her. She'd done this to him. All because she thought she could help. When would she learn to think before acting?

"Can you stand?" Frank asked her.

"I'm okay." She made it to her knees and stopped. Her back no longer throbbed, but a cramp skittered across her abdomen. Was it possible she didn't protect herself enough in the shade? Or was it from being shot? She reached back under her shirt. Blood wasn't dripping down her back and she relaxed. She had lost some, but not nearly the amount Jack had.

Frank went over to Jack and helped him up. "We don't have much time. The cops will be here soon. You got a plan?"

"Go on upstairs and get me a clean shirt."

While Jack's voice had lost the gurgling sound, he sounded bossy, using the tone she recognized as his Committee voice. Frank had no problem following orders, he dashed up the stairs without an argument.

She unbuttoned the top button of her coat.

"Keep your coat on," Jack said. "And whatever you do, do not turn your back on them. We can't have them thinking we were hit."

"If we weren't hit, what were we then?" she asked. "Won't they see the stakes?"

"I'll take care of the stakes, but it will be easier if I don't have to cover up everything." Slowly, he lifted his t-shirt, but only reached mid-chest before he stopped and winced.

She hated seeing him hurt. She scooted over to him and eased his arms out from the sleeves before lifting it over his head. She cleaned off the blood on his mouth and chin. He took the shirt and wiped his chest, unveiling his wounds. They puckered, but were no

My Sunny Vampire

longer bleeding. She reached out, planning to touch them, but stopped, afraid of hurting him more. Sadness overcame her, causing her eyes to ache with unshed tears.

"I'm so sorry, Jack. I'm such an idiot."

He took her hand and kissed the palm. "You didn't know. How are you doing?"

"Better than you, I think." She rose and the room remained steady, a good sign.

Frank returned with a shirt and he and Sunny helped Jack put it on. He didn't cry out, but she could see the pain in his eyes.

The siren cut off as a car pulled up outside. Dang it. They weren't ready.

"Sunshine, pick up the stakes. Frank, help me up and take me to the couch."

As she picked up the arrows, someone knocked on the front door. Fudge. She jumped and dropped the pieces of wood. They clattered and skittered across the floor. Her heartbeat kicked up a few notches and her nerves were fried.

"Come here, sweetheart." Jack patted the cushion on his right.

Frank helped pick up the arrows and handed them to her. She ran to Jack and sat beside him. Just being close to him gave her some strength.

He put his arm around her shoulders. "It's okay if you look scared. Just don't say anything, okay?"

That wouldn't be too hard. She wasn't sure any coherent words would come out of her mouth anyway. "What about the stakes?"

He took them and nodded to Frank. How was he able to keep his cool when she felt ready to burst out of her skin?

"Hey." Jack touched her cheek. "It'll be okay. I promise."

Easy for him to say. He'd probably done this a hundred times.

Another knock sounded. Frank opened the door.

"We heard there was a disturbance here. Did someone get shot?" The visitor spoke as if he'd gargled one too many razor blades.

"Not quite. Come on in officer."

He wore the standard policeman uniform, but with the addition of a jacket. Cops always seemed to be loaded for anything--walkie-talkie, baton, gun. Sunny had never cared for the police. They always seemed to take her father's side and never hers. Suddenly, she felt like a teenager in trouble. Her heart thumped wildly in her chest and her breathing became erratic. Jack gave her shoulder a gentle squeeze, but now even his presence wasn't helping.

The cop came inside and Frank leaned against the wall, keeping out of the way. "Hello, sir, ma'am. I'm Officer Stanton. Can you tell me what happened here today? From the calls we received, it sounded like you were under attack."

Jack laughed. "I guess it would seem that way. Please, sit." As the officer removed his hat and took the chair, Jack continued, "Apparently someone shot some plastic darts at us. As you can see, they are harmless. While we were scared at first, no one was hurt."

Stanton picked up one of the bloody stakes and examined it. Jack must be sending a visual message, but the officer looked unfazed. No glazed-over eyes. No zombie look. Man, how did Jack do that?

"Do you wish to press charges?" Stanton placed the arrow on the table.

"No. I'm sure whoever it was is long gone by now."

The cop stared at her. "Why do you look familiar?"

She glanced at Jack. He smiled and nodded. Guess she didn't have to keep quiet after all. A lump formed in her throat and she swallowed. "Umm, I'm Sunshine Petersen?" She didn't mean for it to sound like a question.

Officer Stanton shook his head. "I don't know who that is."

"She's the governor's daughter," Jack said. The cop still looked confused. "Of Florida. You know, vampire girl?"

The cop's eyes lit up at those words. "Oh, you're her. You look better than I pictured. Weren't you burned or something?"

Sunny couldn't answer. Her lying abilities left a lot to be desired, especially when scared out of her wits.

Jack answered for her. "She had an allergic reaction. As you can see, she's fine."

"I guess that kind of explains what happened here, doesn't it? But wouldn't they have used wooden stakes?"

Jack shrugged. "You'd think, huh? Problem is, we didn't think anyone but her father knew she was here. Now we're being hounded by the media and freaks who think vampires live here. Maybe you can relay to the nice reporters out there that she's not a vampire, so they will go home and leave us alone."

"I can try, but won't guarantee anything. I've learned that reporters won't leave until they're ready to leave." Stanton rose and replaced the hat on his head. "If you're not going to press charges, there's nothing for me to do here."

Jack thanked him for coming and Frank showed him to the door. Once it clicked shut, Jack doubled over. "I didn't think he would ever leave."

She wrapped an arm around his back and leaned with him. "Why didn't you keep him here to feed from?"

"I didn't want him here any longer than necessary, especially since we're being watched."

Frank sat in the chair. "How bad is it?"

Jack lifted his head and smiled at Sunny. "To quote a famous redhead, 'like I've been staked.'"

He meant it as a joke, she was sure of it, but deep down her heart weighed heavy at his words. She pulled away and covered her face. "I'm so sorry."

"Hey, this isn't your fault," Jack said.

"How do you figure that?" Frank asked. "She went outside when you told her not to."

"The reporters didn't shoot us. Those men who staked her did. I'm sure they would have attacked tonight when we left to feed." Jack pulled her head down onto his shoulder. "This isn't your fault, Sunshine. If anyone is at fault, it's me. I thought I heard something this morning and didn't check it out."

"So what do we do now? I can't bear to see you suffer until nightfall." She wasn't feeling too perky herself, but she certainly wouldn't tell him that. Small cramps flitted across her stomach and it would only take an hour or so before they caused her enough pain to double over.

"Frank, how many people can you control at a time?"

"Two, if I'm not distracted. Why?"

"I think we may need to invite the reporters inside."

Chapter 24

"Why don't we go upstairs and take a shower?" Jack leaned over and kissed her on the cheek. "I know I'm feeling a little sticky."

Sunny sat on the couch criss-cross-style, with her arms folded across her chest. She didn't want to take a shower. Well, she did, it felt like someone had glued her shirt to her back, but she would do it on her own terms, not his. Ever since those reporters came inside, she'd been practically invisible to Jack. She had offered to help, but he refused her services and Frank just went along with him.

"Why wouldn't you let me help? You keep saying I need practice to get better, but if you won't let me help, how am I supposed to get better?"

"Sweetheart." His condescending tone only inflamed her more. "Now wasn't a good time. When there's one person, then you can practice. You can always practice with Carrie, too. I'm sure she wouldn't mind."

"Hmmpf. I don't plan on feeding from Carrie. You could have let me try to control the woman I fed from."

"How many times do I have to tell you? I wasn't in any shape to help you if you lost control."

"No, but Frank was here. You keep telling me I'm not broken, but you act just the opposite. I think you don't want me to get better."

"That's not true."

My Sunny Vampire

She stood. "Could have fooled me. I'm going upstairs to take a shower. Alone."

* * * *

Sunshine stormed up the steps and seconds later a door slammed. The walls and windows shook as if a small earthquake hit. Jack shook his head. What the heck was her problem? "Damn, I hope she didn't crack the drywall." Frank glanced up at the ceiling. "She has quite a temper, doesn't she?"

"I'd worry more about the door frame. You'd think I'd done something wrong."

Frank plopped down on the chair and laughed. "You did plenty wrong. You took over everything, just like you always do. She's right, too. I could have helped her. Why didn't you want her trying?"

Jack lowered his head. "It's not that. Her powers are unpredictable. I hate seeing her struggle, or seeing her discouraged. It breaks my heart."

"She's never going to get better if you keep taking over. Sure, she'll make mistakes. Isn't that how we learn? Did you ever think that maybe you're the cause of her inconsistencies?"

"Me? I've done nothing but help her."

"Yeah, and you're a huge crutch. Face it, you like how she depends on you, don't you?"

Ah, hell. He couldn't deny it. Ever since he declared his love, he'd stopped teaching and started doing. Was it because a tiny part of him loved being needed? He didn't want her to fail or see her get hurt, but in the process he'd done just that.

"She's not Clara," Frank whispered. "Do you think Sunny will leave you if she no longer needs you? If you do, you're blind. That woman is in love with you."

"When did you become such an expert?"

"Since Linda." Pain flashed in Frank's eyes. He stood and went into the kitchen.

"Frank." Jack followed his friend.

He hadn't been in the kitchen since Linda's death. She had hated leaving the spaces intended for the refrigerator and stove barren and had filled those areas with racks of plants. Now the racks stood like skeletons. He touched the small square table, surrounded by four chairs. He had played cards with Frank, Linda and Linda's pick of the month--so sure she'd eventually find Jack a mate--many times on that same table, but now it seemed lonely and out of place. Frank stood in front of the back door and toyed with the blinds, which were currently closed. An awning prevented any sun from filtering inside, but the snow made it too bright.

"She would have loved Sunny because you love her," Frank said. "I always thought her one goal in life was to get you hitched."

Jack smiled at the memory. "She did try her darndest. You still miss her a great deal, don't you?"

"She was the love of my life. I think I died a little with her on that day."

"Is that when you started drinking?" Jack regretted the words, but the truth was Frank hadn't been the same since Linda's death. Not that Jack blamed him.

Frank spun around, rolling his eyes. "How many times do I have to tell you I don't have a drinking problem?"

"Something is wrong, then. Do you think Linda would be happy with the way you've been acting since her death?"

"Probably not."

"You're not cheating on her with Carrie. You know that, don't you?"

Frank turned his back to Jack. "It feels like it, though."

Jack came up to Frank and put a hand on his back. "Linda would want you to be happy."

"I know." He sighed heavily. "I like Carrie, I really do. But I don't want to forget Linda, either. And if you're smart, you'll go and apologize to Sunny. I believe you have something with her like I did with Linda. You can't screw that up, Jack. It's too rare."

Leave it to Frank to flip the subject back to Jack. "You have to stop beating yourself up, too. God, we're a couple of imbeciles."

"Yeah, well, you're a bigger one than me. Have you told her about Clara? Have you told her anything?"

"No. She wouldn't understand."

"What about that picture you carry around in your wallet? Aren't you afraid she'll see it?"

"I took it out, and a good thing, too. She found my wallet the other day and I'm sure she went through it."

"Jack, you can't base your relationship on a lie."

"I'm not lying to her. I'm only omitting information."

"Same difference. Have you told her you love her?"

"Yes."

My Sunny Vampire

"Good. Now show her. Words mean nothing if you don't follow through."

Frank made sense, but Jack wasn't sure what kind of relationship he could have with Sunshine if she suspected he had an ulterior motive to turn her. No, he couldn't tell her everything about Clara. Not yet. Not until he found the person responsible for her turning. If he was the one responsible, their relationship was already doomed.

"Go on up there," Frank said. "I'll be okay. Guess I have some of my own thinking to do."

Jack might not be able to tell her about Clara, but he could certainly apologize. He left his friend standing in the kitchen and rushed up the stairs, taking two steps at a time. The door to the bathroom loomed in front of him. Sure enough, tiny cracks trailed along the wood frame. He would have to make sure to repair the damage since he was basically the cause. Fully expecting to hear the sound of a shower running, he frowned at the silence. Well, not totally silent. Muted sobbing came from the other side of the door.

Each hitch in her throat pierced his heart. He did this to her. He caused her grief. All because he wanted to protect her. Some protector he was.

He opened the door. She was sitting in the tub, her back to him. If her plans included taking a shower, it might have helped if she had turned on the water or even undressed. She still wore her coat.

Sunshine looked over her shoulder at the click of the door closing. Her dry eyes turned to slits when she spotted him. "Get out. I don't want to see you right now."

"That's too bad 'cause I'm not going anywhere."

She stood. "Fine. You stay. I'll leave."

He placed a hand on her shoulder and pushed her back down into the tub. "You're not going anywhere until we talk."

She shrugged his hand away and stared at the wall. "I don't want to talk."

He sat on the floor beside the tub, facing her. "Okay, then listen. You're right. It wasn't my intent, but apparently I have been holding you back. Not because I don't want you to get better. But because..." Damn it, nothing he could say would soften the blow.

"Because you don't think I will get better," she finished. "Is that it?"

"It's wrong of me to think that. You've only been a vampire for four days. I have to remind myself of that."

"But if you think it, then maybe it's true." She brought her knees up and rested her head on top.

"No, I won't believe that. Tell you what. When we go out tonight, you choose the donor. We'll pretend you're on your own. I'll stay out of it."

"But what if--"

"No buts. I'll stay out. I promise. You'll be on your own." Of course, he would intervene if she was truly in trouble. He would have to make sure she didn't notice. "I'm so sorry, Sunshine. I screwed up. If you would prefer Frank went with you instead, I'd understand."

She leapt out of the tub and tackled him, smothering his face with kisses. "I don't want Frank, I want you. I'll always want you."

While he loved her enthusiasm, his chest still hurt and he gritted his teeth. She attempted to pull away, but he held her close. If he could hold her forever, he would. The pain be damned.

"I'm hurting you." She squirmed in his arms.

"You won't if you hold still."

He brushed her silky tresses back from her face. His lips found hers and he softly kissed her. She opened up, inviting him inside and he obliged, tasting the sweetness that was all her.

He needed to get them out of these blasted clothes. "Can we take that shower now?"

* * * *

Sunny stood still in the tub, away from the shower spray. Jack rubbed the soapy washcloth over her back, being especially gentle around her wounds. His touch set her on fire. If her injuries hurt, she couldn't tell.

Nuzzling her neck, he brought the washcloth around to her front and cleaned her breasts in lazy strokes while embracing her with his other arm. Even Little Jack made his presence known, rubbing up against her backside.

"Are you finished?" she asked. "Is it my turn to clean you?"

He rubbed his chest against her back, slipping over the soapy skin. "Nah, I'm good."

She turned around and laughed. Pink-tinged soap suds clung to his skin, but he was far from clean. "Give that to me." She snatched the wash cloth from his hand and shook her head.

My Sunny Vampire

Chuckling, he stood still while she scrubbed away the blood. Well, most of him stood still.

"You need to go lower," he said.

Lower, huh? His desire bobbed up and down, but he could wait. Doing her best not to smile and playing it as innocent as she could, she ran the cloth down to his abdomen and stopped. "Here?"

"Lower."

She moved the cloth down an inch. A laugh tried to escape, but she squelched it.

"You wench." He took the washcloth and dropped it in the tub.

Unable to hold it any longer, she snorted. Shaking his head, he grabbed her shoulders and turned her around, pulling her in close. Little Jack nudged her, creating a fire in her belly. If she bent forward he'd take her, she just knew it. Before she could suggest it, he wrapped an arm around her waist and walked them under the shower spray, washing off the soap. He pulled her hair to the side. His lips skimmed the spot between her neck and shoulder and she tilted her head, giving him better access. His breath electrified her skin.

"I love the way you smell. Like roses. I always thought it was a perfume, but it's not. It's just you."

"It's not me, it's the soap, silly."

He sniffed at his shoulder and then came back to her, breathing deep. "Nope. Definitely you, sweetheart." His hand slid over her stomach, going lower, not quite touching her sex. Her breath sped up. "Give me a kiss," he said.

She turned her head and his lips covered hers. Passionate. Possessive. No one had ever claimed her before, she'd never let them. But his kisses told her she was his, no one else's.

His tongue invaded her mouth, and he reached down and rubbed her clit. Like an electrical charge, desire surged through her body. Her breath hitched and her heart slammed against her ribs. He continued to rub her, delving deeper. Her body tightened, riding the waves he created with each stroke. Using his free hand, he teased a nipple. Spasms ripped through her body and she threw her head back, breaking the kiss.

"I love watching you come." He kissed her throat as she continued to shudder.

Before she could recover, he bent her over his arm, supporting her. She was primed for him and he slipped inside, filling her up. The sensation of him thrusting while she was still in the throes of an orgasm made her clench even tighter. He found just the right spot to rub and brought her to the pinnacle again. The orgasm caught her off balance. She slipped in the tub and reached out for support, grabbing the first thing she came in contact with. The rings of the shower curtain clanged against the rod and the material ripped, but Jack held her tight.

Two times in a matter of minutes. Definitely a record for her.

He continued to pound into her and she relished each thrust. She could easily see coming a third time if he could hold out. Didn't seem probable, though. His breath came in bursts and he grunted. She reached between her legs and stroked his balls, they tightened at her touch.

"Oh Sunshine, I love you." His climax came like an explosion. He grabbed her hips and buried himself deep inside her. When he started to relax, she straightened up and brought his arms around her, hugging him tight.

"I love you, too. I hope it's like this forever." Their forever might not be very long, though. Even if he wasn't found guilty of turning her, he could grow tired of her, just like every other man in her life had. That thought made her heart heavy. She couldn't lose him. Not when she'd finally found the one.

* * * *

Jack rested his chin on her shoulder and kissed her cheek. He caught a snippet of her thoughts about forever not being very long, and knew she was sad. However, her words held more meaning. "You'd want to spend forever with me?"

Sunshine lowered her head. "Only if you'd want me."

His heart warmed. Oh, he wanted. He wanted very much. Didn't she know that? "Where is this coming from? Why would you think I don't want you?"

"Because I've made your life a mess since I've come into it. I know how much you enjoy the sex, but--"

"You're more than sex to me. I thought you knew that."

"Well, you seem to have the need to protect me. Maybe when I'm more independent--"

"Stop. Yes, it's true, I like protecting you. I don't want you to get hurt."

"I don't need protecting, Jack. I don't want you to feel an obligation."

"Sunshine, I don't feel obligated." He let out an exasperated breath. Damn, the woman certainly knew how to twist things around.

"I also frustrate you. You might grow tired of that."

He squeezed her. "I could never grow tired of you, Sunshine. I love you. I'll say it a hundred times if it'll get you to believe me. I love you. All parts of you."

She turned her head and gazed at him with doubt on her face.

"Why?"

Why would anyone not love her? He brought a hand up and cupped her face. "You're wild. Carefree. I've never known anyone like you. You've opened this old heart of mine. I didn't think I'd ever find love again."

"Are you telling me there hasn't been anyone since your wife?"

"I won't deny I've been with many women, but do you know how many I told I loved?"

She frowned and shook her head.

He turned her around and placed his brow against hers. "Two."

Her eyes widened. "Two?"

"Yes. Clara...and you."

She hugged him and placed her cheek against his. "You must have lived a lonely life."

He'd never thought it was lonely. Now he couldn't imagine his life without her. "The past doesn't matter. What matters is now."

"I want now to last forever, though." She sighed and her breath felt like feathers against his skin. "But I know better."

Jack continued to block his thoughts. She sounded melancholy. Probably thinking about what their future held, if they had a future. Could he trust the Committee to help him find the vampire who turned her or would they just condemn him? He'd been with them for over a hundred years. In all that time, they'd never been given the opportunity to show compassion. The guilt evident, the guilty punished. Jack would be the first under circumstantial evidence. It wasn't a risk he was willing to take. Not if it meant losing her.

"You're awfully quiet," she said, looking up at him. "You're going to have to teach me that."

"Teach you what? How to keep your mouth shut?" He ran a finger down her lips and smiled, to let her know he was joking.

She laughed. "No, and good luck, there. I mean blocking your thoughts. I figure that's what you must do. I rarely ever hear them."

He reached back and turned off the shower. Their private time was over and he didn't need to run up Frank's water bill. "Blocking thoughts consistently takes practice, but you've been improving. Your thoughts aren't coming across like they used to. I only catch snippets."

"So you're saying I probably won't be able to do it, is that it?"

He moved the part of the shower curtain still hanging and stepped out of the tub. He grabbed two towels and handed one to her. "No. I'm saying with more practice…"

"I'm probably the only vampire who's ever had to do that." She pouted as she dried herself off.

"I wouldn't know. I'm not that old." He tossed the wet towel on the floor.

"Not that old? But you were turned in 1778, right? Oh never mind. I don't think I want to know." She wrapped the towel around her and stepped out of the tub. Then she picked up his towel and draped it over the shower rod. "So, if you don't mind me asking, who called you earlier? Before I was stupid enough to think I could get answers from the media?"

Shit. Barnet. He'd completely forgotten about him. "Nobody important."

"Committee business, huh? I guess you haven't told them about me, yet?"

No, no, no. He wasn't having this conversation with her. He walked to the door, avoiding eye contact.

She grabbed his arm. "Did I say something wrong?"

Say? No. Do? Yes. He kept his gaze on the knob. "No, of course not."

She lowered her arm. "If it concerns me, shouldn't I know?"

"Who said it concerned you?"

"Because you're acting all defensive. Geez, Jack. I'm not fragile, you know. I'm a big girl. If you have bad news, spill it. I can take it."

He could tell her part of the conversation. "If you must know, Barnet Groves, the Committee Head, saw the vampire girl story."

"So he knows about me?"

My Sunny Vampire

"Only what he saw on the news. He called to have me check it out. Then I lied to him. I lied and hung up on him, and it makes me sick to think what kind of trouble I can be in." That, and the fact Harris hadn't said anything yet. What was that guy up to anyway?

"You hung up on him? Why?"

"Because that's when Frank decided to tell me that my girlfriend went outside to talk to the media." The words came out harsher than he intended. The look of horror on her face made him feel like a tiny man. "Sunshine, I'm sorry. I didn't mean to make it sound like it was your fault."

She walked to the toilet and sat. "But it is my fault."

He knelt in front of her. "No, sweetheart, no. I panicked. It was my fault."

"You? Panicked? But you were so calm with the police officer and the reporters. I didn't think anything got to you."

He sat back on his legs. "I've had more experience dealing with mortals than explaining my personal life to Barnet. What I did with them I did on autopilot."

"So, what are you going to do? Are you going to call him back?"

What could he say? That he knew all about the vampire girl and was dating her? Not likely. "I haven't thought that far ahead. Guess I expected to find out more by now."

"Do you think you could try going through my memories again?"

"What would that accomplish? I didn't get anything of value."

"Yeah, but that was before."

"Before? Before what?"

"Before us." She wagged her finger between them. "I was so afraid of getting too close. Afraid of boinking you. Maybe I held back. You can try again, can't you? What do we have to lose?"

He laughed. "Boinking? Where do you come up with these words?"

"Hey, I didn't make that one up."

He stood and offered his hand. "Hell, who's to say we don't end up 'boinking' after I try again, huh?"

She took his hand and smiled. "That's the spirit."

219

Chapter 25

Sunny removed her towel and placed it on the dresser as Jack closed the bedroom door. Getting staked and shot was ruining her clothes. She sifted through the pile on the floor, snatched her backpack and sat on the bed.

Looking inside, she found only one pair of underwear. "I need to do some laundry. Blood comes out in cold water, right?"

"I think they're beyond the laundry. You should throw them in the trash." Jack stretched out on the bed and patted the mattress. "Don't bother getting dressed. Come up here and lay down."

She crawled to him. "What am I going to do for clothes? I don't have anything else clean to wear. You expect me to just walk around in the buff all day?"

"Hmmm, why not? I can always blindfold Frank."

Settling in next to him, she draped a leg over his and an arm over his waist. One of her favorite places to be. Little Jack stirred. "You'd like me naked all the time, now, wouldn't you?"

"Well, yeah. I'm a guy, aren't I?"

She would think with all the sex they just had that neither one of them would be interested, but heck, with Jack, she was always interested. Apparently, he felt the same since Little Jack rose a fraction of an inch. But sex would have to come later. Even though he'd never admit it, she was sure he was in trouble with the Committee.

"Maybe we should cover up." She jumped off the bed and tugged on the sheets. "Get up."

My Sunny Vampire

"Why?" When she pointed at his growing penis, he rolled his eyes and climbed off the bed. "Covering up isn't going to stop me wanting you."

"That's nice to know sweetie, but it can't hurt."

They slipped in between the sheets and she settled back in against him.

"Now, how is this any different?" he asked as the sheet slowly tented.

"If it isn't any different to you, then why are you complaining?" Of course, he did have a point. She molded her body next to his, enjoying the feel of his muscles. At least she couldn't see him, and that did help some. "Now, what do you need me to do?"

"Just remember that night, like you did the last time."

"Okay." Something occurred to her and she sat up. "Before we start, why is it that my memory before turning is fuzzy, but every memory since is remembered in detail? Was it because I was drunk?"

He shook his head. "Most mortals don't retain every detail. Therefore, the memory seems fuzzy because you only remembered the important parts. When you became a vampire, you were gifted with a photographic memory."

"Wouldn't that mean you have a memory of that night?"

"It should, but I'm not getting anything. That only tells me that whatever I ingested interfered with my ability to remember."

There had to be a way. He was awake that night. "Could someone help you remember?"

"Maybe, but I'd rather figure this out on my own."

"Can I help you remember?"

He smiled and smoothed her hair away from her face. "There are only a handful of vampires with the skill to dig. I'd rather not get them involved right now."

Dig? That sounded painful. She had a feeling her first encounter with the Committee wouldn't go well. They certainly didn't seem to have any compassion.

Jack rubbed her back. "Sunshine, relax. It'll be okay. I have faith we'll find the person."

His touch was soothing and she hadn't even realized she'd gotten tense. She took a deep breath and settled in once again. "I'll start at the beginning, when Carrie and I got to the bar."

Sunny replayed the memory in her head.

She and Carrie entered the crowded club. Carrie saw a friend and stopped. Sunny headed for the bar. Three men hit on her before she reached it. The third one offered his stool. She declined to dance with all of them.

"You stole his stool and then rejected him?"

"I didn't steal his stool, he gave it to me. Besides, my feet hurt. Carrie made me wear those stupid heels. Do any of them look familiar?"

He chuckled. "No. Go on."

Sunny was chatting with the bartender when Carrie tapped her on the shoulder. "I'm going dancing," she said, placing her handbag on the bar where Sunny could watch it. She headed to the dance floor with a blond-haired gentleman.

"Did you get a better look at him?"

The music turned to something slow and the man pulled Carrie close. She laid her head against his chest. During the whole dance, the man faced Sunny twice.

"Was your eyesight bad? His face is fuzzy."

"There was nothing wrong with my eyesight. Cigarette smoke does make them burn, maybe that's what happened."

"How long was she gone?"

"Just the dance. See? She came back alone."

"*That was quick,*" Sunny said. "*Didn't you like him?*"

Carrie ordered a beer. "He smelled like Juicy Fruit. I prefer my men to smell manly. So, are you just going to sit here all night? We could have done that at my apartment."

"*Maybe I'm just waiting for Mr. Right.*"

"I can't believe you said that," Jack said.

She couldn't either. "Can I make stuff up? If so, I'll change the line."

He smiled. "I bet you would. So why were you just sitting there? That doesn't seem like you."

"You're right. It didn't seem like me. Do you think someone programmed me to wait for you?"

"If it was all set up like I suspect, then yes."

She shuddered. "Someone controlled me? Can you tell who? When?"

He rubbed her back again. "Not unless I happened to be accessing that particular memory. It'd be like finding a needle in a haystack. Quit worrying. No one can manipulate your mind anymore. Go on, what happened next?"

My Sunny Vampire

She took a deep breath.

Carrie took a long swig of her beer. "That's a laugh. How do you expect to find him sitting on your butt? I thought you wanted to have fun. There's lots of guys in here just waiting to hook up." She pointed animatedly. "How about him? Or him?" Her hand knocked over a drink, spilling the contents. Carrie hustled to pick up the ice cubes.

Jack placed his hand on her arm. "Wait. I saw that."

"You were there then?"

"Yes. We'd just arrived. Shortly after, Frank and I went out to feed."

She looked up at him. "That's when you drank from Bobby? Why'd you do that? I get the feeling that's not normal for you."

"It's not, but Frank thought it would help me relax and it seemed like a good idea at the time."

"Dang. Was I that scary?"

He looked away for a second. "Maybe I was afraid you'd turn me down like all those other guys."

His heart rate sped up a bit. Was he lying? She placed her chin on his chest. "But I didn't turn you down, now did I?"

Of course, if someone programmed her what choice did she really have?

He brushed her hair with his fingers, but didn't look her in the eye. "No, I guess you didn't. Wish I could remember it, though."

Maybe that's all it was. She remembered what it felt like when she had no memory, lost. No one was controlling her now. If she didn't want to be with Jack, she wouldn't.

"Well, I do remember," she said. "So I'll share. Now, back to our feature."

Carrie downed her beer and ordered a second. "Must be hot in here. I can't believe how thirsty I am."

Sunny bolted upright, disconnecting the memory. "That's when it started."

He sat up with her. "When what started? What do you remember?"

* * * *

Jack's heart raced at the thought of a breakthrough. He hadn't seen anything unusual, but apparently Sunshine had.

"Carrie. Her drinking. It started after that dance. Are you sure you didn't recognize him?"

"Sweetheart, the only identifying mark was his blond hair. Just like the guy who staked you. Do you think it was him?"

"If it was, he's certainly no vampire. It can't be a coincidence, can it?"

There were too many coincidences, he didn't know what to believe. "I wouldn't get your hopes up. If it'll make you feel better, we can access Carrie's memory and see what she remembers."

She shuddered and held herself.

He gently held her shoulders. "You act like we're going to skewer her. It doesn't hurt. You know that."

"I just hate using her like that."

"Then ask her. Do you honestly think she'll turn you down?"

"No, I don't. But that's just it. She doesn't think any vampire is dangerous."

"Sunshine, we're no more dangerous than mortals. There are good and evil in both our species. Just because we have special powers doesn't mean we abuse them. We have them to survive and we use them without harming anyone. If we break the rules, we're punished." He leaned back, taking her with him. "Come on, show me more."

"Will Frank be punished?" she whispered.

Jack closed his eyes. Should he lie and quiet her down, or tell the truth and face her wrath? How about neither? "We'll talk about that later."

She moaned. "That just means no. Dang it, it's not fair what he's doing to her."

Jack took her face into his hands. "Didn't you tell Carrie you would stay out of it?"

"Yes, but--"

"Do you want to go back on your word?" She shook her head and he kissed her lightly. "Then drop it. What he's doing isn't good for their relationship, but he's not hurting her. If he were, I would intervene. I promise."

His heart ached at seeing her upset.

She relaxed at his promise, and it was a promise he would keep. Frank was walking a thin line, Jack couldn't deny that, but until Frank actually did anything to hurt Carrie, Jack's hands were tied.

"Why don't you show me what else you remember."

Sunshine played out everything that happened that night. None of it useful. If the vampire hung around, she didn't see him.

My Sunny Vampire

Although, it amused him how nervous he seemed when he first talked to her and how brazen he became as the night wore on.

"I'm sorry," she said. "I was really hoping I saw something."

He kissed the top of her head. "You did see something. You saw the start of Carrie's strange drinking behavior. We have something to go on, now. If I were smart, I would have checked her memories long before now. That was my mistake."

She snuggled up against him, causing a rise in Little Jack. Damn, he just couldn't get enough of her. No wonder he wasn't thinking straight. His stupid penis took over. And lying naked on the bed beside her wasn't exactly the smartest thing he could do to clear his mind. The sheet did nothing to curb his appetite.

"As much as I moaned and groaned at the beginning, I'm still glad I came to Pittsburgh. Although, it would have been nicer if I was prepared to be a vampire. Maybe then I wouldn't have such a hard time."

He blocked his thoughts. A slow ache spread across his chest. He loved her, no doubt about it. But would he have pursued her after that night if not for her turning? Or would he have fallen for her anyway? Could it be fate that she was in that bar, or did someone intervene? So many questions and very few answers.

"When did you come to Pittsburgh?"

"I arrived a week before Christmas."

"You didn't spend the holiday with your father?"

"Nope, and I'm sure he didn't miss me, either. I haven't lived with him since my marriage. Saw no sense going back after the divorce. I didn't want to spend Christmas with him or alone, and since I was between jobs, I called Carrie. It'd been a couple of years since I'd seen her, so I was glad she accepted me inviting myself up."

"Between jobs?"

"Yeah, even during the holidays I couldn't seem to hold a job. Taking pictures of screaming kids isn't my idea of fun."

"Is that why you brought your portfolio with you? Hoping to get work?"

"No. I just wanted to show my pictures to Carrie."

"Can I see them someday?"

She sat up. "You're interested?"

"Sweetheart, I'm interested in anything you do."

She grinned. "Don't suppose vampires have a use for a photographer, do they?"

"They might. Certainly wouldn't have to worry about any screaming kids."

She laughed. "I'm glad to hear you don't turn children."

"I'm glad, too, but it's only because we can't that we don't. A mortal cannot be changed until after puberty. Something in their brain or glands prevents us from turning them sooner."

"Does that mean someone tried?"

He nodded. "Many someones tried. Mostly female vampires who wanted children."

"How horrible."

"It happened long before I was born and no one got hurt, so don't worry about it. So, whose idea was it to go to the bar on New Year's Eve?"

"Carrie's. She suggested it the day after Christmas."

"Wasn't that the day you got the call regarding your job interview?"

She nodded. "Sure was."

"Did you go anywhere between the day you arrived in Pittsburgh and received that call?"

Resting an arm on his abdomen, she said, "I went lots of places between those two days. I mean, it was Christmas and I shopped."

"I meant at night. Did you go to any parties?"

"Carrie took me to a Christmas party on Christmas Eve."

Shit. Could it have been that simple? Was he looking at it all wrong? Could the vampire have met them earlier? "Show me."

"But, Jack, I really didn't do much there."

"I don't care. Just show me."

Carrie and Sunshine walked up the stairs toward the sounds of Christmas music playing. Carrie knocked and a young, bearded man opened the door, wearing a huge grin on his face to match the Santa smiley face on his shirt. He gave her a hug and welcomed them inside.

The room was spacious, one of those loft apartments where no inside walls existed. People milled about holding cups or plates and Sunshine avoided knocking over anyone's drink as she made her way with Carrie to the refreshment table. A Christmas tree stood to the side, lighting the table with a colorful array. Carrie grabbed a cup and dipped a ladle into the huge bowl filled with pink liquid while Sunshine took a plate and filled it with food bits.

My Sunny Vampire

A man in the corner stared at her and smiled. He lifted a tidbit from his plate as a toast and she looked away, scanning the crowd.
"I'm afraid most of the night was like this. They were Carrie's friends, not mine."
"What about the guy who was staring? Did he approach you?"
"Yes and no. He tried. I avoided."
"Was Carrie with you the whole time?"
She laughed. "No. She was hounded shortly after we got some food. When I gave her my blessing to leave me, I found some people watching *It's a Wonderful Life* and that's pretty much where I spent my time. I'm sorry, Jack. I wish I had more to show."

Someone must have spotted her there. Was it Harris? Was he even in town then? To have Carrie decide to go to the dance club for New Year's Eve, Sunshine to receive a job interview and the Committee informed about Frank's behavior all on the same day was too coincidental. If it wasn't Harris, Jack would definitely need the Committee's help. There were too many vampires out there who held a grudge. Of course, they held the grudge against the whole Committee, so why single Jack out?

Sunshine held him tight. "What are you going to do? I don't want you to get into any more trouble."

Her heart was racing and she trembled. How could he comfort her when he had no idea what to do next? He probably should contact Barnet, but at what cost? The only bright spot was Carrie. She might be the answer he was looking for, but she wouldn't be off work until five-thirty. That left them with several hours in which he could worry or have fun. Jack voted for fun.

"First off, I'm not in trouble." Yet. "Second, I can't do anything until Carrie gets off work." He smoothed the hair from her face as she looked up at him. "That leaves..." Slowly he rolled her to her back and straddled her.

She raised an eyebrow. "That leaves what?"

He kissed her brow. "Lots." He kissed her nose. "And lots." His lips hovered over her mouth. "Of boinking."

She laughed and he silenced her with a kiss. He felt her fingers on the back of his scalp, holding him tight. Her tongue played with his. Oh yes, the next several hours were definitely going to be fun.

Chapter 26

The dryer buzzed from deep in the basement. Sunny tightened the sheet around herself and headed for the laundry room. What she wouldn't give for a pin or something to secure the stupid thing. She wouldn't be walking around looking like the next toga party attendee if Jack or Frank owned a robe.

Her shirts had come clean okay, but the holes were another matter. The t-shirt she wore when she'd been staked was indeed ruined. Washing only made the hole bigger. No way would she wear that and she tossed it in the trash. The shirt Jack had lent her hadn't fared much better, but at least those holes were smaller and in the back. She wouldn't flash her boobs to anyone.

The sheet loosened in her movements of unloading and folding. She rewrapped it around her body the best she could before picking up the folded laundry. Climbing the stairs became a chore what with holding the basket and tripping over the stupid sheet.

"Where would you like me to put your clothes?" she asked Frank in the most cordial tone she could offer. She was still miffed at him and wouldn't have washed his clothes at all if she hadn't needed to use his soap.

He was sitting in a chair reading and lifted his nose out of his book. "Just put them in front of my bedroom door, thanks."

What? Didn't he trust her to go inside his room? Whatever.

Jack, lounging on the couch, blew her a kiss and smiled. "Why didn't you change downstairs? Isn't that sheet a little hard to maneuver in?"

My Sunny Vampire

She mentally slapped herself. Well, duh, changing downstairs would have only made sense. Since she'd been with Jack, her brain must have taken a vacation. She certainly wasn't thinking straight. She shrugged and returned the kiss before ascending the stairs, being careful not to trip on the sheet.

What would life be like once Jack solved her case? Would she live with him or in a house full of vampires? Holy moly. Listen to her, jumping to conclusions, assuming they were a couple. Would they be a couple? Did he want them to be a couple? Maybe he was waiting until he cleared his name before he said anything. She hoped that's all it was.

She reached Frank's bedroom door and deposited his clothes on the floor. She carried the remainder of the laundry to the room she and Jack shared and placed them on the bed. Ready to ditch the sheet, she unwound it and tossed it next to the stack of clothes. She got dressed and packed her backpack. Tonight she would go to Carrie's or the safe house with Jack. She'd had it with Frank.

Sunny went to the bathroom and stopped when she caught her reflection. Yikes. Her hair was a tangled mess. Why didn't Jack say anything? Or did he like seeing her like this? She wouldn't put it past him, keeping her looking like she'd just had sex--with him, of course. Using her wide-toothed comb, she gently worked out the tangles. Tempted to braid the wild mane, she refrained, knowing how much Jack hated it.

After gathering her things, she carried them to the bedroom and stuffed them in the backpack. She turned to go downstairs, but her neatness gene wouldn't let her leave the bed unmade. Making it as is was out of the question, though. The sheets weren't exactly clean. There must be a clean set somewhere in the house.

No sheets in the bathroom cabinets and the hallway didn't possess a storage closet of any kind. Back in the bedroom, she searched the only remaining place--the dresser. She opened a drawer and found it stuffed with Jack's clothes. Geez, didn't the guy know how to put stuff away? It looked as if he had dumped his suitcase into the drawer. She couldn't ignore the mess, something about wrinkled clothes bugged her. With a sigh, she scooped up the underwear and shirts and deposited them on the bed. She wouldn't go so far as packing. He might not want to leave Frank's. Taking the folded shirts, she went to place them in the drawer and stopped. She hadn't noticed the picture when she'd emptied the drawer.

* * * *

Jack lay back against the armrest after Sunshine nearly tripped over that stupid sheet. She looked adorable all wrapped up. And her hair was a wild mess, as if she'd just made love--to him, of course. He was tempted to follow her and unwrap her, but even he had his limits. Small cramps flittered across his stomach, an indication he'd overdone it in the lovemaking department.

"I was thinking of taking Sunshine to the safe house. If Harris is still there, I'm sure our arrival will boot him out."

Frank lowered his book and stared at Jack. "Don't like my company anymore, is that it?"

"Aw, Frank. It's not that--"

Frank's laughter caught Jack off guard. "Relax, man. You need to learn to lighten up, you know that? Actually, that sounds like a good plan. Maybe I can get him to stay here. I want to get proof he isn't involved in Sunny's turning and convince him we're not involved, either. Then maybe the three of us could be friends again."

How could Jack tell his friend that that would never occur? Harris didn't want to be his friend any more than he wanted to be Harris's, and it had nothing to do with Ivy's death.

In 1930, after a six-year-long crush, Frank had insisted Jack introduce him to Linda. Harris accused Jack of stealing his friend away, and maybe it had seemed that way to Harris, as he and Frank had been together since their turning back in 1843. Didn't matter that Frank was in love, Harris blamed Jack.

Jack never told Frank about the conversation. Up until Ivy, Harris had appeared to be a friend to both Frank and Linda, but had ignored Jack, which suited him just fine.

Jack's cellphone vibrated next to his hip. He pulled it out. "Speak of the devil." It could have been worse, it could have been Barnet. Flipping it open, he sat up and greeted Harris in the friendliest tone he could muster.

"No need to fake it, Jack I'm not buying it."

"What do you want?"

"Just thought you should know that I'm headed down to Atlanta. Want to know why?"

My Sunny Vampire

Jack tensed. The casing of his phone crackled in his ear and he loosened his grip. This man was nothing but a thorn in his side.

"Because you'd rather have an audience than tell them over the phone?"

"You can joke all you want, but you'll pay. I saw you on YouTube today. You and Sunny in front of Frank's house. Wouldn't the Committee be interested in seeing that?"

"What? No. We wiped those reporters' minds. Cleared their cameras."

"Apparently you missed someone. It's not movie quality, but you can see the two of you being shot. Or was that staked? You're getting sloppy. Why don't you just give it up? I know you turned her."

* * * *

Sunny lifted the frame and turned it over. A black and white wedding picture. Based on the clothing, it had been taken many years ago. Frank looked the same, but was that Linda? Sunny had never seen him smile like that. He was grinning for the camera. Clearly happy, and in love. It practically radiated out of the picture. She might not be Frank's fan, but her chest ached for the loss he had suffered.

So why stuff it in a drawer? Didn't Jack see it when he dumped his clothes in there? Knowing him, probably not. Still, wouldn't Frank want to display the event, or was it still too painful for him? Or maybe vampires just didn't display their pictures. There weren't any of Jack in the house, either.

She replaced the photo and put the folded clothes in the drawer. She still needed sheets and proceeded to open each drawer, finding them empty until she opened the bottom drawer.

Hallelujah! She hit pay dirt. Blue flowered sheets filled the compartment. They seemed a bit frilly for Frank's taste so they must have belonged to his late wife. When she lifted them out, she uncovered a small wallet-sized card. Now what had Frank hidden? And why would he need to hide anything? She put the sheets on the dresser and bent over to pick up the card.

This was no ordinary card. Too slick, more like a photo. She turned it over and her heart thumped heavily against her ribs.

Oh God. A photo. Of a painting. An old painting. The young woman sat in a chair, wearing a blue dress similar to those worn during the colonial times. This woman, wearing her red hair pulled back into a bun or braid, was the spitting image of Sunny.

Sunny dropped the picture as if it burnt her fingers. Her heart stung.

Nooo! Harris was right.

* * * *

Jack stood and paced. If Harris had proof, he'd have already reported it to the Committee.

"What's the matter?" Frank asked.

Jack raised his hand and shook his head. He couldn't deal with Frank yet. "If you're so sure I turned her, why haven't you told the Committee?"

"Yeah, like they'd believe me. You're the wonder boy of the Committee. They'd never suspect you of doing any wrong. But this video will help. And that amnesia bit? I'm sure they'll find that suspicious, too. So I thought I'd speed up the process of them finding out what you did, because they will find out eventually. You Committee members always do. Isn't that what you told me?"

"This is about Ivy, isn't it? You still hold a grudge."

"I still blame you, yes. You didn't have to tell her. I would have gotten around to it eventually. But this has nothing to do with her. This has to do with Sunny and how you think it's okay for you to break the rules, but not anyone else."

Nothing Jack said would change Harris's mind. He would think what he wanted, he always did. "Do what you need to do. I'll get the proof I need showing I wasn't responsible."

Harris cackled. "Yeah, good luck there. Can't get what isn't there."

The connection ended. Jack continued to pace the room. He clenched his free hand, itching to strike at something, anything.

"Well?" Frank asked.

"Harris is on his way to Atlanta. Apparently we were on YouTube." He threw the phone at the couch and it disappeared between the seat cushions. What the hell was he going to do? How did everything get so out of hand?

"Jack, I think it's time you told Sunny everything. Then you need to come clean with Barnet."

"No. I just need more time."

My Sunny Vampire

Frank put his book down, stood and blocked Jack's pacing. "You haven't gotten any proof yet. What makes you think you will?"

Jack clenched and unclenched his fists, trying to keep his anger under control. "The proof is out there. It has to be. No one's that good."

Frank placed his hands on Jack's shoulders. "I know you don't want to think this, but maybe you can't find any proof because..."

Jack shrugged free. "Not you, too."

"But isn't that what you believe? If you're so sure you didn't do it, why haven't you had someone dig into your memories?"

Why, indeed. Jack's anger dissipated with Frank's question. He was a member of the Committee, dammit. He'd cracked tougher cases. Maybe he just didn't want to crack this one. "I hear it's painful."

"I never took you for a coward."

Frank's words landed like a punch in the gut. Jack fell back onto the couch. "What if I did it, Frank? What if I did turn her? She'd never forgive me. Hell, I wouldn't forgive myself, not to mention I'd be dead."

"You don't know that. How many cases have there been of illegal turnings since the law was written?"

He could answer that easily enough. He was on the Committee when they wrote the law. "Two, if you count Sunshine."

"How many of those were committed by an incapacitated vampire?"

"Incapacitated from a drug or incapacitated from love? Because we all know what love can do to a person."

Frank smacked Jack on the shoulder. "You know what I mean. Besides Sunny's case, did the vamp know what she was doing?"

Frank knew the answer to that, all vampires knew the answer to that, but Jack supposed he was just trying to make a point.

"Yes, she was fully aware of what she did. But that doesn't mean--"

"Don't be an idiot," Frank interrupted. "It means a lot, and you know it. You have no idea how they'll treat your case, because they've never had one like it. They could be lenient, especially if Sunny's on your side. And she won't be on your side if you don't come clean."

Oh, hell. What choice did he have? He could lose her either way. Better to tell her the truth and beg for forgiveness. Was that asking too much? Probably. He couldn't forgive himself.

He glanced at the staircase. Sunshine had been up there for quite some time, probably avoiding Frank. Or packing. She made it perfectly clear she wanted out.

"I guess I should go on up there." So why was he still sitting on the couch? He looked at Frank. "I'll pay for any damage she makes."

"You expecting her to throw something?"

"Yeah. Me."

A heavy weight pressed down upon his shoulders and he rose in slow motion. More cramps flitted across his stomach. He shuffled to the stairs and stopped. His heart pounded so hard, he wouldn't be surprised if it exploded out of his chest.

Wasn't it just a few short hours ago he rushed upstairs to apologize? So why couldn't he rush now? He placed his right foot on the first step, but his left one felt like it was glued to the floor. One step at a time, he could do this.

Each step brought him closer to the woman he loved.

Each step brought him closer to losing her forever.

Step after agonizing step, he finally reached the top. The door to their room stood open. A breeze brushed against his face, the scent of fresh air tickled his nose.

Sheets were piled on the floor, the bed bare. The curtains flapped. Why was the window open? "Sunshine?"

No answer. He stepped inside the room. The bottom drawer was open and the sheets he had carefully put Clara's picture under were on the dresser. His blood froze and his heart stopped momentarily.

Clara stared at him like she always did, but this time with accusation in her eyes. Even with the breeze through the open window, it felt as if someone sucked all the air out of the room. He fell to his knees and picked up the photograph.

"Ah, shit. What have I done?"

Chapter 27

The snow drift softened her fall. It also kept her footsteps quiet. Sunny landed in the side yard, toward the back of the house--the same side as the living room. She didn't have much time if she wanted to leave undetected. Luckily for her, Jack was arguing with someone, either on the phone or with Frank, so maybe he hadn't heard the window opening. She wouldn't stick around and find out.

Of course, in her haste, she'd left her coat inside. The temperature had probably dipped since the sun set, if it was even warm to begin with. The snow certainly hadn't melted much. Not many people walked around without some sort of coat on, making her stand out. She couldn't worry about that, she needed to beat feet.

Snow was definitely a hindrance. She left footprints wherever she walked. So, did she risk being discovered running to the plowed street and hope no one noticed her lack of outerwear? Or did she climb the backyard fence and stay hidden, but leave a trail behind?

One way familiar, the other, new territory. The street it was. She'd have only gotten lost the other way.

She inched her way to the front. Jack and Frank were still talking, but she couldn't make out the words. They probably kept their voices low because they thought she was upstairs. Good, that meant she could still get away undetected.

Jack's voice, however faint, made her pause. Was he congratulating himself on tricking her for so long? Frank must have

235

known she looked like Clara, which meant he was in on it. Pain slashed through her heart. She should have known better than to believe Jack's declaration of love. Men only said that to get something. He may have told only two women he loved them, but did it count when he thought they were the same person? Her eyes ached to shed tears. Fudge. She needed to stop dwelling on it and get a move on.

The street was deserted. A quick dash and she'd be free of the house. One breath. Two breaths. Three breaths. She dashed. No one called her name. No steps sounded behind her. Zipping down the street, she slowed to a normal gait whenever she came upon traffic. She couldn't afford anyone noticing her super-human speed, not with her spotty mind control ability.

She arrived on Carrie's street and stopped. What was she thinking? Carrie's place would be the first place Jack looked. She dashed between two buildings, feeling safer out of sight. This was all Jack's fault. He wanted his late wife back and took his chance when he spotted her. Turn the redhead, pretend amnesia, how hard was that?

But had he stopped with her? No. He let Frank control Carrie. Now she was caught in his trap. How could Sunny save her friend? Carrie wouldn't believe her, not without proof, and Sunny didn't have any. Could she control her friend? She shuddered at the thought. But what choice did she have? Carrie's life depended on it. She'd eventually come around and see the truth.

So, how could Sunny reach her friend without Frank or Jack's knowledge? She needed help. But there wasn't anyone she could trust. No, wait. Shoot. Why didn't she think of him earlier? He'd said he would help.

She opened up her backpack and rummaged through it--her brush and comb, some underwear. Where was it? She had put it in here, she was sure of it. Finally, her fingers brushed against the stiff card.

* * * *

The front door opened.

"Frankie!" Carrie's joy floated up the stairs.

Shit. Jack straightened up. How long had he been up here? And why didn't Frank even bother to check on him?

"Damn, it's cold in here," she complained. "You got a window open or something?"

My Sunny Vampire

He was still holding Clara's picture. He rose, placed the photo face down on the dresser and walked over to the window.

"Jack?" Frank called up the stairs. "Everything okay up there?"

No, everything wasn't okay. The woman he loved more than life itself had jumped out the window and left him. He slammed the window shut, vibrating the glass in the process.

"Jack?"

Jack jumped. Frank stood at the door. Damn. The man was quiet, or Jack was off his game. Most likely the latter.

"What happened? Where's Sunny?"

Carrie poked her head around the big guy and smiled. How long would that last when she heard what he'd done to Sunshine?

He couldn't talk. The words stuck in his throat. He turned toward the wall and leaned against it. His body shook. It felt like someone squeezed his heart, taking all the life out of it. A moan escaped his lips.

"Carrie, sweetie, can you wait downstairs? I need to talk to Jack in private."

"Is something wrong with Sunny? Where is she?"

"I'm sure she's fine. Why don't you go downstairs and try and call her."

"Okay, Frankie." Her footsteps faded.

Frank's hand landed on Jack's shoulder. "She didn't take it well, I guess?"

Jack turned around and whispered, "I never told her. She was gone when I got up here. She found Clara's picture."

"Holy shit. I'm so sorry, Jack."

"Don't you mean to say 'I told you so'?"

"I'm sure she'll be back once she's had a chance to cool off. You know how she can fly off the handle. She loves you, Jack."

"I don't know. She's probably thinking I turned her now. Can't say I blame her. I have to find the man responsible. Which means…" Carrie. Jack took a deep breath and rushed down the stairs.

Frank followed behind. "Which means, what?"

Carrie placed her phone inside her purse. "She's not answering her phone. Did you two have a fight?"

Jack took her hand. "She's a little mad at me right now. I'm sure she's over at your place plotting her revenge, but right now I need you to do me a big favor."

She looked between him and Frank. "What kind of favor?"

"I just want to see your version of New Year's Eve."

Frank pulled Jack away and stood between the two. "Why would you need to do that?"

"I'm not going to hurt her. Sunshine remembered Carrie dancing with someone before we showed up. I need to know who that was."

Carrie peered around Frank. "You mean the guy with the rug?"

"Rug?" Jack looked to Frank for help, but he only shrugged.

She rolled her eyes. "Honestly, I would have thought you two knew a rug was a wig."

"So he wasn't blond?"

"He might have been. I just assumed he was bald."

"So, will you do it?" Please say yes, please say yes, Jack ranted inside his head. He didn't want a fight with Frank if it came to forcing Carrie.

"Sure, if it'll help find the person who turned Sunny. What do you need me to do?"

"Just relax and remember the night," Jack said, leading her to the sofa. He sat on her left. "We'll both be watching, in a sense."

Frank sat on the other side of her and held her hand. "It'll be okay. I wouldn't let him do it if it hurt, okay?"

Let Frank believe what he wanted. Jack needed him as a witness to testify he wasn't manipulating her, but he would get to the truth of the matter regardless of who got hurt.

"Do you think I could have a beer first?" she asked. "I'm real thirsty."

Frank stroked the back of her head. "Baby, you don't need a beer. Besides, we don't have any."

"I know that, that's why I brought my own. It's out on the porch, keeping cold. Please, just one?"

"Maybe when we're done," Jack said. "I need your head clear. Liquor will only fog it."

She lowered her head. "Oh, okay."

He placed his hand on her arm and waited. Slowly, a vision appeared.

She and Sunshine entered the crowded club. Someone grabbed Carrie's arm and she stopped. Sunshine headed for the bar.

"Hey sweetness, you staying all night?"

My Sunny Vampire

"Hi, Parker." *She kissed him on the cheek.* "Happy New Year. Haven't decided if I'm staying, yet. I brought a friend tonight."

"Who's Parker?" Jack asked.

"He's a regular at the club." *She glanced at Frank and smiled.* "No one special."

"Can you skip to the blond?" Jack asked.

"Be patient. I'm getting there."

Carrie left Parker and headed for the bar, when a body blocked her way.

"Care to dance?"

She looked up. His hair didn't sit right on his head. "Sure, let me tell my friend."

"Wait," Jack said. "Can't you remember what he looks like?"

"Yeah," Frank said. "He's all blurry."

"I'm trying."

"Go on. Maybe something will show up later."

Sunshine was chatting with the bartender when Carrie tapped her on the shoulder. "I'm going dancing," she said, placing her handbag on the bar. She looped her arm around the blond and he led her to the dance floor.

The music turned to something slow and the man pulled her close and danced across the floor. No words were exchanged.

"This isn't working," Jack said. "We have to go deeper."

"Deeper?"

Frank caressed her cheek. "He means he'll have to control you. You apparently can't remember. If he connects with you, he can get more detail. It won't hurt and I'll be right here."

She nodded and closed her eyes. "Okay. Have at it."

Jack admired her. She was willing to do anything for her friend.

"Frank, I need you as a witness. When I link, you know what to do."

Frank nodded. He knew two vampires couldn't control one person. So while Jack was linked with Carrie, Frank would watch through Jack.

Jack linked with her, putting her in a hypnotic state. Frank took Jack's hand.

"*Show me the blond man. Did he give you a name?*"

"No."

The man's face was still blurred, but a buzzing sound could be heard.

"Frank, can you hear that?"

"She was being controlled, wasn't she?"

Jack's heart thumped wildly. He had found the vampire. He was sure of it.

"*Carrie, go back to your dance with him.*"

Her head rested against his chest. The buzzing was just as bad, but Jack concentrated and caught bits of words. B*zzz*...*bzzz*...*thirsty*...*bzzz*...*liquor*...*bzzz*...*Frank*...*bzzz*...*feed.*

"Damn it," Frank said. "Was she programmed to like me, too?"

"*Carrie, did you notice anything unusual about him? A mark? A scent?*"

She inhaled as if she were back there at the club. She scrunched her nose. "He smelled fruity."

"*Fruity? What kind of fruit?*"

"Not one in particular. Like the gum. Juicy Fruit."

Okay, now he was getting somewhere. Both Sunshine's and Carrie's versions mentioned Juicy Fruit. Now if he could only figure out if it meant anything.

"Oh, shit." Frank said, wide-eyed.

"You know who he is?"

"You were right. Think about it. What vampire do you know who chews gum?"

Damn it. How stupid could he be? Of course. He disconnected with Carrie and stood. "When I get my hands on that bastard, I'll kill him."

"What happened?" Carrie said. "Kill who?"

* * * *

A car pulled up to the curb and stopped as the passenger window lowered. Harris waved her over. Trepidation eased its way into her thoughts and she stutter-stepped. Could she trust him?

"I'm not the enemy, Sunny. Come on in."

What choice did she have, really? She inched her way to the front of the building and then dashed for the car. Once inside, she slunk down, making sure no one could recognize her. Not so much Jack, but anyone who might recognize Vampire Girl, especially Tom and his blond friend.

Harris chuckled. "What are you doing?"

"Just making sure no one sees me."

He put the car in gear and drove off. "Relax. No one's going to see you. The windows are tinted. Didn't you notice?"

No, she hadn't. Relief eased the tension she'd held since she made the phone call and she straightened up.

"Have you fed yet?"

The instant he mentioned food, a cramp skittered across her midsection. She'd been getting them for the last thirty minutes, but couldn't get up enough nerve to try and feed on her own. "I'm okay. We need to get Carrie, first. Who knows what they'll do to her."

"About Carrie. I think it would be best if I get you to Atlanta first. The Committee can take care of Jack and Frank, in essence helping your friend."

"No, no, no. I can't leave Carrie. She's defenseless against them."

"Do you think they'll hurt her?"

"Not so much hurt her as use her. She hasn't been acting the same since we met them. I'm pretty sure Frank has a drinking problem and is feeding from Carrie to get his fix. I think he's been manipulating her mind to do it, too."

"Frank and not Jack?"

"No, not Jack, not directly. If he wanted to stop Frank, he would have. Wouldn't he?"

Harris furrowed his eyebrows. "You would think. Still, the Committee is better suited to these kinds of things."

"But Jack is part of that Committee. How do I know they won't side with him?"

"Jack is a sick man. He should have been removed long ago. Once the Committee sees the proof of his madness, they will set things right. He had no right to turn you."

"If you can't help me, then let me out. I'll do it on my own."

"Okay, okay. Let me go park where we can discuss our options."

* * * *

Frank placed a protective arm around Carrie and she went silent. "I'm not happy about what he did, but don't talk about killing. You're scaring her."

"I'm sorry, but Harris makes my blood boil." Jack clenched his fists. The wall looked like a good punching bag. It was all starting to make sense. Harris must have seen Sunshine and immediately called the Committee regarding Frank, knowing Jack would be sent to check out his friend. Just how long had Harris waited for such an opportunity?

"So who turned Sunny? Harris or Beanie?" she asked.

Frank kissed the top of Carrie's head. "They're the same person. And since he controlled you…"

Carrie's eyes closed and she slumped over.

"What did you do to her?" Jack asked.

Frank held her close and stroked her hair. "Do you think Beanie told her to like me? Has it all been a farce?"

Aw, shit. Another reason to kill the bastard. If Harris faked Carrie's affection, Frank might not ever recover. "Do you really want to know?"

"I think I love her, Jack. I…" He choked on his words.

"Then wake her."

Frank nodded. Carrie's eyes opened. "What happened?"

"Carrie," Jack said. "Look at me." When she did as he requested, he smiled, getting her to smile in return. "Do you like me?"

Carrie furrowed her eyes. "Yeah, you're okay. What does this have--?"

"You love Sunshine?"

She grinned. "Sure. She's my best friend."

"How do you feel about Frank?"

Her face lit up and her eyes got all dreamy. No vampire could create those emotions. What she felt for Frank was real.

"He's the best thing that's ever happened to me." She turned and faced him. "Don't you know that?"

Frank hugged Carrie. "I do now." He looked at Jack. "So why would he do this?"

"It has to be Ivy. It's the only thing that makes sense."

"But you didn't cause Ivy's death. I'm the one who told her."

"And you told her because you knew I would."

"Stop," Carrie said. "Who's Ivy and what did you tell her?"

"Ivy was Beanie's girl," Frank said, "but she was a little unstable."

Jack snorted. "Unstable? She was just plain crazy. Harris wanted to turn her without her consent or the consent of the Committee."

"So you stopped him?"

"There was no stopping Beanie," Frank said. "He was going to go through with it. I didn't want him to get in trouble, so I told Ivy what he was planning to do."

"I guess she didn't take it well?"

My Sunny Vampire

"She might have if I gave her time. When she freaked out, I panicked. I sent a suggestion to calm down and to help her see the value of becoming a vampire. I had no idea she'd know I was in her head and she screamed she heard voices. When she ran into her bedroom, I let her be, but I should have followed her. She jumped out the window to her death."

"Oh, Frankie. How horrible." She caressed the back of his head. "That doesn't explain why he would turn Sunny. What does she have to do with it?"

Jack faced the wall. How much should he come clean? Shit. Keeping secrets got him in this mess to begin with. "Frank, you might as well tell her. I'm going to Carrie's to talk to Sunshine. Call me if you need me."

"Hey." Frank stuck his hand between the sofa cushions and pulled out Jack's cellphone. "Won't you need this?"

Jack indicated for Frank throw it. "Thanks." He headed for the door.

"Wait." Carrie pulled a set of keys from her purse. After unhooking one key, she tossed it to him. "In case she won't let you in."

He chuckled. Would she have given it to him after Frank told her? He wasn't about to stick around and find out.

Chapter 28

Harris drove up a hill and stopped on a snow-covered lot containing a shed. More than one set of car tracks marred the snow. Either Harris visited often, or the place was a popular hangout. The city lit up below them.

"What is this place?"

"I have no idea. I like to come up here to think because it's so quiet." He glanced through the windshield. "Apparently so do others." Turning back toward Sunny, he said, "Have you thought of any way to get Carrie away from Jack and Frank?"

Sunny shook her head. "Everything I think of, she'd only tell them, or worse, they'd follow her."

"Why don't we go outside? I always find fresh air helps me think clearer."

"I don't have my coat."

"Who's going to see you? But if it'll make you feel better, I'll take mine off, too." He climbed out of the vehicle and removed his coat.

She opened her door and got out. The pine-scented air did smell refreshing.

Harris reached inside a pocket of his coat and pulled out a pack of gum. He placed the coat on the back seat. "Did you want a piece?" He held the yellow pack out.

"Won't it make you sick?"

"There's not enough to get you sick and I like sweets. I guess you could say it's my guilty pleasure."

My Sunny Vampire

She'd never been much of a gum chewer. "No thanks, I think I'll pass."

"Suit yourself." He shoved a stick into his mouth and returned the pack to his pocket. "Do you think Jack and Frank will tell Carrie why you ran away?"

"Probably not. What logical reason would they have to tell her? I need to call her." Her phone was in the car and she pulled on the door handle.

Harris grabbed her arm. "Whoa. Hold up. What are you going to tell her? You should have it all planned out before you start talking."

"You sound like Jack."

Harris scowled. "Please. We have nothing in common."

"You don't like him much, do you?"

"I never liked him, but he's Frank's friend, so I tolerated him."

"So, you've known Frank a long time?"

He nodded. "The same person turned us, so I guess you could say we're brothers. But enough about me. Think about what you'll say to Carrie. How much do you want her to know? I'm guessing you don't want her to know that Jack has betrayed you?"

"If she knew that, she might ask them questions."

"Exactly. So, why did you run off?"

Oh, shoot. She didn't care what he said, he still sounded like Jack. She was a doer, not a thinker, and it was going to take some work for her to change. She inhaled the crisp air and leaned against the vehicle. Okay, so what could she say to Carrie that would sound believable?

* * * *

Jack arrived at the safe house. He wanted to see Sunshine badly, but he needed to know if Harris had left or not. If Harris was in town, he was a dead man.

He punched in the code forcibly, taking his frustration out on the metal box. The door clicked and he swung it open. Deserted. In fact, it didn't appear anyone had lived here since the day he spent with Sunshine. So, where did Harris spend his days if not here? A hotel? It certainly had more to offer than this safe house. Damn, if he had known Harris wasn't staying here, he would have brought Sunshine and then maybe she wouldn't have found out. He sighed. Oh hell. She would have found out eventually. He only wished he'd been the one who told her. He couldn't imagine the pain she must have suffered seeing Clara's picture the way she had.

After checking the second floor and finding it just as undisturbed as the first, he went back downstairs. How did he manage to screw things up so royally? He'd been doing his best with her, trying to stay away. But his heart wanted what it wanted, and it spread the word to the rest of his body. There was no one else for him but her.

He must make things right. First order of business, a conversation he should have had four days ago.

He pulled his cell out of his pocket. Barnet would have a fit, but at least now Jack had answers, more than he did earlier at least.

* * * *

"Okay, so I call her and tell her I want a girl's night out, that I need new clothes." Sunny said. "I can have her meet me at the mall."

Harris shook his head. "Not the mall. Too many people. Jack and Frank could easily hide. You need a place that's not so busy."

"But wouldn't the crowd be to our advantage? We could hide in it better. I don't want to stick out like a sore thumb. The clothes shopping thing sounds genuine." Honestly, the man didn't have a clue how to avoid someone.

"I don't know…"

"Trust me, Harris. It'll work." She leaned inside the car and pulled her cell out of the backpack. When she straightened up, she bumped into him. "What are you doing?"

"Sorry. Just wanted to listen in if it's okay. If things get out of hand, I can talk to you mentally, tell you what to say. It's best if she doesn't know I'm with you, don't you think?" His breath smelled fruity. Why did that seem familiar?

"I suppose." She punched in Carrie's number and waited. Harris stood much too close, but how could she tell him to back off without offending the man? He was doing her a huge favor.

"Sunny?"

"Hey, Carrie. Whatcha doing?"

"I'm at Frank's. Are you okay? Jack said you two had a fight."

Interesting. At least he knew she was mad. "I'm fine, but I was wondering if I could pull you away from Frank tonight. I need a new coat and thought we could go shopping at the Robinson Mall. Can you meet me there?"

My Sunny Vampire

"I don't know. Have you talked to Jack?"

"I don't want to talk to Jack. Can you meet me or not?"

"Sure, Sunny. Frank won't mind."

"Thanks, Carrie. I'll meet you inside the mall, on the lower level, in front of Macy's. Please don't tell Jack or Frank. I need some girl time right now."

"Girl time it is, then. I'll see you there."

She said goodbye and pocketed the phone. "See, I told you it would work. Can she come to Atlanta with us?"

Harris walked around the car. "I don't see why not. She'll probably be safer with us in any case. So, where is this mall we're going to?"

"The mall in Robinson Township. It's out of the way. I just don't want to be too close, if you know what I mean."

While he programmed the GPS, she climbed inside. When she moved her backpack out of the way, the strap got tangled with something under the seat. She bent over to free it.

"There's The Mall at Robinson or Robinson Town Centre, which one is it?" Harris asked.

"The Mall at Robinson." With the car door open, she planted one leg outside as she untangled the strap from the seat adjuster. Something hairy was under the seat. What the heck? Had an animal crawled inside? She grabbed it, almost expecting it to skitter away. No animal, a blond wig. "Is this yours?"

Harris wasn't behind the driver's seat. Something crackled in the air and pierced the side of her neck.

Fudge. Her body seized and she fell out into the snow. She couldn't move her arms to sit up. "What happened?" And why did she sound drunk?

Harris stood over her, holding what appeared to be a cellphone. "I wish you hadn't found that wig. Kind of puts a crimp in my plans. I'll manage, though."

The wig. Juicy Fruit. If she could hit her head, she'd be smacking it. He was the guy Carrie danced with at the bar, making the odds fairly high he was her maker. Cold fear prickled her skin.

He scooped her up and walked over to the shed. She felt sluggish and her arms refused to listen to her brain. He hadn't staked her, so what the heck had he done?

"Stun guns do a number on vampires, don't they? When I hit Jack with it, he blacked out. But then, he had some help. It's

247

amazing what absinth can do to a vampire when zapped with electricity. Voila, I not only knocked him out, but got him to forget, too."

"Who was drinking absinth? Bobby?"

"Who's Bobby? Oh, that druggie. No, honey, it was you. I made the bartender lace your drinks and then I made you keep ordering. One taste of you and Jack couldn't stop, it sure is addictive. When I saw Frank sample you, I had to make sure Carrie's drinks were also laced. Couldn't have them fight over you now, could I? That would have spoiled everything."

Why the heck hadn't she listened to her intuition the first time she met him? She needed to escape, but at the moment would have been glad to move. A vampire may be immortal, but they sure could be incapacitated in a variety of ways. She was pretty sure she'd experienced them all.

He opened the door to the shed and entered. The room looked like some sort of torture chamber. The far wall contained a narrow cage. Attached to the back of the cage were two prongs with shiny, sharp points. At the bottom corner was a small black box. Another cage, shorter and squarer, sat catty-cornered to the first. A leather collar hung from a chain inside the top and a pile of rope lay outside.

She could move her fingers on command. Thank God, it was only temporary. "What is this place? Why are you doing this?"

He placed her on the floor and pressed the gun on her neck. No, no, no. Not again. She tried to push it away. Her fingers might have worked, but her arms were still in denial and she couldn't get to it fast enough. A crackling sound echoed in the enclosure. Pain burned her neck and spread. She cried out. The room wavered in and out of focus.

"I'll answer your questions later, but right now, I need to get you set up."

Set up? Set up for what? Nothing was making any sense.

He picked her up under her arms. Her feet dangled in the air. His face was close enough to smell the fruity gum on his breath. If she could gather up enough saliva she'd spit on him, but those jolts left her mouth dry as a desert.

"This will probably sting a little." He carried her over to the cage.

My Sunny Vampire

Sting? She wasn't moving. Why would he need to zap her again? Then she remembered the hooks. Panic surged as he approached the taller cage. She didn't want to be skewered. She tried to kick, but her legs refused to cooperate. She tried to hold onto the opening of the cage, but her arms were stubborn.

He walked inside the narrow enclosure and shoved her against the wall. The metal pierced her just above her armpits and she screamed. The points punctured her muscles, making squishy noises. He continued to push. She continued to scream. Bones cracked. After what seemed like an eternity, the prongs poked out. He bent the tips upward to hold her in place. Blood poured down the sides of her shirt. She took shallow breaths to relieve the pain, but it didn't work. The hooks were up high, only her toes could touch the floor and she used what she could to keep the pressure off her wounds.

He patted her cheek. "See, that wasn't so bad now, was it?"

Easy for him to say, he wasn't hanging like a side of beef. If she could move her arms, she would have strangled the son of a gun. He closed the gate on the cage. Long, sharp spikes were arranged every few inches, pointing at her. If she moved her arms or legs forward, she would get stabbed. She wouldn't be able to free herself without committing serious damage. Not that getting out of the hooks would be easy. She'd need a stool or another person.

A cord hung from the shed's ceiling. With one tug, he pulled the ceiling back, exposing the sky and a full moon. He yanked out something from his pants pocket that looked like a key fob, aimed it at her and pushed a button. Nothing beeped or honked, but her cage hummed. Dang, was it wired for an explosion? She twisted her head to get a better look, but any kind of movement caused her shoulders to shift, bringing excruciating pain.

"My insurance." He looked up at the opening. "If I'm not back in time, I'm afraid it's toast for you."

Her stomach cramped, but was nothing compared to the throbbing in her shoulders. "Hey, buster! What'd I ever do to you?"

"Sunny, this was never about you. You just have the unfortunate luck to look like Jack's late wife. I do have to say, it's worked out so much better than I imagined. I thought just turning you would be enough to get him in trouble, but I decided I wanted more, especially when I saw how much he liked you that night.

He'll suffer when he's killed you and then get in trouble for your turning and I couldn't be happier. Now don't go anywhere." He snickered. "I've got to go get your friend."

"What? Why do you need Carrie? She hasn't done anything."

He shut the door behind him, leaving her alone with the moonlight.

"Get back here! I'll just scream until someone comes."

"Scream all you want, Sunny. No one's going to hear you."

A car door slammed. The motor roared to life. Sunny lowered her head and sobbed.

* * * *

Jack knocked on the door, but didn't announce himself. He figured his chances of Sunshine opening it were better that way. On the way over, he'd thought about what he would say to her, but nothing sounded adequate. He deserved every curse she aimed at him.

Knowing he hadn't turned Sunshine and talking to Barnet had eased some of the tension he'd been holding. And if Harris was doing what he said he would, going to Atlanta to report Jack, then maybe everything would work out. Barnet and the rest of the Committee were ready to arrest Harris.

All Jack had to do now was make it right with Sunshine. He knocked again and waited. Silence. Was she even here? He used the key and opened the door. No sign of her. It didn't appear she had even come home. So where the hell was she?

He entered her bedroom. Her rosy scent lingered in the air and his chest tightened. She hadn't been gone all that long and he already missed her. If he gave her some space, would she come to forgive him? Somehow he would prove he loved her for her, not for her likeness, but even that wouldn't erase his part in all this. He might not have been the one who bit her, but if not for him, she'd still be mortal. Would that matter to her? Would that make a difference?

He would wait for her. Forever, if that's what it took. He couldn't imagine his life without her, didn't want to spend it without her. He would do anything it took to earn her trust once again.

A portfolio leaned up against the wall, on the floor. He picked it up and sat on the bed. Her pictures. Too bad her interview was a sham. While she went about it all wrong, he understood her need for control of her life. And there wasn't technically anything wrong with having a career in the arts. It would just be hard to do anonymously. Maybe together they could figure something out. That was if she could ever forgive him.

His phone vibrated against his hip. His hopes rose for a split second until he saw Frank's name.

"Jack, I don't think Sunny is at Carrie's."

No kidding. "Why do you say that?"

"Because she just called Carrie to meet at the mall. Said she wanted to go shopping."

That sounded like Sunshine. Most of her clothes were ruined, so why not go shopping. At least she hadn't left yet. Still, didn't the woman realize she was famous? Someone was liable to spot her. Being labeled Vampire Girl wasn't helping their cause any, but telling her not to go wouldn't do any good. Like she'd listen to reason. "Did Carrie tell her about Harris?"

"No. She thought it would be better to tell her in person. I'm driving Carrie there now, but thought you might want to come."

He'd love nothing better than to see her again, but not in a crowded mall. He wanted her alone--to talk, to explain, to apologize. "I'll think about it. You might want to make sure she doesn't spot you. She's probably still mad at you."

"If you change your mind, give me a call. I'll give you directions. You'll need your car, though. It's outside the city limits."

Jack said goodbye and closed the phone. He had nearly pocketed it when an idea struck him. A silly, foolish idea, but one that wouldn't leave his head. If he called Sunshine, would she answer the phone? Would she be willing to talk to him?

If he only heard her voice for a second, it would be worth it. He opened his phone and selected her number, hoping against hope she wouldn't automatically send him to voice mail.

* * * *

Sunny breathed through the pain. The initial throbbing dulled to an ache, but only if she stayed still. Any sudden movement would most likely be excruciating.

Her stomach continued to cramp, but feeding was the least of her problems. How the heck could she escape? She was not only trapped inside the cage, but Harris had apparently rigged it to go off if anyone opened the door.

The theme from *Friends* played and her pocket vibrated. Her phone. She'd completely forgotten about it, but then, so had Harris.

Slowly, she raised her hand, keeping it close to her body and clear of the spikes. Her shoulder screamed in pain, but she wouldn't give up. She couldn't. She reached inside her pocket, pulled out the phone. Using her thumb, she pushed the talk button. It hurt way too much to raise the phone to her ear. "Hello? Can you hear me?"

"Sunshine? I'm so glad you answered."

Jack. Hope surged through her. He could save Carrie. He could stop Harris. "Jack, listen. You need to get Carrie. She's in danger. You can find her at the lower level of the Robinson Mall in front of Macy's."

"Whoa, slow down. How is Carrie in danger?"

"Harris is after her. You have to stop him. She's defenseless against him."

"She's not defenseless. Frank is with her. Where are you? I'll come get you."

"I don't know where I am. Some hill overlooking the city. Jack, there's no time. Stop talking to me. Call her."

"I will. But why didn't you call her?" A door slammed on his end of the line.

She couldn't tell him the truth. If he knew the extent of her injuries, he'd ditch Carrie and look for her. "I forgot I had my phone on me. I thought it was in my backpack."

"Are you okay? You sound like you're in pain. Did Harris hurt you?"

"I'm okay. I'm just worried about Carrie. Just call her. Please. I'd do it if I could. Then get Harris. He's driving a black Ford Taurus. You need to get him to find out where I am."

"Sunshine, you're not making any sense. How is it you can answer your phone, but not call anyone?"

"Jack, I promise I'll tell you everything later. If you can't get to Carrie in time, Harris will bring her back here and I don't even want to think about what he's planning to do. If you can't get Harris and find out where I am, I'm liable to burn. Now go find him. I'm hanging up now." She used her thumb to disconnect, but the phone slipped out of her hand. On instinct, she reached out for it. The hooks held her in place and pain ripped through her

My Sunny Vampire

shoulders. She cried out. The phone clanged against the wall of the cage and landed with a squish. She reached for the phone with her foot, but no luck. Her only link to the world, to Jack, was now inaccessible. She couldn't tell if the call ended or not. Maybe she was still connected. "Jack? Are you there?"

No sound. Okay, so she wasn't connected. She might be toast, as Harris put it, but at least Carrie would be saved.

* * * *

"Sunshine!" Jack yelled into the phone. Damn, she hung up on him. He called her back, but was sent to her voice mail. Something wasn't right with her. What wasn't she telling him?

He ran toward his car and punched in Frank's number.

"Hey, Jack. Did you change your mind about coming?"

"Harris is on his way to the mall. He's done something to Sunshine and now he's after Carrie. You need to make sure he doesn't leave until I get there."

"What? Shit. I need to go get her."

"Aren't you with her?"

"No. I'm waiting in the car. She didn't want Sunny to see me. I need to get her out of here."

"No. Frank, you can't leave until I get there. Have her go in another store. If you control her, Harris won't be able to get to her. If he doesn't spot her, he might think she hasn't shown up yet. You can't let him get away. I need to know where he's keeping Sunshine."

"Dammit, Jack. I'm not using Carrie as bait."

"I'm not asking you to. Hide Carrie and keep an eye out for him." Jack reached his car, a 1965 Ford Mustang. He hadn't driven it since arriving and it was covered in snow. Shit. He couldn't drive like that. "Give me the directions. I'm leaving now."

After Frank gave him the directions, Jack used vampire speed and cleaned the car in record time. If anyone spotted him doing it, he didn't care. He had Harris in his sights and he wouldn't let anyone get in the way.

Once he hit the road, he called Sunshine again. And again he was sent to voice mail. Something was wrong. Something was terribly wrong. He felt it in his bones, his heart, his being. But how could he help her when he didn't know where she was?

All the more reason to find Harris.

Chapter 29

The ring tone stopped for the second time. Jack was probably having a fit wondering if she wouldn't or couldn't answer the phone. At least it still worked. As if that did her any good right now. Unless she got free, she could have one hundred working phones and it wouldn't matter. Shoot.

Somehow she had to get free. She couldn't just hang around and wait for Harris to kill her. She was a vampire, dag-burnit. She possessed abilities. Time to put them to use. If they refused to work or got her killed, well, at least she died trying.

Slowly, Sunny reached for the top of the cage. Her shoulders screamed in protest, but she breathed through the pain, determined to get free. If she could get her fingers wrapped around the metal, maybe she could pull herself loose.

Another cramp seized her stomach. Stupid hunger. At least the bleeding had stopped. Of course, that would change if she freed herself and aggravated the wounds. She could render herself weaker, or worse, become paralyzed like she had earlier.

But what choice did she have? Carrie's life depended on her. If Jack couldn't stop Harris, then Sunny was the only one who could. The essence of surprise was on her side.

She poked her fingers through the openings and gripped tight. Pulling up only put pressure on her wounds, but didn't move her like she hoped. Maybe if she straightened out the hooks. Could she slip off that way?

My Sunny Vampire

The metal gave easier than she imagined, but not without causing a searing pain through her shoulders. Every movement she made with her arms made the pain worse. Short breaths weren't even helping this time, but dang, she had managed to straighten the hooks. "What would happen if I pulled them down?"

Bracing herself for the anticipated pain, she took several cleansing breaths. She could do this. Once free, she'd feel better. It was a given. She closed her eyes, said a silent prayer, and pushed down on the prongs.

Nothing happened.

She gritted her teeth and wriggled her shoulders.

All that accomplished was more pain. She still hung there.

"Dang it." What the heck did it take to get free? An engraved invitation? She fisted her hands and pounded behind her, against the back of the cage. She wished she were pummeling Harris. He could use a good kick or two.

Stabbing pain sliced through her shoulders. "Ow, ow, ow."

She slipped down.

And forward.

Into the spikes.

* * * *

Jack sneaked inside the mall and scanned the area. Even with only a couple hours left to shop, the place was crowded. More than he expected. Finding Harris might be difficult.

"You got here quick," Frank whispered as he walked past. "Speed much?" He disappeared into the Victoria's Secret store.

A bunch of women cackling like hens headed for the exit. Jack leaned against the wall of a perfume store to get out of their way.

Frank bolted out of the store. "Jack, she's gone! I knew I shouldn't have left her alone."

"Weren't you controlling her?"

"I didn't think I needed to."

Shit. Could she have been in that mass of women who just left? "The parking lot."

They rushed outside. Carrie was walking down an aisle, two aisles over. Jack held Frank's arm to keep him from darting over there. "Easy. I don't see Harris, yet."

Frank tugged free. "She's not bait."

Like hell she wasn't. Jack couldn't let Harris get away. "At least wait until she approaches his car."

"No." With vampire speed, Frank zipped to her.

"Shit." Jack followed, scanning the lot. "Where is he?"

Frank had almost reached Carrie when he flew through the air as if shoved by someone really strong. Harris. He appeared out of nowhere, scooped her up and ran. Jack sprinted as fast as he dared. Harris wouldn't be able to get inside his car without putting Carrie down.

A trunk to a black sedan opened and Harris headed for it. Without a bulky load, Jack arrived moments before Harris. Now he had him.

Harris stopped and set Carrie on her feet. "It's too late for you, Jack. I suggest you let me go."

"You're not going to get away with this. We know you turned Sunshine."

"How would you know something that isn't true? You have proof?"

"Carrie's our proof."

Harris hugged her close. "No, she's my proof. I'm only trying to save this young woman from the same fate as Sunny."

"Let her go, Beanie," Frank said.

"Why? So you can continue to feed from her? You've been using this poor woman all along. I think the Committee would be interested in knowing that. Give it up, you two. You can't win."

Frank approached Harris.

"I wouldn't come any closer."

"Why, so you can kill her in front of witnesses? I don't think so." Frank touched Carrie's cheek, but she didn't react.

In a fraction of a second, Harris pulled a cellphone out of his pocket and pointed it at Frank's neck. Crackling sounds rent the air. Frank convulsed and went down. What the hell? Jack rushed at Harris, knocking him to the ground. Harris swung the weapon toward Jack, but Jack blocked his arm. The device skittered across the pavement.

Harris shoved Jack. He flew backwards and crashed into the back of a parked SUV, triggering the alarm. The continuous honking blared throughout the lot. He scrambled up to rush Harris, but the man was gone. No. He climbed up on top of the honking vehicle and searched the parking lot. Shit. No sign of him anywhere.

My Sunny Vampire

Carrie hovered over Frank, who was still lying on the ground. "What's the matter with him?"

Jack jumped down and found the object Harris used. From a distance it looked like a cellphone, but this wasn't a device that made calls. "A stun gun?" He knelt beside his friend. "How bad off are you?"

Frank touched his forehead. "I'm okay. Just need to get my equilibrium." He sat up and shook his head. Carrie hugged him. "Not something I want to experience again."

Jack stood and looked out over the sea of cars. Damn Harris and his crazy mind. Sunshine hadn't done anything to that bastard except look like Clara and now she might have to pay for it with her life.

* * * *

"Fudge." The spikes not only looked sharp, they were sharp, like tiny knives. Sunny fell back on her butt and pried her arm free only to be stabbed in the leg. Dag-burnit. Blood trickled down her arm and her pants were getting wet. Great, just what she needed, more wounds.

She grabbed the back of the cage to stand, but her bloody hand slipped free. Looking to avoid being stabbed again, she twisted sideways and slid down. Something crunched underneath her. "Please be the black box."

She lifted up one butt cheek and pulled out her phone, or what was left of it. "Nooo!" Despair sunk her heart. The cover was cracked. The screen a lifeless black. She choked on a sob. Couldn't anything go her way? True, she couldn't give Jack her location, but now she couldn't find out if Carrie was safe. She threw the phone. It clattered against the bars and bounced off her chest.

"Oww. Nice going, Sunny." She rubbed the offended site. At least she could move around. Time to see what Harris had wired.

Moving in the cage wasn't impossible, just difficult. The floor was slippery with her blood and she didn't wish to add anymore to it. Once she got turned around, she sat and pried the black box open. There were wires, wires and more wires, a battery and some kind of clay. Oh, not clay, C4. How the heck did Harris get C4? Stupid question. He was a vampire. He probably suggested it out of someone.

She was no expert by any means, but the device seemed rather simple. If the door opened, she went ka-boom. What if she yanked the wires out of the C4 at the same time? Would that prevent it from exploding? What was the worst that could happen? Probably a big ka-boom. But what were the odds Harris had made this difficult? It's not like he expected she'd get free and examine his handiwork.

Her fingers hovered over the wires. Grab and yank. That's all. Just grab and yank. Fear trickled down her spine. She took a deep breath, wrapped her hand around the wires, then…

Closed her eyes.

"Come on, you chicken, you can do this."

She pulled.

Nothing happened. No ka-boom. She opened her eyes. "Whoo hoo!" Now maybe she could get out of this torture chamber.

She reached for the door and skewered her hand. "Shoot!" When would she learn to think first? She couldn't afford to lose any more blood. Not if she wanted to remain mobile. Just to make her point, a severe cramp rippled across her abdomen. She clutched her stomach and breathed through it. Be strong. She must stay strong if she wanted out.

The bars to the cage interlaced close enough, with the alignment of the spikes, she could barely get her fingers through the holes. She needed something to pull the lock sideways.

Well, heck, what about the wire? Would that work? She picked it up and ran her fingers down the length to start a slip knot. A shot of electricity zapped her fingers. Son of a gun. She dropped the wire and rubbed the pain away. Stupid battery. One good yank snapped the wire free and she continued with her knot. Feeding it through a square opening, she aimed to loop it around the knob on the lock. Dag-burn spikes. They kept getting in the way.

After several tries, and more holes in her hands and fingers, frustration set in. Why was this so hard? She needed to get her anger under control or she'd still be in the cage if Jack didn't come through and Harris returned. After a cleansing breath, she tried again, finally nabbing the lock. She pulled the wire and the door swung open. Hallelujah! She was free.

She crawled out on her hands and knees, afraid if she stood she'd fall into the spikes again. Once she cleared the cage, she lay on her side to rest. Wiped out, that's what she was. She needed blood, but since she was pretty much stuck in no-man's-land, she knew better than to hope someone might stop in for a visit.

Postponing the celebration of her freedom, she plotted her next move. The shed wasn't all that big to begin with. If she hid along the wall of the exit, he wouldn't spot her right away. That'd give her time to what? Tackle him? Yeah, that wasn't happening.

No, she needed a weapon, something that would disable him, like a stake. She couldn't find anything similar from her position on the floor. That meant she needed to stand up. She rolled to her stomach and brought her knees up. Her wounds weren't nearly as bad as before, but they were still pretty sore and she winced with every movement she made. In four hours she might be healed, if she fed. Who knew how long it took otherwise? Maybe she couldn't heal in the state she was in. She would just have to buck it up, then. It beat being dead.

Slowly, she straightened her torso, keeping her knees on the floor. The room didn't sway. That was a good sign. She still couldn't locate any suitable staking material, though. She knee-walked to the shorter cage and used it as leverage to stand. That's when she saw it.

How could she have missed that? She'd been practically staring at it from the blasted cage. A wooden ladder hung sideways above the door. She would only need a small piece of wood to make a stake, but could she break off a piece? A folded knife lay beside the pile of rope. Even better. Now to get the ladder down.

Easier said than done.

Jumping was out of the question. It used too much energy. Could she climb? Would she have enough strength? Using the door handle, she braced a knee against it and reached for the ladder. Only two hooks held it up. Shouldn't be too difficult to slide it right off.

Instead, her knee slid off the door handle and she landed on the floor. "Fudge!" Maybe she should just jump anyway. Any more falls would defeat the whole purpose of trying to save energy.

Served her right. Jumping turned out to be the best way to slide the ladder free. She broke off one of the skinnier pieces of wood and leaned the ladder up against the wall. By the time Harris noticed, she hoped to have him staked.

Whittling a point proved to be more exhaustive work than she imagined. She wanted to sit and save energy, but couldn't risk the sound of rising, or worse, not being able to rise, if Harris came back with Carrie. So she stood beside the door, leaning against the wall, straightening up every so often as she slid to one side or the other.

Would it have been smarter to escape and get Jack or Frank? Probably. She looked down at her bloody t-shirt. Probably not. If she didn't get lost, she would either be avoided or arrested. Her telepathic abilities struggled while healthy, would they even work in her weakened condition?

So, no escaping. Not worth Carrie's life.

Footsteps crunched in the snow outside. She tensed. Harris. Had she missed hearing his car? Was she that far out of it? She hoped not. Now was her chance, her only chance.

She held her breath. The door slowly creaked opened, blocking her view. Her heart raced. This was it. Harris would notice she'd escaped. That didn't give her much time. She raised her hand, stake ready.

Sunny bumped into the door, exposing her target. He was alone. She lunged.

He turned around and grabbed her wrist as it came down.

"Nooo!" she screamed in frustration.

"Sunshine!"

"Jack?"

Hours ago she could have spit in his face. Now she couldn't imagine a more beautiful sight. Relief rushed through her, washing the adrenaline away, or whatever kept her standing. Her legs buckled. Jack caught her on the way down.

Chapter 30

Jack held Sunshine's limp body as he eased his way to the floor. He cradled her, thankful to be holding her. "Sweetheart. What did he do to you?"

Sunshine winced. "Nothing that blood and time won't heal. Right?"

He'd expected her to be immobile or trapped, not used as a pincushion. There were wounds in her back, chest, arms and fingers. He picked up her hand and licked away the blood on her fingers, healing what he could.

"Well, dang. Why didn't I think of that?"

He smiled. "Maybe you were a bit preoccupied." A piece of wood, sharpened on one end, lay in her lap. He picked it up. "You know, you nearly stabbed me."

She snatched it back. "I thought you were Harris. Guess I won't need it now. Carrie's okay? You caught the son of a gun?"

How could he tell her he failed? That all her hard work was for nothing? He toyed with her hair. "We got to Carrie in time. She's safe with Frank."

"As safe as she can be with him. What about Harris? You have him stashed at the safe house or what?"

"Sweetheart, I'm sorry. Harris got away."

Her eyes widened. "Then he'll be back. We need to be ready."

"What? Are you crazy? There's no getting ready. We're getting out of here."

She shook her head. "No. Don't you see? He won't be expecting you. By the way, how did you find me?"

A stroke of luck? He'd been ready to kick in the side of Harris's car for the sheer fun of it when Carrie spotted the GPS. So he took his frustration out on the back seat cushions via the open trunk. Lucky for Jack, Harris had left the unit on and there was a reverse feature. Led Jack straight to Sunshine. "I'll tell you later. We're not staying."

"Jack, we have to stay. He'll be back. We can surprise him and capture him. If we don't, he'll only go after Carrie and she's no match for him."

"Fine, I'll stay. But you're going."

"No. He'll leave if he doesn't sense me."

Why'd she have to be so damned logical? "How do you expect to fight Harris? You can barely stand."

"I don't have to fight him. I just have to distract him." She handed him the stake. "You can stake him when he's not looking."

He was beginning to understand Frank's displeasure at using Carrie as bait, but how could he object when Sunshine was more than willing? The woman was fearless "You're brilliant, you know that?"

"I do have my moments." Her smile warmed his heart.

"I don't need that." He pushed the wood away and pulled out the stun gun. "I have something better."

Her smile turned devious. "Perfect. He'll never suspect a thing." Her brows furrowed. "Except for your car. Is it out front?"

"Shit. Let me go take care of it and I'll be right back." He kissed the top of her head and she shied away, causing a minor pain in his chest. God, he loved this woman. She was everything to him. He would have preferred a better place and time, but they were together, and alone. When would he have this chance again to explain? All the more reason to hurry.

* * * *

Being in Jack's arms felt way too familiar, too comfortable, too intimate.

Sunny still loved him, there was no denying that, but she wouldn't make the same mistake twice. When she married Aaron Petersen, she thought he loved her as much as she loved him. But he had only wanted her family connection and she realized it too late. Young and stupid. Well, she was older and wiser now.

My Sunny Vampire

It still hurt.

She needed to distance herself now or it would hurt more.

Jack returned and sat beside her. He reached out to pull her onto his lap.

"I was thinking I should just stay here on the floor and you could stand where I did by the door. He won't see you when he comes in." She scooted to put some distance between them, but he pulled her back and held her tight. In her weakened condition, she couldn't fight him. Deep down, she didn't want to.

"There's no need to hurry. He's not here." He took a deep breath as if he were trying to gather up some courage. "Sunshine. I need to apologize."

"Apologize?" For what? For breaking her heart? She couldn't let him know how much he'd hurt her.

"I'm sorry for not coming clean from the start. I thought once I found out who turned you, that would be it and you'd be on your way. But then this funny thing happened. I got to know you. I fell in love. I thought if you knew about Clara…hell. Let's just say I wasn't thinking my best."

"It's because I look like her that you even approached me, isn't it? You see me as a replacement?"

His eyes widened. "Never. You're not a replacement." He looked over her head and snickered. "As for approaching you… When I first saw you, I was prepared to avoid you at all costs. I was afraid of the memories you'd conjure up. So I guess I have Harris to thank, because it would have been my greatest mistake if I had never met you."

His gaze traveled back to her and he caressed her cheek. Love shone in his eyes, but she was afraid to get her hopes up, so she didn't speak.

"I loved Clara. If I hadn't have been turned, I would have had a good life with her. But I would have never experienced the joy you bring to my heart. The passion of our love making. Or the fun you put in my life. You are my heartbeat, my reason for living. Yes, I loved Clara, but I'm in love with you, Sunshine.

"I should have trusted you, and for that, I'm sorry. I let my fears get in the way. If it takes the rest of my life to make it up to you, I'll do it. I'll do whatever it takes for you to trust me again."

It wasn't fair a vampire couldn't cry. It wasn't fair to feel the need and not get the release. Her eyes ached. Her chest ached. She desperately wanted to believe him. So why couldn't she? She covered her face with her hands.

"I know I hurt you," he whispered into her ear. "You don't know how sorry I am for hurting you. Maybe I'm asking too much too soon, but I know you're not Clara. I don't want you to be her."

"Won't I always be a reminder?"

"My dear, sweet, Sunshine. You only remind me of you."

She looked up at him. "I want to believe you."

He cupped her face. "You can. I won't let you down again. I promise. I don't ever want to hurt you again."

She sucked in her bottom lip. "Oh, Jack. I do love you."

"No more than I love you." He kissed her. Light, hesitant. She opened up to him, wanting more.

A severe cramp clutched her stomach. She broke the kiss and sucked in her breath. Fudge. The pains were getting worse. She could bear it if it meant getting Harris. That creep had done enough damage, time to put him away. She hoped it happened soon.

Jack pulled her close and wrapped his arms around her. She buried her head against his chest, his jacket soft on her face. Okay, maybe not so soon. Safe and secure, that's what she felt when he held her.

* * * *

Sunshine was his. All this time she was his, he was just too stupid to realize it. Jack kissed the top of her head, nuzzled his nose into her silky hair and took in a scent he hoped to never lose. He would love her forever.

An engine sounded in the distance. Since the Taurus was sitting at the mall parking lot with four flat tires, Harris must have stolen a car.

She lifted her head. "Someone's coming."

Her abilities were getting better and Jack was proud. "You ready?"

He could feel her heart race, but she nodded.

Using her as bait still made him uncomfortable, but if he was quick, Harris would never have a chance to touch her again. Jack lightly kissed her lips and found it hard to break away.

She patted his cheek and smiled. "Go on. I'll be fine."

She might be fine, but he was far from it, not until this whole mess ended. He rose and trudged to the wall. A moonlight beam

My Sunny Vampire

cut across her body as she lay on the floor, acting the invalid. Hell, it wasn't much of an act. She put on a brave front, but he knew how much she hurt. The woman had guts.

Jack took the stun gun from the pocket of his jacket, which he slipped off and placed on the floor. After seeing Frank go down the way he had, Jack respected the small weapon. His heart thudded with anticipation. He was ready to end this.

A car door slammed. Snow crunched underfoot.

Sunshine put a finger up to her lips and winked. "Hello? Is someone out there? I'm trapped and need help."

Jack held his breath. This would work. He pictured Harris trussed up like a pig at a luau and smiled.

The door opened and nearly hit him.

"I told you no one--What the fuck?" Harris's bellow echoed inside the small enclosure. "How did you get out? Isn't anything working out right?"

The sound of a kick was followed by Sunshine crying out. By the time Jack cleared the door, she had crashed into the cage. Rage flowed through his body like a wildfire. He rushed at Harris and tackled him from behind. Harris grunted. Jack took the weapon and placed it against Harris's neck. He pushed the button.

Nothing happened.

Shit.

Harris reached over his shoulder and grabbed Jack. In one swift movement, Jack crashed into the smaller cage. The gun dislodged, clattering across the floor. Pain shot through his back. He scrambled to a crouching position before Harris could attack.

Jack waved away the dust cloud caused by their struggle and stupidly took a breath. He coughed, but kept his gaze on Harris. "Give it up. The Committee might go easy on you."

"Yeah, right. Next you'll tell me Santa is real." Harris zipped to the gun and picked it up. His eyes reflected a glint of moonlight making him appear maniacal. "Did you know these things have a safety?"

He was bluffing. He had to be. When would he have had time to set the safety?

After Harris pushed multiple buttons, a red light came on.

Shit. Jack lowered his shoulder and charged, grunting on impact, driving them into the wall. On the force of impact, metal groaned and buckled. Jack reached for the gun.

Harris slapped Jack's arm away and shoved. Jack crashed into the door and fell to the floor. Slightly dazed, he stood on wobbly legs. Harris plowed into him. He brought the gun up. Jack grabbed his wrist.

The crackling of static echoed within the enclosure.

Chapter 31

Pain shot through Jack's nervous system. Sunshine's cry sounded from a great distance. He lost control of his limbs and fell hard to the concrete floor. Damn it all to hell. In one small zap, he became a lifeless pile of meat. If rage could fuel him, he would rip Harris's head clean off, but even moving his fingers took an effort.

"Wish I had a stake, but this will have to do. Enjoy the show." Harris smiled down at him before strolling over to Sunshine. "I should have killed you earlier, but toying with Jack was too irresistible to pass up. Too bad he couldn't go along with the plan. Oh well, better late than never."

She was lying on her side and glanced at Jack. How could he help her when he could barely move? He concentrated, but every command failed. He'd failed Clara in her time of need. Was he destined to repeat history?

"How exactly do you kill a vampire? The sun's not out." She sounded weak, defeated. Was she giving up or was it part of her act?

"That's true. The sun is a very thorough and painful way to kill a vampire. So is fire. That worked on Linda, anyway. Sent a tanker truck into her car and boom! Went up in flames. She never had a chance."

"What?" Sunshine brought her hand up to her mouth. "Her death wasn't an accident?"

Harris deserved to die for each life he'd destroyed. Jack's heart ached for his friend. If only he could--wait. Did his hand just move?

"If you were to live longer, you might learn there are no true accidents in this world. But hey, I have nothing against you, so I'll be quicker...humane. Jack will suffer regardless." Harris laughed as he approached the pile of rope. He picked up a knife and turned it in his hand. Moonlight reflected off the blade. "All I have to do is cut your head off before setting you on fire. It's quite messy, but less painful." He shrugged. "Or so I'm told."

Over Jack's dead body, and if he didn't get moving, it could very well end that way. Control of his hands traveled to control of his arms and he struggled to sit up. He needed to be quick. Shit, he needed to be stealthy. He was neither.

"Ah, ah, ah." Harris walked over to Jack and zapped him in the neck.

Damn it. Jack flopped back to the floor. He could tolerate the burn, but hated losing control.

"Listen, once I'm done with her, I don't care what you do. You and Frank took away the only person that mattered. So I took Linda from Frank. Now I'll take Sunny from you. I'm tired of your meddling, of you thinking you're better than everyone else. Well, guess what? You're not."

While Harris ranted, Sunshine slowly made it to her knees. The stake had been underneath her and she moved it behind her back. Could she stab Harris in the heart? Did she have enough energy? Enough nerve? What was he thinking, she always had enough nerve.

He needed to distract Harris and give Sunshine a chance. "Ivy was never yours, Harris. She was sick. When are you going to realize that?"

"Don't talk about her like that!" Harris took the knife and plunged it into Jack's stomach.

Oh crap. What was that bit about forgetting what a bayonet felt like? This brought it all back and then some. Jack cried out. He barely heard Sunshine's cry along with his own.

"See? You're not that special." Harris removed the knife and sent a kick into Jack's side. "You bleed just like the rest of us. So I assume you'll feel her loss as deeply as I felt Ivy's."

My Sunny Vampire

And just to make Jack feel totally helpless, Harris zapped him again.

Jack felt numb. Dead. And he would die if Harris went through with his threat.

With the stake pointed outward, Sunshine sprang to her feet and rushed Harris. He spun around just as she plowed into him with a warrior-like cry. Her momentum sent them crashing into the wall. The knife and gun he held clattered to the floor while a red stain bloomed on the front of his shirt.

"Nooo!" Harris went limp and slid to the floor. She wasn't far behind.

Great almighty, hallelujah, she did it!

Scowling, she wiped her hand on his shirt and found the stun gun. The red light was still on. She pressed it against his neck. "This is for sticking me in that cage." Her voice was cold as she zapped him. Harris's body convulsed. "Doesn't feel so good, does it?" She pushed the button a second time. "And that's for Linda."

"Sunshine," Jack said.

With a wild spark in her eyes, she kept zapping Harris until the weapon only clicked.

"Sunshine." *Click.* "Sunshine." *Click.* "Sunshine!"

She looked up. At last he got her attention.

"Jack." She dragged herself over and collapsed alongside him. "Are you okay?"

He propped up on an elbow and brushed the hair from her face. She didn't need him or anyone else to help her. She was the strongest woman he knew. "I think I'm doing better than you." He shook his head. "I'll never underestimate you again."

"What are you talking about? What did I do?"

"Let's just say I'm glad you're on my side." He sat up. "Now, let's go feed off him. I need him alive, but I don't want him talking."

"Why not?"

"Because Frank doesn't need to hear what Harris did to Linda. He's finally getting over her death and it will only cause him pain. Pain he doesn't deserve. Let him believe it was an accident. I think he can live with that a whole lot easier than knowing she was murdered. He already feels guilty about Ivy's death. Imagine the guilt he'd feel if he thought he was responsible for Linda's."

"But Frank didn't kill Linda."

"No, but Frank won't see it that way. Come on. Let's go fill up. If we drain Harris dry, he'll remain quiet."

"Won't that kill him?"

"No, but it'll be a step in the right direction."

They crawled to Harris. She bit his wrist almost gingerly, but Jack took the neck in one violent bite. Harris cried out. His blood was sweeter than a mortal's and not as potent, but would aid in healing.

Eventually Harris quieted down as they drained him into paralysis. Jack was still sore, and would be for a while, but not nearly as exhausted. Nothing a proper feeding and a good bath wouldn't take care of.

Hmmm. Yes, a bath. With Sunshine. The night was looking better by the second.

Chapter 32

Jack shut the trunk of his Mustang with a satisfying slam. Harris would be cramped, but the guy had it coming.

After driving Sunshine to Carrie's, he and Frank had come back to the shed for Harris. Jack originally planned to put Harris in the backseat, but Frank came up with the great idea of stuffing the louse in the trunk.

"I can't believe I trusted that man," Frank said. "We should have just killed him."

Frank would have if Jack hadn't intervened. Instead, Frank accidentally kicked Harris, numerous times.

"Normally, I'd agree, but I kind of need him to clear my name. He'll be dead soon enough, though."

"So, did I pass?"

Jack knocked the snow off his shoes and opened the car door. "Pass?"

"Hey, I know you came up here to spy on me. I'm not that much of a fool."

If anyone was the fool, it was Jack. "There was nothing to pass. Harris set us up. I should have known you were okay. You were always the level-headed guy." He slid behind the wheel.

Frank climbed in on the passenger side. "I was only level-headed with Linda around."

"So, everything's okay with you and Carrie?"

The smile slowly spread across his friend's face. "Everything's great. I didn't think it was possible to get lucky again. I especially didn't think it would happen this soon."

"Hey. Linda would want you to be happy. You know that, right?"

"I know. I still miss her, though."

Jack patted his friend on the shoulder. "I'd tell you to take it slow, but that's your mode of operation."

"I wasted a lot of time before I made a decision with Linda. Time I could have spent with her. I'm not going to do that with Carrie."

And Jack wasn't going to do that with Sunshine. He knew what he wanted. He only hoped she wanted the same.

First he needed to clean up and pack. That bath with Sunshine would have to wait.

* * * *

Sunny had folded and packed the last shirt when Carrie entered her room.

"You really going to Atlanta?"

"Seems so. Would you believe their headquarters is located in the Underground? We have to turn over Harris and apparently I have to check in. If Gary calls again, tell him I left for home. If that doesn't get the ball rolling on my missing status, Frank will let you know what to do." Sunny's life in Florida was over, she knew that. And Pittsburgh hadn't been her home for over ten years. She'd like to think her new life would be in Atlanta with Jack, but he hadn't said anything. Yet.

"Okay. You'll still call, right? And send e-mails?"

"As soon as I get my new identity."

Carrie walked around the room and plopped down on the bed. "Maybe I'll see you down there some day."

"Oh?"

Carrie fell backwards and flung out her arms. "I think I love him."

Sunny zipped up the suitcase and placed it on the floor. "I don't mean to make light of your statement, but you have uttered those same words about Brad and Rick and Jarrod."

Her friend propped her arms up on the bed in a semi-sitting position. "Frank's different. And not because he's a vampire. No

My Sunny Vampire

one's ever made me feel so special before and I'm not letting him get away. I really think he's the one."

"Yeah, but how does he feel?"

"He didn't come right out and say it, but I think he feels the same." Sunny sat on the bed. "You still having any urges to drink?" Jack had said Carrie's obsession should disappear once Harris was incapacitated, since Harris had to continually reinforce his suggestions to Carrie.

"Nope. Not a drop."

"What about Frank's urges?"

"He told me what he'd done and apologized. But he only did it to be with me. I can forgive him that. It wasn't like I didn't flaunt my blood under his nose. The poor man didn't stand a chance against me. I should probably ask for his forgiveness."

"You were being controlled. He wasn't."

"Yes, but he was also trying to protect me. You need to let up on him. He's a good man."

Carrie was right. She wasn't being fair to Frank. The man had suffered enough from Harris, he didn't need to suffer from her, too. "Well, you better hope he works faster with you than he did with Linda. Jack told me it took Frank ten years to propose."

Carrie's eyes widened. "If we ever get that serious, then I guess I'll be the one proposing. I don't want to wait until I'm an old woman. So, what about you and Jack? You two have plans?"

Sunny stood and walked over to the window. "We haven't really talked about any. Although he said he would help me with my photography. Since turning into a vampire, I can take these amazing night shots."

"All your shots are amazing, Sunny. But if Jack's helping, I'm sure it'll go great. The guy's crazy for you."

Yeah, but being crazy in love and offering to help weren't the same as a commitment. Sunny wanted a life with him and she wanted him to want one with her.

She pulled the curtain back. The window faced the neighboring building, but the parking lot was in sight, as was the driveway. No sign of Jack, yet. However, one familiar body loitered among the trees.

"Son of a gun. Doesn't that guy ever give up?"

Carrie appeared beside her and peeked out the window. "Who? Where?"

"Tom. Out there." Sunny pointed.

Carrie squinted. "Oh, man. The security lights are out again. I can't see shit. Damn, I hope I'm a vampire someday. I'd never need light."

Sunny rushed to the door. Time to put an end to that fool's errand. He wasn't Buffy and he was liable to get himself hurt.

She exited out the front and snuck around to the back, keeping to the shadows. Tom leaned against the fence, bundled up in winter gear. He held the binoculars to his eyes, pointed toward the building. What exactly was he looking for?

Sunny took a deep breath. After she told Jack that Harris had incapacitated him with absinth, Jack smiled. Not quite the reaction she expected until he told her the liquor most likely caused her inconsistencies. With time, she would be just like any other vampire. How long, he didn't know. The drug worked differently on different people and with her being a newborn and all, it probably affected her worse.

That was good news, but she still had a mortal to control and she worried she might fail. How many times had Jack told her to relax? So she rolled her shoulders as if preparing to lift weights and stared at her target as if she were talking to Carrie. *"Tom, put the binoculars down."*

The man did as he was told and he didn't look like a zombie. Adrenaline coursed through her veins. Hot dang. She did it. Wait. No sense getting ahead of herself. She was far from finished.

She walked up to Tom and took his hand, starting a connection. *"Show me how you found Vampire Girl."*

The memories played out in her head and her jaw dropped. It worked, it actually worked. She took a deep breath to keep from hyperventilating.

Tom had seen Sunny on TV and it was pure luck he ran into her at the bar. Just as she suspected, he and his friend had followed her that night and followed Jack when he carried her to Frank's after the staking. Harris wasn't involved at all. Just two guys who thought they would be vampire slayers.

"Where is your blond buddy?"

"He went out to buy some coffee. He'll be back soon."

My Sunny Vampire

Coffee? What, were they on a stakeout? She would be so glad to see these two out of her life.

"Tom, *you'll forget you ever saw Vampire Girl. You don't believe in vampires. They're a myth and you'll argue with anyone who says they exist. So Tom, do vampires exist?*"

"Hell, no. They're a myth."

"*Very good. Now sit down and sleep until you're shaken awake.*"

Sunny released him. He sat on the ground and slumped forward. His breathing deepened.

She pumped her fist in the air and jumped with glee. Holy moly. She was a vampire. An honest to goodness vampire. With powers, even. Hot diggity-dog. She couldn't wait to tell Jack.

Headlights lit the parking lot as a newer, more modern car pulled in. Not Jack's Mustang.

Well, she'd tell Jack after she finished her job here.

* * * *

The last hour had been maddening. Jack couldn't shower and pack fast enough. Now it seemed as if he stopped at every traffic light between Frank and Carrie's. He gunned it through the last one.

Frank placed a hand on Jack's shoulder. "Easy, Jack. If you get pulled over, it will only delay you more. What are you in such a hurry for anyway? She's not going anywhere."

Jack pulled in front of the apartment building. His life was beginning now, at this very moment and he couldn't wait to get it started.

He left Frank and flew up the stairs. Without knocking, he opened the door and followed her scent to the living room. Sunshine stood when she saw him and grinned. Her hair was down, flowing over her shoulders. Radiant, that's what she was. And his.

She flew into his arms. "Oh, Jack. I work. I actually work!"

Her exuberance rubbed off and he laughed. "What are you talking about?"

"I just did what you've always told me and it worked. Those two vampire slayers won't be bothering us anymore. I made sure they don't believe in vampires."

He held her face in his hands. She was grinning, joyous. He'd never been prouder.

"I never thought you were broken." He kissed her--deeply, completely. Tasting every morsel she offered. Little Jack sprang to life. Too bad they had a long drive ahead of them.

Carrie cleared her throat. "Do I need to leave?"

Reluctantly, he broke the kiss. "No." He caressed Sunshine's face. "Do you know how much I love you?"

She pulled herself closer, rubbing up against his erection. An evil glint showed in her eyes and her smile turned devious. "No. Why don't you tell me?"

"I'd like to show you, but I'm afraid I haven't been able to go shopping."

She raised one beautiful eyebrow. "Shopping? What for?"

"Because that's what a gentleman does before he proposes. He buys a ring."

Her mouth hung open. He pushed her chin up.

"Will you make an honest man out of me and be my wife?"

She threw her arms around him and laughed. "You betcha."

Someone might have cheered. Someone might have patted him on the back. But he only saw Sunshine. Her answer became his favorite two words in the English language.

Acknowledgements

As with any book, feedback is invaluable and I have the following to thank for giving me the best: my writing friends with the Western Ohio Writers Association (you only saw the first few pages, but your comments were enough to put me on the right track); my critique partners, Todd (you're my first and I hope you stick around) and Melissa (without you, this book wouldn't be what it is today and it certainly wouldn't have such a cool title); my first readers, Stephanie (don't hold back, tell me how you *really* feel), Kathleen (simply the best, I wish you weren't so popular), and Mary (no, I'm not sorry I made you late for work); my editor, Paige Christian (you opened my eyes and made my first editing experience practically painless); and my husband, Jim (I don't want to research with anyone but you; your love and support mean more than I can say).

About the Author

Stacy McKitrick always had stories in her head; she just never knew what to do with them. Then one day she decided to give writing a try and discovered the passion she'd been looking for all her life. Her stories contain paranormal characters, but her practical nature needs to make their existence plausible, as well as give them that happy ending (because it's all about the love). Living in her own happy ending, she resides in Ohio with her husband, Jim and their two grown children.

You can find her at www.stacymckitrick.com

Thank you for purchasing this book

Sign up for Stacy's newsletter to receive new release announcements, sneak peeks of future books, and bonus content. She sometimes even gives away stuff.

http://eepurl.com/-Auwz

Now read further for the first chapter of
Bite Me, I'm Yours
Book 2 in the
Bitten by Love Series.

Bite Me, I'm Yours
Chapter 1

If Sarah Daugherty were smart, she'd live somewhere it never got cold. If she were smart, she'd have never let her mother get the best of her. If she were smart, she'd have never married Steven. Yeah, if she were smart.

She stared at her reflection in the mirrored elevator doors. Somewhere beneath the white down-filled coat and pink scarf, a pathetic, twenty-four-year-old divorcee waited for doors to open and blast her with air that belonged in a freezer. They didn't disappoint.

Her friend, Lori, laughed. "What a wimp. We're not even outside and you act like it's below zero."

"It's below zero in Celsius." Ever since the events that unfolded prior to her divorce, Sarah had been cold. No matter what she did, she couldn't get warm enough. Winter wasn't helping any, either.

"Yeah, but last I saw, Dayton still measured temps in Fahrenheit." Lori stepped out and looked up. "Gee, what happened to the lights? It looks like a freakin' tomb in here. You're the workaholic. Do they normally go off after seven?"

"They never did before." Sarah examined the ceiling while the elevator still provided some light. Bulbs nearby were broken, meaning the ones leading to her car were probably the same way. The doors shut behind her. If it weren't for the oil and gasoline odors, she could be in a dungeon.

Lori unlocked her car. "Told my sister I would babysit tonight and I'm already late. Do you want to come?"

Babysit? Lori's niece was only six months old. Sarah's heart hadn't mended enough for that kind of torture. "Thanks, but I think I'll pass."

Lori frowned as she opened the driver's door. "Shit. Wasn't thinking. Sorry."

Sarah smiled her no-worries smile. She'd gotten pretty good at it the past few months. "It's okay. Now get out of here."

After a brief hug, Lori slid behind the wheel. "I'll see you tomorrow, kiddo."

Sarah headed for her little Civic, looking for her landmark. If the owner of the bright yellow Nissan Xterra ever quit his or her job, or decided to drive it to lunch, she'd be heartbroken. Ever since she started using this garage, she'd parked beside The Bumblebee—the name she'd come to call it—where it remained by quitting time. Seeing the tall vehicle brought a smile to her face. What did it mean when a yellow SUV was a bright spot in her life? Maybe that she needed a better life.

The roar of an engine echoed. Lights from behind cast long shadows ahead. Sarah waved as her friend drove by. Darkness surrounded her Civic and the SUV, and as she walked between them she stepped in something crunchy. Bits of white glass dotted the floor, glinting faintly from what little light remained. Another broken bulb.

Crunch, crunch.

She jerked upright. Was someone else here? She walked to the rear of the vehicles, making more crunchy sounds of her own. No one approached from the elevators or stairs, not that she could see much. Her heart crept up her throat and she swallowed.

The only sounds came from the pounding in her chest.

"You're hearing things, you idiot," she mumbled. Still, pinpricks of fear raced over her skin and she itched to go home. On legs that were no longer steady, she turned back to her car. She opened her purse with shaky hands.

Crunch, crunch.

She hadn't imagined that. Something scratchy and wet with a sweet smell cupped her nose and mouth.

What the— Holding her breath, she grabbed at the mask. Her purse fell and landed with a thud. The assailant wrapped his free arm around her waist and yanked her against his hard body.

"Time to sleep," he whispered, his breath warm against her ear.

Nooo! She hadn't escaped Steven's abuse only to have some stranger take his place. She clawed at his hand, but her gloves prevented her from scratching him. Taking hold of his fingers, she pulled. Bones cracked, but he held on. She yanked harder. His shriek pierced her ear, and he pulled away, scratching her face with the stiff material. Mouth free, she took a clean breath and screamed. Someone had to hear. The place echoed like a canyon. He clamped his hand across her mouth, cutting off her cry for help. Damn it. What would it take to stop him? She kicked him in the legs.

"God damn it," he muttered.

The attacker lost his balance and loosened his hold. Freedom seemed in reach. She leaned forward, using whatever leverage she could. He righted himself and pulled her back with arms that doubled for a vise. No amount of twisting and turning got her free. She reached behind, hoping to gouge his eyes, but he bent her head back against his shoulder. The mask scraped her face and her neck screamed in pain.

"Keep it up and I'll snap your neck," he growled.

Her heart raced. He might not kill her now, but there was no way this would end well. Wasn't there anyone around to help? Tears welled in her eyes and her chest burned for oxygen. With no choice left, she breathed in the sweet scent. Her world went dark.

* * * *

John Pennington emerged from the stairwell into the parking garage with a playful bounce. Sporadic lighting made him glance up. A few steps later, he stepped in something crunchy. Broken glass glittered in the remaining light. He shook his head. Who would do such a thing? He made a mental note to report the incident. Good thing he didn't need the light.

He headed for his SUV. A lady's loafer lay on its side in the aisle. Was some poor woman limping around with one shoe, or had it been used to break the bulbs? He picked it up. A familiar scent hit him, one that always lingered around his vehicle. Strawberries.

A man softly grunted as if straining. Always willing to lend a helping hand, John walked toward the sound and came to a sedan backed in against the wall. The trunk was open and the grunter, a man in his late twenties, struggled with loading his cargo. Cargo he had no right to load. A woman's shoeless foot stuck out to the side.

John stopped cold. "Hey! What the hell are you doing?"

The culprit jumped, dropping the woman. Her head hit the trunk floor with a thud. John winced. That had to hurt. While he stood there gaping at the woman, the man dashed off.

"Oh no you don't." John transmitted instructions to the man telepathically, "Come back here."

Like a robot, the man stopped and shuffled back to John, jerking with each step. John grimaced. One of these days he'd get better at manipulating mortals. When others took control, the human looked…well…human. For John, they looked like zombies, right down to the glazed-over eyes.

"What's your name?"

"Ray Brian Fowler."

"Ray, go over to the wall and sit down."

The would-be kidnapper followed the instructions.

John crouched before the low-life. "Tell me your plans for this woman."

"I'm going to take her home and play with her like I did all the others."

The others? Ray sounded like a boy talking about his favorite toy.

John grabbed Ray's hand, getting the skin contact needed to link. "Show me the others."

The grisly scene emerged in his mind. John gasped. Four dead and disfigured women, cut beyond recognition. Their features were not clear, but they all possessed long brown hair, and were all similar in size. Just like the woman in the trunk.

A smile spread across Ray's face as the memories played out in John's head. Cutting them had given Ray the thrill he'd needed to rape them. Death had been an unfortunate by-product. All four were buried side-by-side at an old farmhouse up north.

"Oh God!" John dropped Ray's arm, stopping the horrifying vision. How could one person be so evil?

"Go to sleep, Ray."

Ray's eyes closed and his head fell forward.

That would keep him out for a good hour or so. John broke the link, stood and moved toward the woman. "You might not think this now, but today's your lucky day."

She didn't respond. She was out cold.

A mask, the type popular during flu season, covered her face. He tossed the shoe in the trunk and leaned forward to unhook the elastic from around her ears. The car reeked of chloroform, explaining why the young woman was out to the world.

John lifted the mask and stared. He couldn't remember the last time he'd seen anyone so lovely. Her long lashes were real, not those fake add-ons, and her full lips... Well, he didn't need to be thinking about those. Best to see if she was seriously injured first.

Three small scratches marred her cheek. He sniffed for any major blood loss. The scent of strawberries hit him again. Lovely. Just like the shoe. Just like around his... Wait a minute. A purse lay beside her and he searched through it, finding her keys. He aimed the fob toward his SUV and hit the unlock button. The vehicle beside his honked and lit up. "Well I'll be damned."

He picked up the shoe. "Okay, Miss Strawberry. Let's get you back to your car." He slid it on her foot, chuckling at the penguin-decorated sock. "Cute."

He grabbed her purse and jogged over to her car. Opening the driver's door gave him another whiff of her perfume. Damn, he could really get used to that. Reminded him of the garden his mother had planted every year.

After tossing her bag inside, he zipped back to Ray's car and lifted her with ease. Her fragrance more noticeable now that he held her, he stared at her lovely face. What was he doing? Damn. Blinking didn't clear his head, so he held his breath. That did the trick. He situated her behind the steering wheel then licked his thumb and applied his saliva over the scratches. As the wound healed, a small heating sensation formed on his thumb and then a rush of warmth filled his palm. He snapped his hand away. What the—

He knelt beside her and slowly ran the back of his hand across her soft cheek, now unmarred. This time the warmth traveled up his arm. Oh sweet Jesus, what was she?

Wonder filled his heart. He removed her glove and took her delicate hand into his own. Luxurious warmth spread. He closed his eyes and sighed as it traveled through his system. He hadn't felt anything this good in years. No, make that decades.

Soft, whispery breaths and the intense strawberry scent caused him to open his eyes. Lips begging to be kissed were mere inches away. When had he leaned forward? His heart raced. The last time he had kissed anyone had been the night of his turning. He hadn't missed it until now.

She moved her head and mumbled. Panic gripped his chest. He jerked backward and stood, establishing a distance and clearing his head. Damn. He'd almost kissed her. What was he thinking? She was helpless. How could he take advantage?

He leaned against his Xterra and slid to the ground, landing in broken glass. Great. He leaned sideways and brushed the debris away.

Now what? In order to ensure Ray reported himself to the police, John would have to leave her alone. But she was vulnerable. John hugged his knees to his chest. He could send Ray on his way alone, and the thought tempted him, but anything could happen between the garage and the police station. He needed more assurance than that. Maybe if he locked her inside her car? No one had entered the garage since his arrival. He stood and went over to the door.

Would she get cold? Her down-filled coat appeared warm enough and she wore a scarf. Plus, she was out of the elements. It couldn't be that cold in the garage, but then, what did he know? He had to trust she would wake up before she froze.

He needed to send her a command in case she left before he returned, but her unconsciousness made transmitting the command more difficult, if not impossible. Cupping her head would be the best way to insure a connection. It would also cause him to lose control. But man, to feel that heat once more... Shit.

Maybe he couldn't avoid the heat, but he could avoid her scent. Holding his breath, he placed his hands on her. Warmth cascaded up his arms and spread throughout his body. The intensity caught him off guard, and he blinked several times before coming to his senses. "When you wake up, you will feel refreshed. You will remember getting in your car and that you were sleepy. Go straight home and stay in for the night."

He released her and stepped back, his breathing ragged, her heat dissipating. It was the best he could do without confusing her any more. "I'll be back to check on you, I promise." He activated the locks and shut the door, cutting off her scent. The loss was immediate. He sighed and trudged back to Ray, kicking him awake.

"Ray, get in the back seat of your car."

The miscreant followed orders while John shut the trunk and got behind the wheel. He drove to the police station and parked on a side street.

Ray didn't deserve to live. He deserved to be treated as he had treated those women. However, killing him, or even maiming him, would only implicate someone else and John wanted Ray to pay for his crimes.

"Go to the police station and tell all officers you encounter every crime you've ever committed. Tell them your conscience finally got the best of you. However, you will not remember me or the lady you abducted tonight. Now, go."

Ray climbed out and stalked, in that jerky, zombie way, toward the station. Once he reached the entrance, John broke the link. Ray looked up at the building and shook his head as if he had just awakened. After a few moments, he walked through the doors.

Okay, one down, one to go.

John walked back to the garage, aiming to look normal, but the closer he got, the faster his pace. He barged through the stairwell door, practically flew down the stairs, and zipped to his car.

Miss Strawberry was gone.

Disappointment squeezed his chest. Sure, he was glad she'd been well enough to drive off, but he should have gotten her name. He snorted at his idea. Right. Like it would have made a difference. He'd probably never see her again. But as he climbed inside his SUV, all he could think about was her and that lovely scent.

Made in the USA
Monee, IL
31 July 2024